The Princess Diaries

Meg Cabot is the author of the phenomenally successful The Princess Diaries series. With vast numbers of copies sold around the world, the books have topped the US and UK bestseller lists for weeks and won several awards. Two movies based on the series have been massively popular throughout the world.

Meg is also the author of the bestselling Airhead trilogy, the Abandon trilogy, *All-American Girl*, *All-American Girl: Ready or Not*, *How to Be Popular*, *Jinx*, *Teen Idol*, *Avalon High*, *Tommy Sullivan Is a Freak*, The Mediator series and the Allie Finkle series as well as many other books for teenagers and adults. She and her husband divide their time between New York and Florida.

Visit Meg Cabot's website at
www.megcabot.co.uk

*Books by Meg Cabot*

The Princess Diaries series

The Mediator series

The Airhead trilogy

The Abandon trilogy

All-American Girl
All-American Girl: Ready or Not

Avalon High
Avalon High manga: The Merlin Prophecy
Teen Idol
How to Be Popular
Jinx
Tommy Sullivan Is a Freak
Nicola and the Viscount
Victoria and the Rogue

*For younger readers*
The Allie Finkle series

*For older readers*
The Boy Book series
Queen of Babble series
The Heather Wells series

# Ten out of Ten

## Princess Amelia Mignonette Grimaldi Thermopolis Renaldo (Mia)

invites you to an exclusive event to celebrate
her 18th birthday and the FABULOUS last
ever instalment of The Princess Diaries

Dress code: Glamorous and gorgeous. Tiaras optional.
And, Lana Weinberger, don't forget your underwear!

Etiquette: No curtsying. No paps. No kissing Prince William.

0138446190

# The Princess Diaries

## Ten out of Ten

## Meg Cabot

MACMILLAN

First published 2008 by Macmillan Children's Books

This edition published 2009 by Macmillan Children's Books
an imprint of Pan Macmillan
20 New Wharf Road, London N1 9RR
Associated companies throughout the world
www.panmacmillan.com

ISBN 978-0-330-45060-7

13

A CIP catalogue record for this book is available from
the British Library.

Typeset by Intype Libra Ltd
Printed and bound by CPI Group (UK) Ltd, Croydon, CR0 4YY

*For my agent, Laura Langlie, with love and many thanks for her endless patience, kindness and, most of all, her sense of humour!*

This series would not have been possible without the help of people too numerous to name, but I'd like to try to thank a few of them, specifically:
Beth Adler, Viviane Basset, Jennifer Brown, Barb Cabot, Sarah Davies, Michele Jaffe, Laura Langlie, Amanda Maciel, Abigail McAden, Rebecca McNally, Fliss Stevens, Benjamin Egnatz, everyone at Macmillan Children's Books who worked so hard on behalf of Princess Mia and her friends, and, most especially of all, the readers, who stuck by her until the end. A royal thank-you to you all!

'It's exactly like the ones in the stories,' she wailed. 'Them pore princess ones that was drove into the world.'

*A Little Princess*
Frances Hodgson Burnett

# *teenSTYLE* Exclusive!

**teenSTYLE chats with Princess Mia Thermopolis on what it means to be royal, her upcoming high-school graduation and prom, and her fashion must-haves!**

*teenSTYLE* caught up with Princess Mia this spring as she was engaged in one of her many volunteer activities – tidying up Central Park along with the rest of her fellow Albert Einstein High School seniors, since they'll all be taking part in commencement ceremonies there in a few weeks!

What could be less princessy than painting park benches? And yet Princess Mia managed to look entirely regal in a pair of 7 For All Mankind dark-rinse low-rise skinny jeans, a simple white crew-neck tee and Emilio Pucci ballerina flats.

This is one royal who truly knows what it means to have *teenSTYLE*!

*teenSTYLE*: Let's cut right to the chase. A lot of people are confused about what's happening with the government in Genovia right now. Our readers really want to know: Are you still a princess?

**Princess Mia**: Yes, of course. Genovia was an absolute monarchy until I found a document last year revealing that my ancestress, Princess Amelie, had declared it a constitutional monarchy – exactly like England – 400 years ago. That document was proven valid by the Genovian parliament last spring, and now we're two weeks away from elections for prime minister.

**teenSTYLE**: But will you still rule?

**Princess Mia**: Much to my chagrin. I mean, yes. I will inherit the throne upon the demise of my father. The people of Genovia will elect a prime minister, the same as the people of England, while still having a reigning monarch . . . in Genovia's case, since we're a principality, a prince or princess.

**teenSTYLE**: That's great! So you'll always have the tiara, the limos, the palace, the beautiful ballgowns . . .

**Princess Mia**: . . . and the bodyguards, the paparazzi, no private life, people like you hounding me, and my grandmother forcing me to agree to meet with you to get my name in your magazine so we can attract more tourists to Genovia? Yes. Not, of course, that we aren't in enough magazines right now, seeing as how my dad is running for prime minister, and his own cousin, Prince René, is running against him.

**teenSTYLE**: And leading in the polls, according to latest new reports. But let's move on to your plans for after high school. You're scheduled to graduate from Manhattan's prestigious Albert Einstein High School on May 7th. What kind of accessories do you plan on wearing to set off your mortar board and gown—

**Princess Mia**: Although frankly, I find Prince René's campaign platform ridiculous. He's been quoted as saying, 'You'd be surprised how many people in the world have never even heard of Genovia. Many of them believe it's a made-up place, something out of a movie. I'm out to change all that.' But his ideas of changing Genovia for the better include generating more income from tourism. He keeps insisting that Genovia could be a vacation destination spot like Miami or Las Vegas! *Vegas!* He wants to install restaurant chains like Applebee's, Outback Steakhouse and McDonald's in order to appeal to cruise-ship tourists visiting from America. Can you imagine? What could be more disastrous to Genovia's delicate infrastructure? Some of our bridges are five centuries old! Not to mention what it would do to the environment, which has already been severely damaged by cruise-ship waste dumping—

**teenSTYLE**: Er . . . we can see this an issue about which you feel passionate. We encourage our readers to take a keen interest in current events – like your eighteenth birthday, which we know is coming up on May 1st! Any truth to the rumours that your grandmother, the Dowager Princess Clarisse, has been in New York City for some time, planning a completely over-the-top eighteenth birthday celebration for you, aboard a yacht?

**Princess Mia**: I'm not saying there isn't necessarily room for improvement in Genovia, but not in the way Prince René means. I believe Dad's response – that if anything, what our citizens need right now is improvements to their daily lives – is utterly correct. My father, not Prince René, has the experience Genovia needs right now. I mean, he's been prince there his entire life, and has ruled for the past ten years. He knows, more than anyone, what his people need and don't need . . . and what they don't need is an Applebee's!

**teenSTYLE**: So . . . you're planning on studying political science in college?

**Princess Mia**: What? Oh, no. I was thinking of majoring in journalism. With a creative-writing minor.

**teenSTYLE**: Really? So you want to be a journalist?

**Princess Mia**: Actually, I'd love to be an author. I know publishing is really hard to break into. But I've heard if you start by writing romance novels you have a better chance.

**teenSTYLE**: Speaking of romance, you must be getting ready for something every girl in America is starting to get excited about! A little something called PROM?

**Princess Mia**: Oh. Um. Yeah. I guess.

**teenSTYLE**: Come on, you can tell us. Of course you're going! We all know things between you and long-time steady boyfriend, Michael Moscovitz, ended last year when he went off to Japan. As far as we know, he hasn't come back yet, right?

**Princess Mia**: Right. He's still in Japan. And we're just friends.

**teenSTYLE**: Right! You've often been seen in the company of fellow AEHS senior John Paul Reynolds-Abernathy IV. That's him painting that bench over there, isn't it?

**Princess Mia**: Uh . . . yeah.

**teenSTYLE**: So . . . don't keep us in suspense! Is J.P. the special guy who'll be escorting you to Albert Einstein High's senior prom? And what will you be wearing? You know metallics are in this season . . . can we count on you to glitter in gold?

**Princess Mia**: Oh, no! I'm so sorry! My bodyguard didn't mean to kick that paint can over on to you. How clumsy of him! Do send me the dry-cleaning bill.

**Lars**: Care of the Royal Genovian press office, Fifth Avenue.

Her Royal Highness
*The Dowager Princess Clarisse Marie Grimaldi Renaldo*
requests the pleasure of your company
at a soirée to celebrate the eighteenth birthday
of Her Royal Highness
*Princess Amelia Mignonette Grimaldi Thermopolis Renaldo*
on Monday May 1st
at 7 p.m.
at South Street Seaport, Pier Eleven
The Royal Genovian Yacht
*Clarisse 3*

YALE University

Dear Princess Amelia

Congratulations on your admission to Yale
College! Announcing the good news to a
candidate is the absolute best part of my job,
and it gives me great pleasure to send you
this letter. You have every reason to feel
proud of our offer of admission. I know that
Yale will be an even richer and more vital
place for your being here –


PRINCETON University

Dear Princess Amelia

Congratulations! Your academic
accomplishments, extra-curricular
achievements and strong personal
qualities were deemed by the
admissions officers to be exceptional
and ones we want here at Princeton. We
are pleased to be sending you this
good news and especially to be
welcoming you to Princeton –

Columbia College

COLUMBIA University

Dear Princess Amelia

Congratulations! The Committee on Admissions joins me in the most rewarding part of this job – informing you that you have been selected for admission to Columbia University in the City of New York. We are fully confident that the gifts you bring to our campus will be unique and valuable and that your abilities will be challenged and developed here –


HARVARD University


Dear Princess Amelia

I am delighted to inform you that the Committee on Admissions and Financial Aid has voted to offer you a place at Harvard. Following an old Harvard tradition, a certificate of admission is enclosed. Please accept my personal congratulations for your outstanding achievements –

BROWN University

Dear Princess Amelia

Congratulations! The Brown Board of Admission has completed its evaluation of more than 19,000 applicants, and it is with great pleasure that I inform you that your application has been included among our acceptances. Your –


Daphne Delacroix
1005 Thompson Street, Apt 4A
New York, NY 10003

Dear Ms Delacroix

Enclosed please find your novel, *Ransom My Heart*. Thank you for giving us the opportunity to read it. However, it does not suit our needs at the present time. Good luck placing it elsewhere.

Sincerely

Ned Christiansen
Editorial Assistant
Brampft Books
520 Madison Avenue
New York, NY 10023

Dear Author

Thank you for the submission of your book. Although it was carefully read, it is not what we are looking for here at Cambridge House. Best of luck in your future endeavours. Faithfully

Cambridge House Books


Dear Ms Delacroix,

Thank you so much for your submission *Ransom My Heart*. We here at AuthorPress were highly impressed by it and we think it shows a lot of promise! However, it's important to keep in mind that publishing houses receive well over 20,000 submissions a year, and in order to stand out your manuscript needs to be PERFECT. For a nominal fee ($5 per page), your manuscript *Ransom My Heart* could be on store shelves by next Christmas –

The Senior Class of
Albert Einstein High School
requests the pleasure of your company
at the senior prom
on Saturday May 6th
at 7 p.m.
at the Waldorf-Astoria ballroom

# Thursday, April 27, Gifted and Talented

Mia – We're going shopping for prom dresses – and something to wear to your birthday shindig – after school. Bendel's and Barneys first, then if we strike out there we'll hit Jeffrey and Stella downtown. You in? – Lana

– – – – – – – – – – – – – – – – – – – –

Sent from my BlackBerry Wireless Handheld

L – I'm sorry. I can't. Have fun though! – M

What, do you mean, you *can't*? What *else* do you have to do? Don't say princess lessons because I know your grandmother has cancelled them while she gets ready for your big pahtay, and don't say therapy either because you only have that on Fridays. So what gives? Don't be such a byotch, we need your limo. I blew all my taxi money for the month on a new pair of D&G patent-leather platform slingbacks.

Wow. Coming clean about Dr Knutz to my friends was freeing and all that, just like he said it would be.

Especially since it turns out most of them have been in therapy too.

But some of them – such as Lana – tend to treat the subject way too casually sometimes.

I'm staying after school to help J.P. with his senior project. You know he's putting on his final performance piece for the senior-project committee next week. I promised I'd be there for him. He's worried about some of the performances his actors are giving. He thinks Amber Cheeseman's little sister,

Stacey, doesn't really seem to be giving it her all. And she's the star, you know.

**OMG, that play he wrote? God, what are you two, attached at the hip? You can spend ten minutes apart, you know. Now come shopping with us. Pinkberry after! My treat!**

Lana thinks Pinkberry solves everything. Or, if not Pinkberry, *Allure* magazine. When Benazir Bhutto got assassinated, and I couldn't stop crying, Lana got me a copy of *Allure* magazine and told me to get in the bathtub and read it cover to cover. Lana was seriously all, 'You'll feel better in no time!'

And I'm pretty sure she really meant it.

The weird thing was, after I did what she said, I sort of *did* feel a little better.

I also knew a lot more about the dangers of SmartLipo.

Still.

Lana. It's an artistic thing. J.P.'s the writer/director. I have to be there to support him. I'm the girlfriend. Just go without me.

**God, what is *with* you? It's PROM. Fine, be that way. I'll forgive you, but only because I know you're freaking out over this election thing of your dad's. Oh, and where you're going to go to school next year. God, I can't believe you didn't get in *anywhere*. I mean, even *I* got in to Penn. And *my* senior project was on the history of eyeliner. Good thing my dad's a legacy, I guess.**

Ha, yeah, well, it's true! I got the lowest math SAT score you can get. Who'd want me? Thank God L'Université de Genovia *has* to accept me, on account of my family being its founder and major benefactor and all.

**You're so lucky! A college with beaches! Can I come over for Spring Break? I promise to bring plenty of Penn hotties . . . Oops, gotta go, Fleener is breathing down my neck. What is UP with these pinheads? Don't they realize we only have two weeks left at this place? Like our grades even MATTER any more!**

Ha, I know! Pinheads! Yeah! Tell me about it!

# Thursday, April 27, French

OK, it's been four years since I started going to this place. And it still feels like all I ever do is lie.

And I don't just mean to Lana or my parents either. Now I'm lying to *everyone*.

You would really think, after all this time, I'd be getting better about that.

But I found out the hard way – a little less than two years ago now actually – what happens when you tell the truth.

And even though I still think I did the right thing – I mean, it did bring democracy to a country that has never known it before and all – I'm not making that mistake again. I hurt so many people – especially people that I really care about – because I told the truth, I really think it's better now just . . . well, to lie.

Not big lies. Just little white lies that don't hurt anybody. It's not like I'm lying for personal gain.

But what am I going to do, *admit* I got into every college I applied to?

Oh yeah, that would go down really well. How would all the people who *didn't* get into their first choice colleges – especially those of them who deserved to . . . and that would be approximately eighty per cent of the current AEHS graduating senior class – feel then?

Besides, you know what they'd say.

Sure, *nice* people – like Tina – would say that I'm lucky.

Like luck had anything to do with it! Unless you count as 'luck' the time my mom ran into my dad at that off-campus party where they met and instantly hated one another. That of course led inevitably to sexual tension and then to l'amour and, one broken condom later, to me.

And – despite Principal Gupta's insistence – I'm not convinced hard work had very much to do with me getting in everywhere either.

OK . . . I did do really well in the verbal and reading sections of my SATs. And my college app essays were good too (I'm not going to lie about *that*, at least not in my own journal. I worked my butt off on those).

I'll admit, when your extra-curriculars are, *Single-handedly brought democracy to a country that otherwise had never known it before*, and *Wrote a 400-page novel for my senior project*, it does look slightly impressive.

But I can be truthful to *myself*: All those colleges I applied to? They only let me in because I'm a princess.

And it's not that I'm not grateful. I know every single one of those schools will give me a wonderful, unique educational opportunity.

It's just . . . it would have been nice for just *one* of those places to have accepted me for . . . well, for *me*, and not the tiara. If only I could have applied under my pen name – Daphne Delacroix – to know for sure.

Whatever. I've got bigger things to worry about right now.

Well, not bigger than where I'm going to spend the next four – or more, if I goof off and don't declare a major right away like Mom did – years of my life.

But there's the whole thing with Dad. What if he doesn't win the election? The election that wouldn't even be happening if it weren't for me telling the truth.

And Grandmere is so upset about the fact that René, of all people, is running against Dad – plus all the rumours that have been going around ever since I made

16

Princess Amelie's declaration public, like that our family was purposefully hiding Amelie's declaration all along, so that the Renaldos could stay in power – that Dad has had to banish her to Manhattan and have her plan this stupid birthday party for me just to distract her so she'll quit driving him insane with her constant barrage of, 'But does this mean we'll have to move out of the palace?'

She – like the readers of *teenSTYLE* – can't seem to understand that the Genovian palace – and royal family – are protected under Amelie's declaration (and besides which are a major source of tourist income, just like the British royal family). I keep explaining to her, 'Grandmere, no matter what happens in the election, Dad is *always* going to be HRH Prince of Genovia, you're *always* going to be HRH Dowager Princess, and I'm *always* going to be HRH Princess of Genovia. I'm still going to have to open new wings on the hospital; I'm still going to have to wear this stupid tiara and attend state funerals and diplomatic dinners . . . I'm just not going to make legislature. That will be the prime minister's job. Dad's job, hopefully. Got it?'

Only she never does.

I guess it's the least I can do for Dad after what I did. Dealing with her, I mean. I figured, when I spilt the beans about this whole Genovia-is-really-a-democracy thing, he'd run for prime minister unopposed. With our apathetic population, who else would be interested in running?

I never dreamed the Contessa Trevanni would put up the money for her son-in-law to campaign against him.

I should have known. It's not like René has ever had an actual job. And now that he and Bella have a baby, he's got to do *something*, I suppose, besides change the Luvs disposables.

But *Applebee's*? I suppose he's getting a kickback from them or something.

What's going to happen if Genovia is overrun by chain restaurants and – my chest seriously gets tight when I think about this – turned into another EuroDisney?

*What can I do to make this not happen?*

Dad says to stay out of it – that I've done enough . . .

Yeah. Like that doesn't make me feel *too* guilty.

It's all just so exhausting.

Not to mention all this other stuff. Like it even matters, in comparison to what's going on with Dad and Genovia, but . . . well, it kind of does. I mean, Dad and Genovia are facing all these changes, and so am I.

The only difference is, they aren't *lying* about it, the way I am. Well, OK, sure, Dad's lying about why Grandmere is in New York (to plan my birthday party, when really she's here because he can't stand having her around).

That's *one* lie. I have *multiple* lies. Lies layered upon lies.

## Mia Thermopolis's List of Big Fat Lies She's Been Telling Everyone

**Lie Number One:** Well, of course, first there's the lie that I didn't get into all those colleges (no one knows the truth but me. And Principal Gupta. And my parents, of course).

**Lie Number Two:** Then there's the lie about my senior project. I mean, that it wasn't *actually* on the history of

Genovian olive-oil pressing, circa 1254–1650, which is what I've told everyone (except Ms Martinez, of course, who was my adviser, and who actually read it . . . or at least the first eighty pages of it, since I noticed she stopped correcting my punctuation after that. Of course, Dr K knows the truth, but he doesn't count).

No one else even asked to read it, because who'd want to read a 400-page paper on the history of Genovian olive-oil pressing, circa 1254–1650?

Well, except for one person.

But I don't want to talk about that right now.

<u>Lie Number Three:</u> Then there's the lie that I just told Lana about how I can't go prom-dress shopping with her because I'm busy hanging out with John Paul Reynolds-Abernathy IV after school today, when the truth is—

Well. That's not the *only* reason why I'm not going prom-dress shopping with her. I just don't want to get into it with her, because I know what she'll say. And I just don't feel like dealing with La Lana right now.

Only Dr Knutz knows the exact extent of my lies. He says he's prepared to clear his schedule for the day when they all blow up in my face, as he's warned me is inevitably going to happen.

And he says I'd better do it soon, because next week is our last session.

He's mentioned it would be far better if I just came clean – confess the truth about having been admitted to every college to which I applied (for some reason, he thinks it *isn't* necessarily just because I'm a princess), tell everyone what my senior project is *really* about, including the one person who wants to read it . . . even fess up about the prom.

If you ask me, a good place for me to start telling the truth would be in Dr K's office – with telling Dr K that I think *he*'s the one in need of therapy. Yeah, he pretty much came to the rescue when I was going through one of the darkest periods of my life (though he made me do all the real work to climb out of that black hole myself).

But he has to be nuts to think I'm simply going to start blurting out the cold hard truth to everyone like that.

It's just that *so* many people would be *so* hurt if I suddenly started telling the truth. Dr K was there when the fallout happened after the Princess Amelie revelation. My dad and Grandmere were in his office for *hours* afterwards. It was *awful*. I don't want that to happen again.

Not, OK, that my friends would end up in my therapist's office. But Kenny Showalter – oh sorry, *Kenneth*, as he wants to be known now – wanted to go to Columbia more than anything, but instead got into his second choice school of MIT. MIT is a fantastic school, but try telling Kenny – I mean, Kenneth – that. I guess the fact that he'll be separated from his one true love, Lilly – who *will* be going to Columbia, just like her brother – is what's bothering him about MIT, which is in Massachusetts, a whole state away from where New York is.

And then there's Tina, who didn't get into *her* first choice of Harvard – but *did* get into NYU. So she's kind of happy, because Boris didn't get into his first choice of

Berklee, which is in Boston. Instead, he got into Juilliard, which is in New York City. So that means Tina and Boris will at least be going to colleges in the same city. Even if they aren't their first-choice colleges.

Oh, and Trisha is going to Duke. And Perin is going Dartmouth. And Ling Su is going to Parsons. And Shameeka is going to Princeton.

Still. None of them is their first-choice college (Lilly wanted to go to Harvard). And no one who wanted to go to school together got into the same place!

Including me and J.P. Well, except that we did. But he doesn't know that. Because I told him I didn't.

I couldn't help it! When everyone was checking online, and all the envelopes were coming, and no one was getting into their first-choice schools and everyone was finding out they were going to be one or even two states apart, and they were all crying and carrying on, I just . . . I don't know what came over me. I felt so badly about getting in everywhere I blurted out, 'I didn't get in anywhere either!'

It was just easier that way than telling the truth and having someone get their feelings hurt. Even though my lie made J.P. turn pale and swallow resolutely and put his arm around me and say, 'It's all right, Mia. We'll get through this. Somehow.'

So, yes. I suck.

But it wasn't like my lie was all that unbelievable. With my math SAT score? I *shouldn't* have gotten in any-where.

And honestly? How can I tell anyone the truth *now*? I can't. I just can't.

Dr K says this is the cowardly way of dealing with things. He says that I'm a brave woman, just like

Eleanor Roosevelt and Princess Amelie, and that I can easily surmount these obstacles (such as having lied to everyone).

But there's just ten more days of school to go! Anyone can fake anything for ten days. Grandmere's faked having eyebrows for the entire time I've known her –

Mia! You're writing in your journal! I haven't seen you do that in ages!

Oh. Hi, Tina. Yeah. Well, yeah, I told you. I was busy with my senior project.

I'll say. You've been working on it for the past two years almost! I had no idea the history of Genovian olive-oil pressing was that fascinating.

It is, believe me! As the main export of Genovia, olive oil and its manufacture is an extremely interesting subject.

I can't believe myself. Listen to me! How sad can I sound??? *As the main export of Genovia, olive oil and its manufacture is an extremely interesting subject?*

If only Tina knew what my book was really about! Tina would *die* if she knew I'd written a 400-page historical romance . . . Tina *adores* romances!

But I can't tell her. I mean, it obviously isn't any good if I can't get it published.

If only she had asked to read it . . . but who'd *want* to read about olive oil and its manufacture?

OK, well, *one* person.

But he was just being nice. Honestly. That's the only reason.

And I can't actually send him a copy. Because then he'll see what it's *really* about.

And I'll die.

Mia. Are you all right?

Of course! Why do you ask?

I don't know. Because you've been acting sort of . . . funny the closer we've gotten to graduation. And as your best friend, I just thought I'd ask. I know you didn't get into any of the colleges you applied to, but surely your dad can pull a few strings, right? I mean, he's still a prince – not to mention soon to be the prime minister! Well, hopefully. He's sure to beat that jerk Prince René. I just know your dad could get you into NYU . . . and then we could be roomies!

Well . . . we'll see! I'm trying not to worry about it too much.

You? Not worry? I'm surprised you haven't had your nose stuck in that journal for the past six months. Anyway, what's this Lana tells me about you not wanting to go prom-dress shopping with us this afternoon? She says you're going to J.P.'s play rehearsal?

Wow, news travels fast around this place. I guess I shouldn't be surprised. It's not like any of us seniors is

23

actually going to do any work the last two weeks of school.

Uh-huh. Gotta support my man!

Right. Except didn't J.P. forbid you from attending all rehearsals of his play because he wants you to be completely surprised by the show when you see it on opening night? So . . . what's really going on, Mia?

Great. Dr K was right. It's all blowing up in my face. Or starting to at least.

Well, all right. If I'm going to start telling people the truth I might as well start with Tina . . . sweet, non-judgemental, always-there-for-me Tina, my best friend and total confidante.

Right?

Actually, I'm not sure I'm going to the prom.

WHAT? Why? Mia, are you taking some kind of feminist stand against dances? Did Lilly put you up to this? I thought you guys still weren't even speaking.

We're speaking! You know we're speaking. We're . . . civil to one another. I mean, we have to be, since she's the editor for *The Atom* this year. And no one has updated ihatemiathermopolis in almost two years. You know, I think she still feels kind of bad about all that. Maybe.

Well – I guess so. I mean, OK, she never did update it again after that day she was so awful to you in the caff. Maybe, whatever it was Lilly was so mad at you about, she got it out of her system that day.

Right. Either that or she's just totally preoccupied with *The Atom*. And Kenny, of course. I mean, Kenneth.

I know! It's sweet Lilly's managed to stick with one guy for so long. But I honestly wish they wouldn't make out in front of me in Advanced Bio. I don't want to see that much of anyone's tongue. Especially now that she's pierced it. But none of this explains why you're not going to the prom!

Well, the truth is . . . J.P. hasn't actually asked me to go. And I'm fine with that because I don't want to go.

Is that all? Oh, Mia! Of course J.P. is going to ask you! I'm sure he's just been so busy with his play – and figuring out what FANTASTIC thing he's going to give you for your birthday – he hasn't gotten around to thinking about the prom yet. Do you want me to have Boris say something to him about it?

Ack! Ack, ack, ack, ack.
Also, why me?

Oh yes, Tina, yes, I do. Yes, I want you to have your

boyfriend remind my boyfriend to ask me to the prom. Because that's super romantic, and just how I always envisioned getting my invitation to the senior prom – via someone else's boyfriend.

I see what you mean. Oh dear, what a mess. And this was supposed to be our special time – you know.

Wait . . .

Can Tina actually be talking about . . .

She is. She actually *is*.

She's referring to that thing we used to talk about during our sophomore year.

You know, that losing-our-virginity-on-prom-night thing.

Doesn't Tina realize a lot of time has passed – and a lot of water gone under the bridge – since we sat in class when we were in tenth grade and fantasized about our perfect prom nights?

She can't possibly think I still feel the same way about it that I did back then.

I'm not the same person I was back then.

And I'm certainly not *with* the same person I was then. I mean, I'm with J.P. now –

And J.P. and I . . .

It's too late now for J.P. to make reservations for a room for after-prom at the Waldorf. Last I heard, they had no rooms left.

Oh my God! She's serious!

It's official: I'm freaking out now.

But he can probably get a room somewhere else. I hear the W is really nice. I just can't believe he hasn't asked you! What's wrong with him? This just isn't like him, you know. Is everything all right between you two? You didn't have a fight or anything, did you?

I seriously can't believe this is happening. This is *way* too weird.
   Should I tell her?
   I can't tell her. Can I?
   . . . No.

No, no fight. There's just been a lot of stuff going on with finals coming up and our projects and graduation and the election and my birthday and all. I think he really just forgot. And didn't you read my last text, Tina? I DON'T WANT TO GO TO THE PROM.

Don't be silly, of course you do. Who doesn't want to go to her senior prom? And why didn't you ask him? This isn't the 1800s. Girls can ask guys to the prom, you know. I know it's not the same, but you two have been going out for like forever! You're a little more than just friends, even if you still haven't . . . well, you know . . . yet. I mean . . . you haven't . . . have you?

Awwww . . . she still calls it *You Know*! That's so cute, I could die.
   Still. Tina brings up some good points. Why *didn't* I

ask him? When the ads for the prom started appearing in *The Atom*, why didn't I clip one out and stick it on J.P.'s locker door with *Are we going to this?* written on it?

Why didn't I just ask him, point-blank, if we were going to the prom, when everybody else was talking about it at lunch? It's true J.P.'s been distracted with his play and Stacey Cheeseman sucking so majorly in it (it would probably help if he wasn't always rewriting it and giving her new lines to memorize).

I easily could have gotten a yes or no answer out of him.

And, of course, because he's J.P., it would have been a yes.

Because J.P., unlike my last boyfriend, has nothing against the prom.

The thing is, I don't need to check in with Dr K to figure out why I didn't ask J.P. about the prom. It isn't exactly a mystery. To Tina, maybe, but not to me.

But I don't want to get into that right now.

You know, prom's not that big a deal to me any more, T. It's really kind of lame. I actually wouldn't mind blowing it off. So why waste time shopping for some dress I might not ever wear? You guys have fun shopping without me. I have stuff to do anyway.

Stuff. When am I going to stop calling my novel 'stuff'? Seriously, if there's one person in the world I can be honest about it with, it's Tina. Tina wouldn't laugh if I told her I'd written a novel . . . especially a *romance* novel. Tina is the person who introduced me to romance novels, who got me to appreciate them and realize how fabulously cool they are, not just as an introduction into the publishing world (although more of them are published than any other genre, so your chances of getting published are statistically higher if you write a romance as opposed to, say, a science-fiction novel), but because they're the perfect story really, because you have a strong female protagonist, a compelling male lead, a conflict that keeps them apart, and then, after a lot of nail-biting, a satisfying conclusion . . . the ultimate happy ending.

Why would anyone want to write anything else really?

If Tina knew I wrote a romance, she'd ask to read it – especially if she knew it was about something *other* than the history of Genovian olive-oil pressing, a subject no rational person would want to read about . . .

Well, except one person.

Which, really, every time I think about it, I want to start crying, because it's just about the sweetest thing anyone's ever said to me. Or emailed me, actually, because that's how Michael sent it to me . . . his request to read my senior project, I mean. We only email randomly a couple of times a month anyway, keeping it strictly light and impersonal, like that first email I sent him after he broke up with me – *Hi, how are you? Things are fine, it's snowing here, isn't that weird? Well, I have to go, bye.*

I'd been shocked when he'd been all, *Your senior project's on the history of Genovian olive-oil pressing, circa 1254-1650? Cool, Thermopolis. Can I read it?*

You could have knocked me over with one of Lana's pompoms. Because *no one* had asked to read my senior project. No one. Not even Mom. I thought I'd picked such a safe fake subject, I was safe from *anybody* asking to read it.

Ever.

And here was Michael Moscovitz, all the way from Japan (where he's been for the past two years, slaving away on his robotic arm – which I'm so sure is never going to get done I've given up asking about it, since it doesn't seem polite to bring it up any more, as he barely acknowledges the question), asking to read it.

I told him it was 400 pages long.

– He said he didn't care.

I told him it was single spaced and in nine-point font.

– He said he'd enlarge it when it came.

I told him it was really boring.

– And he said he didn't believe anything I wrote could be boring.

That's when I stopped emailing him back.

What else could I do? I couldn't send it to him! Yeah, I can send it to publishers I've never even met before. But not my ex-boyfriend! Not Michael! I mean . . . it's got *sex* in it!

It's just . . . how could he *say* that? That he didn't believe anything I wrote could be boring? What was he *talking* about? Of *course* something I wrote could be boring! The history of Genovian olive-oil pressing, circa 1254–1650. That's boring! That's really, really boring!

And OK, that's not what my book is really about.

But still! He doesn't know that.

How could he *say* something like that? How *could* he? That's not the kind of thing exes – or even mere friends – say to one another.

And that's all we're supposed to be now.

Anyway. Whatever.

It's not like I can show it to Tina either, and she's my *best friend*. Although I don't know what I'm so embarrassed about really. There are people who slap their novels all over the Internet, begging other people to read them.

But I can't do that. I don't know why. Except . . .

Well, I *know* why: Because I'm afraid Tina – not to mention Michael or J.P. or *who*ever really – might not like it.

Just like every single publisher I've sent it to hasn't liked it. Well, except AuthorPress.

But they want me to pay THEM to publish it! REAL publishers are supposed to pay YOU!!

Of course, Ms Martinez claimed to like it.

But I'm not convinced she even read the whole thing.

The thing is, what if I'm wrong, and I'm a terrible writer? What if I just wasted almost two years of my life? I know everybody *thinks* I did, writing about Genovian olive-oil pressing.

But what if I *really* did?

Oh no. Tina is still texting me about the prom!

Mia! Prom isn't lame! What's wrong with you? You're not going through a depression thingy again, are you?

'Depression thingy.' Great.

OK. I can't fight Tina. I can't. She's a force too strong for me.

No! No depression thingy. Tina, I didn't mean it. I don't know what's wrong with me. Senioritis, I guess –

the same thing that's keeping all of us from paying attention in class. I just meant – forget it. I'll talk to J.P. about the prom.

Do you mean it???? You really will???? You're not just saying that????

Yes, I'll ask him. I'm sorry. I just have a lot of stuff on my mind.

And you'll go shopping with us today after school?

Oh, man. I so don't want to go shopping with them today after school. Anything but that. I'd take *princess lessons* over that.

Wow. I can't believe I just wrote that.

Yeah. Sure. Why not.

YAY! We're going to have so much fun! Don't worry, we'll make you forget ALL about what's going on with your dad - eep!

*Je ne ferai pas le texte dans la classe.*
*Je ne ferai pas le texte dans la classe.*
*Je ne ferai pas le texte dans la classe.*
*Je ne ferai pas le texte dans la classe.*
*Je ne ferai pas le texte dans la classe.*
*Je ne ferai pas le texte dans la classe.*

Wow. Madame Wheeton has been on the *warpath* this month.

I swear they're going to take away all our iPhones and Sidekicks one of these days.

Except, if you ask me, the teachers all have senioritis too though, because they've been threatening for weeks, and so far nobody's actually carried out that threat.

# Thursday, April 27, Psychology

OK! So I told someone the truth about something . . .

And nothing earth-shattering happened (well, except that Madame Wheeton flipped out over finding us texting one another while she was trying to do her review session for the final).

I told Tina the truth about J.P. not having asked me to the prom . . . and my not really wanting to go anyway. And nothing earth-shattering happened. Tina didn't faint dead away.

She did try to convince me I'm wrong, of course.

But what else did I expect? Tina is such a romantic, of course she thinks the prom is the height of teen l'amour.

I know there was a time when I thought so too. All I have to do is look through the pages of my old journals. I used to be *crazy* for the prom. I would sooner have DIED than missed it.

I guess in a way I wish I could recapture that old excitement.

But we all have to grow up one day.

And the truth is, I really don't see what the big deal is about going to a dinner (rubbery chicken and wilted lettuce under disgusting dressing) and dance (to bad music) at the Waldorf (which I've been to a million times before anyway, most notably last time where I gave a speech that may have ruined my family's reputation, not to mention my native country, for all time).

I just wish –

AHHHHH!!!! God, I *have* to get used to that thing vibrating in my pocket . . .

Ameliaaaaaaa – I need an updated guesssssstlist from you for Mondayyyyyy. I'm quite put outtttttttt. *Everyone* I've invited has RSVP-ed yesssssss, according to Vigo. Even your cousin Hankkkkkkkkkkkk is coming in from the Milan shows to attend. And I just heard from your motherrrrrrrr that your dreadful grandparents from Indianaaaaaaaaaa will be flying into town for the event. I am most upset about thisssssssss. Of course they had to be invited, but I never expected them actually to say *yesssssssssssssssss*. It's all most disturbing . . . I may need for you to disinvite a few of your guests. You know the yacht only holds 300 comfortably. Call me immediately – Clarisse, your grandmotherrrrrrrrrrrrrr

– – – – – – – – – – – – – – – – – – – – – – –

**Sent from my BlackBerry Wireless Handheld**

God! Why did Dad get Grandmere a BlackBerry? Is he trying to ruin my life?

And who, exactly, was stupid enough to show her how to *use* it? I could kill Vigo.

Bystander effect: a psychological phenomenon in which someone is less likely to intervene in an emergency situation when other people are present and able to help than when he or she is alone. See Kitty Genovese, case in which a young woman was brutally attacked within hearing of a dozen neighbours, but none of them called the police, each thinking someone else would do it.

**Homework**

World History: Whatever

English Lit: Bite me

Trig: God, I hate this class

Gifted and Talented: I know Boris is playing at Carnegie Hall for his senior project, but WHY WON'T HE STOP PLAYING THE CHOPIN?????

French: *J'ai mal à la tête*

Psychology II: I can't believe I even bother taking notes in this class. I have lived this class.

## Thursday, April 27, Jeffrey

Great.

J.P. saw us in the hallway heading out towards the limo and was all, 'Where are you girls going, looking so happy?' and Lars went, before I could stop him, 'Prom-dress shopping.'

And then Lana and Tina and Shameeka and Trisha looked at J.P. expectantly with their eyebrows raised like, *Hello? Prom? Remember? Did you forget something? Would you like to ask your girlfriend to go with you?*

I guess news travels fast. The part about J.P. not having asked me to the prom, I mean. Thanks, Tina!

Not that she doesn't mean well.

Of course J.P. just smiled at us tolerantly and went, 'Well, have fun, girls, Lars.'

Then he kept walking towards the auditorium, where he was holding a play rehearsal.

They were all totally flabbergasted – Lana and those guys, I mean. That he didn't smack himself in the fore-head and go, 'Doh! Prom! Of course!' Then drop on to one knee and take my hands tenderly in his and ask me to forgive him for being a churlish lout and beg me to go with him.

But I told them they shouldn't be so shocked. I don't take it personally. J.P. can't think about *anything* but his play, *A Prince Among Men*.

Which I totally understand, because when I was writing my book I felt the same way. I couldn't think about *anything* else. Every chance I got, I just curled up in bed with Fat Louie at my side (he proved to be *such* an excellent writing cat) and my laptop, and *wrote*.

I mean, that's why I didn't keep up with my journal

or anything, not for almost two whole years. It's hard, when you're really concentrating on a creative project, to keep your mind on anything else.

Or at least it was for me.

Which, in a way, I guess, was why Dr K suggested it. That I write a book. To get my mind off . . . well, other things.

Or other people.

And it wasn't like I had anything *else* to do, since my parents took away my TV, and it was really hard to watch my shows out in the living room. It's kind of embarrassing to veg out in front of *Too Young to Be So Fat: The Shocking Truth*, when people know you're watching it.

Anyway, writing my book was great therapy, because it really worked. I didn't feel like writing in my journal once while I was writing and researching it. Everything just went into *Ransom My Heart*.

Now that the book's done, of course (and getting rejected everywhere), I suddenly find myself feeling like writing in my journal again.

Is that a good thing? I don't know.

Sometimes I think maybe I should write another book instead.

Anyway, I'm just saying I understand J.P.'s preoccupation with his play.

The thing is, unlike me, J.P. has a solid chance of actually getting *A Prince* produced, at least Off Broadway, because his dad is such a mover and shaker in the theatre world and all.

And Stacey Cheeseman has done all those GapKids commercials and had that part in that Sean Penn movie. J.P.'s even got Andrew Lowenstein, Brad Pitt's third cousin's nephew, playing the part of the male lead. The thing is bound to be HUGE. I hear, from people who've seen it, it might even have Hollywood potential.

Anyway, back to the whole prom thing: it's not like I don't know J.P. loves me. He tells me so like ten times a day –

Oh God, I forgot how annoyed everyone gets when I start writing in my journal instead of paying attention to what's going on. Lana is making me try on a strapless Badgley Mischka now.

Look, I get the fashion thing now. I do. How you look on the outside is a reflection of how you feel about yourself on the inside. If you let yourself go – not washing your hair, wearing the same clothes you slept in all day or clothes that don't fit or are out of style – that says, 'I do not care about myself. And you shouldn't care about me either.'

You have to Make An Effort, because that says to other people I Am Worth Getting To Know. Your clothes don't have to be *expensive*. You just have to look good in them.

I realize that now, and acknowledge that in the past I may have slacked off in that area (although I still wear my overalls at home on the weekends when no one is around).

And since I've stopped binge eating, my weight has stopped fluctuating and I'm back down to a B cup.

So I get the fashion thing. I do.

But honestly – why does Lana think I look good in purple? Just because it's the colour of royalty doesn't mean it looks good on every royal! Not to be mean, but has anyone taken a good look at Queen Elizabeth lately? She so needs neutral colours.

An Excerpt from *Ransom My Heart* by
Daphne Delacroix

Shropshire, England, 1291

Hugo stared down at the lovely apparition
swimming naked below him, his thoughts
ajumble in his head. Foremost amongst them
was the question, *Who is she?*, though he
knew the answer to that. Finnula Crais, the
miller's daughter. There had been a family of
that name in villeinage to his father, Hugo
remembered.

This, then, must be one of their offspring.
But what was this miller about, allowing a
defenceless maid to roam the countryside
unescorted and dressed in such provocative
garb – or completely undressed, as the case
now stood?

As soon as Hugo arrived at Stephensgate
Manor, he would send for the miller, and see
to it that the girl was better protected in the
future. Did the man not ken the riff-raff that
travelled the roads these days, the footpads
and cut-throats and despoilers of young
women such as the one below him?

So fixed was Hugo upon his musings that, for
a moment, he did not realize that the maid
had paddled out of view. Where the waterfall
cascaded, the pool below was out of his line of
vision, being blocked off by the rock outcrop
on which he lay. He assumed that the girl had

ducked beneath the waterfall, perhaps to rinse her hair.

Hugo waited, pleasantly anticipating the girl's reappearance. He wondered to himself whether the chivalrous thing to do was to creep away now, without drawing attention to himself, then meet up with her again upon the road, as if by accident, and offer to escort her home to Stephensgate.

It was as he was deciding that he heard a soft sound behind him, and then suddenly something very sharp was at his throat and someone very light was astride his back.

It was with an effort that Hugo controlled his soldierly instinct to strike first and question later.

But he had never before felt so slim an arm circle his neck, nor such slight thighs straddle his back. Nor had his head ever been jerked back against such a temptingly soft cushion.

'Stay perfectly still,' advised his captor, and Hugo, enjoying the warmth from her thighs and, more particularly, the softness of the hollow between her breasts, where she kept the back of his head firmly anchored, was happy to oblige her.

'I've a knife at your throat,' the maid informed him in her boyishly throaty voice, 'but I won't use it unless I have to. If you do as I say, you shan't be harmed. Do you understand?'

## Thursday, April 27, 7 p.m., the Loft

```
Daphne Delacroix
1005 Thompson Street, Apt 4A
New York, NY 10003

Dear Author

Thank you for giving us the opportunity
to read your manuscript. However, it
does not suit our needs at the present
time.
```

Not even a signature! Thanks for nothing.

I just walked in the door and Mom wants to know why someone named Daphne Delacroix keeps getting all this mail from publishing houses addressed to our apartment.

Busted!

I thought about lying to her too, but there's no point really. She's going to catch me eventually, especially if *Ransom My Heart* does get published some day and I build my own wing on to the Royal Genovian Hospital or whatever.

OK, well, I have no idea how much published novelists get paid, but I heard the forensic mystery writer Patricia Cornwell bought a helicopter with her book money.

Not that I need a helicopter, because I have my own jet (well, Dad does).

So I was just like, 'I sent out my book under a fake name just to see if I could get it published.'

My mom already suspects what I wrote wasn't a

really long history paper. I couldn't lie to *her* about it. She saw me in my room, listening to the *Marie Antoinette* movie soundtrack with my headphones on and Fat Louie by my side, typing away all the time . . . well, whenever I wasn't at school, princess lessons, therapy or out with Tina or J.P.

I know it's bad to lie to your own mother. But if I told her what my book was *really* about, she'd want to read it.

And there's *no way* I want Helen Thermopolis reading what I actually wrote. I mean, sex scenes and your mother? No thank you.

'Well,' Mom said, pointing to my letter, 'what did they say?'

'Oh,' I said. 'Not interested.'

'Hmmm,' Mom said. 'It's a tough market these days. Especially for a history of Genovian olive-oil pressing.'

'Yeah,' I said. 'Tell me about it.'

God, what if TMZ got hold of the truth about me? What a liar I am, I mean? What kind of role model am I? I make Vanessa Hudgens look like Mother Freaking Teresa. Minus the whole nudity thing. Because I'm not about to take naked photos of myself and send them to my boyfriend.

Thankfully it was kind of hard to have a conversation with Mom because Mr Gianini was practising his drums, with Rocky banging along on his toy drum set.

When he saw me, Rocky dropped his drumsticks and ran over to throw his arms around my knees, screaming, 'Meeeeeeaaaaaaahhhhhh!'

It's nice to be able to come home to someone who's always happy to see you, even if it's only an almost three-year-old.

'Yeah, hi, I'm home,' I said. It's no joke trying to walk with a toddler attached to you. 'What's for dinner?'

'It's two-for-one pizza night at Tre Giovanni,' Mr G said, hanging up his sticks. 'How can you even ask?'

'Where were you?' Rocky wanted to know.

'I had to go shopping with my friends,' I said.

'But you din't buy anything,' Rocky said, looking at my empty hands.

'I know,' I explained, heading to the kitchen drawer where we keep the silverware with him still attached to me. It's my job to set the table. I may be a princess, but I still have chores. That's one thing we established during Family Sessions with Dr K. 'That's because we went prom-dress shopping, and I'm not going to the prom, because it's lame.'

'Since when is the prom lame?' Mr G wanted to know, wrapping a towel around his neck. Drumming can make you sweaty, as I know all too well from the small damp person attached to my legs.

'Since she became a bitingly sarcastic, soon-to-be college girl,' Mom said, pointing at me. 'Speaking of which, Family Meeting after dinner. Oh, hello.'

She said this last part into the phone, then gave Tre's our standard order of two medium pies, one all meat for herself and Mr G, and one all cheese for Rocky and me. I'm back on the vegetarian bandwagon. Well, I'm really more of a flexatarian . . . I don't order meat for myself except in times of extreme stress when I need a quick source of high protein, such as beef tacos (so irresistible, though I try to abstain). But when someone else serves meat to me – for instance, such as at last week's meeting of the Domina Reis – I'll eat it to be polite.

'Family meeting about what?' I demanded when Mom hung up.

'You,' she said. 'Your father's scheduled a conference call.'

Great. There's really nothing I look forward to more than a nice call from my dad in Genovia in the evening. That's always a big guarantee a good time will be had by all. Not.

'What did I do now?' I wanted to know. Because, seriously, I haven't done anything (except lie to everyone I know about . . . well, everything). But other than that, I'm always home by curfew, and it isn't even because I have a bodyguard who basically ensures it either. My boyfriend is way conscientious. J.P. doesn't want to get on the bad side of my father (or mother or stepfather), and when we get together he basically freaks if I'm not on my way home a half-hour before I'm supposed to be, and so he literally hurls me into Lars's arms every time.

So whatever Dad's calling about – I didn't do it.

Not this time, anyway.

I went in to my room to visit Fat Louie before the pizzas came. I worry about him so much. Because let's just say I do choose to make everyone I know furious with me, and go to a college in the US instead of L'Université de Genovia, which really no one but the sons and daughters of celebrity plastic surgeons and dentists who couldn't get in anywhere else attends (Spencer Pratt from *The Hills* probably would have gone there, if he hadn't leeched his way on to his girlfriend's ex-friend's TV show. *Lana* probably would have had to go there, if I hadn't forced her to make studying, not getting on to lastnightsparty.com, a priority in her junior year).

The thing is, none of the colleges I got into has

dorms that let you bring your cat. Which means if I go to one of them and I want to take Fat Louie, I'll have to live off-campus. So I won't meet anyone, and I'll be a bigger social leper than I would be otherwise.

But how can I leave Fat Louie behind? He's afraid of Rocky . . . understandably, because Rocky adores Fat Louie and every time he sees him he runs and tries to grab him and pick him up and squeeze him, which, of course, has given Fat Louie a complex, because he doesn't like being grabbed and squeezed.

So now Fat Louie just stays in my room (which Rocky is forbidden from entering because he messes with my *Buffy the Vampire Slayer* action figures) when I'm not around to protect him.

And if I go off to college, that means Fat Louie'll just be hiding in my room for four years with no one to sleep with him and scratch him under the ears, just the way he likes.

That's just wrong.

Oh sure, Mom *says* that he can move into *her* room (which Rocky is also forbidden from entering – unsupervised, anyway – because he's obsessed with her make-up and once ate one of her entire Lancôme Au Currant Velvet lipsticks, so she had to put one of those slippy things on her doorknob too).

But I don't know if Fat Louie will really like sleeping with Mr G, who snores.

My phone! It's J.P.

## Thursday, April 27, 7.30 p.m., the Loft

J.P. wanted to know how prom-dress shopping went. I lied to him, of course. I was like, 'Great!'

Our conversation slipped into the twilight zone from there.

'Did you get anything?' he wanted to know.

I couldn't believe he was asking. I was truly shocked. You know, what with the whole *his-having-neglected-to-ask-me-to-the-prom* thing and all. Silly me to assume we weren't going.

I said, 'No . . .'

My shock grew beyond all bounds when he then went on to say, 'Well, when you do, you have to let me know what colour it is, so I'll know what colour corsage to get you.'

Hello?

'Wait,' I said. 'So . . . we're *going* to the prom?'

J.P. actually laughed. 'Of course!' he said. 'I've had the tickets for weeks now.'

!!!!!!!!!

Then, when I didn't laugh along with him, he stopped laughing and said, 'Wait. We *are* going, aren't we, Mia?'

I was so stunned, I didn't know what to say. I mean, I –

I love J.P. I do!

It's just that for some reason, I don't love the idea of going to the prom with J.P.

Only I wasn't quite sure how I was going to explain that to him without hurting his feelings. Telling him that I thought the prom was lame, like I'd said to Tina, didn't seem like it was going to cut it.

Especially since he'd just admitted he'd had the tickets for weeks. And those things aren't cheap.

Instead I heard myself muttering, 'I don't know. You . . . you never asked.'

Which is *true*. I mean, I was telling the *truth*. Dr K would have been proud of me.

But all J.P. said to this was, 'Mia! We've been going out for almost two years. I didn't think I had to ask.'

*I didn't think I had to ask?*

I couldn't believe he said this. Even if it's true, well . . . a girl still wants to be asked! Right?

I don't think I'm the girliest girl in the world – I don't have fake nails (any more) and I don't diet or anything, even though I'm far from the skinniest girl for my height in our class. I'm WAY less girly than Lana. And I'm a *princess*.

But still. If a guy wants to take a girl to the prom, he should *ask* her . . .

. . . even if they have been dating exclusively for almost two years.

Because she might not want to go.

Really, is it me? Am I asking too much? I don't think so.

But maybe I am. Maybe expecting to be asked to the prom, rather than just assuming I'm going, is too much.

I don't know. I don't know anything any more, I guess.

J.P. must have realized from my silence that he'd said the wrong thing. Because finally, he said, 'Wait . . . are you saying that I *do* have to ask?'

I said, 'Um.' Because I didn't know what to say! A part of me was like, *Yeah! Yeah, you should have asked!* But another part of me was like, *You know what, Mia? Don't rock the boat. You're graduating in ten days. TEN DAYS. Just let it go.*

On the other hand, Dr K told me to start telling the truth. I'd already not lied to Tina today. I figured I might as well stop lying to my boyfriend too. So . . .

'It'd have been nice if you'd asked,' I heard myself say, to my own horror.

J.P. did the strangest thing then:

He laughed!

Really. Like he thought that was the funniest thing he'd ever heard.

'Is *that* how it is?' he asked.

What was *that* supposed to mean?

I had no idea what he was talking about. He sounded a little bit crazy, which wasn't at all like J.P. I mean, true, he does make me sit through a lot of Sean Penn films, because Sean Penn is his new favourite actor/director.

I have nothing against Sean Penn. I don't even mind that he ended up divorcing Madonna. I mean, I still like Shia LaBeouf even though he was in *Transformers,* which turned out to be a movie about robots from space.

That talk.

Which is just as bad as divorcing Madonna, if you ask me.

Still. That doesn't mean J.P. is crazy. Even though he was laughing like that.

'I know you bought tickets,' I said, going on as if I didn't actually suspect him of a cognitive imbalance. 'So I'll pay you back for mine. Unless you want to take someone else.'

'Mia!' J.P. stopped laughing all of a sudden. 'I don't

want to take anyone but you! Who else would I want to take?'

'Well, I don't know,' I said. It's funny, but I couldn't get the thought of Stacey Cheeseman out of my head. She'd been really good in that Sean Penn movie, playing a teenaged hooker. She's only a sophomore, but she's very curvaceous. And I think she has a little bit of a crush on J.P. If he asked her to the prom, I'm sure she'd go in a New York minute. 'I'm just saying. It's your senior prom too. You should ask who you want.'

'I'm asking *you*,' J.P. said, sounding grumbly, which he used to do sometimes when he felt like going out and I felt like staying in and writing. Only I couldn't tell him that's what I was doing, because of course he didn't know I was writing a real book and not just a paper for my senior project.

'Are you?' I asked, a little surprised. 'You're asking me right now?'

'Well, not right this minute,' J.P. said quickly. 'I realize I may have fallen down in the romantic prom-invitation department. I plan to do it right. So expect an invitation soon. A real invitation that you won't be able to resist.'

I have to admit, my heart kind of sped up when I heard this. And not in a happy, oh-he's-so-sweet kind of way either. More in like a oh-no-what's-he-going-to-do sort of way. Because I honestly couldn't think of any way J.P. could ask me to the prom that could make dry chicken and bad music at the Waldorf at all appealing.

'Um,' I said. 'You're not going to do something that's going to embarrass me in front of the whole school, are you?'

'No,' J.P. said, sounding taken aback. 'What are you talking about?'

'Well,' I said. I knew I probably sounded insane, but I had to say it. So I said it fast, to get it out. 'I saw this Lifetime movie once, where to make a grand romantic gesture this guy wearing a full suit of armour rode up to this woman's office building to propose to her on a white horse. You know, because he wanted to be her knight in shining armour? You aren't going to ride up to Albert Einstein High wearing a suit of armour on a white horse and ask me to the prom, are you? Because that would truly be about nineteen levels of wrong. Oh, and the guy couldn't find a white horse so he painted a brown one white, which is cruelty to animals, and also, the white paint rubbed off on the inside of his jeans, so when he got off the horse to kneel down to propose, he looked really dumb.'

'Mia,' J.P. said, sounding annoyed. Which, really, I guess I couldn't blame him. 'I'm not going to ride up to Albert Einstein High in a suit of armour on a horse painted white to ask you to the prom. I think I can manage to think of something a little more romantic than *that*.'

For some reason this assertion didn't make me feel any better though.

'You know, J.P.,' I said, 'prom is pretty lame. I mean, it's just dancing at the Waldorf. We can do that any time.'

'Not with all our friends,' J.P. pointed out. 'Right before we all graduate and go off to different colleges and possibly never see one another ever again.'

'But we're going to do that,' I reminded him, 'at my

birthday blowout on the Royal Genovian yacht Monday night.'

'True,' J.P. said. 'But that won't be the same. All your relatives are going to be there. And it's not like we'll really get a chance to be alone afterwards.'

What was he talking about?

Oh . . . right. The paparazzi.

Wow. J.P. *really* wants to go to the prom. And do all the after-prom stuff, it sounds like.

I guess I can't really blame him. It *is* the last event we'll ever attend as AEHS students, besides graduation, which the administration has cleverly scheduled for the next day, in order to avoid what happened last year, when a few seniors got so drunk at a downtown club they had to be admitted to St Vincent's Hospital for alcohol poisoning, after spray-painting *The WMDs were hidden in my vagina* all over Washington Square Park. Principal Gupta seems to feel that if people know they have graduation the next day, they won't let themselves get *quite* that intoxicated this year.

So I said, 'OK. Well, I look forward to the invitation.' Then I thought it might be better to change the subject, since we both seemed to be getting a little irritated with one another. 'So. How did play rehearsal go?'

Then J.P. complained about Stacey Cheeseman's inability to remember her lines (which, honestly, I think she'd be able to do if he didn't keep changing them) for about five minutes until I said I had to go because the pizzas had come. But that was a lie (*Mia Thermopolis's Big Fat Lie Number Four*), since the pizzas hadn't come.

The truth is, I'm scared. I know he's not going to ride up to the school in a full suit of armour on a painted horse in order to ask me to the prom, because he said he wouldn't.

But he might do something equally embarrassing.

I love J.P. – I know I keep writing that, but it's because I do. I don't love *him the same way* I loved Michael, it's true, but I still love him. J.P. and I have so much in common with the writing thing, and we're the same age, and Grandmere loves him and most of my friends (except Boris, for some reason) do too.

But sometimes I wish – God, I can't believe I'm even writing this – but sometimes . . .

Well. I worry that my mom might be right. She's the one who pointed out the fact that if I say I want to do something, J.P. *always* wants to do it too. And if I say I don't want to do something, he *always* agrees he doesn't want to do it either.

The only time he hasn't agreed with me, in fact, was when I used to say I didn't want to hang out with him, back when I was working on my book.

But that was just because he couldn't be with me. It was so romantic really. All the girls said so. Especially Tina, who would know. I mean, what girl wouldn't want a boyfriend who wanted to be with her *all* the time and always do whatever she wanted to do?

Mom was the only one who noticed this and asked me if it drove me crazy. And when I asked her what she meant, she said, 'Dating a chameleon. Does he even *have* his own personality, or is it all about accommodating yours?'

That's when we got into a huge argument about it. So huge we had to have an emergency therapy session with Dr K.

She promised to keep her opinions about my love life

to herself after that, since I pointed out I've never mentioned how I feel about hers (although, the truth is, I like Mr G. Without him I wouldn't have Rocky).

I've totally never brought up *the other thing* about J.P. though. Not to Dr K, and certainly not to my mom.

For one thing, it would probably make my mom happy. And for another . . . well, no relationship is perfect anyway. Look at Tina and Boris. He *still* tucks his sweaters into his pants, despite her repeated requests that he not do so. But they're happy together. And Mr G snores, but Mom solved that by wearing earplugs and using a white-noise machine.

I can deal with the fact that my boyfriend likes all the same things that I do and always wants to do everything that I do all the time.

It's *the other thing* about him I'm not sure I can deal with . . .

And now the pizzas really *are* here, so I have to go.

# Friday, April 28, Midnight, the Loft

OK. Deep breath. Calming down. It's going to be fine.

Just fine. I'm sure of it! More than sure. A hundred per cent positive everything is going to be—

Oh God. Who am I kidding? I'm a wreck!

So . . . the family meeting turned out to be about a little more than just the election and Dad nagging me about which college I'm going to go to – in other words: it was a disaster.

It started out with Dad trying to give me a deadline: election day. I've got until ED (also known as the prom) to decide where I'm going to spend the next four years of my life.

Then I've got to make a decision.

You'd think Dad would have more important things to worry about, what with René breathing down his neck at the polls.

Grandmere conferenced herself in, of course, and was giving her two cents (she wants me to go to Sarah Lawrence. Because that's where she would have gone, back in the age of drawn-on stockings, if she'd gone to college instead of marrying Grandpere). We all tried to ignore her, just like in family therapy, but it's impossible with Rocky around, because for some reason he loves Grandmere, even the sound of her voice (question: WHY?), and ran over to the phone and kept yelling, 'Gwanmare, Gwanmare, you come over soon? Give Wocky big kiss?'

Can you imagine *wanting* that big wonk looming over you? She's not even technically related to him (lucky kid).

Anyway, yeah. That's what the big meeting was about – or at least, what it *started off* being about. Me deciding, in nine days' time, where I am going to go school.

Thanks, guys! No pressure!

Dad *says* he doesn't care where I go, so long as I'm happy. But he's made it more than clear that if I don't go to an Ivy or Sarah Lawrence or one of the Seven Sisters, I might as well be committing hara-kiri.

'Why don't you go to Yale?' he kept saying. 'Isn't that where J.P. wants to go? You could go with him.'

Of course Yale is where J.P. wants to go, because they have a fantastic drama department.

Except I can't go to Yale. It's too far from Manhattan. What if something were to happen to Rocky or Fat Louie – a freak flash fire or building collapse? – and I had to get back to the loft fast?

Besides, J.P. thinks I'm going to L'Université de Genovia, and has already applied and resigned himself to going there with me. Even though L'Université de Genovia has no drama department and I explained to him that by going there he's shooting all his own career aspirations in the foot. He said it didn't matter, so long as we can be together.

I guess it actually *doesn't* matter, since his dad will always be able to get his plays produced.

But anyway, none of that is what I'm freaking out about. It's what happened *afterwards*.

It was after Grandmere had harangued me some more about the invitation list to my party – and said to Mr G, 'Do your niece and nephew *have* to attend? Because you know if I could scratch them off I could make room for the Beckhams' – and then finally hung up that Dad said, 'I think you ought to show it to her now,' and Mom said, 'Really, Philippe, I think you're being just a tad dramatic, there's no need for you to stay on the phone, I'll give it to her later,' and Dad said, 'I'm part of this family too, and I want to be here to support her, even if I can't actually be there in the flesh,' and Mom said, 'You're overreacting. But if you insist.' And she got up and went into her room.

And I went, starting to feel a bit nervous, 'What's going on?'

And Mr G said, 'Oh, nothing. Your dad just emailed something he saw on international business CNN.'

'And I want you to see it, Mia,' Dad said through the speakerphone, 'before someone tells you about it at school.'

And my heart sank, because I figured it was some new scheme of René's to junk up Genovia in order to get more tourists to go there. Maybe he was going to put a Hard Rock Cafe in there, and try to get Clay Aiken to come and play at its grand opening.

Only it wasn't. When Mom came out of her bedroom with a printout of what Dad had emailed her, I saw that it had nothing to do with René at all.

It was this:

NEW YORK (AP) - Robotic arms are the future for surgery, and one in particular, dubbed the CardioArm, will be revolutionizing cardiac surgery, already making its creator - Michael Moscovitz, 21, Manhattan - a very wealthy man.

Billed as the first surgical robot compatible

with advanced imaging technology, Moscovitz has spent two years leading a team of Japanese scientists designing CardioArm for his small company, Pavlov Surgical.

The stock of Pavlov Surgical, Moscovitz's high-tech company with a monopoly on selling robotic surgical arms in the United States, has surged nearly 500 per cent over the last year. Analysts believe that the rally is far from over.

That's because demand for Moscovitz's product is growing, and so far his small company has the market all to itself.

The surgical arm, which is controlled remotely by surgeons, was approved by the Food and Drug Administration for general surgery last year.

The CardioArm system is considered to be more precise and less invasive than traditional surgical tools that include small handheld surgical cameras inserted into the body during surgery. Recovery from surgery performed by the CardioArm system is considerably faster than recovery from traditional surgery.

'What you can do with the robotic arm – with the capabilities in manipulation and visualization – you just can't do any other way,' said Dr Arthur Ward, Head of Cardiology, Columbia University Medical Center.

There are already fifty CardioArms operating in American hospitals, with a waiting list of hundreds more, but with a price tag ranging from $1 million to $1.5 million, the systems don't come cheap. Moscovitz has donated several CardioArm systems to children's hospitals nationwide, and will be donating a new one to Columbia University Medical Center this weekend, a fact for which the university, his Alma Mater, is grateful.

'This is a highly perfected, highly sought after, very unique technology,' said Ward. 'In terms of robotics, CardioArm is the clear leader. Moscovitz has done something extraordinary for the field of surgical medicine.'

!!!!!!!!!!

Wow. The ex-girlfriend is always the last to know.

But whatever. It's not like this changes anything.

I mean, so what? So Michael's genius is universally acknowledged, the way it always should have been. He deserves all the money and acclaim. He worked really hard for it. I knew he was going to save children's lives, and now he's doing it.

I just . . . I guess I just . . .

Well, I just can't believe he didn't tell me!

On the other hand, what was he going to say in his last email exactly? *Oh, by the way, my robotic surgical arm is a huge success, it's saving lives nationwide, and my company has the fastest trading stock on Wall Street?*

Oh no, that wouldn't be too braggy.

And anyway, *I'm* the one who freaked out and stopped emailing him when he asked if he could read my senior project. For all I know, maybe he *was* going to mention that his CardioArm is selling for $1.5 million a pop and has a stronghold on the robotic-surgical-arm market.

Or, *I'm coming back to America and donating one of my robotical surgical arms to Columbia University Medical Center on Saturday, so maybe I'll see you.*

I just never gave him the chance, being the super rude one who never wrote back after the last time we corresponded.

And for all I know, Michael's been back to America a dozen times since we broke up, to visit his family and whatnot. Why would he mention it to me? It's not like we're going to get together for coffee or anything. We're broken up.

*And hello, I already have a boyfriend.*

It's just . . . in the article, it said, Michael Moscovitz, 21, *Manhattan*. Not Tsukuba, Japan.

So. He's obviously living here now. He's *here*. He asked to read my senior project, and he's *here*.

Panic attack.

I mean, before, when he was in Japan, and he asked to see my senior project, I could have been like, *Oh, I sent it to you, didn't you get it? No? That's so weird. Let me try sending it again.*

But now, if I see him, and he asks . . .

Oh my God. What am I going to do?????

Wait . . . whatever. It's not like he's asked to see me! I mean, he's here, isn't he? And has he called? No.

Emailed? No.

Of course . . . I'm the one who owes him an email. He's politely observed email etiquette and waited for me to email him back. What must he think, since I totally stopped communicating when he asked to read my book? He must think I'm the biggest byotch, as Lana would say. Here he made the nicest offer – an offer my own boyfriend has never made, by the way – and I totally went missing in action . . .

God, remember that weird thing where I used to want to smell his neck all the time? It's like I couldn't feel calm or happy or something unless I smelt his neck. That was so . . . geek, as Lana would say.

Of course . . . if I remember correctly, Michael always *did* smell a lot better than J.P., who continues to smell like dry-cleaning. I tried buying him some cologne for his birthday, like Lana suggested—

It didn't work. He wears it, but now he just smells like cologne. Over dry-cleaning fluid.

I just can't believe Michael's been back in town and I didn't even know it! I'm so glad Dad told me! I could have run into him at Bigelow's or Forbidden Planet and, without having any advanced warning he was back, I might have done something incredibly stupid when I saw him. Such as pee myself. Or blurt out, 'You look *incredible*!'

Providing he does look incredible, which I'm guessing he probably does. That would have been *awful* (although peeing myself would be worse).

No, actually, showing up at either place and bumping into him without any make-up on and my hair a big mess would be worse . . . except I have to say my hair is looking better than it ever has now that Paolo has layered it and it's grown out and I've got a real proper hairstyle that I can actually tuck behind my ears and give a sexy side part to and put up in a hairband and all. Even *teenSTYLE* agreed about *that* in their year-end fashion Hot and Not columns (I was in the Hot columns for once instead of the Not. I so owe Lana).

Which isn't why Dad told me about Michael coming back of course (so I can make sure I look Hot at all times now, in case I run into my ex).

Dad says he told me so I wouldn't be caught off guard if a paparazzo asked me about it.

Which, now that there's been this press release, is bound to happen.

And there was no need to provide that quote for me from the Genovian press office – that I'm truly happy for Mr Moscovitz and so glad to see that he's moved on, like I have. I can make up my own quotes for the press, thank you very much.

It's fine. He's back in Manhattan, and I'm totally OK with that. I'm *more* than OK with that. I'm happy for him. He's probably forgotten all about me, much less about asking to read my book. I mean, senior project. Now that he's a bazillionaire robot-arm inventor, I'm sure a silly email exchange with a high-school girl he used to date is the last thing Michael is thinking about.

Honestly, I don't care if I never see him again. I have a boyfriend. A perfectly wonderful boyfriend who is, even now, planning a completely romantic way to ask me to the prom, that won't involve painting a brown horse white. Probably.

I'm going to bed now, and I'm going to go to sleep right away, and NOT lay awake half the night thinking about Michael being back in Manhattan, and having asked to read my book.

I'm *not*.

Watch me.

# Friday, April 28, Homeroom

Uck, I feel awful, and I look worse, I was up all night freaking out about Michael being back in town!

And, to make things worse, I skipped *The Atom* staff meeting this morning before school. I know Dr K would highly disapprove, because a brave woman, such as Eleanor Roosevelt, would have gone.

But I didn't feel very Eleanor Roosevelt this morning. I just didn't know if Lilly was going to assign someone to cover Michael's donation of one of his CardioArms to the Columbia University Medical Center or not. It seems like she would. I mean, he's an AEHS grad. An AEHS grad inventing something that's saving children's lives and then donating it to a major local university would constitute news . . .

I couldn't run the risk that Lilly might assign *me* to be the person to cover the story in the last issue. Lilly isn't actively doing stuff to antagonize me — we're totally staying out of each other's way.

But she might have done it anyway, just out of a perverse sense of irony.

And I do not *want* to see Michael. I mean, not as a high-school reporter covering the story of his brilliant comeback. That would probably kill me.

Plus, what if he asks about my senior project?????

I know it's highly unlikely he remembers. But it could happen.

Plus, my hair is doing that weird flippy thing in the back this morning. I totally ran out of Phytodéfrisant.

No, the next time I see Michael, I want my hair to look good and I want to be a published author. Oh, please, God, make both these things happen!

And I know, OK, I already helped a small European country achieve democracy. And that is a *major* accomplishment. It's ridiculous of me to want to be a published author by the age of eighteen (which gives me approximately three days, a totally unrealistic goal) as well.

But I worked so hard on that book! I poured almost two years of my life into that book! I mean, first there was all the research – I had to read like 500 romance novels, so I'd know how to write one myself.

Then I had to read fifty billion books on medieval England, so I could get the setting and at least some of the dialogue and stuff right in mine.

Then I had to actually write it.

And I *know* one small historical romance novel isn't going to change the world.

But it would be lovely if it made a few people as happy reading it as it made me when I was writing it.

Oh God, why am I obsessing about this when I don't even care? I've already got a wonderful boyfriend who tells me constantly that he loves me and takes me out all the time and who everyone in the entire universe says is perfect for me.

And, all right, he forgot to ask me to the prom. And then there's *the other thing*.

But I don't even want to go to the prom anyway, because the prom is for children, which I'm not, I'll be eighteen in three days, at which point I'll legally be an adult . . .

OK. I need to get a grip.

Maybe Hans can go get me another chai latte – I don't think my first one took this morning. Except Dad says I have to stop sending my limo driver out on personal errands. But what else am I supposed to do? Lars totally refuses to duck out and get me hot foamy drinks, even though I've pointed out to him it's *highly* unlikely anyone is going to kidnap me between the time he leaves for Starbucks and the time he gets back.

No one has mentioned the CardioArm story yet, and I've seen Tina, Shameeka, Perin and of course J.P.

Maybe it hasn't broken anywhere but international business CNN.com.

Please God, let it not break anywhere else.

# Friday, April 28, third-floor stairwell

I just got a 911 text from Tina telling me to grab a bathroom pass and meet her here!

I can't imagine what could have happened! It has to be serious because we've been really good about skipping lately, considering the fact that we've all gotten into college and there's basically no reason to attend classes any more, except to admire what kind of shoes we're buying to wear for commencement.

I really hope she and Boris haven't had a fight. They're so cute together. He does get on my nerves sometimes, but you can tell he just adores T. And he asked her to the prom in the cutest way, by presenting her with a prom ticket attached to a single half-blown red rose with a Tiffany's box dangling from it.

Yes! It wasn't even from Kay Jewelers, which has always been Tina's favourite. Boris decided to upgrade (which, good for him. Her attachment to Kay's was starting to get kind of sad).

And inside the box was another box, a velvet ring box (Tina said she nearly had a heart attack when she saw it).

And inside that was the most gorgeous emerald ring (a *promise* ring, not an engagement ring, Boris hastened to assure her). And inside the band of the ring were Tina's and Boris's initials entwined, and the date of the prom.

Tina said she nearly threw up a lung, if such a thing were physically possible, she was that excited. She came into school on Monday and showed the ring to all of us (Boris gave it to her at dinner at Per Se, which is like the most expensive restaurant in New York right now.

But he can afford it because he's recording an album, just like his idol, Joshua Bell. His ego hasn't been *too* inflated ever since. Especially since he also got asked to play a gig at Carnegie Hall next week, which is going to be his senior project. We're all invited. J.P. and I are going as a date. Except I'm bringing my iPod. I've already heard everything in Boris's repetoire like 900 million times, thanks to his playing it in the supply closet in the Gifted and Talented room. I can't believe anyone would pay *money* to hear him, to be honest, but whatever).

Tina's dad wasn't too thrilled about the ring. But he was plenty thrilled about the shipment of frozen Omaha Steaks Boris had sent to him (that part was *my* suggestion. Boris so owes me).

So Mr Hakim Baba might even come round to the idea of Boris being part of the family one day (poor man. I feel so bad for him. He'll have to listen to that mouth-breathing every time he sits down with his daughter and her boyfriend for a meal).

Oh, here she comes – she's not crying, so maybe it's –

# Friday, April 28, Trig

Yeah. OK. So it wasn't about Boris.

It was about Michael.

I should have known.

Tina has her phone set to receive Google Alerts about me. So this morning she got one when the *New York Post* ran an item about Michael's donation to the Columbia University Medical Center (only because it was the *Post* and not CNN international business news, the primary focus of the story was that Michael used to go out with me).

Tina's so sweet. She wanted to let me know that he was back in town before someone else did. She was afraid, just like my dad was, that I might hear it from a paparazzo.

I let her know I already knew.

This was a mistake.

'You *knew*?' Tina cried. 'And didn't tell me right away? Mia, how could you?'

See? I can't do anything right any more. Every time I tell the truth, I get in trouble!

'I just found out myself,' I assured her. 'Last night. And I'm OK with it. Really. I'm over Michael. I'm with J.P. now. It's completely cool with me that Michael's back.'

God, I'm such a *liar*.

And not even a very good one. At least not about this. Because Tina didn't look very convinced.

'And he didn't tell you?' Tina demanded. 'Michael didn't say anything in any of his emails about how he was coming back?'

Of course I couldn't tell her the truth. About how

Michael offered to read my senior project and that freaked me out so much I stopped emailing him.

Because then Tina would want to know why that freaked me out. And then I'd have to explain that my senior project is actually a romance novel I'm trying to get published.

And I'm just not ready to hear the amount of shrieking this response would engender from Tina. Not to mention her demand to read the book.

And when she gets to the sex scene – OK, sex *scenes* – I think there's a good chance Tina's head might actually explode.

'No,' I said in response to Tina's question instead.

'That's just weird,' Tina said flatly. 'I mean, you guys are friends now. At least, that's what you keep telling me. That you're friends, just like you used to be. Friends tell each other if one of them is moving back to the same country – the same *city* – as the other. That *has* to mean something, that he didn't say anything.'

'No it doesn't,' I said quickly. 'It probably happened really fast. He just didn't have time to tell me—'

'To send you a text message? *Mia, I'm moving back to Manhattan.* How long does that take? No.' Tina shook her head, her long dark hair swinging past her shoulders. 'Something else is going on.' She narrowed her eyes. 'And I think I know what it is.'

I love Tina so much. I'm going to miss her when I go away to college (no *way* am I going to NYU with her, even though I got in there. NYU just seems way too high-pressure for me. Tina wants to be a thoracic surgeon, so odds are, with all the pre-med classes she'll be taking, I'd hardly ever seen her anyway).

But I really wasn't in the mood to hear another one

of her wacky theories. It's true sometimes they're right. I mean, she was right about J.P. being in love with me.

But whatever she was about to say about Michael – I just didn't want to hear it. So much so, I actually put my hand over her mouth.

'No,' I said.

Tina blinked at me with her big brown eyes, looking very surprised.

'Wha?' she said, from behind my hand.

'Don't say it,' I said. 'Whatever it is you're about to say.'

'It's nofing bad,' Tina said, against my palm.

'I don't care,' I said. 'I don't want to hear it. Do you promise not to say it?'

Tina nodded. I dropped my hand.

'Do you need a tissue?' Tina asked, nodding to my hand. Because of course my fingers were covered in lip-gloss.

It was my turn to nod. Tina handed me a tissue from her bag. I wiped off my hand, purposefully not acknowledging the fact that Tina looked as if she was literally dying to tell me what she wanted to tell me.

Well, OK, maybe not *literally* dying. But metaphorically.

Finally Tina said, 'So. What are you going to do?'

'What do you mean, what am I going to do?' I asked. I couldn't help feeling this total sense of impending doom . . . not unlike what I felt concerning J.P.'s forthcoming prom invitation. Well, I guess that wasn't as much doom as it was dread. 'I'm not going to *do* anything.'

'But, Mia –' Tina appeared to be choosing her words with care – 'I know you and J.P. are totally and blissfully happy. But aren't you the least bit *curious* to see Michael? After all this time?'

Fortunately it was right then that the bell rang and we had to grab our stuff and 'skedaddle' as Rocky is fond of saying (I have no idea where he picked up the word 'skedaddle', much less 'skedaddling shoes', which are what he calls his sneakers. Oh God, how am I going to go away to college for four whole years and miss out on all his formative development . . . not to mention his cuteness? I know I'll be back for holidays – the ones I don't spend in Genovia – but it won't be the same!).

So I didn't have to answer Tina's question.

I sort of wish now that I hadn't stopped Tina as she was about to tell me her theory. I mean, now that my heart rate has slowed down (it was totally pounding back there in the stairwell for some reason. I have no idea why).

I bet, whatever it was, it would have made me laugh.

Oh well. I'll ask her about it later.

Or not.

Actually, probably not.

# Friday, April 28, Gifted and Talented

OK. They've descended into madness.

I guess some of them (namely Lana, Trisha, Shameeka and Tina) didn't have that far to go anyway.

But I think they've taken the word senioritis to new extremes.

So Tina and I were out in the hallway just before lunch, when we ran into Lana, Trisha and Shameeka, and Tina yelled, over the din of everyone passing by, 'Did you guys hear? Michael is back! And his robotic arm is a huge success! And he's a millionaire!'

Lana and Trisha, as one might predict, both let out shrieks that I swear could have burst the glass in all the emergency fire pulls nearby. Shameeka was more subdued, but even she got a crazed look in her eyes.

Then, when we got into the jet line to get our yogurts and salads (well, those guys. They're all trying to lose five pounds before the prom. I was getting a tofurkey burger), Tina started telling them about Michael donating a CardioArm to the Columbia University Medical Center, and Lana went, 'Oh my God, when is that, tomorrow? We are so going.'

'Uh,' I said, my heart sliding up into my throat. 'No, *we* aren't.'

'Seriously,' Trisha said, agreeing with me (I could have kissed her). 'I've got a tanning appointment. I'm totally building up a golden glow for prom next weekend. I'm wearing white, you know.'

'Whatever,' Lana said, picking out diet sodas for all of us. 'You can tan after.'

'But we've got Mia's party Monday,' Trisha said.

'There're going to be celebrities there. I don't want to look pasty in front of celebrities.'

'Trisha really has her priorities straight,' I pointed out. 'Not looking pasty in front of celebrities comes before stalking my ex-boyfriends.'

'I don't want to stalk Michael,' Shameeka said. 'But I agree with Lana that we should at least check out this event. I want to see how Michael looks. Aren't you curious, Mia?'

'No,' I said firmly. 'And besides, I'm sure we won't be able to get in. It's probably closed to everyone but invited guests and press.'

'Oh, that won't be a problem,' Lana said. 'You can get us in. You're a princess. And besides, even if you can't – you're on the staff of *The Atom*. Get us press passes. Just ask Lilly.'

Lifting up my lunch tray, I shot her a very sarcastic look. It took Lana a second or two to realize what she'd said. Then, when she finally did, she went, 'Oh. Yeah. He's her brother. And she was really mad at you about dumping him last year or something. Right?'

'Let's just drop it,' I said. I swear I wasn't even hungry any more. My tofurkey burger, sitting on its plate in front of me, looked completely unappetizing. I thought about ditching it for tacos. If ever there'd been a day I could have used some spicy beef, it seemed like today.

'Isn't your little sister writing for *The Atom* this year?' Shameeka asked Lana.

Lana looked over at her little sister, Gretchen, who was sitting with the other cheerleaders at a table by the door.

'Ooh,' Lana said. 'Good suggestion. She's such a little butt kisser, trying to get extra-curriculars for college, she'll have been to *The Atom* meeting this morning for sure. Let me go check and see if she got assigned to the Michael story.'

I could have stabbed them both with my spork.

'I am going to go sit down now,' I said from between gritted teeth. 'With my boyfriend. You guys can come sit with me, but if you do, I don't want you to be talking about this. *In front of my boyfriend*. Do you understand? Good.'

I kept my gaze locked on J.P. as I made my way across the caff to our table, determined not to glance in Lana's direction. J.P., chatting with Boris, Perin and Ling Su, noticed me coming, looked up and smiled. I smiled back.

Still, out of the corner of my eye, I managed to see Lana hit her sister on the back of the head, grab her Miu Miu purse and dig around in it.

Great. That could only mean one thing. Gretchen had press passes to tomorrow's event.

'How's it going?' J.P. asked me as I sat down.

'Great,' I lied. (Mia Thermopolis's Big Fat Lie Number Five.)

'Fantastic,' J.P. said. 'Hey, there's something I wanted to ask you.'

I froze with my tofurkey burger halfway to my lips. Oh God. Here? *Now?* He was going to ask me to the prom in the cafeteria, in front of everybody? This was J.P.'s idea of romantic?

No. It couldn't be. Because J.P.'s made me dinner at his apartment before when his parents were out of town, and he's pulled out all the stops . . . candles, jazz on the stereo, delicious fettuccine Alfredo, chocolate mousse for dessert. The guy knows romantic.

And he's no slouch on Valentine's Day either. He got me a beautiful heart locket (from Tiffany, of course) with our initials entwined on it for our first, and a diamond journey necklace (to show how far we'd come from that first kiss outside my building) for our second.

Surely he wasn't going to ask me to the prom as I was biting into a tofurkey burger in the cafeteria.

Then again . . . he thought he didn't have to bother asking me to the prom at all. So . . .

Tina, overhearing J.P.'s question as she slid her tray down next to Boris's, gasped.

Well, let's face it. She would. This is another reason I can never tell her about *Ransom My Heart*. She'd never be able to keep it to herself. Especially the steamier parts. She'd want to know how I researched them.

Then she recovered herself and said, 'Oh? You have a question for Mia, J.P.?'

'Uh,' J.P. said. 'Yeah . . .'

'How nice.' Tina tried not to look like she was the cat who'd just swallowed the canary. 'Everybody? J.P. wants to ask Mia something.'

'Uh,' J.P. said, a light pink shade tinging his cheeks as a hush fell over the cafeteria table and everyone looked at him expectantly. 'I just wanted to ask what you were getting Principal Gupta and the rest of them as thank you gifts for writing your letters of recommendation?'

Oh. Also, phew.

'I'm getting them each a set of six hand-blown Genovian crystal water goblets,' I said. 'With the Royal Genovian crest on them.'

'Oh,' he said, gulping. 'I think my mom's just going to get them each a gift certificate to Barnes and Noble.'

'I'm sure they'll like that much better,' I said, feeling

bad. Grandmere was always so over the top with her gift-giving.

'We're giving them Swarovski crystal apples,' Ling Su and Perin said at the same time. This made them sound nerdier than they are. They'd actually completely given up sitting with the Backpack Patrol, as J.P. refers to Kenny's – I mean, Kenneth's – gang, across the caff, who'd taken to travelling everywhere with their giant backpacks of books, even this late in the school year, knowing full well they'd already gotten into their colleges of choice (well, second choice). Some of them had so many books, in fact, they used wheelie suitcases to cart them around. It was like they'd never heard of using their lockers.

Lilly, who used to sit among them – until *Lilly Tells It Like It Is* took off and her lunch hour became too busy for her to spend it in the caff – with her multiple piercings and often variantly coloured hair, looked like an exotic flower. I think they were all pretty sorry to see her go – although I'm not sure any of them but Kenny – I mean, Kenneth – really noticed, seeing as how their heads were all buried in their Advanced Chem books.

'Well, that's taken care of,' Lana announced, setting her tray down. 'Two o'clock tomorrow, geek.'

She was addressing me. Geek is Lana's pet name for me. I've learned she means it as a term of endearment.

'What's at two o'clock tomorrow?' J.P. wanted to know.

'Nothing,' I said quickly, just as Shameeka slid her tray down too and said, covering for me, 'Mani-pedi appointments. Who's got the Diet Cokes? Oh, thanks, Mia.'

'This is so lame.' Trisha took one of the Diet Cokes

I'd bought too. 'Did I mention how lame this is? I *have* to tan.'

'What are they talking about?' J.P. asked Boris.

'Don't ask,' Boris advised him. 'Just ignore them, and maybe they'll go away.'

And that was that. It was decided – sort of non-verbally, but more verbally after lunch was over and we were all walking to class and the guys were gone. Lana got press passes (two of them: one for a reporter and one for a photographer) from her sister Gretchen for Michael's donation of one of his CardioArms to Columbia.

Apparently they all think we're going tomorrow (to them, two press passes equals permission for the five of us to enter, in Lana Fantasy Land).

But the REAL fantasy is that they think I'm actually going to go, because no way I am setting foot anywhere near that place. I mean, nothing has changed – I still don't want to see Michael – I still *can't* see Michael . . . not sneaking in to see him on Lana Weinberger's little sister's high-school newspaper's press pass. I mean, that is insane. That's like something out of a book – something that's just not going to happen.

Ever.

God, Boris is really scraping away on that thing!

And Lilly isn't even here. Which is no big surprise, she hasn't been in G and T since her show got picked up by a television network in Seoul. She tapes every day during lunch and fifth period. They actually let her out of school to do this, and give her class credit and everything.

Which is cool. I guess she's a huge star in Korea.

Well, I always knew she'd be a star.

For some reason I just always thought I'd be friends with her when it happened.

Well, things change, I guess.

# Friday, April 28, French

Tina won't stop texting me, even though I'm not texting back (I don't need a repeat performance of yesterday's debacle).

She wants to know what I'm going to wear tomorrow when we go to see Michael donate a CardioArm to Columbia's Medical Center.

I wonder what it's like to live in Tinaville.

I get the feeling it's very shiny there.

# Friday, April 28, Psychology

I finally texted Tina back that I'm not going tomorrow.

There has been radio silence ever since, so I'm just slightly suspicious about what's going on between her and the rest of the gang.

It's slightly restful, however, not to have my phone buzzing every five seconds.

**Amelia – I still haven't had your answerrrrrrr. I need you to disinvite twenty-ffiveeeee people to your party. The captain is telling me we won't be able to set saillllllll with 300. Weeeeeeeeee need to cut it down to two seventy-five max. I think Nathan and Claire, Frank's niece and nephew, can go, obviously. What about your mother? You don't need her there, do you? She'll understandddddd. And Frank tooooooo. I'll be waiting for your call. Clarisse, your grandmotherrrrrrr**

— — — — — — — — — — — — — — — — —

**Sent from my BlackBerry Wireless Handheld**

Oh my *God*.

Major histocompatibility complex – MHC: gene family found in most mammals. Believed to play an important role in mate selection through olfactory (scent) recognition. In studies, female college students asked to smell the unwashed T-shirts worn by male college students invariably chose ones worn by males possessing MHC that was entirely dissimilar to their own. This is believed to be due to the fact that these males would make the most genetically desirable mates (pairing opposite MHC genes would create offspring with the strongest immune systems). The more genetically *dissimilar* mates are to one another, the stronger the immune system of the offspring, a fact believed detected through the olfactory senses of the female of the species.

**Homework**
World History: Study for final
English Lit: Ditto
Trig: Ditto
Gifted and Talented: Ugh, I'm so SICK of Chopin
French: Final
Psychology II: Final

# Friday, April 28, Dr Knutz's waiting room

Great. I walked in here today for my next-to-last session and who should be sitting here but none other than the Dowager Princess of Genovia herself.

I was like, 'What the –?' but fortunately managed to control myself at the last minute.

'Oh, Amelia, there you are,' she said, like we were meeting for tea at the Carlyle or whatever. 'Why haven't you phoned back?'

I just stared at her in horror. 'Grandmere,' I said. 'This is my *therapy session*.'

'Well, I know that, Amelia.' She smiled at the receptionist, as if to apologize for my idiocy. 'I'm not slow, you know. But how else am I supposed to get you to communicate with me, when you won't return my calls and you refuse to write back to my emails, which is the method of communication I *thought* was all the rage with you young people today? Really, I had no choice but to hunt you down here.'

'Grandmere.' I was seriously about to bubble over with rage. 'If this is about my party, I am NOT disinviting my own mother and stepfather to make room for your society friends. Disinvite Nathan and Claire if you want, I don't care. And can I just add, it is totally inappropriate of you to show up at therapy to talk to me about this. I realize we've had joint therapy sessions in the past, but those were scheduled beforehand. You can't just show up at therapy and expect me to—'

'Oh, that.' Grandmere made a little waving motion in the air, the sapphire cocktail ring the Shah of Iran had given her sparkling as she did so. 'Please. Vigo has straightened out the difficulties with the invitation list.

And don't worry, your mother is safe. Though I wouldn't say the same for her parents. I hope they'll enjoy the view of the party from the steering deck. No, no, I'm here about *That Boy*.'

I couldn't figure out what she was talking about at first. 'J.P.?' She never calls J.P. *That Boy*. Grandmere loves J.P. I mean seriously loves him. When the two of them get together, they talk about old Broadway shows I've never even heard of until I practically have to drag J.P. away. Grandmere is more than a little convinced she could have had a great career on the stage if she hadn't chosen to marry my grandfather and been the princess of a small European country instead of a huge Broadway star a la that girl who stars in *Legally Blonde*, the musical. Only of course in Grandmere's mind, she's better than her.

'Not John Paul,' Grandmere said, looking shocked at the very idea. 'The other one. And this . . . thing he's invented.'

*Michael?* Grandmere had invited herself to my therapy session to talk to me about *Michael?*

Also, great. Thanks, Vigo. Had he set her BlackBerry to receive Google Alerts about me too?

'Are you serious?' I swear at this point I had no idea what she was up to. I really hadn't put two and two together. I still thought she was worried about the party. 'You want to invite Michael now too? Well, sorry, Grandmere, but no. Just because he's a famous millionaire inventor now doesn't mean I want him at my party. If you invite him, I swear I'll—'

'No. Amelia.' Grandmere reached out and grabbed my hand. It wasn't one of her usual grasping, needy grabs, where she tries to force me to give her sciatica a massage. It was as if she was taking my hand to . . . well, to *hold* it.

I was so surprised, I actually sank down on to the leather couch and looked at her like, *What? What's going on?*

'The arm,' Grandmere said. Like a normal person, and not like she was telling me not to lift my pinky up when I drank my tea or anything. 'The robot arm he's made.'

I blinked at her. '*What?*'

'We need one,' she said. 'For the hospital. You have to get us one.'

I blinked even harder. I've suspected Grandmere might be losing her mind for . . . well, the entire time I've known her, actually.

But now it was clear she'd gone completely around the bend.

'Grandmere.' I discreetly felt for her pulse. 'Have you been taking your heart medication?'

'Not a donation,' Grandmere hastened to explain, sounding more like her usual self. 'Tell him we'll pay. But, Amelia, you do know if we had something like that in our hospital in Genovia, we'd . . . well, it would improve the state of care we're able to give our own citizens to such an incredible degree. They wouldn't have to go to Paris or Switzerland for heart surgery. Surely you see what a—'

I ripped my hand out from hers. Suddenly I saw that she wasn't crazy at all. Or suffering from a stroke or a heart attack. Her pulse had been strong and steady.

'Oh my God!' I cried. '*Grandmere!*'

'What?' Grandmere looked bewildered by my outburst. 'What is the matter? I'm asking you to ask

85

Michael for one of his machines. Not donate it. I said we'd pay—'

'But you want me to use my relationship with him,' I cried, 'so Dad can gain an edge over René in the election!'

Grandmere's drawn-on eyebrows furrowed.

'I never said a word about the election!' she declared in her most imperious voice. 'But I did think, Amelia, if you were to go to this event at Columbia tomorrow—'

'Grandmere!' I sprang up from the couch. 'You're horrible! Do you really think the people of Genovia would be more likely to vote for Dad because he managed to buy them a CardioArm, as opposed to René, who's only managed to promise them an Applebee's?'

Grandmere looked at me blankly.

'Well,' she said, 'yes. Which would you rather have? Easy access to heart surgery, or a Bloomin' Onion?'

'That's Outback Steakhouse,' I informed her acidly. 'And the point of a democracy is that no one's vote can be bought!'

'Oh, Amelia,' Grandmere said with a snort. 'Don't be naive. Everyone can be bought. And anyway, how would you feel if I told you at my recent visit to the royal physician that he told me my heart condition has gotten more serious and I might need bypass surgery?'

I hesitated. She looked totally sincere.

'D-do you?' I stammered.

'Well,' Grandmere said, 'not yet. But he did tell me I have to cut back to three Sidecars a week!'

I should have known.

'Grandmere,' I said. 'Leave. Now.'

Grandmere frowned at me.

'You know, Amelia,' she said, 'if your father loses this

election, it will kill him. I know he'll still be prince of Genovia and all that, but he won't rule it, and that, young lady, will be no one's fault but your own.'

I groaned in frustration and said, 'GET OUT!'

Which she did, muttering very darkly to Lars and to the receptionist, both of whom had watched our entire exchange with a great deal of amusement.

But honestly, I don't see what's so funny about it.

I guess to Grandmere, using an ex-boyfriend to jump to the head of the waiting list (as if Michael would even consider such a thing) to get a million-dollar piece of medical equipment is just a normal day's work.

But though we may share the same gene pool, I am nothing like my grandmother.

NOTHING.

## Friday, April 28, the limo home from Dr Knutz's office

Dr K, as usual, was less than sympathetic to my problems. He seems to feel I've brought them all down upon myself.

Why can't I have a nice normal therapist, who asks me, 'And how do you feel about that?' and hands me anti-anxiety medication, like everyone else I go to school with?

Oh no. I have to have the one therapist in all Manhattan who doesn't believe in psychopharmaceuticals. And who thinks every crummy thing that happens to me (lately, anyway) is my own fault for not being emotionally honest with myself.

'How is my boyfriend not asking me to our senior prom my fault for not being honest with my emotions?' I asked him at one point.

'When he asks you,' Dr Knutz said, countering my question with another question, in classic psychotherapist style, 'are you going to say yes?'

'Well,' I said, feeling uncomfortable (yes! I am honest with myself to admit I felt uncomfortable at that question!), 'I really don't want to go to the prom.'

'I think you've answered your own question,' he said, a self-satisfied gleam shining behind the lenses of his glasses.

What is that even supposed to *mean*? How does that help me?

I'll tell you. It doesn't.

And you know what else? I'm just going to say it:

Therapy doesn't help me any more.

Oh, don't get me wrong. There was a time when it did, when Dr K's long rambling stories about the many horses he'd owned really helped me through my depression and what was going on with my dad and Genovia and the rumours about him and our family having known about Princess Amelie's declaration all along – not to mention getting me through the SATs and the college application process and losing Michael and Lilly and all that.

Maybe since I'm not depressed any more and the pressure's off (somewhat) and he's a child psychologist and I'm not really a kid any more – or won't be after Monday – I'm just ready to cut the cord now. Which is why our last therapy session is next week.

Anyway.

I tried to ask him what I should do about choosing a college, and the thing Grandmere had brought up, about getting Michael to sell one of his CardioArms to Genovia in time for Dad's election, and if I should just tell people the truth about *Ransom My Heart*.

Instead of offering constructive advice, Dr K started telling me this long story about a mare he'd once had, named Sugar; this thoroughbred he'd bought from a dealer, who everyone said was such a great horse and he knew was a great horse too.

On paper.

Even though *on paper* Sugar was this fantastic horse, Dr Knutz could just never find his place in the saddle with her, and their rides were totally uncomfortable, and eventually he had to sell her, because it wasn't fair to Sugar, as he'd started avoiding her and riding all his other horses instead.

Seriously. What does this story have to do with me?

Plus, I'm so sick of horse stories I could scream.

And I still don't know where I'm going to go to college, what I'm going to do about J.P. (or Michael), or how I'm going to stop lying to everyone.

Maybe I should just tell people I want to be a romance writer? I mean, I know everyone laughs at romance writers (until they actually read a romance). But what do I care? Everyone laughs at princesses too. I'm pretty much used to it by now.

But . . . what if people read my book and think it's about . . . I don't know.

Me?

Because it's so not. I don't even know how to shoot a bow and arrow (despite the erroneous movies made of my life).

Who would even name a horse Sugar? That's a little bit of a cliché, right?

# Friday, April 28, 7 p.m., the Loft

Dear Ms Delacroix

Thank you for your submission. After a great deal of consideration, we have decided *Ransom My Heart* is not right for us at this time.

Sincerely

Pembroke Publishing

Rejected again!

Seriously, is the entire publishing world on crack? How can no one want to publish my novel? I mean, I know it's not *War and Peace*, but I've seen way worse out there. My book is better than that! I mean, at least my book doesn't have spanking sex robots in it or anything.

Maybe if I'd put spanking sex robots in it, someone would want to publish it. But I can't put spanking sex robots in it now. It's too late, and besides, that wouldn't be historically accurate.

Anyway.

Things are insane here with preparations for arrivals for the birthday extravaganza. Mamaw and Papaw will be staying at the Tribeca Grand this time, and every effort is being undertaken to see that Mom and Mr G have as little one-on-one time with them as possible. They're being sent on tours of Ellis Island, Liberty Island, Little Italy, Harlem, the Metropolitan Museum of Art, Madame Tussauds, Ripley's Believe It Or Not! and M&M's World (the last three at their request).

Of course, they want to spend time with me and

Rocky (mostly Rocky), but Mom keeps saying, 'Oh, there'll be plenty of time for that.' They're only staying for three days. How there'll be time for visiting and all that touring, as well as the party, is a secret known only to Mom.

Uh-oh, an IM from Tina:

```
Iluvromance: So we're meeting on Broadway and
             168th Street tomorrow at 1.30
             p.m. The dedication ceremony or
             whatever it is starts at two, so
             that should give us plenty of
             time to get good seats so we can
             see Michael up close.
```

What is it going to take to get through to these girls that I am NOT going to this thing?

```
FtLouie:     Sounds good!
```

'Sounds good' isn't a lie. I mean, what she said does *sound* good.

It'll be sad and all when they're standing on the corner of Broadway and 168th all by themselves. But no one said life was fair.

```
Iluvromance: Wait . . . Mia, you are coming,
             right?
```

Whoa. How did she guess????

```
FtLouie:     No. I told you I wasn't.
>
```

```
Iluvromance: Mia, you HAVE to come! The whole
             thing is for nothing if you're
             not there! I mean, aren't you
             the least bit curious about how
             Michael looks after all this
             time? And whether or not - be
             serious now  - he cares? You
             know, in THAT way?
```

Oh, God. She *would* have to play the 'If he still cares'
card.

```
FtLouie:    Tina, I already have a boyfriend
            who loves me and who I love back.
            And anyway, how am I going to be
            able to tell if Michael still
            cares 'in THAT way' just by see-
            ing him at some public event?
>
Iluvromance: You'll be able to tell. You just
             will. Your eyes will meet across
             the room and you'll *know*. So.
             What are you going to wear????
```

Fortunately I just got a call from J.P. He's done with
rehearsal for the day and wants to grab some sushi at
Blue Ribbon. Using his dad's producer connections, he's
gotten a table for two (virtually impossible at a place
like that on a Friday night). He wants to know if I can
join him for some crispy salmon skin and dragon rolls.

My other choice for dinner is leftover pizza from last
night or two-nights'-old Number One Noodle Son cold
sesame noodles.

Or I could shoot up to Grandmere's newly renovated condo at the Plaza and join her and Vigo for salads as they strategize for my party.

Hmmm, what to choose, what to choose? It's so *hard*.

And, OK, J.P. *might* use the opportunity to ask me to the prom . . . like maybe he'll slip a written invitation into an oyster shell or under a piece of unagi or something.

But I'm willing to risk it if only I can end this conversation.

```
FtLouie:     Sorry, T, going out with J.P.
             I'll text you later!
```

## Saturday, April 29, Midnight, the Loft

It turns out I needn't have worried about J.P. asking me to the prom at dinner tonight. He was too exhausted from rehearsal – and frustrated: he spent almost the whole time complaining about Stacey – even to be thinking about it, apparently.

And then after dinner, we had other concerns. It's so weird how everywhere I go with J.P. the paparazzi seems to show up. This *never* happened when I dated Michael.

I guess that's the difference between going out with a lowly college student (which Michael was at the time), and a rich theatre producer's son like J.P.

Anyway, as we were coming out of Blue Ribbon, the paps were out in full force. I thought at first Drew Barrymore must have been in there with her latest toy boy or whatever, and I was looking around for her.

But it turned out they were all trying to get pictures of ME.

At first it was fine, just . . . whatever. I had on my new Christian Louboutin boots, so I was feeling OK about it. It's like Lana says . . . if you have on your CLs, nothing bad can happen to you (shallow . . . but true).

But then one of them yelled, 'Hey, Princess, how does it feel to know your father is going to lose the election . . . and to your cousin, René, who's never run so much as a laundromat, let alone a whole country?'

I haven't had nearly four years of princess lessons (well, on and off) for nothing. It wasn't like I was unprepared for this. I just said, 'No comment.'

Except that might have been a mistake, because of course if you say *anything*, that just baits them to ask you more, and even though J.P. and Lars and I were trying to walk back to the loft (it's literally like two blocks from the restaurant, so we hadn't bothered with the limo), the paps crowded all around us, and we couldn't walk fast enough, especially since my CLs have like four-inch heels and I haven't really practised walking in them enough and I was kind of teetering in them (just a little) like Big Bird.

So the reporters were totally able to keep up even though I had Lars on one side and J.P. on the other, hustling me along.

'But your dad is losing in the polls,' the 'journalist' said. 'Come on. That's gotta hurt. Especially since if you had just kept your mouth shut, none of this would be happening.'

Man! These guys are brutal. Also, their grasp on politics is somewhat lacking.

'I did what was right for the people of Genovia,' I said, trying to keep a pleasant smile plastered across my face, the way Grandmere had taught me. 'Now, if you'll excuse us, we're just trying to get home—'

'Yeah, guys,' J.P. said while Lars was opening his coat to make sure his gun showed. Not that this ever scared the paps, because they knew good and well he couldn't shoot them (although he had, upon occasion, shoulder rolled a few of them). 'Just leave her alone, will you?'

'You're the boyfriend, right?' one of the paps wanted to know. 'Is that Abernathy-Reynolds, or Reynolds-Abernathy?'

'Reynolds-Abernathy,' J.P. said. 'And quit pushing!'

'The people of Genovia sure do seem to want Bloomin' Onions,' another of the paparazzi pointed out. 'Don't they, Princess? How does that make you feel?'

'I've been trained in a special technique that can

send your nasal cartilage into your brain using only the heel of my hand,' Lars informed the pap. 'How does that make YOU feel?'

I know I should be used to this stuff by now. Really, there are other people who have it so much worse than me. I mean, at least the 'press' lets me go to and from school in relative anonymity.

Still. Sometimes . . . .

'Is it true Sir Paul McCartney is bringing Martha Stewart to your birthday party Monday night, Princess?' one of the reporters yelled.

'Is it true Prince William will be there?' yelled another.

'What about your ex-boyfriend?' yelled a third. 'Now that he's back in—'

That was the exact moment when Lars physically threw me into an empty cab he'd signalled to pull over, and commanded it to take us around SoHo a few times until he was sure we'd shaken off all the reporters (who've given up staking out the loft, due to the fact that all the residents, including Mom, Mr G and me, routinely water-balloon bomb them from above).

All I can say is, thank God J.P. is so busy with his play that he had no idea what that last reporter had been talking about. He no sooner checks the Internet for Google Alerts on me (or Michael Moscovitz) than he remembers to eat breakfast. That's how crazed he is right now.

Anyway, when we got back to the loft, there was no sign of any reporters lurking around (thanks to their having gotten soaked one too many times with Mom's expert aim).

That was when J.P. asked if he could come up.

I knew what he wanted, of course. I also knew Mom and Mr G would be asleep, because they always crash early on Fridays after a long working week.

Really, the last thing I felt like doing after the paparazzi incident was to mess around in my room with my boyfriend.

But as he pointed out (beneath his breath, so Lars couldn't overhear), it had been ages since we'd been alone together, what with his rehearsal schedule and my princess stuff.

So I said goodbye to Lars at the vestibule and let J.P. come up. I mean, he WAS sweet, defending me from the paparazzi like that.

And he let me have that extra piece of crispy salmon skin, even though I know he wanted it.

I feel terrible about lying to him about all the things I'm lying to him about. He really deserves a better, nicer girlfriend than me. He really does.

An Excerpt from *Ransom My Heart* by Daphne Delacroix

'I told you not to move!' said the diminutive captor astride Hugo's back.

Hugo, admiring the slim arch of the foot, the only part of her that he could actually see, decided he ought to apologize now. Surely the girl had a right to be angry: in all innocence, she had come to the spring to bathe, not to be spied upon. And while he was greatly enjoying the feel of her nubile body against him, he was not enjoying her wrath. Better that he calm the spirited wench and see her back on the road to Stephensgate, where he could make sure that she was kept from straddling other men's backs and thereby getting herself into mischief.

'I earnestly beg your pardon, demoiselle,' he began in what he hoped was a contrite tone, though it was difficult for him to speak without laughing. 'I stumbled upon you in your most private hour, and for that I must ask your forgiveness—'

'I took you for simple, but not completely stupid,' was the girl's surprising reply. Hugo was amazed to hear that her voice was as rich with amusement as his own.

'I *meant* for you to stumble upon me, of course,' she elaborated. Quick as lightning, the knife left his throat, and the maid seized both his wrists and had them trussed behind him before he was even aware of what was happening.

'You're my prisoner now,' Finnula Crais said with evident satisfaction at a job well done. 'To gain your freedom, you'll have to pay for it. Handsomely.'

Ever since I've woken up, all I can think about is what that reporter said . . . about Dad losing in the polls and it being all my fault.

I know it's not true. I mean, yes, it's true we're having an election.

But the fact that Dad is losing isn't my fault.

And then, naturally, my mind keeps turning back to what Grandmere said, back in Dr Knutz's office. About how if we could get our hands on one of Michael's CardioArms, Dad might stand a better chance against René.

Except I know how wrong it is to think that way. The reason we need a CardioArm is because it would make the lives of the citizens of Genovia so much easier.

A CardioArm at the Royal Genovian Hospital wouldn't stimulate the economy or bring tourists to Genovia or even help Dad in the polls or anything like that, like Grandmere seems to believe.

But it *would* help Genovians who are sick not to have to travel to hospitals outside our country to get medical care, because instead they could easily get non-invasive heart surgery right inside our own borders. They'd save time and expense.

Plus, like the article said, they'd heal faster, because of the CardioArm's precision.

I'm *not* saying if we got one people would be more likely to vote for Dad. I'm just saying getting one would be the right thing to do – the princessy thing to do – for my own people.

And I'm *not* saying by going to the thing today that I want to get back together with Michael. I mean, if he'd even have me, which he fully wouldn't, because he's moved on, as is illustrated by the fact that, clearly, he's been in Manhattan for a while now and hasn't even so much as called. Or emailed.

I'm just saying obviously I *should* go to the thing at Columbia today. Because it's what a true princess would do for her people. Get them the most up-to-date medical technology available.

Just how I'm going to do that without looking like the world's biggest tool, I have no idea. I mean, I can't go, 'Um, Michael, due to the fact that we used to date, even though I treated you horribly, can you jump Genovia to the top of the waiting list and get us a CardioArm right away? Here's a cheque.'

But I think that's pretty much the way it's going to go. Part of being a princess means swallowing your pride and doing the right thing for your people, no matter how personally humiliating it might be.

And anyway, he still owes me for the Judith Gershner thing. I understand now that the reason Michael didn't tell me about how he had sex with her before he and I started going out was because he knew I wasn't mature enough at the time to handle the information.

He was right: I wasn't.

And though it might be really manipulative and awful of me to use my past romantic relationship with Michael to try to get him to let us jump to the head of the CardioArm waiting list, this is *Genovia* we're talking about.

And it is my royal duty to do whatever I have to do for my country.

I haven't spent the past four years with the combs of a tiara digging into my head for nothing, you know.

I guess I didn't *just* learn which one was the soup spoon from Grandmere, after all.

I better go call Tina.

## Saturday, April 29, 1.45 p.m., Columbia University Medical Center, Simon and Louise Templeman Patient Care Pavilion

This. Was. The. Worst. Idea. Ever.

I know this morning when I woke up I had some big noble idea that I was doing something way important for the people of Genovia.

And – OK, I'll admit it, maybe in some twisted way, I guess, for my dad.

But in actuality, this is just insane. I mean, Michael's entire family is here. *All* the Moscovitzes! Even his *grandma*! Yes! Nana Moscovitz is here!

I'm so embarrassed I could die.

And, OK, I've made us all sit in the very back row (security here is very lax: they let us all in, even though we had only the two passes), where, thank God, it doesn't appear there's any chance any of them is going to see us (but Lars and Wahim, Tina's bodyguard, are so tall, what are the chances of them not being noticed? I've made them wait outside. They're so mad at me. But what am I supposed to do? I can't risk the chance of Lilly seeing them).

And I know the whole point of this was my actually speaking to Michael.

But I didn't know *Lilly* was going to be here! Which was incredibly stupid of me. I should have assumed, of course. I mean, that Michael's family (including his sister, who brought Kenny, I mean, Kenneth, who is wearing a SUIT. And Lilly is wearing a dress . . . and she's taken out all her piercings. I barely recognized her) would of course be at such an important and prestigious event.

How can I go up and talk to Michael in front of her? It's true Lilly and I are not exactly at each other's throats any more, but we're definitely not *friends* either. The last thing I need right now is her revving up ihatemiathermopolis.com again.

Which I could totally see her doing if she suspected I was trying to use her brother to, oh, I don't know, get a CardioArm for my country or something.

Lana says it's no big deal and I should just go up to the Drs Moscovitz and say Hi. Lana says she's totally on friendly terms with all her exes' parents (which, considering it's Lana, is like, half of the population of the Upper East Side), even though she's used most of their sons for sex, and even worse things (. . . such as? What is worse than using a boy for sex? I don't even want to know. Lana took Tina and me to the Pink Pussycat Boutique last year because she said we needed educating in that department, and while I did make a purchase, it was only a Hello Kitty personal massager. But you don't even want to know what Lana bought).

But Lana's never dated any guy for as long as Michael and I dated. And she wasn't best friends with any of those guys' sisters, and she didn't make them as mad at her as Lilly was mad at me. So going up to them at public events and being all, 'Hey, how's it going?' is no big deal for *Lana*.

I, on the other hand, cannot go up to the Drs Moscovitz and go, 'Oh, hey, hi, Dr and Dr Moscovitz. How you *doing*? Remember me? The girl who acted like a total byotch to your son and who used to be best friends with your daughter? Oh, and hey, Nana

Moscovitz. How's that rugelach you used to make? Yum, I used to love that stuff!! Good times.'

Anyway. This donation thing is turning out to be a huge event (fortunately, because there are a ton of people I can slouch behind and remain unseen). There's press from *everywhere*, *Anesthesia* magazine to *PC World*. They've got hors d'oeuvres and stuff too, and a lot of model-looking types, slinking around in tight red dresses, passing around champagne.

There's no sign of Michael so far though. He's probably in a green room somewhere, getting a massage from one of those slinky-dress girls. That's what bazillionaire robotic-arm inventors do before giving away major donations to their Alma Maters. I'm just guessing.

Tina says I should stop writing in my journal and pay attention in case Michael comes in (she doesn't believe my slinky-model-massage theory). Also, she thinks the dark sunglasses and beret I'm wearing are only drawing attention to myself, not serving as a good disguise.

But what does Tina know? This has never happened to her before. She –

Oh.

My.

God.

Michael just walked in . . .

I can't breathe.

## Saturday, April 29, 3 p.m., Columbia University Medical Center, ladies' room

OK. I messed up.

Really, *really* messed up.

It's just . . . he looks so incredibly good.

I don't know what he's been doing to work out while he was overseas . . . fighting monks in the Himalayas like Christian Bale in *Batman Begins* is what Lana thinks. Trisha says plain old weightlifting, while Shameeka says probably a combination of lifting and cardio.

Tina thinks he just 'got hit with a stick of pure awesomeness'.

But whatever it was, he's almost as wide in the shoulders now as Lars, and I highly doubt it's because he's wearing an shoulder holster under his Hugo Boss suit coat, which Lana suggested.

And he's got a real haircut, like a grown-up man, and his hands look huge for some reason, and he didn't seem at all nervous coming out on to that stage and shaking Dr Arthur Ward's hand. He was totally at ease, like he comes out and speaks in front of hundreds of people all the time!

And that's because he probably does.

And he was smiling and looking all the audience members in the eye, just like Grandmere always tells me to do, and he didn't need notecards to give his speech, he had the whole thing memorized (just like Grandmere *also* always tells me to do).

And he was funny and smart and I sat up and took my beret off and also my sunglasses so I could see him better, and all my insides melted in on themselves and I knew I had made the worst mistake coming here. *Ever.*

Because all it did was make me realize all over again how much I wish we hadn't broken up.

I'm not saying I don't love J.P. and all that.

I just wish . . . I . . .

I don't even know.

But I do know I wish I hadn't come here! And I knew for sure, the minute Michael started speaking, and thanking everyone for having him and describing how he'd come up with the idea for Pavlov Surgical (which I already knew of course – he'd named it for his dog, Pavlov, which is the most adorable thing ever), that there was no way I was going to go up to him afterwards. Even if Lilly and his parents and Nana Moscovitz hadn't been there.

Not even for the people of Genovia. No way. Not ever.

I just couldn't trust myself to go up and speak to him and not throw my arms around his neck and plunge my tongue down his throat, like Finnula does to Hugo in *Ransom My Heart*.

I know! And I have a boyfriend! A boyfriend I love! Even if – well. There's *the other thing*.

So I was like, *It's fine, we're in the last row, we'll just sneak out when he's done talking.*

I really thought it wouldn't be any big deal. Lars was still out in the hallway with Wahim, even though I could see him peeking in at me and giving me the evil eye (which he completely learned from Grandmere). There was no chance of us getting busted unless Lana or Trisha began making out with one of the other members of the press who was sitting around us, none of whom was cute anyway, so that seemed pretty unlikely.

But then Michael started introducing the other members of the CardioArm team – you know, who'd helped him invent it or make it or market it or whatever?

And one of them was this totally cute girl named Midori, and when she came out on the stage she gave Michael this big hug, and I could tell . . . I mean, I could just tell . . .

Well, anyway, that's when I knew they were a couple and also when I could feel the oatmeal with raisins I'd had for breakfast almost coming up into my throat. Which made no sense because we're broken up and, oh yeah, as mentioned previously, I HAVE A BOYFRIEND.

Anyway, Tina saw the hug too, and leaned over to whisper, 'I'm sure they're just friends and they work together. Seriously, don't worry about it.'

To which I whispered back, 'Yeah, right. Because all guys just ignore the girl in the micromini at work.'

Which of course Tina had no reply for. Because Midori's micromini looked as supercute as she did. And every guy in the room was ignoring it. NOT.

And then Michael presented his CardioArm – which was way bigger than I thought it would be – and everyone clapped, and he ducked his dark head and looked adorably modest.

And then Dr Arthur Ward surprised him by giving him an honorary master's degree in science. Just, you know, like that.

So then everyone clapped some more, and the Drs Moscovitz came up on stage with Nana and Lilly (Kenny – I mean, Kenneth – hung back, until Lilly finally signalled for him to join them, which he did, after a lot of hesitation and her waving at him, and finally stamping her foot kind of imperiously, which was very Lilly-like, and made people laugh, even people who didn't know her) and the whole family hugged, and I just . . .

I started bawling. Really.

Not because Michael has a new girlfriend now, or anything lame like that.

But because it was just so sweet, to see them all up there hugging like that, a family that I personally know, and who has been through so much, what with Michael and Lilly's parents' almost-divorce and now their getting back together and Lilly's general psycho-ness and Michael's going off to Japan and working so hard and . . .

. . . and they were all just so happy. It was just so . . . *nice*. It was this wonderful moment of success and triumph and *wonderfulness*.

And there I was, *spying* on them. Because I wanted to use Michael, to get something that, yes, my country needs, but I don't in any way deserve. I mean, we can wait, like everybody else.

Basically, I felt like I was totally invading their privacy, and that I had no right to be there. Because I didn't. I was there on false pretences.

And it was time to leave.

So I looked at all the other girls – as best I could see them through my tears – and I was like, 'Let's go.'

'But you haven't even talked to him!' Tina cried.

'And I'm not going to,' I said. I knew as I said it that *this* was the princessy thing to do. To leave Michael alone. He was happy now. He didn't need crazy, neurotic me, messing up his life any more. He had sweet, smart Micromini Midori – or if not her, someone like her. The last thing he needed was lying, romance-writing Princess Mia.

Who by the way already had a boyfriend.

'Let's sneak out one at a time,' I said. 'I'll go first, I have to stop in the bathroom.' I knew I had to write all this down while it was still fresh in my mind. Besides which, I had to reapply my eyeliner and mascara, since I'd just cried it all off. 'I'll meet you guys back at Broadway and One-sixty-eighth.'

'This blows,' Lana said. She is very in touch with her feelings.

'The limo's waiting there,' I said. 'I'll take you to Pinkberry. My treat.'

'Pinkberry, my butt,' Lana said. 'You're taking us to Nobu.'

'Fine,' I said.

So I snuck in here. Where I've reapplied my make-up, and I'm writing this.

Really, it's better this way. To let him go. Not that I ever truly had him, or could have, really, but . . . well, *'tis a far, far better thing I do*, and all that. I'm sure Grandmere wouldn't think so. But this really is the more princessy thing to do. The Moscovitzes looked so *happy*. Even Lilly.

And she's *never* happy.

OK, I better go meet those guys. I think Lars might actually shoot me if I make him wait any longer. I –

Hey, those shoes look really familiar.

Oh *no*.

Oh *yes*.

Lilly. It was *Lilly*.

In the stall next to mine.

She totally recognized my platform Mary Janes. My new Prada ones, not the old ones I had from two years ago, which she so mercilessly savaged on her website.

She was like, 'Mia? Is that you in there? I thought I saw Lars in the hallway . . .'

What could I do? I couldn't say it wasn't me. Obviously.

So I came out and there she was, looking totally confused like, *What are* you *doing here?*

Fortunately the whole time I was sitting in the audience I'd totally had a chance to make up a story for what I would say if this happened.

Mia Thermopolis's Big Fat Lie Number Six:

'Oh, hi, Lilly.' I was so Ms Casual. Even though I had given myself a complete MAC makeover and blow-dry and was in my best Nanette Lepore top and black lace-trimmed leggings, I acted like the whole thing was no big deal. 'Gretchen Weinberger couldn't make it today, so she gave me her press pass and asked me to cover the story of Michael's donation for her.' I even pulled Gretchen's press pass out of my bag to prove my colossal lie. 'I hope that's OK with you?'

Lilly just stared at the press pass. Then she looked up at me (because I still tower over her by about six inches, especially in my platforms, even though she was wearing heels).

Honestly, I didn't like the way she was looking at me. Like she didn't believe me.

Too late, I remembered the way Lilly could always tell when I was lying (because my nostrils flare).

However, I've been practising lying in the mirror, and also in front of Grandmere, to stop this from happening, because people being able to tell you're lying is totally detrimental to one's future career as a princess, or whatever you want to be really, as white lies are really crucial to all professions ('Oh no, you have much longer than six months to live actually.').

And Grandmere says I've gotten much better about it (J.P. too. Well, obviously. Otherwise he'd have known when I said I hadn't gotten into any of the colleges I said I hadn't gotten into. Not to mention any of the other multiple lies I've told him. I could *kill* Lilly for having told him about the nostril thing. Sometimes I wonder if there's anything *else* she told him about me that he hasn't told me she told him).

I was pretty sure Lilly couldn't tell I was lying. But just to be sure, I added, 'I hope you don't mind I'm here. I tried to stay out of your way and in the background as much as possible. I know this is a special day for you and your family, and I . . . I think it's really great about Michael.'

This last part wasn't a lie, so I didn't need to worry about my nostrils. Not even a little bit.

Lilly narrowed her eyes at me. For once she hadn't smeared them all over with black kohl. I knew she'd done this out of deference for Nana Moscovitz, who thinks kohl is slutty.

I thought she was going to hit me. I really did.

'You're really here to cover the story for *The Atom*?' she asked in a hard voice.

I have never concentrated on my nostrils more in my entire life.

'Yes,' I said. And anyway, it wasn't a lie, because I plan on going home now and writing a 400-hundred word story about this whole thing and submitting it Monday morning. After throwing up about 900 times.

Lilly's mean-eyed gaze didn't change.

'And did you really mean that about my brother, Mia?' she asked.

'Of course I do,' I said.

This too was the truth.

Just as I'd suspected, Lilly was totally staring at my nose. When she didn't see my nostrils move, she seemed to relax a little.

What she said next shocked me so much, I momentarily lost the ability to speak.

'It was really great of you to come. In Gretchen's place, I mean,' she said, sounding a hundred per cent sincere. 'And I know the fact that you came will mean a lot to Michael. And since you're here, you can't leave without coming to say hi to him.'

That's when I nearly threw up my oatmeal again. *What?*

'Uh,' I said, backing up so fast I almost collided with this old lady who was coming out of another bathroom stall. 'No, thanks. That's OK! I think I have enough for the story for *The Atom*. This is family time for you guys. I don't want to intrude. In fact, my ride is waiting, so I have to go.'

'Don't be an idiot,' Lilly said, reaching out and grabbing my wrist. Not in a nice, friendly, *Come on* kind of way. But in a *You're busted and you're coming with me, young lady* kind of way. I'll admit it. I was a little scared.

'You're a princess, remember? You can tell your ride when it's time to go. As your editor, I'm telling you you need a direct quote from Michael for the paper. And he'd be hurt if he found out you were here and didn't say hi. And,' she said, giving my wrist an ominous squeeze, along with a glare that could have frozen molten lava, 'you're not hurting him again, Mia. Not on my watch.'

*Me*, hurt *him*? Hello? Did I need to remind her that her brother was the one who dumped *me*?

And OK, I acted like a complete jackass and completely deserved to be dumped. But still.

What was going on here, anyway? Was this some kind of continuation of the revenge for whatever it was I did to her last year? Was she going to drag me into that room and then do or say something horrible to humiliate me in front of everyone – especially her brother?

If so, it wasn't like I had any choice but to let her pull me back into the crowded pavilion. Her grip on my wrist was like iron.

But . . . what if this *wasn't* about revenge? What if Lilly was over whatever it was she'd been so mad at me about for nearly two years? Maybe it was worth the risk.

Because in spite of everything – even ihatemiathermopolis.com – I missed having Lilly as a friend. At least, when she wasn't trying to get revenge on me for things I'd supposedly done to her.

I saw Lars look up in surprise as we came out of the ladies' room together, and his eyes widen – he knows perfectly well Lilly and I aren't exactly bosom buddies any more. And I guess seeing the way she had hold of my wrist was probably a bit of a tip-off to him that I wasn't exactly going with her of my own volition.

Still, I shook my head at him to let him know he shouldn't go for his taser. This was my own mess and I was going to take care of it. Somehow.

I also saw Tina down the hall notice us, and throw us a startled look. Lilly, thank God, didn't see her. Tina's jaw dropped when she spied the way Lilly's hand was clamped over my wrist, which I suppose did not look exactly friendly-ish. Tina thrust her cellphone to her ear and mouthed *Call me!*

I nodded. Oh, I was going to call Tina all right.

Call her and give her a piece of my mind for getting me into this mess in the first place (though I suppose it was my big plan to Do The Princessy Thing that got me here really).

The next thing I knew, Lilly was dragging me across the Simon and Louise Templeman Patient Care Pavilion towards the stage where Michael and her parents and Nana Moscovitz and Kenny – I mean, Kenneth – and the other employees of Pavlov Surgical were still standing, drinking champagne.

I felt like I was going to die. I really did.

But then I remembered something of which Grandmere had once assured me: No one has ever died of embarrassment – never, not once in the whole history of time.

Of which I am living proof, having a grandmother like mine.

So at least I had the assurance I would escape from all this with my life.

'Michael,' Lilly started bellowing when we were halfway across the stage. She'd dropped my wrist and taken my hand – which felt so weird. Lilly and I used to hold hands all the time when we were crossing the street together back when we were kids, because our mothers made us, thinking somehow this would ensure we wouldn't get run over by an M1 bus (instead, it basically meant we'd *both* get ploughed down). Lilly's hand had always been sweaty and sticky with candy back then.

Now it felt smooth and cool. A grown-up's hand really. It was strange.

Michael was busy talking to a whole group of people – in Japanese. Lilly had to say his name twice more before he finally looked over and saw us.

I wish I could say that when Michael's dark eyes met mine, I was completely cool and collected about seeing him again after all this time, and that I laughed airily and said all the right things. I wish I could say that after having pretty much single-handedly brought democracy to a country I happen to be princess of and written a 400-page romance novel and gotten into every college to which I applied (even if it's just because I'm a princess), I handled meeting Michael for the first time again after throwing my snowflake in his face almost two years ago with total grace and aplomb.

But I totally didn't. I could feel my whole face start to heat up when his gaze met mine. Also, my hands began to sweat right away. And I was pretty sure the floor was going to come swinging up and smack me in the head, I suddenly felt so light-headed and dizzy.

'Mia,' Michael said, in his deep Michael-y voice, after excusing himself from the people he'd been talking to. Then he smiled, and my light-headedness increased by about ten million. I was positive I was going to pass out.

'Um,' I said. I think I smiled back. I have no idea. 'Hi.'

'Mia's here representing *The Atom*,' Lilly explained to Michael when I didn't say anything more. I *couldn't* say anything more. It was all I could do just to keep from falling over like a tree that had been gnawed on by a beaver. 'She's doing a story on you, Michael. Aren't you, Mia?'

I nodded. Story? *The Atom*? What was she talking about?

Oh, right. The school paper.

'How are you doing?' Michael asked me. He was talking to me. He was talking to me in a friendly, non-confrontational manner.

And yet no words would formulate in my head, much less come out of my mouth. I was mute, just like Rob Lowe's character in the TV movie of Stephen King's *The Stand*. Only I wasn't as good-looking.

'Why don't you ask Michael a question for your story, Mia?' Lilly poked me. *Poked* me. In the shoulder. And it didn't not hurt.

'Ow,' I said.

Wow! A word!

'Where's Lars?' Michael asked with a laugh. 'You better watch out, Lil. She generally travels with an armed escort.'

'He's around here somewhere,' I managed to get out. Finally! A sentence. Accompanied by a shaky laugh. 'And I'm fine, thanks for asking before. How are you doing, Michael?'

Yes! It speaks!

'I'm great,' Michael said.

Right then his mother came up and said, 'Honey, this man over here is with *The New York Times*. He wants to

118

talk to you. Can you just –' Then she saw me, and her eyes went totally huge. 'Oh. *Mia.*'

Yeah. As in: *Oh. It's You. The Girl Who Ruined Both My Children's Lives.*

I seriously don't think it was my imagination either. I mean, it would take an imagination the size of Tina's to turn it into: *Oh. It's You. The Girl For Whom My Son Has Secretly Been Pining Away For Almost The Past Two Years.*

Which, having seen Micromini Midori, I knew wasn't the case.

'Hi, Dr Moscovitz,' I said, in the world's smallest voice. 'How are you?'

'I'm fine, sweetheart,' Dr Moscovitz said, smiling and leaning over to kiss my cheek. 'I haven't seen you in so long. It's lovely you were able to come.'

'I'm covering the event for the school paper,' I explained hastily, knowing even as I said it how incredibly stupid it sounded. But I didn't want her to think I'd come for any of the real reasons I'd actually come. 'But I know he's busy. Michael, go talk to the *Times*—'

'No,' Michael said, 'that's OK. There's plenty of time for that.'

'Are you kidding me?' I would have liked to have reached out and pushed him towards the reporter, but we're not going out any more, so touching isn't allowed. Even though I really would have liked to put my hand on that suit-coat sleeve, and have felt what was underneath it. Which is really shocking, because I have a boyfriend. 'It's the *Times*!'

'Maybe you two could get together for coffee or something tomorrow,' Lilly said casually, just as Kenneth – ha! I finally remembered! – came sauntering up. 'For like a private interview.'

119

What was she *doing*? What was she *saying*? It was like Lilly had suddenly forgotten how much she hated me. Or Evil Lilly had been replaced, when no one was looking, by Good Lilly.

'Hey,' Michael said, brightening. 'That's a good idea. What do you say, Mia? Are you around tomorrow? Want to meet at Caffe Dante, say, around one?'

Before I knew what I was doing, buoyed by popular sentiment, I was nodding, and saying, 'Yes, one tomorrow is fine. OK, great, see you then.'

And then Michael was walking away . . . only to turn at the last minute and say, 'Oh, and bring that senior project of yours. I still can't wait to read it!'

Oh my God.

I fully thought I was going to be sick all over Kenneth's shiny dress shoes.

Lilly must have noticed, since she poked me in the back (not very gently) and asked, 'Mia? Are you *all right*?'

Michael was out of earshot by then, talking to the *Times* reporter, and his mom had drifted off to talk to his dad and Nana Moscovitz. I just looked at Lilly miserably and said the first thing that popped into my head, which was, 'Why are you being so nice to me all of a sudden?'

Lilly opened her mouth and started to say something, but Kenneth put his arm around her and glared at me and went, 'Are you still going out with J.P.?'

I just blinked at him in confusion. 'Yes,' I said.

'Then never mind,' Kenneth said, and swung Lilly away from me like he was mad at her or something.

And she didn't try to stop him.

Which is weird, because Lilly isn't exactly the type of

girl to let a guy tell her what to do. Even Kenneth, who she really likes. More than likes, I'm pretty sure.

Anyway, that was the end of my big first meeting with Michael after almost two years. I got down off the stage with as much dignity as I could (it helps when you have a bodyguard to escort you), and we headed to the limo, where the girls were waiting, and they demanded every detail, which I was able to give them as I wrote this (although I left out a few things of course).

I have to take them to Nobu, where they say we're going to sample every type of sushi on the menu.

But I don't know how I'm going to be able to concentrate on appreciating the subtle flavours of Chef Matsuhisa when the whole time I'm going to be all, *What am I going to do about showing my book to Michael?*

Seriously. Not to sound common – as Grandmere would say – but I am pretty much screwed right now.

Because I can't give my book to Michael. He invented a robotic arm that saves people's lives. I wrote a romance novel. One of these things is not like the other.

And I really don't want the guy who just got an honorary master's degree in science from Columbia (and who's had his hand down my shirt on numerous occasions) reading my sex scenes.

Talk about embarrassing.

## Saturday, April 29, 7 p.m., the Loft

I decided that Dr K is right.

I really have to stop lying so much. I mean, if I'm going to meet Michael tomorrow for this newspaper-interview thing (which there's no way I can get out of, because if I don't do it then I have to admit that I *wasn't* there today to interview him for *The Atom*, and there is absolutely *no way* I'm fessing up that I was *really* there to ask him for a CardioArm . . . or, worse, to spy on him with my giggling girlfriends), then I'm going to have to give him a copy of my senior project.

I'm just going to have to. There's no way I can get around it. He totally remembered – don't ask me how, when he's obviously the busiest man in the universe.

And if I'm going to come clean with my ex-boyfriend regarding the truth about my senior project, well, that means I have to tell the truth about it to the people in my life who are more important than he is. Such as my best friend and my actual boyfriend.

Because otherwise, it's just not fair. I mean, for Michael to know the truth about *Ransom My Heart*, but not Tina or J.P.

So I decided that I'm just going to bite the bullet and give ALL of them a copy. This weekend.

In fact, I emailed Tina hers just now. I've got nothing but free time tonight, since J.P. is at rehearsal and I'm babysitting Rocky while Mom and Mr G are at a community meeting to discuss NYU's rampant expansionism and what they can do to stop it before the only people who can afford to live in the Village are twenty-year-old Tisch film students with trust funds.

I sent Tina a copy of my manuscript with this message:

*Dear T*

*I hope you won't be mad, but remember when I said my senior project was about Genovian olive-oil pressing, circa 1254–1650? Well, I was sort of lying. Actually, my senior project was a 400-page medieval romance novel called* Ransom My Heart, *set in England in 1291, about a girl named Finnula, who kidnaps and holds for ransom a knight just back from the Crusades, so she can get money for her pregnant sister to buy hops and barley to make beer (a common practice in those days).*

*However, what Finnula doesn't know is that knight is really the earl of her village. And Finnula has some secrets the earl doesn't know as well.*

*I'm sending* Ransom My Heart *to you now. You don't have to read it or anything (unless you want to). I just hope you'll forgive me for lying. I feel really stupid for that. I don't know why I did it, I guess because I was embarrassed as I wasn't sure if it was any good. Plus, there are a lot of sex scenes in it.*

*I really hope you'll still be my friend.*

*Love*
*Mia*

I haven't heard back from her, but that's because the Hakim Babas usually have dinner all together at this time of day, and Tina's not allowed to check her messages at the table. It's a family rule that even Mr Hakim Baba follows now that his doctor warned him about his high blood pressure.

I kind of feel sick – sick and excited at the same time. About sending *Ransom My Heart* to Tina, I mean. I can't imagine what she's going to say. Will she be mad at me for lying to her? Or stoked, because romance novels are her favourite thing in the whole world? It's true she prefers contemporary romance novels, and usually ones with sheiks in them.

But it's possible she might like mine. I put a ton of references to the desert in it.

More importantly, what's J.P. going to say about it when I tell him? I mean, he knows I love writing and that I want to be an author some day.

But I've never actually mentioned *romance* writing to him before.

Well, I guess I'm going to find out what he thinks soon enough. I'm sending him a copy too.

Although who knows when he'll actually open it up and read it. His play rehearsals have been known to go on until midnight.

And now Rocky is begging me to watch *Dora the Explorer* with him. I understand that millions of kids love Dora and have learned to read or whatever from her show. But I wouldn't mind if Dora fell off a cliff and took her little pals with her.

## Saturday, April 29, 8.30 p.m.

I just got a text from Tina!

OMG I CAN'T BELIEVE YOU WROTE A ROMANCE NOVEL AND YOU NEVER TOLD ME!!!!!!!! YOU R SO AWESOME!!!!!!!! I LUV U!!!!!!!! ROMANCE NOVELS 4EVER!!!!!!!! I'VE STARTED IT ALREADY AND IT'S SO CUTE!!!!!!!! YOU HAVE TO TRY TO GET THIS PUBLISHED!!!!!!!! I CAN'T BELIEVE YOU WROTE A WHOLE BOOK!!!!!!!! Tina☺

PS I have to talk to you about something. It's nothing I can put in a text. It's not a bad thing. But it's something I thought of because of your book. CALL ME ASAP!!!!!

It was as I was reading this that my phone rang and I saw it was J.P. I picked up, and before I could say anything, even *Hello*, he was all, 'Wait . . . you wrote a *romance novel?*'

He was laughing. But not in a mean way. In an affectionate, *I can't believe it* way.

Before I knew it, I was laughing too.

'Yeah,' I said. 'Remember my senior project?'

'The one about the history of Genovian olive-oil pressing, circa 1254–1650?' J.P. sounded incredulous. 'Of course.'

'Yeah,' I said. 'Well, actually, I sort of . . . lied about that.' Oh, dear God in heaven, I prayed. Don't let him hate me for lying. 'My senior project was really a historical romance novel. The one I just sent you. It's medieval, set in 1291 England. Do you hate me?'

'Hate you?' J.P. laughed some more. 'Of course I don't hate you. I could never hate you. But a *romance novel*?' he said again. 'Like the kind Tina reads?'

'Yeah,' I said. Why did he sound like that? It wasn't *that* strange. 'Well, not *exactly* like the kind she likes to read. But sort of. See, Dr K told me it was great that I helped Genovia become a constitutional monarchy and all, but that I should really do something for *myself*, not just for the people of Genovia. And since I love writing, I thought – and Dr K agreed – maybe I should write a book, because I want to be an author and all, and I was always writing in my journal anyway. And, well, I love romance novels . . . they're so satisfying, and proven to be stress relievers – did you know, many of the Domina Reis, leaders in the business and political world, read romance novels to relax? I did some research, and over twenty-five per cent of all books sold are romances. So, I figured if I was going to write something that had a hope of being published, statistically, a romance had the best shot –'

OK. I was babbling. I mean, did I really just tell him over twenty-five per cent of all books sold were romances? No wonder he wasn't saying anything.

'You wrote a *romance novel*?' he finally said. Again.

Weirdly, J.P. was turning out to be less upset about the fact that I'd lied to him than he was about the fact that I'd written a romance novel.

'Um, yeah,' I went on, trying not to focus too much on how stunned he sounded. 'See, I did a whole lot of research on medieval times – you know, like when

Princess Amelie lived? Then I wrote my book. And now I'm trying to get it published—'

'You're trying to get it *published*!?' J.P. echoed, his voice breaking a little on the word *published*.

'Yes,' I said, a little surprised by his surprise. What was up with that? Isn't that what you did when you wrote a book? I mean, he'd written a play, and I was pretty sure he was trying to get it produced. Right? 'Only not very successfully. No one seems to want it. Except vanity presses of course, who want *me* to pay *them*. But that's not unusual, I guess. I mean, J. K. Rowling's first Harry Potter novel got rejected numerous times before she—'

'Do the publishers know the book is by *you*?' J.P. interrupted. 'The Princess of Genovia?'

'Well, no, of course not,' I said. 'I'm using a pseudonym. If I said it was by me, they'd totally want to publish it. But then I wouldn't know for sure if they really liked it and thought it was good and worth publishing, or if they just wanted to publish a book written by the Princess of Genovia. Do you see the difference? I don't even want to be published if it's going to happen that way. I mean, I just want to see if I can do it – be a published author – without it happening because I'm a princess. I want it to happen because what I wrote is good – maybe not the best. But OK enough to be sold at Wal-Mart or wherever.'

J.P. just sighed.

'Mia,' he said. 'What are you *doing*?'

I blinked. 'Doing? What do you mean?'

'I mean, why are you selling yourself short? Why are you writing commercial fiction?'

I had to admit, he completely lost me there. What

was he talking about, 'selling myself short'? And commercial fiction? What other kind of fiction was I supposed to write? Fiction based on real people? I'd tried that once . . . a long time ago. I wrote a short story based on real people – it was about J.P., as a matter of fact, before I had gotten to know him.

And I'd had the character based on him kill himself at the end by throwing himself under the F train!

Thank GOD I'd realized at the last minute – just before the story was about to be distributed to the entire school via Lilly's literary magazine – that you just can't *do* that. You can't write stories based on real people and have them throwing themselves under the F train at the end.

Because you'll just end up hurting their feelings if they happen to read it and recognize themselves in it.

And I don't want to hurt anybody!

But I couldn't tell J.P. that. He didn't know about the short story I'd written about him. I'd kept that a secret this whole time we'd been going out.

So, in answer to his commercial-fiction question, I said, 'Well. Because . . . it's fun. And I like it.'

'But you're so much better than that, Mia,' he said.

I have to admit, this kind of stung. It was like he was saying my book – which I'd spent almost two years working on, and which he hadn't even read yet – wasn't worth anything.

Wow. This was *really* not the reaction I'd hoped for from him.

'Maybe you should read it first,' I said, trying to keep the tears that had suddenly popped into my eyes – I don't know from where, I'm really not usually that sensitive – from spilling over, 'before you make judgements about it.'

J.P. sounded instantly contrite.

'Of course,' he said. 'You're right. Sorry. Listen . . . I have to get back to rehearsal. Can we talk more about this tomorrow?'

'Sure,' I said. 'Call me.'

'I will,' he said. 'I love you.'

'Love you too,' I said. And hung up.

The thing is, it's going to be fine. I know it is. He'll read *Ransom My Heart* and he'll love it. I know he will. Just like I'll see *A Prince Among Men* on opening night next week and I'll love it. Everything's going to be fine! That's why we're so well suited to each other. Because we're both so creative. We're artists.

I mean, J.P. will probably have a few editorial notes to make about *Ransom My Heart*. No book is perfect. But that's OK, because that's how creative couples are. Like Stephen and Tabitha King. I welcome his input! I'll probably have a few notes on *A Prince Among Men* as well. We'll go over his notes on my book together tomorrow and –

OH MY GOD I'M MEETING MICHAEL FOR COFFEE TOMORROW!!!!!!!!!!

How am I ever going to get to sleep NOW?????

# Sunday, April 30, 3 a.m., the Loft

## Questions to ask Michael for *The Atom*:

1) What inspired you to the invent the CardioArm?

2) What was it like to live in Japan for twenty-one months, assuming you were there this whole time and not actually back in this country before now and just not calling me, which would have been totally fine because we're broken up anyway?

3) What did you miss most about America?

4) ~~What did you like best about Japan?~~
(I can't ask him this! What if he says Micromini Midori? I won't be able to bear it! Plus, I can't put that answer in a school paper! Oh . . . maybe I should just ask it anyway . . . he could say something like sushi . . .)

4) What did you like best about Japan? (PLEASE DON'T LET HIM SAY MICROMINI MIDORI!!!!)

5) ~~How long is the waiting list for one of Pavlov Surgical's CardioArms?~~ I can't ask this either! Because it sounds like I'm asking to see how long it would take Genovia to get one, and that I'm hinting that I want one . . .

6) Hypothetically, if a very small country were to request a CardioArm for one of its hospitals (and was willing to pay cash for it, of course), what type of procedure would it follow? Does Pavlov Surgical accept cheques, or could a country pay with a black

American Express card and if so could I possibly pay for it now?

7) If you could be any animal what would it be and why? (God, this is the stupidest question, but it seems like everyone who ever interviews me asks this, so I guess I'd better ask it too.)

8) How long do you plan on staying in New York? Is this a permanent move or do you think you'll go back to Japan? Or do you see yourself moving, perhaps to Silicon Valley in California, which is where all the young computer titans, such as the founders of Google and Facebook, seem to live these days?

9) As an AEHS grad, what is your best memory of your time at our school? (Non-Denominational Winter Dance. Please say Non-Denominational Winter Dance your senior year.)

10) Do you have any words of inspiration for this year's AEHS graduating class?

AAAAAAAAAAHHHHH THESE ARE SO LAME!!!!!!

## Sunday, April 30, Noon, the Loft

OK, I still haven't thought of any better questions for Michael, but those were the best I could come up with after what happened with J.P. being all *You wrote a romance?* Not to mention the 900 text messages I've received from Tina telling me to we have to talk 'in person'. I have no idea what could be so important that we can't discuss it over the phone.

But Tina is totally convinced that René might have hackers secretly taping my cellphone transmissions (just like Prince Charles and Camilla and the 'tampon' incident), so for the moment she won't say or text anything too inflammatory to me via cellular transmission.

Which makes me think whatever it is that's on her mind, I probably don't want to hear it.

Possibly the reason that I can't come up with any better questions for Michael might have something to do with the fact that I woke up this morning to Rocky banging on my face with his fist, yelling, 'Soopwise!'

I was 'soopwised' all right. Surprised he was in my room, since he isn't supposed to be allowed in it – and he isn't supposed to be able to get in it with the special slippy thing I put over the doorknob that only adults know how to work.

Only it turned out an adult had opened the door for him. An adult who was peering down at me with a big happy grin on her face.

'Well, hey there, Mia! How you doin'?'

Oh my God. It was Mamaw. With Papaw right next to her. In my room. My *BEDROOM*.

That's it. I'm moving out of this place. Just as soon as

I can figure out where I'm going to go to college. Which I have exactly six more days to decide.

'Happy birthday, in advance!' Mamaw yelled. 'Look atchoo, lying in bed at ten o'clock! Who do you think you are, anyway? Some kinda princess?'

This caused Mamaw and Papaw to explode with laughter. At their own joke. It caused me to pull the covers up over my head and yell, 'MO-O-OOOM!!!'

'Mother.' I could hear Mom show up. 'Please. I'm sure Mia's very excited to see you, but let's give her a chance to get up and greet you properly. You'll have plenty of time to visit one another.'

'I don't see when,' Mamaw said. I could tell by her voice that she was scowling. 'Ya'll have us visitin' so many museums and tours and whatnot.'

'Well, I'm sure Mia will be more than happy to go on some of those tours with you,' I heard Mom say.

It was at that point I flipped the covers down and glared at her. Mom just glared right back.

So, apparently, I'm taking Mamaw and Papaw to the Central Park Zoo later today.

I understand that it's the least I can do in my capacity as their only granddaughter. Still. *It's not like I don't exactly have other things to do.*

One of them being get ready for my ~~coffee date~~, I mean interview, with Michael. Which I need to continue doing right now. Even though it's hard because my hands are trembling so much I can barely hold my eye pencil to outline my lids.

And I really wish Lana would quit texting me to tell me what to wear, because that's not helping either.

Although I refuse to take her advice, and I'm going with something casual. Just my 7 For All Mankind jeans, the Christian Louboutin boots, my off-the-shoulder Sweet Robin Alexandra top, all my bangles, my Subversive lava-bead cameo choker and my chandelier earrings. That's not too much at all! I mean, it's not like I'm trying to get him to like me in a sexy way. We're just friends now.

I'm going to brush my teeth one more time though, just to be safe.

Mr G and Rocky are putting on a drum recital for Mamaw and Papaw.

Please let me get out of here without developing a cluster headache.

# Sunday, April 30, 12.55 p.m., Caffe Dante, MacDougal Street

My hands are sweating so much. This kind of weakness is insufferable, especially in a member of the House of Renaldo. We're all feminists. Even Dad. He has the endorsement of NOWG, the National Organization of the Women of Genovia, after all. Even Grandmere is a member.

Speaking of Grandmere, she's emailed me like FOUR times today about the party and/or Dad's election. I've deleted each one. I don't have time to read her insane messages! And why can't she learn to email properly? I realize she's 400 years old, and I have to respect my elders (even though, if you ask me, she is in no way deserving of my respect). But still, she could let go of the R button once she's pressed it the first time.

Where IS Michael? Lars and I are here. And I realize we're five minutes early (I wanted to get rid of the paparazzi if I had to, but there's none here, strangely. I also wanted to have the first choice of seat so I could make sure I got the best lighting. Lana assures me this is vitally important in boy/girl meetings, even of the Friends Only variety. Also, I wanted to snag a table close by for my bodyguard, yet far enough away that he wasn't breathing down our necks, no offence of course, Lars, if you're reading this over my shoulder, which, don't lie, I know you do when the battery on your Treo runs down). So where is –

Oh God. There he is. He's looking around for us.

He looks SO good. Even better than yesterday,

because today he's wearing jeans and they're fitting him SO PERFECTLY in all the right places.

Wow. I'm turning *into* Lana.

And he's also wearing a totally nice black short-sleeved polo shirt, and I'm just going to come right out and say that everything we suspected lay under the sleeves of his suit jacket yesterday REALLY DOES. As in, muscles. Not hideous bulked-up steroidy ones either.

But Lana was not far off in her Christian Bale *Batman Begins* assessment.

And I know I have a boyfriend. I am merely observing this in my capacity as an investigative journalist. !!!!!

He's seen me!!!!! He's coming!!!!!

I'm dying now, goodbye.

<u>Interview with Michael Moscovitz for *The Atom*,</u>
<u>as recorded by Mia Thermopolis on Sunday, April 30,</u>
<u>via iPhone (to be transcribed later)</u>

**Mia:**              So, it's OK if I record this?

**Michael**
(laughing):           I said it was.

**Mia:**              I know, but I need to record you saying it. I know it's stupid.

**Michael**
(still laughing):  It's not stupid. It's just kind of weird. I mean, to be sitting here being interviewed by you. First of all, it's you.

|              | Second of all . . . well, you were always the celebrity. |
|--------------|----------------------------------------------------------|
| **Mia:**     | Well, now it's your turn. And thanks again, so much, for doing this. I know how busy you must be, and I want you to know I really appreciate your taking the time out to meet with me. |
| **Michael:** | Mia . . . of course.                                     |
| **Mia:**     | OK, so first question: What inspired you to invent the CardioArm? |
| **Michael:** | Well, I saw a need in the medical community and felt I had the technical knowledge to fill it. There've been other attempts in the past to create similar products, but mine is the first to incorporate advanced imaging technology. Which I can explain to you if you want, but I don't think you're going to have room for it in your article, if I remember how long the stories are in *The Atom*. |
| **Mia** (laughing): | Uh, no, that's OK—                               |
| **Michael:** | And, of course, you.                                     |
| **Mia:**     | What?                                                    |

**Michael:** You asked what my inspiration was for inventing the CardioArm. Part of it was you. You remember, I told you before I left for Japan, I wanted to do something to show the world I was worthy of dating a princess. I know it sounds dumb now, but . . . that was a big part of it. Back then.

**Mia:** R-right. Back then.

**Michael:** You don't have to put that in the article if it embarrasses you though. I can't imagine you'd want your boyfriend reading that.

**Mia:** J.P.? No . . . no, he'd be fine with that. Are you kidding? I mean, he knows about all that. We tell each other everything.

**Michael:** Right. So he knows you're here with me?

**Mia:** Um. Of course! So where was I? Oh, right. What was it like to live in Japan for so long?

**Michael:** Great! Japan's great. Highly recommend it.

**Mia:** Really? So are you planning on . . . Oh, wait, that question's later . . . Sorry, my grandmother woke me up really early this morning and I'm all disorganized.

**Michael:** Oh, right. How is the Dowager Princess Clarisse?

**Mia:** Oh, not her. The other one. Mamaw. She's in town for my birthday party.

**Michael:** Oh, right. I wanted to thank you for the invitations to your party.

**Mia:** . . . the invitations to my *party*?

**Michael:** Right. Mine arrived this morning. And my mom said hers and Dad's and Lilly's came last night. That was really nice of you, to let bygones be bygones with Lilly. I know she and Kenny are planning on going tomorrow night. My parents too. I'm going to try to make it as well.

**Mia**
(under breath): *Grandmere!*

**Michael:** What was that?

**Mia:** Nothing. OK . . . so what did you miss most about America while you were gone?

**Michael:** Uh . . . you?

| | |
|---|---|
| **Mia:** | Oh, ha ha. Be serious. |
| **Michael:** | Sorry. OK. My dog. |
| **Mia:** | What did you like best about Japan? |
| **Michael:** | Probably the people. I met a lot of really great people there. I'm going to miss some of them – the ones I haven't brought over here with the rest of my team – a lot. |
| **Mia:** | Oh. Really? So you're moving permanently back to America now? |
| **Michael:** | Yeah, I have a place here in Manhattan. Pavlov Surgical will have its corporate offices here, though the bulk of the manufacturing will be done out of Palo Alto in California. |
| **Mia:** | Oh. So— |
| **Michael:** | Can I ask *you* a question now? |
| **Mia:** | Um . . . sure. |
| **Michael:** | When am I going to get to read your senior project? |
| **Mia:** | I knew you were going to ask me that— |

| Michael: | So, if you knew, where is it? |
|----------|-------------------------------|
| Mia: | I have to tell you something. |
| Michael: | Uh-oh. I know that look. |
| Mia: | Yeah. My project's not about the history of Genovian olive-oil pressing, circa 1254–1650. |
| Michael: | It's not? |
| Mia: | No. It's actually a 400-hundred-page medieval historical romance novel. |
| Michael: | Sweet. Hand it over. |
| Mia: | Seriously. Michael – you're just being nice. You don't have to read it. |
| Michael: | *Have* to? If you don't think I want to read it now, you're high. Have you been smoking some of Clarisse's Gitanes? Because I'm pretty sure I got high once on the secondhand smoke from those. |
| Mia: | She had to quit smoking. Look, if I email you a copy, will you just promise to not start reading it until I've left? |
| Michael: | What, now? You mean this minute? To |

my phone? I completely and totally swear.

| | |
|---|---|
| **Mia:** | OK. Fine. Here it is. |
| **Michael:** | Outstanding. Wait. Who's Daphne Delacroix? |
| **Mia:** | You said you wouldn't read it! |
| **Michael:** | Oh my God, you should see your face. It's the same colour red as my Converse. |
| **Mia:** | Thanks for pointing that out. Actually, I changed my mind. I don't want you to have a copy any more. Give me your phone, I'm deleting it. |
| **Michael:** | What? No way. I'm reading this thing tonight. Hey – cut it out! Lars, help, she's attacking me! |
| **Lars:** | I'm only supposed to intervene if someone is attacking her, not if the princess is attacking someone else. |
| **Mia:** | Give it to me! |
| **Michael:** | No— |
| **Waiter:** | Is there a problem here? |

| | |
|---|---|
| **Michael:** | No. |
| **Mia:** | No. |
| **Lars:** | No. Please excuse them. Too much caffeine. |
| **Mia:** | Sorry, Michael. I'll pay for dry-cleaning . . . |
| **Michael:** | Don't be stupid . . . are you still *recording* this? |

End recording.

## Sunday, April 30, 2.30 p.m., a bench in Washington Square Park

Yeah, so, that didn't work out so well.

And it got even worse when I was saying goodbye to Michael – after I'd tried, then failed, to wrestle his iPhone away from him so I could delete that copy of my book I'd so stupidly sent him – and we got up to leave, and I stuck out my hand to shake his hand goodbye, and he looked at it and said, 'I think we can do a little better than that, can't we?'

And held out his arms to give me a hug – an obviously *friendly* hug, I mean, it was nothing more than that.

And I laughed said, 'Of course.'

And I hugged him back.

And I accidentally smelt him.

And it all came rushing back. How safe and warm I'd always felt in his arms, and how every time he'd held me like that, I'd never wanted him to let go. I didn't want him to let go of me there, right in the middle of Caffe Dante, where I was just interviewing him for *The Atom*, not on a date or anything. It was so stupid. It was so awful. I mean, I had to practically *force* myself to let go of him, to stop breathing in his Michael-y smell, which I hadn't smelt in so long.

What is *wrong* with me?

And now I can't go home, because I don't think I can deal with running into any of my various family members from Indiana (or Genovia) who might be there. I just have to sit out here in the park and try to forget what a complete idiot I was back there (while Lars stands guard to protect me from the drug dealers who keep asking me to 'Smoke? Smoke?', the homeless people who want to know if I can give them a five dollars, and the packs of touring NYU kids with their parents, who keep going, 'Oh my God, is that – It is! It's Princess Mia of Genovia!') and hope eventually I'll go back to normal and my fingers will stop shaking and my heart will stop beating *Mi-chael, Mi-chael, Mi-chael* like I'm back in freaking ninth grade again.

I really hope that hot chocolate washes out of his jeans.

Also, I would just like to ask the gods or anyone else who might be listening . . . why can't I conduct myself in a grown-up fashion around guys I used to date and with whom I broke up and with whom I should be completely and one hundred per cent OVER?

It was just so . . . *weird* sitting so close to him again. Even *before* I could smell him. And I get that we're just friends now – and of course I know I have a boyfriend, and Michael's got a girlfriend (probably – I never did get a straight answer about this).

But he's just so . . . I don't know! I can't explain it! He sort of emanates this . . . *touchable* quality.

And of course I knew I couldn't touch him (before I did touch him . . . which he ASKED me to do. He couldn't have known what that hug would do to me. Did he know? No, he couldn't have. He isn't a sadist. Not like his sister).

But being there in the cafe with him, it was like . . . well, it was like no time had gone by. Except of course a lot of time had gone by. Only in the best way, you know? Like, even though I might have sounded stupid on the tape (I just played it back. I sounded like a complete idiot), I didn't *feel* stupid while I was saying it – not the way I used to when I was younger around Michael. I think it's because . . . well, a lot of stuff has happened since I was last in Michael's company, and I just feel more confident about things (OK, well . . . about men) than I used to. Recent hug-related freak-out aside.

For instance – now that I've played the tape back, I realize Michael was kind of flirting with me! Just a little.

But that's OK. It's *more* than OK actually.

Oh no. Did I just write that?

Not that it matters, because I'm pretty sure he thinks the only reason I was there was because I'm doing an article for *The Atom* (although some reporter I am, since I didn't even ask him all my questions, once I got so preoccupied wrestling him over his phone).

Wrestling! In a restaurant! Like a seven-year-old! Great. When am I ever going to learn to act like a grown-up? I really thought I'd reached the point of being able to maintain a somewhat dignified demeanour in a public place.

And then I wrestled my ex-boyfriend in a cafe over his iPhone! And spilt hot chocolate over him!

Then I smelt him.

I think I lost one of my chandelier earrings too.

Thank God no paparazzi showed to get photos of *that*.

Anyway, I guess it was . . . sweet? Michael, I mean, and his reaction to my telling him I wrote a romance novel. Even though I completely regret sending it to him.

He says he's going to read it! Tonight!

Of course, J.P. said the same thing. But J.P. also told

me I shouldn't sell myself short. Michael didn't say anything like that.

Then again, Michael's not my boyfriend. He doesn't have my best interests at heart the way J.P. does.

It was just so adorable how he said I was the inspiration for his inventing the CardioArm though. Even if that was ages ago, and before we broke up.

He also said it was nice of me to let bygones be bygones with Lilly. He obviously doesn't know the truth. I mean that *I'm* not the one who's been holding a grudge all this time, but –

Oh no. Grandmere's calling. I'm going to pick up, because I have a few things I want to say to her.

'Amelia?' Grandmere sounds like she's in a tunnel. I hear blow-drying in the background, though, so I know it's only because she's getting her hair done. 'Where are you? Why aren't you answering any of my emails?'

'I have a better question for you, Grandmere. Why did you invite my ex-boyfriend and his family to my birthday party tomorrow night? And you better not say it's to butter him up so I can ask him for a CardioArm, because—'

'Well, of course that's why, Amelia,' Grandmere says. I hear a slapping noise, and then she says, *'Stop that, Paolo. I said not so much hairspray.'* To me she says, in a louder voice, 'Amelia? Are you still there?'

Really, nothing she says or does should surprise me any more. And yet it does. Continuously.

'Grandmere,' I say. I'm mad. Really. This isn't just any ex-boyfriend. It's *Michael*. 'You can't do this. You can't *use* people like this.'

'Amelia, don't be stupid. You want your father to win the election, don't you? We need one of those arm contraptions. As I think I told you. If you had done what I asked you and requested one from him, I wouldn't have had to send him and that horrible sister of his an invitation, and you wouldn't be placed in the awkward position of having to entertain your former paramour at your birthday soirée tomorrow night in front of your current paramour. Which I admit will be tricky . . .'

'Former –' I sputter. There's a pack of pubescent boys skateboarding nearby. I watch as one of them wipes out on a cement mound placed in the park for this purpose. I know exactly how he feels. 'Grandmere, Michael was *not* my paramour. That word suggests that we were lovers, and we were *not*—'

'Paolo, I *told* you, not so much hairspray. Are you trying to gas me? Just look at poor Rommel, he's practically hyperventilating – his lung capacity isn't the same as a human's, you know!' Grandmere's voice is fading in and out. 'Now, Mia, about your gown for tomorrow night. Chanel will be delivering it in the morning. Kindly let your mother know someone needs to be at your flat to receive it. This means your mother will have to stay home from her little art studio for once. Do you think she can handle that, or is it too much responsibility? Never mind, I already know the answer to that question—'

My call waiting is going off. It's Tina!

'Grandmere. This isn't over,' I inform her. 'But I'm going now—'

'Don't you dare disconnect me, young lady. We haven't spoken about what we're going to do if the Domina Reis make an offer of membership to you tomorrow, as you know they're likely to. You—'

I know it's rude, but I'd had quite enough of Grandmere. Really, thirty seconds of her is plenty.

'Bye, Grandmere,' I said. And switched over to Tina. I'll deal with Grandmere's wrath later.

'Oh my God,' Tina said, the minute I picked up. 'Where are you?'

'Washington Square Park,' I said. 'Sitting on a bench. I just met Michael and spilt hot chocolate on his pants. We hugged goodbye. I smelt him.'

'You spilt hot chocolate on his pants?' Tina sounded confused. 'You *smelt* him?'

'Yeah.' The skateboarders were all trying to outdo each other with their jumps, but most of them just kept crashing. Lars was watching them with a little smile on his face. I really hoped he wasn't thinking about asking one of them to borrow his skateboard and show them how it was done. 'He smelt really, really good.'

There was a long pause as Tina digested this.

'Mia,' she said, 'did Michael smell better to you than J.P.?'

'Yes,' I said in a small voice. 'But he always has. J.P. smells like his dry-cleaner.'

'Mia,' Tina said, 'I thought you bought him some cologne.'

'I did. It didn't take.'

'Mia,' Tina said, 'I *have* to talk to you. I think you better come over.'

'I can't,' I said. 'I have to take my grandparents to the Central Park Zoo.'

'Then I'll meet you,' Tina said, 'at the zoo.'

'Tina,' I said, 'what's going on? What's so important that you can't tell me what you need to say over the phone?'

'Mia,' Tina said, 'you *know*.'

She was wrong. I had no idea!

And it had to be something pretty bad if she was afraid TMZ might pick it up, and it would damage my dad in the polls even more.

'Meet me inside the Edge of the Icepack penguin exhibit at four fifteen,' she said, sounding just like Kim Possible. If Kim Possible ever asked people to meet her inside penguin enclosures.

Still, I'm not surprised. Somehow, the Central Park Zoo penguin enclosure is where I always end up during my hours of darkest need.

'Can you just give me a hint?' I asked. 'What does it have to do with? Boris? Michael? J.P.?'

'Your book,' Tina said. And hung up.

My *book*? What could my book have to do with anything? Unless . . .

Could it be *that* bad?

Great. And both J.P. and Michael are reading copies of it *right now. RIGHT THIS VERY MINUTE!*

I could throw up just thinking about it.

I should just go over to Eighth Street, buy a wig from one of the drag-queen stores and ditch town. I'm practically legal, and there's nothing left for me here. I've been humiliated in every way a person possibly can be. I might as well just grab a bus for Canada.

If only I could figure out a way to get rid of my bodyguard . . .

# Sunday, April 30, 4 p.m., Edge of the Icepack penguin exhibit at the Central Park Zoo

Wow.

Between having my current boyfriend tell me I'm selling myself short writing popular fiction, then spilling hot chocolate all over the jeans of my ex-boyfriend (who is currently reading my book – RIGHT THIS VERY MOMENT), then having my best friend say she has to meet me because there's a PROBLEM with that book – the same book I spent twenty-one months working on – I really didn't think my twenty-four hours could get any worse.

But that was before I got to the zoo with my mother, stepfather, baby brother, grandparents and bodyguard in tow.

I guess I was just born under a particularly lucky star seventeen years, 364 days ago.

The Central Park Zoo wasn't too crowded on the first perfectly sunny Sunday afternoon of the spring, so it wasn't like we had any problems navigating Rocky's enormous stroller through the crowds (NOT!!!!!).

Or that anyone noticed my huge bodyguard, who discreetly chose to wear a pair of wrap-around shades with his black suit jacket and matching black shirt, tie and pants.

And Mamaw didn't stand out too much in her hot-pink extra-large Juicy Couture knock-off sweatsuit (instead of Juicy it says Spicy on the butt. Spicy is one word you definitely don't want to associate with your grandma's butt. Or juicy, for that matter).

Good thing Papaw refused to conform to New York

City fashion dictates and kept on his good old green-and-yellow John Deere baseball cap – though he did let Mamaw buy him a new one that said *Legally Blonde, The Musical*. Which I will pay hard cash to see him wear.

Much was made over showing Rocky the polar bears and monkeys, his two favourite animals. And I will admit, my kid brother is cute, especially when it comes to doing a monkey imitation, with the underarm scratching and whatnot (an ability he clearly inherited from his father. No offence, Mr G).

Mamaw was pretty excited to be spending time with me, not just her grandson. The good thing is, after this, we get to spend even more time together . . . we're spending quality time over dinner at a restaurant of Mamaw and Papaw's choice. And the restaurant they chose was . . . Applebee's.

Yes! It turns out there is an Applebee's in Times Square, and that is where my grandparents want to go. I turned to Lars when I heard this and said, 'Please put a bullet in my brain now,' but he wouldn't do it.

And Mom told me to shut my piehole or she'd shut it for me.

Seriously though. Applebee's? Out of all the restaurants in Manhattan? Why a chain restaurant that can be found in nearly every city in America?

I told Mamaw that I have a black American Express card and could afford to take them to any restaurant they wanted if price was a problem. Mamaw said it wasn't the price. It was Papaw. He didn't like eating strange food. He liked always going to the same place, so he'd know exactly what he was getting.

The whole fun of eating out is getting to try new things!

But Papaw said trying new things isn't fun at all.

I just pray to every single god that exists in the heavens – Yahweh, Allah, Vishnu, etc. – that no paparazzo shows up and snaps photos of me, the Princess of Genovia, coming out of an Applebee's during this crucial time in my father's campaign.

Anyway, Mamaw keeps wanting to talk about college. As in, where I'm going (welcome to the club, Mamaw). She's got a lot of advice as to what I ought to be studying. In her opinion, what I ought to be studying is . . . nursing. She says there are always jobs for nurses, and as the American population ages, good nurses will always be in high demand.

I told Mamaw that while she's quite right, and that nursing is a very noble profession, I didn't think I'd be able to pursue it, what with my being a princess and all. I mean, I have to choose a career where I'll be able to spend at least a largish chunk of my time in Genovia, doing princess stuff like christening ships and hosting benefits and all that.

Being a nurse wouldn't exactly be conducive to that.

But being a writer would, because you can do that in the privacy of your own palace.

Plus with my SAT score I think the last thing anyone wants me doing is trying to measure out their medicine. I would probably kill way more people than I'd save.

Thank God we have people like Tina, who are good at math, going into the medical profession instead of me.

Speaking of Tina, I've snuck into the penguin enclosure to wait for her while Mom and those guys are getting Rocky a freeze pop or something he saw someone else eating and threw a very special soon-to-be-three-year-old tantrum for. They've fixed this place up a bit since the last time I was here. It isn't nearly as smelly and the light's a lot better to write by. But there are so many more people! I swear, New York City is becoming the Disneyland of the north-east. I thought I heard someone ask where the monorail was. But maybe they were joking.

Even so, how am I supposed to leave this place to go to college? How??? I love it so much!!!!

Oh, here's Tina now. She looks . . . *concerned*. Possibly she heard where I'm going to dinner?

I'm kidding . . .

## Sunday, April 30, 6.30 p.m., the ladies' room at the Times Square Applebee's

OK, I am FREAKING OUT OVER WHAT TINA TOLD ME IN THE EDGE OF THE ICEPACK PENGUIN EXHIBIT.

I'm just going to write this down the way it happened and try to ignore the squashed French fry on the floor underneath me (who eats French fries on the toilet? WHO??? Who eats ANYTHING on the toilet???? Excuse me, but gross, also, ew) and the fact that I am writing this in an Applebee's ladies' room, the only place I could go to get away from my grandparents.

So, Tina comes up to me in the penguin house and is like, 'Mia, I'm so glad I found you. We have to talk.'

And I'm all, 'Tina, what's wrong? Did you hate my book or something?'

Because I have to admit, I mean, I know my book isn't the greatest or anything – if it was, I'm sure someone would have wanted to publish it by now.

But I didn't think it could be SO bad that Tina would have to meet me in the Edge of the Icepack penguin exhibit at the Central Park Zoo to tell me in person.

Plus, she looked kind of pale underneath her kohl and lipstick. But it could have been the blue glow from the penguin tank.

But then she grabbed my arm and was like, 'Oh my God, Mia, no! I loved your book! It was so cute! And it had beer in it! I thought that was so funny, because of your bad experience with beer, remember, in tenth grade, when you tried to be a party princess, and you drank that beer and did the sexy dance with J.P. in front of Michael?'

I glared at her. 'I thought we agreed we were never going to speak of the sexy dance again.'

She bit her lip. 'Oops. Sorry,' she said. 'But it's just so cute. I mean, that you wrote about beer! I love that! No, when I said I needed to talk to you about your book, what I meant was –'

And she gave Lars this total look like – *GO AWAY!*

And he got the message, and went over to join Wahim, Tina's bodyguard, looking at the cute penguins swimming around, both of them keeping an eye on the two of us, but out of earshot.

And the whole time I'm like, in my head, OK, I wrote about beer, I mean, there's beer in my book, does Tina think I'm an alcoholic? Is she here to perform an intervention on me? I've totally seen that show *Intervention* on TV. Is that what's happening right now? Is Tina here to do an intervention because she thinks I need one?

And I'm looking around for the camera crew, wondering how I'm going to get out of going to rehab, because, seriously, I don't even *like* beer –

Then Tina turned to me and asked me the question that still has me shaking to my very core. I mean, she was smiling as she asked it, and her eyes were shining, but she looked super serious too.

And as I'm writing this, I still can't believe it. I mean – TINA! TINA HAKIM BABA! Of all people.

I'm not judging. I just never, ever expected it.

Or suspected it.

It's just . . . TINA!

Anyway, she turned to me and goes, 'Mia, I just had to ask – I mean, I was reading your book and – don't get me wrong, I like it, but – I started wondering – and I know it's none of my business, but – have you and J.P. had sex?'

I could only stare at her. This was so far from anything I'd been expecting her to say – especially in the Edge of the Icepack penguin exhibit, with our bodyguards a few yards away, and all the little kids around going, 'Look, Mommy! *Happy Feet!*' – that for a few seconds I think I was simply too shocked to speak.

'It's just,' Tina went on quickly, seeing that I had been rendered mute, 'the sex scenes in your book seem kind of realistic, and I just couldn't help thinking that maybe you and J.P. have. Had sex, I mean. And if you have, I want you to know, I'm not judging you or anything for not waiting until prom night, like we agreed. I totally understand. In fact, I *more* than understand, Mia. The truth is, I've been wanting to tell you for a long time that Boris and I . . . well, we already had sex too.'

!!!!!!!!!!!!!!!!!!!!!!!!

'The first time was last summer,' she went on, after I just stared at her in total mute silence, doing my Rob Lowe in *The Stand* imitation again. 'At the house my parents rented in Martha's Vineyard? You remember, Boris came out for two weeks to visit? Well, that's when it first happened. I tried to wait, Mia. I really did. But seeing him every day in his swimsuit – it was just too much to resist. I finally just . . . well, we did it. After my parents went to sleep. And we've been doing it pretty regularly ever since, whenever Mr and Mrs Pelkowski aren't home.'

I think my eyes must have looked like they were

about to roll out of my sockets, because Tina reached over to shake my arm.

'Mia?' she asked, looking concerned. 'Are you all right?'

'*You?*' I finally managed to choke out. 'And *Boris?*' I wasn't sure if I was going to throw up or pass out. Or both. Then we'd have REALLY needed an intervention.

It wasn't so much the fact that Tina – TINA! – of all people had given up on her dream of losing her virginity on prom night.

It was that she'd just said the sight of Boris in a swimsuit had been too much for her to resist. I'm sorry, but . . .

While it's true that Boris had undergone an incredible transformation from nottie to hottie in recent years – and actually has annoying violin groupies who worship him and follow him around begging him to sign his headshot whenever he appears in recital halls – I just couldn't – CANNOT – see him in that way.

Maybe if I had never known him back when he'd worn a bionater and been such a scrawny sweater tucker-inner – and dated Lilly – I could see it.

But the truth is, I just can't look at him and see the tall, muscular, godlike figure he is today. I just can't. I CAN'T! He's like . . . I don't know. My *brother* or something.

Tina, of course, completely mistook my revulsion for something else.

'Don't worry, Mia,' she said, taking my hand and gazing worriedly into my eyes. 'We're totally safe. You know neither of us has ever been with anybody else. And I've been on the Pill since I was fourteen, because of my dysmenorrhoea.'

I blinked at her some more. Oh, right. Tina's dysmenorrhoea. She used to get out of PE because of it every month. Lucky duck.

Tina looked at me uncertainly. 'So . . . you don't think I'm a slut for not waiting until the prom?'

My mouth fell open. 'What? No! Of course not! Tina!'

'Well.' Tina winced. 'I just . . . I wasn't sure. I wanted to tell you, but I didn't know how you'd feel about it. I mean, we had our plan for prom night and I . . . I ruined it because I couldn't wait.' Then she brightened. 'But then, when you said you thought prom was lame, and J.P. didn't ask you – and then when I read your book – well, I just put it all together and thought, you must have had sex already too! Only now that you and Michael—'

I looked around the penguin enclosure quickly. There were people everywhere! Most of whom were five years old! And screaming about penguins! And we were having this totally intimate conversation! About *sex*!

'Now that Michael and me what?' I interrupted. 'There's no Michael and me, Tina. I told you, I just spilt hot chocolate on him. That's all!'

'But you smelt him,' Tina said, looking concerned.

'Yeah, I smelt him,' I said. 'But that's it!'

'But you said he smelt better than J.P.' Tina still looked concerned.

'Yeah,' I said, starting to feel panicky. Suddenly, the penguin exhibit was making me feel a little claustrophobic. There were way too many people in there. Plus, the echoing shrieks of all the sticky-fingered kids – not to mention the faint odour of penguin – was getting a little overwhelming. 'But that doesn't mean anything!

It's not like we're getting back together or anything. We're just friends.'

'Mia.' Tina looked stern. 'I read your book, remember?'

'My book?' I could feel myself getting hot, even though it was super air-conditioned in the penguin house. 'What does my book have to do with anything?'

'A handsome knight who's been away from home for a long, long time returns?' Tina said meaningfully. 'Weren't you writing about Michael?'

'No!' I insisted. Oh my God! Was everyone who read it going to think this? Was J.P. going to think it? Was *Michael*? OH NO! HE WAS READING IT RIGHT NOW!!!! Maybe he was reading it WITH MICROMINI MIDORI! AND LAUGHING ABOUT IT!

'What about the girl who felt obligated to care for her people?' Tina went on. 'Weren't you really writing about yourself? And the people were the Genovians?'

'No!' I cried, my voice cracking. Some of the parents, holding the smaller kids up to see the penguins, looked over to see what the two teenaged girls in the dark corner were talking about.

If only they knew the truth. They'd probably have run screaming from the zoo. They might even have asked the wardens to shoot us.

'Oh.' Tina looked let down. 'Well . . . it seemed like it. It seemed like . . . you were writing about you and Michael, getting back together.'

'Tina, I wasn't,' I said. My chest was starting to feel tight. 'I swear.'

'So . . .' Tina looked at me intently in the blue glow from the penguin tank. 'What are you going to do about J.P.? I mean . . . you two *are* having sex – aren't you?'

I don't know how what happened next happened – what heavenly miracle occurred to save me – but at that very moment Mamaw and Papaw showed up with Rocky in tow, screaming my name. I mean, Rocky was screaming my name. Not Mamaw and Papaw.

Then the zoo was closing, so we all had to leave. Which pretty much closed the discussion on Tina's sex life. And mine. Thank GOD.

So now I'm here at Applebee's.

And I don't think I will ever be the same. Because Tina just confessed that she and Boris have been having sex regularly.

I should have known. They have been showing little to no public displays of affection at school all year – no kissing, no holding hands in the hallway, nothing like this – which should have been an indication to me that something serious was going on.

Such as major play under the sheets after school when Mr and Mrs Pelkowski weren't home.

God! I'm so blind!

Oh no – my cellphone is going off. It's J.P.! He must be calling to tell me what he thinks of *Ransom My Heart*.

I just answered, even though I'm in the ladies' room and there are people and flushing and stuff all around me. I personally think it's disgusting when people answer their cellphones in the ladies' room, but I haven't heard from J.P. all day, and I left a message with him earlier. I *do* want to see what he thinks of my book. I didn't want to sound needy or anything, but, you know. You'd have thought he'd have called already to let me know. What if HE thinks my book is about Michael and me too, just like Tina?

But it turns out I needn't have worried: He hasn't

had a chance to read it yet, because he's been in rehearsal all afternoon.

He wanted to know what I'm doing for dinner.

I said I was at Applebee's with Mamaw and Papaw and my mom and Mr G and Rocky, and that he was welcome (that I was even DYING for him) to join us.

But he laughed and said that was OK.

I don't think he really comprehended the gravity of the situation.

So then I said, 'No, you don't understand. You NEED to come join us.'

Because I realized I *really* needed to see him, after the day I'd had . . . what with smelling Michael and finding out from Tina about her and Boris and all.

But J.P. said, 'Mia . . . it's *Applebee's*.'

I said, feeling a little desperate (OK – a lot desperate): 'J.P., I know it's Applebee's. But that's the kind of restaurant my family likes. Well, some of my family. And I'm stuck here. It would really cheer me up so much if you could stop by. And Mamaw would really like to meet you. She's been asking about you all day.'

This was a complete and total lie. But whatever, I lie so much, what difference could one more lie make?

Mamaw hadn't mentioned J.P. at all, though she'd asked me if I had ever thought of asking out 'that cute boy from that show *High School Musical*. Because, as a princess, I'm sure you could get him to go out with you'. Um . . . thanks, Mamaw, but I don't date boys who wear more make-up than me!

'Besides,' I said to J.P., 'I miss you. It seems like I hardly ever get to see you any more, you're so busy with your play.'

'Aw. But that's what happens when two creative

people get together,' J.P. reminded me. 'Remember how busy you were when you were working on what I now know was your novel?' His reluctance to set foot in the horror that is the Times Square Applebee's was palpable. Also, may I just add, perfectly understandable. Still. 'And you'll see me in school tomorrow. And all night at your party tomorrow. I'm just really zonked from rehearsal. You don't mind, do you?'

I looked down at the squashed fry beneath my shoe.

'No,' I said. What else could I say? Besides, is there anything more pathetic than a nearly eighteen-year-old girl in a bathroom stall, begging her boyfriend to come meet her and her parents and grandparents at Applebee's for dinner?

I don't think so.

'See you later,' I said instead. And hung up.

I wanted to cry. I really, really did. Sitting there, thinking how my ex-boyfriend was maybe – probably – reading my book and thinking it was about him . . . and my current boyfriend hadn't read my book at all . . . well . . .

Honestly, I think I must be the most pathetic night-before-her-birthday girl in all Manhattan. Possibly on the entire East Coast.

Maybe in all of North America.

Maybe in the whole world.

An Excerpt from *Ransom My Heart* by Daphne Delacroix

Hugo lay beneath her, hardly daring to believe his good fortune. He had been pursued by a great many women in his time, women more beautiful than Finnula Crais, women with more sophistication and worldly knowledge. But none of them had ever appealed to him as immediately as this girl. She boldly announced that she wanted him for his money and she wasn't going to resort to seductions and stratagems to get it. Her game was abduction, pure and simple, and Hugo was so amused he thought he might laugh out loud.

Every other woman he'd ever known, in both the literal and biblical sense, had a single goal in mind – to become the chatelaine of Stephensgate Manor. Hugo had nothing against the institution of marriage, but he had never met a woman with whom he felt he wanted to spend the rest of his life. And here was a girl who stated, plain as day, that all she wanted from him was money. It was as if a gust of fresh English air had blown through him, renewing his faith in womankind.

'So it's your hostage I'm to be,' Hugo said, to the stones beneath him. 'And what makes you so certain I'll be able to pay your ransom?'

'Do you think I'm daft? I saw the coin you tossed Simon back at the Fox and Hare. You oughtn't be so showy with your spoils. You're lucky 'tis me that's waylaid you, and not some of Dick and Timmy's friends. They have rather unsavoury companions, you know. You could have come to serious harm.'

Hugo smiled to himself. He'd been worried about the girl meeting up with trouble on her way back to Stephensgate, never suspecting that she was sharing the same concern for him.

'Here, what are you smiling at?' the girl demanded, and to his regret, she slid down from his back and prodded him, none too gently, in the side with a sharp toe. 'Sit up now, and stop sneering. There isn't anything amusing about me abducting you, you know. I know I don't look like much, but I think I proved back at the Fox and Hare that I truly am the finest shot with a short bow in all the county, and I'll thank you to remember it.'

Sitting up, Hugo found his hands well tied behind his back. There was certainly nothing lacking in the girl's knot-tying education. His bonds were not tight enough to cut off the circulation, yet not loose enough to give way.

Lifting his gaze, he found his fair captor kneeling a few feet away from him, her elfin face pale in a halo of wildly curling red hair, hair so long that the ends of it twined amongst the violets below her knees. Her lawn shirt was untucked and sticking to her still-wet body in places, so that her nipples were plainly visible through the thin material.

Quirking up an eyebrow, Hugo realized that the girl was completely unaware of the dcvastating effect her looks had on him. Or at least, aware only that when naked she made a fetching distraction.

## Monday, May 1, 7.45 a.m., Limo on the way to school

I got up this morning when the alarm rang (even though I hadn't slept a BIT, wondering if Michael had read my book – I KNOW!!! All I could think, all night, was, 'Has he read it yet? What about now? Do you think he's read it now?' And then I'd freak out, going, 'What do I care if my EX-boyfriend has read my book? Pull yourself together, Mia! It doesn't matter what HE thinks! What about your CURRENT boyfriend?' and then I'd lay awake freaking out about J.P. Had HE read it? What had HE thought about it? Had HE liked it? What if he hadn't?), and pulled Fat Louie off my chest and staggered to the bathroom to shower and brush my teeth, and as I was staring at myself in the mirror (and the way my hair was sticking up in funny clumps – thank God I finally got more Phytodéfrisant), it suddenly hit me.

I'm eighteen.

And a legal adult.

And a princess (of course).

But now, thanks to the information Tina gave me yesterday, I'm pretty sure I'm basically the only virgin left in this year's Albert Einstein High's graduating class.

Yeah. Do the math: Tina and Boris – lost it this past summer.

Lilly and Kenneth? Obviously, they've been having sex for ages. You can just tell by the way they fondle one another in the hallway (which, thanks: I so want to see that on my way to Trig). So inappropriate.

Lana? Please. She left her virginity behind back in the days of one Mr Josh Richter.

Trisha? Ditto, although not with Josh. At least, I'm pretty sure, unless he's an even bigger dog than any of us suspect (likely).

Shameeka? The way her dad guards her like she's all the gold in Fort Knox combined? She told me last year she busted out in the tenth grade (not that any of us ever suspected, she was *that* discreet about it) with that senior she was dating, what's-his-name.

Perin and Ling Su? No comment.

And then there's my boyfriend, J.P. He says he's been waiting his whole life for the right person, and he knows that person is me, and when I'm ready, he'll be ready too. He can wait for all eternity, if he has to.

Which leaves who?

Oh yeah. Me.

And God knows *I've* never done it, despite what everyone (well, OK, Tina) apparently seems to think.

Honestly? It's just never come up. Between J.P. and me, I mean. Except for the whole J.P. being willing to wait for all eternity thing (such a refreshing change from my *last* boyfriend). I mean, for one thing, J.P. is the epitome of gentlemanlike behaviour. He is *completely* unlike Michael in that regard. He has never let his hands drift below my neck for so much as a *second* while we're kissing.

Truthfully, I'd be worried he wasn't interested if he hadn't told me that he respects my boundaries and doesn't want to go any further than I'm prepared to.

Which is very nice of him.

The thing is, I don't really know what my boundaries

are. I've never had a chance to test my boundaries out. With J.P., anyway.

It was just so . . . different, I guess, when I was going out with Michael. I mean, he never asked about my boundaries. He just sort of went for it, and if I had any objections I was supposed to speak up. Or move his hand. Which I did. Frequently. Not because I didn't like where it was, but because his – or my – parents or roommate were always walking in.

The problem with Michael was that when things started getting going, in the heat of the moment and all, I often didn't *want* to say something – or move his hand – because I liked what was going on too much.

That's my problem – *the other thing* – my horrible, terrible secret that I can never tell anyone, not even Dr K: With J.P. I never feel that way. Partly because things never get that far. But also because . . . well.

I suppose I could just do what Tina did with Boris and jump his bones. I've seen J.P. in his bathing suit (he's come to visit me in Genovia) plenty of times. But jumping his bones has just never occurred to me. It's not like he's not hot or anything. He totally works out. Lana says J.P. makes Matt Damon from the *Bourne* movies look like Oliver from *Hannah Montana*.

I just don't know what's wrong with me! It's not like I've lost my sex drive, because yesterday during the wrestling match over the iPhone with Michael, and again when he hugged me – it was there all right.

It just doesn't seem to be there with J.P. That's *the other thing*. My boyfriend doesn't seem to really turn me on.

This isn't something I particularly want to think about on my birthday though. Not when I've already had the joyous wonder of waking up in the morning and looking at myself in the mirror and realizing I'm eighteen; I'm a princess; and I'm a virgin.

You know what? At this point in my life, I might as well be a unicorn.

Happy freaking birthday to me.

Anyway, Mom, Mr G and Rocky were all up waiting for me with homemade heart-shaped waffles as a breakfast surprise (the heart-shaped waffle maker was a gift for them from Martha Stewart). Which was super sweet of them. I mean, they didn't know about my discovery (that I'm such a societal freak, I might as well be a unicorn).

Then Dad called from Genovia while we were eating to wish me a happy birthday and remind me today is the day I come into my full allowance as princess royale (not enough money to buy my own penthouse on Park Avenue, but enough to rent one if I need to), and not to spend it all in one place (ha ha ha, he hasn't forgotten my spending spree at Bendel's that one time, the subsequent donation I gave to Amnesty International) because it only gets replenished once a year.

I'll admit, he got a little choked up on the phone and said he never thought, back when he met me at the Plaza nearly four years ago to explain to me that I was actually the heir to the throne and I got the hiccups and acted like such a little freak about finding out I was a princess and all, that I'd turn out this well (if you consider this well).

I got a little choked up myself, and said I hoped there were no ill feelings about the constitutional monarchy thing, especially since we still get to keep the title, the throne, the palace, the crowns, the jewels and the jet and all that.

He said not to be ridiculous all gruffly, which I knew meant he was about to cry from the emotion of it all, and hung up.

Poor Dad. He'd be a lot better off if he'd just meet and marry a nice girl (and not a supermodel, like the President of France did, though I'm sure she's very nice).

But he's still looking for love in all the wrong places. Like fancy underwear catalogues.

At least he knows enough not to date while he's campaigning.

Then Mom came out with her present to me, which was a collage incorporating all the things from our lives together, including things like ticket stubs from train rides to women's productive rights rallies in Washington, DC, and my old overalls from when I was six, and pictures of Rocky when he was a baby, and pictures of Mom and me painting the loft, and Fat Louie's collar from when was a kitten, and snapshots of me in my Halloween costume as Joan of Arc and stuff.

Mom said it was so I wouldn't be homesick when I went to college.

Which was totally sweet of her and completely brought tears to my eyes.

Until she reminded me that I need to hurry up and make my decision about where I'm going to college next year.

OK! Yeah, I'll be sure to get right on that! Push me out of the loft, why don't you?

I know she and Dad and Mr G mean well. But it's not that easy. I have a lot of things on my mind right now.

Like how yesterday my best friend confessed she's been having sex regularly with her boyfriend and never told me until now, and like how before that I gave my novel to my ex-boyfriend to read, and how now I have to go turn in the article I wrote on said ex-boyfriend to his sister, who hates me, and later on tonight I have to attend a party on a yacht with 300 of my closest friends, most of whom I don't even know because they're celebrities my grandma, who's the dowager princess of a small European country, invited.

And, oh yeah, my actual boyfriend has had my novel for more than twenty-four hours and hasn't read it and wouldn't come to eat at Applebee's with me.

Could someone possibly cut me a tiny piece of slack?

Life's not easy for unicorns, you know. We're a dying breed.

# Monday, May 1, Homeroom

OK, so I just left the offices of *The Atom*. I'm still shaking a little.

There was no one in there but Lilly when I went in just now. I put on a big fake smile (like I always do when I see my ex-best friend) and went, 'Hi, Lilly. Here's the story on your brother,' and handed the article to her (I was up until one o'clock last night writing it. How do you write 400 words on your ex-boyfriend and keep it a piece of impartial journalism? Answer: you can't. I nearly had an embolism doing it. But I don't think you can tell, reading it, that I spilt hot chocolate on and then smelt the subject).

Lilly looked up from whatever she was doing on the school computer (I couldn't help remembering that stage she went through when she used to put the names of deities and then dirty words into Google just to see what kind of websites she'd come up with. God, those were the days. I *miss* those days. We used to laugh so hard that my undies were always just a little damp), and went, 'Oh, hi, Mia. Thanks.'

Then she added, sort of hesitantly, 'Happy birthday.'

!!!! She remembered!!!!

Well, I guess the fact that Grandmere sent her an invitation to my party might have been a slight reminder.

Surprised, I said, 'Um . . . thanks.'

I figured that was it and was halfway out the door when she stopped me by going, 'Look, I hope you won't be weirded out if Kenneth and I come tonight. To your party, I mean.'

'No, not at all,' I said. (<u>Mia Thermopolis's Big Fat Lie Number Seven.</u>) 'I'd love for you both to come.'

Which is just an example of how well all those princess lessons have paid off. The truth, of course, is that inside my head I was going, *Oh my God. She's coming??? Why? She can only be coming because she's plotting some horrible revenge on me. Like, she and Kenny – I mean Kenneth – are going to hijack the yacht once it sets sail and steer it out into international waters and detonate it in the name of Free Love once we've all been put into life rafts or something. Good thing Vigo made Grandmere hire extra security in case Jennifer Aniston shows up and Brad Pitt is there too.*

'Thanks,' Lilly said. 'There's something I really want to give you for your birthday, but I can only do it if I come to your party.'

Something she wants to *give* me for my birthday? But she can only give it to me on the Royal Genovian yacht? Great! My hijack theory confirmed.

'Um,' I stammered, 'you d-don't actually have to give me anything, Lilly.'

This was the wrong thing to say, though, because Lilly scowled at me and said, 'Well, I know you already have everything, Mia, but I think there's something *I* can give you that no one else can.'

I got super nervous then (not that I wasn't before), and said, 'I didn't mean it the way it sounded. What I meant was—'

Lilly seemed to regret her caustic outburst, and said, 'I didn't mean it like that either. Look, I don't want to fight any more.'

This was the first time in two years Lilly had referred to the fact that we even used to be friends, and that we'd been fighting. I was so surprised I didn't know what to say at first. I mean, it had never even occurred to me that not fighting was an option. I just figured the only option was what we'd been doing . . . basically ignoring one another.

'I don't want to fight any more either,' I said, meaning it.

But if she didn't want to fight any more, what DID she want? Surely not to be my friend. I'm not cool enough for her. I don't have any piercings, I'm a princess, I go on shopping sprees with Lana Weinberger, I wear pink ballgowns sometimes, I have a Prada tote, I'm a virgin, and, oh yeah – she thinks I stole her boyfriend.

'Anyway,' Lilly said, reaching into her backpack, which was covered all over with badges in Korean . . . I suppose promoting her TV show there, 'my brother told me to give you this.'

And she pulled out an envelope and handed it to me. It was a white envelope with a blue letterhead engraved on it where the return address was supposed to go. The letterhead said *Pavlov Surgical*, and there was a little illustration of Michael's sheltie, Pavlov. The envelope was kind of lumpy, like there was something in it besides a letter.

'Oh,' I said. I could feel myself blushing, like I do whenever Michael's name comes up. I knew I was turning the colour of his high-tops. Great. 'Thanks.'

'No problem,' Lilly said.

Thank GOD the first bell rang just then. So I said, 'See you later.'

And then I turned around and ran.

It was just so . . . WEIRD. Why is Lilly being so NICE to me? She must have something planned for tonight.

She and Kenneth. Obviously they're going to do something to ruin my party.

Although maybe not, because Michael and his parents are going to be there. Why would she do something to hurt me when it might endanger her parents and brother? I could tell how much she loves them Saturday at the thing at Columbia – and of course, from having known her almost my whole life, despite us not talking the past two years.

Anyway. I looked around for Tina or Lana or Shameeka or someone with whom to discuss what had just happened, but I couldn't find anyone. Which was strange, because you'd think they'd have come up to me at my locker to wish me a happy birthday or something. But nothing.

I couldn't help thinking – in an example of the marked paranoia I've been exhibiting lately – that maybe they were all avoiding me because Tina told them about my book. I know she said it was cute, but that's just what she said to my face. Maybe behind my back she thinks it's awful and she sent it to everyone else and they all think it's awful too and the reason the haven't stopped by to say happy birthday is because they're afraid they won't be able to stop laughing long enough in my face.

Or maybe they really *are* planning an intervention.

It's not unlikely.

Now I'm hyperventilating because when I got here to Homeroom and I was sure no one was looking, I tore open the envelope Lilly gave me and this is what I found inside. A handwritten note from Michael that said:

*Dear Mia*

*What can I say? I don't know all that much about romance novels, but I think you must be the Stephen King of the genre. Your book is hot. Thanks for letting me read it. Anyone who doesn't want to publish it is a fool.*

*Anyway, since I know it's your birthday, and I also know you never remember to back anything up, here's a little something I made for you. It would be a shame if Ransom My Heart got lost before it ever saw the light of day because your hard drive crashed. See you tonight.*

*Love*
*Michael*

Inside the envelope with the letter was a little Princess Leia action figure USB flash drive. For me to store my novel on, since he was right – I never back up my computer's hard drive.

The sight of it – it's Princess Leia in her Hoth outfit, my favourite of her costumes (how had he remembered?) – brought tears to my eyes.

He said he liked my book!

He said I'm the Stephen King of the genre!

He gave me a personally designed USB flash drive to store it so it wouldn't get lost!

Really, is there any higher compliment a boy can give a girl?

I don't think so.

I don't think I've ever had a nicer birthday gift.

Except Fat Louie of course.

Plus . . . he signed his letter *Love*.

*Love Michael*.

That doesn't mean anything of course. People sign things *Love* all the time. That doesn't mean they love you in a romantic way. My mom signs all her notes to me *Love Mom*. Mr G writes notes to me and signs them *Love Frank* (which, ew).

But still. The fact that he wrote the word . . .

Love. *Love!*

Oh my God. I know. I'm pathetic.

A pathetic unicorn.

# Monday, May 1, World History

I just saw J.P. in the hallway. He gave me a great big hug and a kiss and wished me a happy birthday and told me I look beautiful (I happen to know I don't look beautiful. I look awful actually. I was up half the night writing the article on Michael, so there are dark circles under my eyes that I tried to hide with concealer, but really there's only so much concealer can do. And I was up the other half of the night freaking out over what Tina told me about her and Boris, and then worrying about how Michael and J.P. would react to my book).

Maybe to J.P. I look beautiful because I'm his girl-friend. J.P. just likes me too much to notice that I am, in fact, a unicorn (but not one of those beautiful ones with the long silky manes from fairy tales. I'm one of those screwed up plastic toy unicorns Rocky's friend Emma from daycare plays with, that My Little Pony unicorn with the bald patches whose head gets sucked on all the time by the little kids).

I waited for J.P. to tell me he'd read my book and liked it, the way Michael did in his letter, but he didn't.

He didn't mention my book at all, as a matter of fact.

I guess he still hasn't gotten around to it. He does have his play and all. It's getting close to opening night, when he has to put it on for the senior project committee (Wednesday night).

But still. You'd have thought he'd have said *something*.

Instead J.P. told me not to expect my present from him just yet. He says he's giving it to me tonight, at my party. He says it's going to blow me away. He says he hasn't forgotten about the prom either.

Which is funny, because I certainly have.

Anyway, still no sign of Tina, Shameeka, Lana or Trisha anywhere. I did see Perin and Ling Su though, and they both wished me a happy birthday. But then they ran off, giggling madly, which is completely unlike them.

So, that about cinches it: They've totally read my book, and hated it. The intervention will probably be at lunch.

I can't believe Tina would do that – send around copies of it without asking me.

I mean it *is* reading day in preparation for finals so there's nothing to do in class BUT read. Obviously it's a perfect time for people to be reading my book.

Maybe I should try flunking all my finals (in the case of Trig, I won't even have to try). Then I really will have no choice but go to L'Université de Genovia next year.

But that won't work. I don't want to be that far from Rocky.

OH NO! Principal Gupta just called for me to come to the office right away due to a family emergency!

# Monday, May 1, Elizabeth Arden Red Door Spa

Yeah. I should have known.

There was no family emergency. Grandmere faked one, as usual, to have me pulled out of school so I could spend my birthday getting pampered with her at her favourite day spa before my birthday bash this evening.

The good thing is, I'm not here alone with her. And this time, she didn't just invite people she thinks I *should* hang out with, like my cousins from the royal family of Monaco or the Windsors or whoever.

No, she actually invited my real friends. Only a few of them (Perin and Ling Su, who actually care about their grades) were conscientious enough to say no and stay in school to study for finals instead. Tina, Shameeka, Lana and Trisha are all here getting pedicures right next to me, while Grandmere is in the next room, having a difficult ingrown toenail removed. Which thank God isn't happening right in front of me, because I think I'd probably throw up. It's bad enough to have to look at Grandmere's toenails when they're au naturel, but an ingrown toenail operation on top of that? No thank you.

It's kind of touching though that after all these years Grandmere finally gets it. I mean, that I have friends that I care about, and that she can't just force me to hang out with whoever she feels would make me a suitable companion (although the majority of the people coming to the party tonight are her friends . . . or Domina Reis).

Sometimes Grandmere does kind of rock.

Although I'm glad she wasn't there at that particular

moment, because the conversation was definitely not one you'd want your grandmother to overhear.

'Oh, the Waldorf,' Trisha was saying in response to a question Shameeka asked her, while the lady doing her feet rubbed gigantic salt granules all over her calves. 'Brad and I got a room.'

'There weren't any rooms left by the time I called,' Shameeka was saying all mournfully.

'Me neither.' Lana had cucumbers over her eyelids. 'Well, there were rooms, but not suites. Derek and I are staying at the Four Seasons instead.'

'But that's across town!' Trisha practically yelled.

'I don't care,' Lana said. 'I won't stay anywhere that only has one bathroom. I'm not sharing a bathroom with some random guy.'

'But you'll have sex with him,' Trisha pointed out.

'That's different,' Lana said. 'I want to be able to use the bathroom without having to wait for someone else to be through with it. I can't be expected to *share*.'

About which, I'd just like to ask, WHO is the princess in the room?

'Where are you and J.P. staying after the prom, Mia?' Shameeka wanted to know, gracefully changing the subject.

'He still hasn't asked her yet,' Tina told them matter-of-factly. 'So they'll probably be joining you at the Four Seasons, Lana.' I didn't have the heart to correct Tina on this. 'Oh, Mia . . . can I tell them?'

Shameeka looked excited. 'Tell us what?'

'About . . . *you* know.' Tina raised her eyebrows excitedly at me.

I seriously panicked when Tina came up with her *Can I tell them, Mia?* I thought – really – that she was referring to our conversation in the penguin enclosure yesterday. About Michael, and how I'd smelt him and all that.

And seeing as how I'd just gotten his note about my book – *Love Michael* – and was holding his Princess Leia USB flash drive in my pocket, and the whole thing had made me feel a little . . . I don't know. I guess *crazy* would be the appropriate word. If unicorns can get crazy.

Plus I was already extra sensitive about the fact that they were all talking about their boyfriends, and where they were taking them after the prom, and mine hadn't even *asked* me properly, let alone ever even touched me below the neck . . .

Well, I guess you could say I overreacted a little.

Because suddenly I heard myself saying, way too loudly, as the woman who was giving me a pedicure ground away at one of my heel calluses, caused from standing around in too high heels at too many royal benefits, 'Look, I've never had sex, all right? J.P. and I have never *done it*. So sue me! I'm eighteen, and I'm a princess, and I'm a virgin. Is that *all right* with everyone? Or should I go wait in the limo until you're all done with your *sexy talk*?'

For a second all four of them (well, nine if you count the ladies who were doing our feet) just stared at me in stunned silence. The silence was finally broken by Tina, who said, 'Mia, I just meant, would it be OK if I told them how you'd written a romance novel.'

'You wrote a romance novel?' Lana wore an expression of shock. 'A book? You like . . . *typed* it?'

'*Why?*' Trisha looked stunned. 'Why would you *do* that?'

'Mia,' Shameeka said, after exchanging nervous glances with everyone else. 'I think it's great you wrote a book. S-seriously! Congratulations!'

It took a minute for it to sink in that they were more shocked by the fact that I'd written a book than that I was a virgin. In fact, they seemed not even to care about the fact that I was a virgin, and were *fixated* on the fact that I'd written a book.

About which, can I just say – well, I was insulted actually.

'But the sex scenes in your book,' Tina said. She looked as shocked as everyone else in the room. 'They were so . . .'

'I told you.' I could feel myself turning as red as Elizabeth Arden's door. 'I read a lot of romance novels.'

'Is it like a real book?' Lana wanted to know. 'Or is it one of those books you make at the mall, where you put your own name in it? Because I wrote one of those when I was seven. It was all about how LANA went to the circus and how LANA got to perform with the trapeze artists and bareback riders because LANA is just as pretty and talented as—'

'Yes, it's a real book,' Tina said, shooting LANA a *look*. 'Mia wrote it herself, and it's really—'

'HELLO!' I yelled. 'I just told all of you that I've never had sex! And all you seem to be able to talk about is the fact that I wrote a book. Can we please FOCUS? *I've* never had *sex*! Do you have nothing to say about that?'

'Well, the book thing is more interesting,' Shameeka said. 'I don't see what the problem is, Mia. Just because we've all done it, doesn't mean you should feel strange about having waited. I'm sure there'll be tons of girls at the University of Genovia who haven't done it either. So you won't be at all out of place.'

'Totally,' Tina said. 'And how sweet is it that J.P. hasn't pressured you?'

'That's not sweet,' Lana said flatly. 'That's weird.'

Tina shot her another dirty look, but Lana refused to back down. 'Well, it is! That's what boys do. It's like their job to try to get you to have sex with them.'

'J.P. is a virgin too,' I informed them. 'He's been saving himself for the right person. And he says he's found her. Me. And he's willing to wait until whenever I'm ready.'

When I said that, everyone in the room looked at one another and sighed dreamily.

All except Lana. She went, 'So what's he waiting for then? Are you sure he's not gay?'

Tina shouted, 'Lana! Could you be serious for one second please?' just as Shameeka asked, 'Mia, if J.P. is willing to wait, then what's the problem?'

I blinked at her. 'There's no problem,' I said. 'I mean, we're fine.' (Mia Thermopolis's Big Fat Lie Number Eight.)

And Tina busted me on it.

'But there *is* a problem,' Tina said. 'Isn't there, Mia? Based on something you mentioned yesterday.'

I widened my eyes at her. I knew what she was going to say, and I really didn't want her to. Not in front of Lana and those guys.

'Uh,' I said, 'no. No problem. I've always been a bit of a late bloomer . . .'

'I'll say.' Lana snorted. 'Geek.'

But Tina didn't notice my subtle hint.

'Do you even *want* to have sex with J.P., Mia?' Tina asked.

*Love Michael.* Now, why did that have to pop into my head?

'Yes, of course!' I cried. 'He's totally foxy.' I was borrowing a phrase from the bathroom wall, about Lana. She'd written it about herself. But I figured it applied to J.P.

'But . . .' Tina looked as if she was trying to choose her words carefully. 'You told me yesterday that you think Michael smells better.'

I saw Trisha and Lana exchange glances. Then Lana rolled her eyes.

'Not the neck thing again,' she said. 'I *told* you, just buy J.P. some cologne.'

'I *did*,' I said. 'It's not that – Look, forget it, OK? You guys all have sex on the brain, anyway. There's more to a relationship than *sex*, you know.'

This caused all the ladies who were doing our feet to start giggling hysterically.

'Well,' I said to them. '*Isn't* there?'

'Oh yes,' they all said, 'Your Highness.'

Why did I get the feeling that they were making fun of me? That they were ALL making fun of me? Look, I knew from my vast romance reading that sex was fun.

But I ALSO knew from my vast romance reading that there were some things more important than sex. *LOVE MICHAEL.*

'Besides,' I added desperately, 'just because I think Michael smells better than J.P. doesn't mean I'm still in love with him or anything.'

'OK,' Lana said. Then she dropped her voice to a whisper and said, '*Except for the part where it totally does.*'

'Oh my God, a love triangle!' Trisha squealed, and the two of them started laughing so hard that they splashed the water in their foot basins, causing their pedicure specialists to have to ask them to please control themselves.

It was at that moment that Grandmere hobbled back into the room wearing her robe and flip-flops and looking particularly frightening, because she'd also just had a facial and so all her pores were still open and her face was devoid of make-up and very shiny and wearing an expression of extreme surprise . . .

But not, it turned out (much to my relief) because she'd overheard us.

It was because no one had drawn her eyebrows back on.

## Monday, May 1, 7 p.m., the Royal Genovian yacht, *Clarisse 3*, master suite

I have never seen so much pre-party psychosis in my life. And I've been to a *lot* of parties.

The florist brought the wrong floral arrangements — whites roses and *purple* lilies, not pink — and the caterer's crispy seafood spring rolls came with a peanut sauce instead of an orange sauce (*I* don't care, but there's some speculation that Princess Aiko of Japan has a peanut allergy).

Grandmere and Vigo are having CORONARIES about it. You would think somebody had forgotten to polish the silver or something.

Don't even get me started on the aneurysm they had when I suggested we use the helicopter landing pad as a dance floor.

Whatever! It's not like anybody's going to be landing the helicopter on it!

At least my dress arrived safely. I've been stuffed into it (it's silver and sparkly and form-fitting and what can I say? It was made especially for me and you can tell. There's not a whole lot left to the imagination), and my hair is all twisted up and tucked into my tiara, and I've been ordered to sit here quietly out of everyone's way and not move until it's time to make my grand entrance, once all the guests have arrived.

Like I'm all that jazzed to go anywhere, seeing as how what awaits me out there are my twin 'surprises' — one from J.P. and the other from Lilly.

I'm sure I'm overreacting. I'm sure whatever J.P. got me, I'm going to like it. Right? I mean, he's my boyfriend. He's not going to do anything to embarrass me in front of my family and friends. The whole thing with the guy who dressed up like the knight and rode up on the horse painted white – I mean, I explained that already. He got the message. I *know* he got the message.

So . . . why do I feel so sick to my stomach?

Because he called me a little while ago to see how I was (I'm actually feeling a little better about *some things* now that I've shared my 'secret' with all the girls. The one about my book AND the one about my being the last *unicorn* in the Albert Einstein High senior class – besides J.P., I mean. The fact that they didn't seem to think it was such a big deal was a pretty big relief. I mean, not that it IS a big deal, because it's not. It's just . . . well, it's good to know *they* don't think it's a big deal.

Although I wish Lana would quit texting me with alternative titles for my book. I don't actually think *Put It In My Candyhole* is that good a name for a novel).

J.P. also wanted to ask if I was 'ready' for my birthday surprise.

Ready for my birthday surprise? What is he *talking* about? Is he trying to freak me out on purpose? Seriously, between him and Lilly – with her talk of how she can only give me my present *tonight* – I'm going to go mental. I really am.

I don't know how anyone can expect me to sit still either. In fact, I haven't been sitting. I've been looking out of one of the portholes at all the people coming up the gangplank (I'm trying to keep myself hidden behind the curtains so no one can see me, keeping in mind Grandmere's golden rule: *If you can see them, they can see you*).

189

I can't believe everyone who's showing up for this shindig. So many celebrities. There's Donald Trump and his wife; Princes William and Harry; Posh Spice and David Beckham; Bill and Hillary Clinton; Will Smith and Jada Pinkett; Bill and Melinda Gates; Tyra Banks; Angelina Jolie and Brad Pitt; Barack and Michelle Obama; Sarah Jessica Parker and Matthew Broderick; Sean Penn; Moby; Michael Bloomberg; Oprah Winfrey; Kevin Bacon and Kyra Sedgwick; Heidi Klum and Seal.

And the evening's entertainment, Madonna and her band, are already setting up. She's promised to do her old-school stuff, in addition to some of her new songs (Grandmere is donating extra money to the charity of Madonna's choice for her to sing 'Into the Groove', 'Crazy for You' and 'Ray of Light').

Hopefully it won't be at all weird for Madonna that her ex, Sean Penn, is also here.

Grandmere had initially planned on having a different musical entertainer for my eighteenth birthday (Pavarotti) but fortunately he died. (No offence, he was awfully nice, but opera is kind of hard to dance to.)

The thing is, in addition to celebrities, there are so many people from my past here! My cousin Sebastiano (stopping to talk to all the paparazzi, snapping pictures where all the limos and taxis are dropping people off), with a supermodel on his arm. He's a famous fashion designer now. He even has a line of jeans in Wal-Mart.

Oh, and there's my cousin Hank, in white leather pants and a black silk top. His stalkers have found their way to the Seaport (they must have read about the party on Page Six, where it was announced this morning), and are screaming for his autograph. Hank pauses suavely and signs for them. It's hard to believe we used to hunt for crawdads together in overalls and our bare feet, back in Versailles, Indiana, all those years ago. Now Hank routinely has giant billboards of himself in his underwear up in Times Square. Who would have thought? I mean, I've seen him squirt Coca-Cola out of his nose.

Aw, and there's Mamaw and Papaw. I see Grandmere got them a stylist. I wonder if she was worried they'd show up in Nascar T-shirts?

But they clean up beautifully! Papaw's in a tux! He looks a little like James Bond. You know, if James Bond chewed tobacco.

And Mamaw's wearing an evening gown! And it looks as if Paolo got to her hair. And OK, she keeps stopping and waving to the paparazzi, none of whom wants to take her picture.

But she looks great! Kind of like Sharon Osbourne. If Sharon Osbourne had bleached blonde hair and a really big butt and said, 'Hey, ya'll!' a lot.

And there's my mom and Mr G and Rocky! My mom looks beautiful, as always. If only I could ever be that pretty some day. Even Mr G isn't a total wash. And doesn't Rocky look cute in his little toddler tux? I wonder how long it will be until he spills something all down the front of it (I give him five minutes). I'm betting it will be the peanut sauce.

And there are Perin and Ling Su and Tina and Boris and Shameeka and Lana and Trisha and their parents . . . oh, don't they all look nice? Well, except Boris.

Oh, all right. Even Boris. When you're wearing a tuxedo, at least you're *supposed* to tuck the shirt into your pants.

And there's Principal Gupta! And Mr and Madame Wheeton! And Mrs Hill and Ms Martinez and Ms Sperry and Mr Hipskin and Nurse Lloyd and Ms Hong and Mrs Potts and just about the entire rest of the staff of Albert Einstein High!

It was nice of Grandmere to let me invite them all, even if it's super weird to see your teachers outside of school. The fact that they're wearing evening clothes makes them basically unrecognizable and, ew, I think Mr Hipskin brought his wife and she looks almost exactly like him, except for the moustache. Sadly I mean hers, not his . . .

Wow, this is actually kind of fun, aside from the fact that eventually I have to—

Oh! And there he is.

J.P., I mean. He's brought his parents.

And he certainly does look GORGEOUS in his evening jacket and white tie.

He doesn't have any large packages with him. So . . . what can it be? His surprise for me, I mean? Because he's not carrying a present, that I can see . . .

Oh look, he's stopping now, with his parents, to talk to the paparazzi. Why does something tell me he's going to mention his play?

Well, if I was writing my book under my own name, would I waste any possible opportunity to mention it? Probably not, right?

On the other hand, considering what – or rather *who* – Tina seemed to think it was about, maybe not . . .

OK, I can't stand this! I think I'm going to be sick. When can I join the party? I'd rather just get it over with than keep waiting like—

Here come the Moscovitzes! They're getting out of a

LIMO! There are the Drs Moscovitz – I'm so glad they got back together! Doesn't Dr Moscovitz look distinguished in his tuxedo? And Lilly and Michael's mom, in her red evening gown, with her hair all up? So pretty! So unlike her normal self, in her glasses and business suit and Lady's Air Jordans . . .

And there's Kenneth, also in a tux, turning around to help – LILLY! Whoa, she actually dressed up – in a really nice black velvet dress. I wonder where she got that, certainly not her normal clothing store of choice, the Salvation Army. And look, she took her piercings out again. Well, most of them, I can't tell about the tongue ring from here . . .

She looks so pretty. I can't imagine she really can be up to anything that devious tonight. Can she? She doesn't appear to be holding anything that could be explosive, except possibly her video camera.

And she *always* has that with her.

Well, they're making everyone put their bags through an X-ray machine (you never can be too sure), so if there's anything wrong with the video camera, I'm sure the Royal Genovian security force will discover it . . . They've been instructed to dust Kenneth's hands for traces of explosives too.

And there's MICHAEL! He CAME! He looks so GORGEOUS in his tuxedo! Oh my God, I think I'm going to—

ACK! It's Grandmere . . . and . . .

The captain!

Great. Captain Johnson says he can't possibly unmoor from the dock, because the boat is already filled to capacity and there are still more limos and taxis pulling up, and if he attempts to head out to sea with more than the maximum capacity than the ship can hold, we'll sink.

'Fine,' Grandmere says. 'Amelia, you're going have to tell your guests to leave.'

I just laughed in her face. She's had WAY too many Sidecars already if she thinks *that's* going to happen.

'*My* guests? Excuse me, who invited Brangelina? *And* all their kids?' I wanted to know. 'I don't even *know* them! I want to have a nice time at my birthday party with my friends. *You* ask *your* celebrity guests to leave!'

Grandmere gasped.

'You know I can't do that,' she cried. 'Angelina is a Domina Rei! There's a strong possibility she's carrying your invitation to join – unless it's Oprah!'

Anyway, we've worked out a compromise: Nobody gets kicked off.

Instead, we're just not going to move. The boat's staying at the dock.

It's just as well. I wouldn't want to be out to sea with some of these lunatics (just in case Lilly IS up to something more than just filming).

Lars just knocked! He says it's time for my big entrance . . . Now I think I really *will* hurl.

It's too bad I'm not being carried in on a couch by half-naked bodybuilders like some of those girls on *My Super Sweet 16.* I'm just walking.

Of course, I have a tiara on my head: So I have to walk tall or it will fall off.

But still.

**Monday, May 1, 11 p.m., the Royal Genovian yacht, *Clarisse 3*, weird overhangy part just off the place where they steer, where Leo and Kate stood in *Titanic*, and Leo said he was the King of the World, I don't know what it's called, I don't know anything about BOATS, but it's cold up here and I wish I had a coat**

Oh God Oh God Oh God Oh God Oh God Oh God Oh God Oh God Oh God Oh God Oh God Oh God Oh God Oh God Oh God Oh God Oh God Oh God Oh God!

OK, I just have to remember to breathe. BREATHE. In and out. IN. Then OUT.

The thing is, it all started off so well. I mean, I came out and Madonna was singing 'Lucky Star', and my tiara didn't fall off, and everyone clapped, and everything looked so nice despite Grandmere's and Vigo's worries, especially the purple flowers and – this was the really amazing thing – it turned out *Dad* had flown in especially for the occasion, all the way from Europe on the Royal Genovian jet, taking time off from the campaign just for the night as a special surprise for me.

Yes! He stepped out from behind the biggest batch of purple flowers and made a speech about how great a daughter – and princess – I am . . . a speech that I barely heard because I was so shocked and teary-eyed at seeing him.

And then the next thing I knew he was hugging me and he'd given me this GIANT black velvet box, and inside was a very sparkly tiara. I thought it looked familiar, and he explained to everyone that it was the one Princess Amelie Virginie was wearing in the portrait I have hanging in my bedroom. He said that if anyone deserved it, I did. It had been missing for nearly 400 years, and he'd had them look all over the palace for it, and finally someone had found it in a dusty corner of the jewellery vault, and they'd polished it all up and cleaned it just for me.

Can you imagine anything so sweet?

It took me five minutes to stop crying. And another five minutes for Paolo to get my old tiara off and the new one on, thanks to all the hairpins.

You know, it fits me a lot better than my old one. It doesn't feel like it's going to slip off *at all*.

After that everyone came up and said such kind things to me like, 'Thanks for inviting me,' and, 'You look so pretty!' and, 'The spring rolls are delicious!'

And Angelina Jolie came up and gave me my formal invitation to join the Domina Reis, which I accepted on the spot (Grandmere told me I had to, but I wanted to of course, because it's a kick-ass organization).

Grandmere spotted us talking and of course figured out *immediately* what was going on, so she came rushing over like Rocky when he hears a box of cookies being opened.

And so Angelina gave her *her* invitation, and all Grandmere's dreams came true.

I wish I could say she went away then, but she spent the rest of the evening, as best I could tell, following Angelina around, thanking her at every chance she got. It was embarrassing.

But then, it was Grandmere. What else is new?

And then I went around and did the princess thing, personally going up to everyone and thanking them for coming, and it wasn't even that awkward, because, whatever, after nearly four years of this I'm pretty much used to it, and I'm not even thrown any more by the bizarre things people sometimes say, which are probably just non sequiturs I've taken out of context, like when Mr Hipskin's wife said, 'You look like a mermaid!'

I'm sure she just meant because my dress is so shiny and not because she's psychic (but only partly) and got mermaids and unicorns mixed up and knows I'm the only virgin left in the graduating senior class of Albert Einstein High, besides my boyfriend, of course.

And Lana and Trisha and Shameeka and Tina and Ling Su and Perin and my *mom* and I had a blast rocking down to 'Express Yourself' ('Come on, girls!'), and then Lana and Trisha made a beeline for the Princes William and Harry (of course), and J.P. and I slow-danced to 'Crazy for You', and my dad and I rumbaed to 'La Isla Bonita'. And even though Lilly was filming everything, which technically wasn't allowed, I told the security force just to let her, rather than to make a big deal of it. She was at least asking people beforehand if it was all right, so that part was OK – but that was *all* she appeared to be up to.

God only knows what she's going to do with the film later. Probably make some kind of documentary about the exorbitant spending habits of the filthy rich – *Real Princesses of New York City* – and run scenes from my party side by side with scenes of people from the slums of Haiti, eating cookies made of dirt.

(Note to self: make a huge donation to hunger organization. One in three children of the world die of hunger *every day*. Seriously. And Grandmere was having a fit over the SAUCE we were supposed to dip the spring rolls in).

But Lilly lowered the camera when she came up to me – Kenneth in tow, and Michael following not far behind – and said, 'Hey, Mia. This is a pretty great party.'

I totally almost choked on the piece of shrimp cocktail I was eating. Because I hadn't been able to eat a thing all night, I'd been so busy dancing and greeting people, and Tina had just come up to me *that minute* with a little plate of food, going, 'Mia, you've got to take a minute to eat something, or you're going to pass out . . .'

'Oh,' I said with my mouth full (a total Grandmere no-no), 'thank you.'

I'll admit, I was speaking to Lilly.

But my gaze had flicked right over her and was totally fixated on Michael, in his tux, behind Kenny – I mean, Kenneth. Michael just looked so . . . incredible, standing there with the glow of the lights of lower Manhattan behind his head, and the little bit of condensation that was in the air having settled over his broad shoulders, making the black material on them look a bit sparkly in all the twinkly party lights.

I don't know. I don't *know* what's wrong with me. I *know* he broke up with me. I *know* Dr Knutz and I worked that all out in therapy already. I know I have a boyfriend, a perfectly good boyfriend who loves me, and at that moment was over at the bar getting me a refill on my sparkling water.

I *know* all that.

Knowing all that and still looking at Michael and seeing him smile at me and thinking he's the handsomest guy in the world (even though, as Lana would be quick to point out, he's not – Christian Bale is) isn't even the problem.

What happened next is.

Which was, Michael said, 'Nice party hat you've got there, Thermopolis,' meaning Princess Amelie Virginie's tiara.

'Oh,' I said, reaching up to touch it. Because I still couldn't quite believe it – that my dad had found it, or even that he'd actually shown up to give it to me. 'Thanks. I'm going to kill him for doing this. He can't afford to take this much time out from the campaign. René is leading in the polls.'

'That guy?' Michael looked shocked. 'He was always kind of a tool. How can people like him more than your dad?'

'Everyone loves a Bloomin' Onion,' Boris, who was standing near Tina, said.

'Applebee's doesn't have Bloomin' Onions,' I growled at him. 'That's Outback!'

'I don't get why your dad wants to be prime minister so bad anyway,' Kenneth said. 'He's always going to be prince, right? Wouldn't he just want to sit back and relax and let some other guy do the political thing, so he can just do the fun prince stuff, like hanging out on yachts like this with . . . well, Ms Martinez, it looks like?'

I looked over to where Kenneth was pointing.

And OK, yeah, my dad was slow-dancing to 'Live to Tell' with Ms Martinez. The two of them looked really . . . snug.

But I'm eighteen now.

So, no, in fact, vomit did not rise up into my mouth.

I very maturely and very wisely turned back to the

conversation at hand and said, 'Actually, Kenneth, yes, my dad could very easily choose not to run for prime minister and simply be happy with his title and his normal royal duties. But he prefers to take a more active role in the shape of the future of his country, and that's why he wants to be prime minister. And that's why I sort of wish he hadn't wasted his time coming here.'

And now that I just saw what I saw, why I REALLY wish he hadn't come.

Oh well. Ms Martinez did read my novel and let it count as my senior project.

I *think* she read it. Some of it, anyway.

But that's not what happened that freaked me out so much either.

Lilly said, in my dad's defence, 'It's nice that he came. You only turn eighteen once. And he's not going to get to see you much after he's elected and you head off to college.'

'He will if Mia goes to the University of Genovia,' Boris said, 'like she's planning.'

Which is when Michael's head whipped around and he looked at me with his eyes wide and he went, 'University of Genovia? Why are you going *there*?' Because of course he knows what a crummy school it is.

I could feel myself blush. Michael and I, in our email conversations with one another, hadn't discussed the fact that I'd gotten into every school I'd applied to, much less the fact that I'd lied about this to all my friends at school.

'Because she didn't get in anywhere else,' Boris helpfully answered for me. 'Her math SAT score was too low.'

This caused Tina to elbow him, deeply enough to make him say, '*Oof.*'

It was at this moment that J.P. came back with my sparkling water. The reason it had taken him so long was because he'd stopped along the way to have a pretty in-depth conversation with Sean Penn – which he must have been pretty stoked about, Sean Penn being his hero and all.

'I find it really hard to believe you got rejected *everywhere* you applied, Mia,' Michael was saying, not noticing who was approaching. 'There are a lot of schools that don't even count SAT scores any more. Some great ones actually, like Sarah Lawrence, which has a really strong writing programme. I can't imagine you didn't apply there. Is it possible maybe you're exaggerating about—'

'Oh, J.P.!' I cried, cutting Michael off. 'Thanks! I'm so thirsty!'

I snatched the water out of his hand and gulped it down. J.P. was standing there, just staring at Michael, looking a little perplexed.

'Mike,' J.P. said. He still seemed a dazed from his conversation with his artistic hero. 'Hey. So. You're back.'

'Michael's been back for a while,' Boris said. 'His robotic surgical arm is a huge financial success. I'm surprised you haven't heard about it. Hospitals everywhere are vying for them, but they cost over a million dollars each and there's a waiting list – *ow.*'

Tina elbowed him again. This time I think she must have nearly broken one of Boris's ribs, because he almost doubled over.

'Wow,' J.P. said with a smile. He didn't look at all

disturbed by Boris's news. In fact, he had his hands in the pockets of his tuxedo pants like he was James Bond or someone. He'd probably gotten Sean Penn's phone number and was fondling it. 'That's great.'

'J.P. wrote a play,' Tina squeaked. Apparently because she was unable to stand the tension and was trying to change the subject.

Everyone just looked at her. I thought Lilly was going to bust a piercing, her eyebrows were so furrowed as she tried to hold in what was apparently a huge horse laugh.

'Wow,' Michael said. 'That's great.'

I honestly didn't know if he was being serious or if he was making fun of J.P., basically repeating the same thing he'd just said, or what. All I knew was, I had to get the heck out of there or the tension was going to kill me. And who wants to stroke out on their eighteenth birthday?

'Well,' I said, handing Tina my plate, 'princess duty calls. I have to go mingle. See you guys later—'

But before I could get even one step away, J.P. grabbed hold of one of my hands and pulled me back and said, 'Actually, Mia, if it's all right with you, I have sort of an announcement I'd like to make, and I can't think of a better time than right now. Will you go with me up to the microphone? Madonna's about to take a break.'

*That* was when I started feeling sick to my stomach. Because what sort of announcement could J.P. be going to make? In front of Mamaw and Papaw? And Madonna and her band? And my dad?

Oh, and Michael.

But before I could say anything, J.P. started gently

tugging – OK, dragging – me up to the stage they'd set up over the yacht's built-in pool.

And the next thing I knew, Madonna was moving graciously out of the way and J.P. had hold of the microphone and was asking for everyone's attention – and getting it. 300 faces were turning our way as my heart thumped inside my chest.

It's true I've given speeches in front of way more people than that. But that was different. Then *I'd* been the one in charge of the microphone. This time, someone else was.

And I had no idea what he was about to say.

But I had sort of an idea.

And I wanted to die.

'Ladies and gentlemen,' J.P. began, his deep voice booming out across the ship's deck . . . and, for all I knew, the entire South Street Seaport. The paparazzi, down below, could probably hear him. 'I'm so proud to be here tonight to celebrate this special occasion with such an extraordinary young woman . . . a young woman who means so much to all of us . . . to her country, to her friends, to her family . . . But the truth is, Princess Mia means more to me, perhaps, than she does to any of you . . .'

Oh God. No. Not *here*. Not *now*! I mean, it was totally sweet of J.P. to be expressing how much he cared about me in this way, in front of everyone – God knew Michael had never had the guts to do such a thing.

But then, I don't think Michael had ever felt that he'd needed to.

'. . . And that's why I want to take the opportunity to show her just how much she means to me by asking her here, in front of all her friends and loved ones . . .'

It was when I saw him reach a hand into one of the pockets of his tuxedo pants that I *really* started to panic that I might need actual CPR in a minute. *Oh God,* was all I could think. *This is way, way worse than riding up to school in a suit of armour on a horse painted white.*

And sure enough, from his pocket, J.P. pulled a black velvet box . . . a much smaller one than Princess Amelie's tiara had been in.

The one J.P. was holding was ring-sized.

As soon as everyone in the crowd saw the box – and then J.P. sink down on to one knee – they went totally bananas. People started cheering and clapping so loudly, I could hardly hear what J.P. said next . . . and I was standing right next to him. I'm sure no one else heard him, even though he was speaking into a microphone.

'. . . Mia,' J.P. went on, looking up into my eyes with a confident smile on his face as he opened the box to reveal an extremely large, pear-shaped diamond on a platinum band, 'will you . . .'

The screaming and cheering from the crowd got even louder. Everything went all swoopy in front of my eyes. The Manhattan skyline, the party lights on the boat, the faces before us, J.P.'s face below me.

I really did think for a second that I was going to pass out. Tina was right: I should have eaten more.

But one thing my vision was still steady enough to take in with perfect clarity:

And that was Michael Moscovitz. Leaving.

Yes, leaving the party. The boat. Whatever. The point was, he was exiting. One minute I saw his face, perfectly expressionless, but there, down below me.

And the next, I was looking at the back of his head. I

saw his broad shoulders, and then his back as he made his way towards the gangplank.

He was going.

Without even waiting to see what I'd say in response to J.P.'s question.

Or even what exactly that question was. Which, it turned out, wasn't at all what everyone seemed to think it was.

'. . . go to the prom with me?' J.P. finished, his smile still wide and full of trust in me.

But I could barely drag my gaze to look in his direction. Because I couldn't stop staring after Michael.

It's just that . . . I don't know. Looking out into the crowd like that, after my vision had gone all kind of wonky from surprise, and seeing Michael turn his back and just walk away, like he couldn't have cared less what happened . . .

It was like something went cold inside me. Something I didn't even realize was still *living* inside me.

Which, it turned out, was this little tiny ember of hope.

Hope that maybe, somehow, some day Michael and I might get back together.

I know! I'm a fool. An idiot! After all this time, why would I keep on hoping? Especially when I have such a fantastic boyfriend, who, by the way, was standing in front of me, holding a RING! (Which excuse me, but what's up with that? Who gives a girl a RING as he's asking her to the *prom*? Well, except for Boris. But excuse me, he's *BORIS*.)

But obviously I was the only one harbouring that little sliver of hope. Michael didn't even care enough to stay and watch what I said in response to my long-time boyfriend's proposal of prom-promise (I guess that's what it was. Wasn't it?).

So. That was that.

It's kind of funny, because I thought Michael broke my heart a long time ago. But he just sort of broke it all over again by walking out like that.

It's amazing how boys can do that.

Fortunately, even though I couldn't see very well because of the tears that filled up my eyes with Michael leaving like that, and my heart that had just been smashed to pieces (again), I could still think clearly. Sort of.

*Obviously* the correct thing to do under such circumstances was give J.P. the speech that Grandmere had made me rehearse nine million times for just such an occasion – when men made unwanted proposals, either of the wedding or *non*-wedding variety (though I'd never actually believed such an occasion would ever arise):

'Oh, *insert name of proposer here*, I'm just so overwhelmed by the intensity of your emotions, I hardly know what to say. You've truly swept me off my feet, and I do believe my head is swimming—'

No lie in this case.

'I'm so young and inexperienced, you see, and you're such a man of the world . . . I just wasn't expecting this.'

Absolutely no lie in this case. Who proposes in high school – even if it is just a promise ring or whatever? Oh, wait, that's right. Boris.

Hold on, where's my dad? Oh, there he is. Oh my God, I've never seen his face that colour. I think his head is literally going to explode, he looks so mad. He must think, like everyone else, that J.P. just proposed.

He didn't hear that all J.P. did was ask me to the prom. He saw the ring, saw J.P. kneel, and just assumed . . . oh, this is awful! Why did J.P. get me a ring? Is that what Michael thought? That J.P. was asking me to marry him? I want to die now.

'I think I need to go have a bit of a lie down in my boudoir – alone – and let my maid apply some lavender oil to my temples while I think this over. I'm just so flattered and thrilled. But, no, don't call me, *I'll* call you.'

The truth is, Grandmere's speech just seemed the tiniest bit . . . *outdated.*

And also it didn't really seem to apply, considering the fact that J.P. and I have been going out for almost two years. So it's not like his promise-ring proposal was completely out of left field.

Come on! I don't even know where I want to college next year. How am I supposed to know who I want to promise to be with for the foreseeable future?

But I have a pretty good clue: *Not* someone who hasn't even *glanced* at my book yet, even though he's had it more than forty-eight hours.

I'm just saying.

The thing is, I'd never say that in front of everyone on the whole boat and humiliate J.P.! I love him. I do. I just . . .

Why oh why did he have to ask me in front of everyone like that?

So instead of Grandmere's speech – and totally aware that there was this growing silence as I just stood there, idiotically saying nothing at all – I said, feeling my cheeks getting hotter and hotter, 'Well, we'll see!'

*Well, we'll see? WELL, WE'LL SEE?*

A totally hot, totally perfect, totally wonderful guy

who, by the way, loves me, and is willing to wait for me for all eternity, asks me to go to the prom with him, and also offers me what looks, at least according to the size chart Grandmere made me memorize in my head, like a three-carat diamond ring, and I say, *Well, we'll see.*

What's *wrong* with me? Seriously, do I have some sort of wish to live alone (well, with Fat Louie) in my room for the rest of my life?

I really think I do.

J.P.'s confident smile wavered . . . but just a little.

'That's my girl,' he said, and stood up and hugged me, while somewhere out in the crowd someone started to clap . . . slowly at first (I recognized that clap . . . it had to have been Boris), and then more rapidly, until everyone was politely applauding.

It was horrible! They were applauding for me saying, 'Well, we'll see!' in response to my boyfriend asking me to the prom! I didn't deserve applause. I deserved to be tossed overboard. They were only doing it because I'm a princess, and their hostess. I know deep down inside, they were thinking, 'What a byotch!'

Why? Why had Michael *left*?

As J.P. hugged me, I whispered, 'We have to talk.'

He whispered back, 'I have certification to prove it's blood free. Is that why you look so freaked out?'

'Partly,' I said, inhaling his mingled scent of dry-cleaning and Carolina Herrera For Men. We'd stepped away from the microphone by then, so there was no chance of anyone overhearing us. 'It's just—'

'It's only a promise ring.' J.P. broke the hug first, but he still held on to one of my hands . . . into which he'd slipped the box holding the ginormous diamond ring.

'You know I'd do anything to make you happy. I thought this was what you wanted.'

I just looked up at him in total confusion. Part of my confusion was over the fact that here was this wonderful, wonderful guy who really did mean what he'd just said – I knew he would do anything to make me happy. So why couldn't I just let him?

And another part of me was wondering what I had ever said to make him think what I wanted was a ring – promise, engagement or otherwise?

'It's what Boris got Tina,' J.P. explained, seeing my lack of comprehension. 'And you were so happy for her.'

'Right,' I said. 'Because that's the kind of thing she likes—'

'I know,' J.P. said. 'The same way she likes romance novels, and you wrote one—'

'So naturally if her boyfriend gave her a promise ring, I'd want one too?' I shook my head. Hello. Couldn't he see there was a big difference between me and Tina?

'Look,' J.P. said, closing my fingers around the velvet box, 'I saw the ring and it reminded me of you. Think of it as a birthday gift if it freaks you out to think of it the other way. I don't know what's been going on with you lately, but I just want you to know . . . I'm not going anywhere, Mia. *I'm* not leaving you, for Japan or anywhere else. I'm staying right here, by your side. So whatever you decide, whenever you decide it . . . you know where to find me.'

That's when he leaned down and kissed me.

And then he too walked away.

Just like Michael.

And that's when I ran for the safety of . . . this. Wherever I am now.

I know I should come down. My guests are probably leaving, and it's rude that I'm not there to say goodbye.

But hello! How many times does a girl get sort-of-proposed to? On her birthday? In front of everyone she knows? And then turns the guy down? Sort of? Only not really?

Also . . . what's wrong with me? Why didn't I just say yes? J.P. is clearly the most amazing guy on the planet . . . he's wonderful, gorgeous, fantastic and sweet. And he loves me. He LOVES me!

So why can't I just love him back, the way he deserves to be loved?

Oh, crud . . . someone's coming. Who do I know who's limber enough to climb all the way up here? Not Grandmere, that's for sure . . .

## Tuesday, May 2, Midnight, Limo home from my party

My dad isn't too happy with me.

He's the one who climbed all the way to the yacht's bow to tell me I had to stop 'sulking' (his word for what I was doing, which isn't completely accurate, in my opinion . . . I'd call it venting, since I'm writing in my journal), and come down and say goodbye to all my guests.

That wasn't all he said either. Not by a long shot.

He said I have to go to the prom with J.P. He said you can't go out with a guy for nearly two years, then decide, a week before the senior prom, that you're not going to go with him, just because you don't feel like going to the prom.

Or, as he so unfairly put it, 'Just because your ex-boyfriend happens to have come back to town.'

I was like, 'Whatever, Dad! Michael and I are just friends!' *Love Michael*. 'Like going to the prom with him had ever even OCCURRED to me!'

Because it totally hasn't. Who takes a twenty-one-year-old college-graduate millionaire robotic-surgical-arm inventor to their high-school prom? Who by the way broke up with me nearly two years ago, and also clearly doesn't care about me now either, so it's not even like he'd go if I asked.

And like I'd even do that to J.P. anyway.

'There's a name for girls like you,' Dad said as he sat down next to me on my precarious perch out over the water. 'And for what you're doing to J.P. And I don't even want to repeat it. Because it's not a nice name.'

'Really?' I was totally curious. No one's ever called me a name before. Except for the names Lana routinely calls me – *geek* and *spazoid* and stuff like that. Well, and all the stuff Lilly called me on ihatemiather-mopolis.com. 'What name?'

'Tease,' Dad said gravely.

I have to admit, that made me start laughing. Even though the situation was supposed to be completely and totally serious, with Dad sitting there on the edge of the yacht, talking me down like I was about to commit suicide or something.

'It's not funny,' Dad said, sounding irritated. 'The last thing we need right now, Mia, is for you to get a reputation.'

This just made me laugh even harder. Considering the fact that I happen to be the last virgin in the graduating senior class of Albert Einstein High School (besides my boyfriend). It was just so ironic that my dad was lecturing me – *me!* – about getting a reputation. I was laughing so hard I had to hold on to the side of the boat to keep from falling into the inky black waters of the East River.

'Dad,' I said when I could finally speak, 'I can assure you, I am *not* a tease.'

'Mia, actions speak louder than words. I'm not saying I think you and J.P. should get engaged. *That*, of course, is completely absurd. I expect you to kindly and gently explain to him that you're much too young to be thinking of that kind of thing right now—'

'Da-ad,' I said, rolling my eyes. 'It's a *promise* ring.'

'Regardless of your personal feelings about the prom,' he went on, ignoring me, 'J.P wants to go, and surely wasn't wrong to have expected to take you—'

'I know,' I said. 'And I told him I wouldn't mind if he takes someone else—'

'He wants to take *you*. His girlfriend. Who he's been seeing for nearly two years. He has certain rights of expectation because of that. One of them is that, barring any sort of gross misconduct on his part, you would go to the prom with him. And so the right thing for you to do is to go with him.'

'But, Dad,' I said, shaking my head, 'you don't understand. I mean . . . I wrote a romance novel, and I gave it to him, and he hasn't even—'

My dad blinked at me. 'You wrote a *romance novel*?'

Oops. Yeah, guess I forgot to mention that part to good old Dad. Maybe I could distract him.

'Um,' I said, 'yeah. About that. You don't have to worry. No one wants to publish it anyway—'

My dad waved a hand like my words were something annoying that was buzzing around his head.

'Mia,' he said, 'I think you know by now that being royal isn't all about being driven around in limos and having a bodyguard and taking private jets and buying the latest handbag or jeans and always being in style. You know what it's really about is always being the bigger person and being kind to others. You chose to date J.P. You chose to date him for nearly two years. You cannot *not* go to the prom with him, unless he's been in some way cruel to you . . . which, from what you describe, it doesn't sound as if he has. Now, stop being such a – what do you kids call it? Oh, right – drama queen and come down from here. My leg is getting cramp.'

I knew my dad was right. I was being stupid. I'd been acting like an idiot all week (so what else was new?). I was going to the prom, and I was going with J.P. J.P. and I were perfect for each other. We always had been.

I wasn't a kid any more, and I needed to stop acting like one. I needed to stop lying to everyone, just like Dr Knutz said.

But most importantly, I needed to stop lying to myself.

Life isn't a romance novel. The truth is, the reason romance novels sell so well – the reason why everyone loves them – is because no one's life is actually like that. Everyone *wants* their life to be like that.

But no one's life really is.

No. The truth was, Michael and I were through – even if he did sign his letter to me *Love Michael*. But that didn't mean anything. That little ember of hope I'd been carrying around – partly, I knew, because my dad had told me that love is always waiting right around the corner – needed to die and stay well and truly dead. I needed to *allow* it to die, and be happy with what I had. Because what I had was pretty freaking great.

I think what happened tonight finally killed that ember of hope about Michael I've been carrying around. I really do.

At least, I'm almost positive that when I climbed down and found J.P. (talking to Sean Penn again, of course) and I went up to him and said, 'Yes,' and showed him I was wearing the ring, that killed it. Killed it pretty much dead.

He gave me a big hug and swung me around. Everyone standing around cheered and clapped.

Except my mom. I saw her give my dad a look, and he shook his head, and she narrowed her eyes at him, like,

*You are so gonna get it*, and he gave her a look like, *It's just a* promise *ring, Helen.*

I suspect I'm due for a breakfast lecture on post-modern feminism from Mom tomorrow morning. As Lana would say, whatevs. Like any lecture of Mom's can make me feel worse than the sight of Michael's back did just now.

Tina and Lana and Trisha and Shameeka and Ling Su and Perin were all over the ring, though Ling Su mainly wanted to know if I could cut plates in half with my new diamond, since she's doing a new installation piece that involves pieces of broken ceramic (we experimented on some of the dishes from the caterer and the answer is yes, my ring can cut plates in half).

The person who seemed most interested was Lilly. She came over and really looked at it and was like, 'So what are you now like engaged?' and I was all, 'No, it's just a promise ring,' and Lilly went, 'That's some big *promise*,' meaning the diamond. Which I'm pretty sure she meant in a semi-insulting way . . .

And she succeeded.

What I couldn't figure out was why Lilly hadn't sprung her 'surprise' on me yet . . . the one she'd said she could only give me if she came to my party. I'd assumed that meant she was going to give it to me *at* my party – or at least on my birthday itself. But so far she'd showed no sign of doing so.

Maybe I'd misunderstood.

Or maybe – just maybe – there was still some sliver of affection for me somewhere in her, and whatever diabolical scheme she'd been planning, she'd decided not to launch it after all.

So remembering what Dad had said about how being

royal is about being the bigger person, I refused to take offence at her 'That's some big *promise*' remark.

And I also refused to ask her where her brother had gone. Though Tina of course sidled up to me and pointed out – in case I'd missed it somehow – that he'd left . . . and that he'd done it as soon as J.P. had whipped out the ring.

'Do you think,' Tina whispered, 'Michael left because he couldn't stand to see the woman he's loved for so long promising herself to another man?'

Really, this was too much.

'No, Tina,' I said flatly. 'I think he left because he just doesn't care about me.'

Tina looked shocked.

'No!' she cried. 'That's not why! I know that's not why! He left because he thinks YOU don't care about him, and knew he couldn't control his unbridled passion for you! He was probably afraid if he stayed, he'd KILL J.P.!'

'Tina,' I said. It was sort of hard to stay calm, but I remembered my new motto – life is a not a romance novel – and that made it a little easier, 'Michael doesn't care about me. Face the facts. I'm with J.P. now, the way I always should have been. And please don't talk to me that way about Michael any more. It really upsets me.'

And that was the end of it. Tina apologized for having upset me – about a million times – and was really concerned about having hurt my feelings. But we hugged it out, and everything was fine after that.

The party went on for a little while longer, but then pretty much fizzled out when the dock master came along and said Madonna's band had to unplug due to complaints from the neighbourhood associations of nearby waterside condos (I guess they'd have preferred Pavarotti).

In all, it was a pretty good party. I cleared some excellent loot: a ton of Marc Jacobs and Miu Miu totes, clutches and wallets and stuff; a lot of scented candles (which you can't even take with you to the dorm – whatever college I end up in – since candles are considered a fire hazard); a Princess Leia cat costume for Fat Louie, which won't be too confusing for him, gender-wise; a Brainy Smurf T-shirt from Fred Flare; a Cinderella Disney castle pendant; diamond and sapphire hairclips (from Grandmere, who always says my hair is in my face now that it's long), and $253,050 in donations to Greenpeace.

Oh, yeah, and one three-carat blood-free diamond promise ring.

I'd add one broken heart to the list, but I'm trying not to be a 'drama queen', like Dad said. Besides, Michael broke my heart a long time ago. He can't break it *again*. And all he did was say he liked my book and write *Love Michael* at the end of his note to me about it. That hardly constitutes wanting to get back together. I have no idea why I got my hopes up in such a ridiculous, girly manner.

Oh, right: because I'm a ridiculous, girly girl.

# Tuesday, May 2, World History final

It probably wasn't such a good idea to have my eighteenth birthday soirée the actual night *of* my birthday, seeing as how finals start today. I've seen more than a few people wandering around looking all bleary-eyed, like they could have used a couple more hours of sleep. Including me.

Thank God the schedules are all topsy-turvy for finals' week and I just have World History and English Lit today, my easiest classes. If I had Trig or French or Psych finals today, I'd die.

Literally. My mom's speech about how women have come a long way from the time when they used to have to get married right out of high school because females weren't allowed in universities, nor were there any jobs open to them either, went on for a really long time. And every time I started to doze during it, she poked me awake again.

I said, 'Mom, duh! J.P. and I aren't getting married after graduation! I'm ambitious, all right? I totally got into every college I applied to already and I wrote a novel and I'm trying to get it published! What more do you want from me?'

But somehow none of this seemed to comfort her. She kept saying, 'But you haven't *chosen* a school. You have less than a week to decide which one you're going to,' and, 'It's a *romance* novel,' like somehow either of these made a difference.

And whatever: the heroine of my romance novel is a total dead shot with a bow and arrow.

I don't even wear J.P.'s ring around the house, so I'm not sure what the problem is. It's not like she even has to see it. What about it is so offensive to her?

# Tuesday, May 2, Lunch

Everyone is forever asking to see my ring. I mean, it's flattering and all, but . . . kind of embarrassing. Then I have to explain it's not an engagement ring. Because of course it looks exactly like one.

And it's so big it keeps getting it snagged on things. Like loose threads of my uniform skirt and once in one of Shameeka's braids. It took like five minutes to get it unsnagged.

I'm not used to being so glamorous at school.

You can tell J.P. is really pleased though.

So. There's that. If he's happy, I'm happy.

# Tuesday, May 2, English Lit final

!!!!!!!!!!!!!!!!!!

OK, once again, I have made a complete and total fool out of myself.

But really, what else is new?

Not that it matters, because I've moved on. I'm eighteen, and an adult, and in four days I will be out of this hellhole FOREVER (just don't ask me where I'll be going instead, because I still have no idea).

Anyway, it's all Tina's fault, because Tina is barely speaking to me. I know I told her not to talk to me about Michael, but that's not the same as saying *Don't talk to me at all*.

You'd think she'd have a lot to talk to me about, seeing as how we're both engaged-to-be-engaged and all.

But maybe she's so scared of saying the wrong thing to me now, for fear of hurting my feelings, she's decided to say nothing to me at all.

I don't know what her problem is. I can't win in the best friend division, apparently. I can't ever seem to make them happy.

I really should just settle for having Lana as my best friend. She's much more easy-going than anyone else I know. She's very excited today because she's got a love bite and she claims it's from Prince William (or so she wishes). She's going around showing it off to everyone. I'm surprised she hasn't drawn a big red circle around it in lipstick, with an arrow, and a sign that says, PRINCE WILLIAM'S (ALLEGED) HICKEY.

Anyway, after lunch I saw Tina in the girls' bathroom and I was like, 'What exactly is your problem?'

And she was all, 'Problem? What problem? There's no problem, Mia,' with her big Bambi eyes.

But I could tell that even though her eyes were all wide and innocent, she was lying. I mean, I don't know how I could tell exactly.

OK, maybe she wasn't lying. Maybe I was just projecting (which is a term we learned in Psych for when you attribute your own unwanted thoughts to someone else as a defence mechanism). Maybe I was still wound up from what had happened the night before, with Michael leaving the party and all.

But in any case, I went, 'There is too a problem. You think I'm doing the wrong thing, saying yes to J.P. when I still have feelings for Michael.' (Yeah, I know. Even as the words were coming out of my mouth, I was like, *What are you saying? Shut up, Mia.* But I couldn't shut myself up. I just kept talking. It was like a nightmare.)

'Well,' I went on, 'I'll have you know that I don't. Have feelings for Michael any more. I've moved on from Michael. Well and truly moved on. Last night when he walked out the way he did was the last straw. And I've decided that after the prom, J.P. and I are going to Do It. Yes. We are.' Honestly, I have no idea where this was coming from. I think I just thought of it at that very moment. 'I'm tired of being the last virgin girl in our senior class. No way am I going to start college with my innocence still intact. Even though I probably lost it a long time ago on a bike or whatever.'

Tina was still doing the big-eyed *I don't know what you're talking about* act.

'OK, Mia,' she said, 'whatever you say. You know I'll support you whatever you decide.'

ARGH! She is so frustratingly NICE sometimes!

'In fact,' I said, whipping out my iPhone, 'I'm going to text J.P. right now. Yes! Right now! And tell him to get a hotel room for after the prom!'

Tina's eyes were HUGE now. She went, 'Mia. Are you really sure you want to do this? You know, there's really nothing wrong with being a virgin. Lot's of people our age—'

'Too late!' I yelled.

I swear I don't know what came over me. Maybe it was because a few minutes before, J.P.'s ring had gotten snagged on Stacey Cheeseman's eyelet ponytail holder as she walked down the hall. Maybe it was all the PRESSURE that was on me . . . finals, Dad's election, everyone telling me I had to choose a college by the end of the week, the thing with Michael, Lilly being so nice to me all of a sudden . . . I don't know. Maybe it was just *everything*.

Anyway, I texted, *MAKE SURE WE R GETTING A HOTEL RM 4 AFTR PROM* to J.P.

It was right after that that a toilet flushed. And a stall door opened.

And Lilly walked out.

I nearly had a synaptic breakdown right there in the girls' bathroom. I just stood there staring at her, realizing she'd overheard everything I'd said – about finally being over Michael *and* about being a virgin . . .

. . . and that I was texting J.P. to get a hotel room for after the prom.

Lilly looked right back at me. She didn't utter a word (neither, needless to say, did I. I couldn't think of a word to say. Later, of course, I thought of a *million* things I should have said. Like that Tina and I had just been rehearsing a scene from a play or something).

Then Lilly turned around, walked over to the sinks, rinsed her hands, dried, tossed her paper towel, and left the room.

All in complete and utter silence.

I looked at Tina, who stared back at me with her huge, troubled eyes . . . eyes, I realized now, that had never been anything but filled with concern for me.

'Don't worry, Mia,' were the first words from Tina's lips. 'She won't tell Michael. She wouldn't. I *know* she wouldn't.'

I nodded. Tina knew no such thing. She was just being nice. The way Tina always is.

'You're right,' I said. Even though she wasn't. 'And even if she does . . . he doesn't care any more. I mean, obviously he doesn't care any more, or he wouldn't have walked out last night like he did.'

This, at least, was true.

Tina bit her lip.

'Of course,' she said. 'You're right. Only, Mia . . . don't you think—'

Only I never found out what it was Tina wanted to know that I thought, because my cellphone buzzed. And there was a text message back from J.P.

And it said:

*HOTEL ROOM ALREADY SECURED. ALL SYSTEMS GO. LUV U.*

So. Great!

That's taken care of. Yay! I'm about to become de-virginized.

Go me.

# Tuesday, May 2, 6 p.m., the Loft

Daphne Delacroix
1005 Thompson Street, Apt 4A
New York, NY 10003

Dear Ms Delacroix

We regret that we are unable to publish the enclosed material. Thank you for giving us the opportunity to read it.

Sincerely
The Editors

And . . . the hits just keep coming.

I walked into the loft and found (besides this letter) Mom with every college acceptance packet I've ever received spread out on the floor, and Rocky sitting in the middle of it all like the stamen of a flower (if the stamen of a flower ever drank from a *Dora the Explorer* sippy cup). Mom looked at me and went, 'We're picking a college for you. *Tonight.*'

'Mom,' I said crankily. 'If this is about J.P. and the ring thing—'

'This is about *you*,' Mom said, 'and your future.'

'I'm going to college, all right? I said I'd choose one by the election. I've got till then. I can't handle this right now, I've got a Trig final tomorrow that I have to study for now.'

Also, I'm going to be devirginized after the prom on Saturday. Only I didn't mention this part to her. Obviously.

'I want to discuss this now,' Mom said. 'I want you to

225

make an informed choice, not just pick any old place because your father is pressuring you.'

'And I don't want to go to some Ivy League college,' I said, 'that I didn't deserve to get into and that just let me in because I'm a princess.' I was fully stalling for time, because all I wanted to do was go into my room and try to digest the whole losing-my-virginity-on-Saturday thing. And the fact that Lilly Moscovitz, my ex-best friend, knew about it. Was she going to tell her brother?

No. She wouldn't. She didn't care about me any more. So why would she?

Except to totally and completely annihilate me in his eyes even further than I have been already by my own idiotic behaviour.

'Then don't go to some Ivy League college,' Mom said. 'Go to some college you might have had a shot at getting into without the princess thing. Let me help you pick a place. Please, Mia, for the love of God. Don't tell me your future degree is an MRS.'

'What's that?' I asked her.

'*Mrs* Reynolds-Abernathy the Fourth,' she said.

'It's a PROMISE ring,' I yelled at her. God! Why doesn't anyone *listen* to me? And why, when I'd been getting my feet done with all those girls who'd had sex, hadn't I asked them more questions about it? I know I wrote about it in my romance novel. I've certainly READ about it quite a bit.

But that's not the same as actually doing it, you know?

'Good,' Mom said, about the promise-ring thing. 'Then PROMISE me you'll let me help narrow it down a little so I can tell your father I'm on this. He's called me *twice* about it today. And he only just got back to Genovia a few hours ago. And I'm slightly worried about it myself, you know.'

I made a face at her. Then I went around the room and picked up the acceptance packets to the schools I thought I could bear to spend at four years. I tried to pay special attention to the ones that didn't count SAT scores (I looked them up on the computer, as per Michael's suggestion . . . even though I didn't do it for HIM. I just did it because . . . well, it was good advice), and that might possibly have let me in despite the whole princess thing.

It was probably the most mature thing I did all day. Besides organize my thank-you notes for all my birthday gifts. I didn't exactly come to a final decision about where I want to go, but I narrowed it down quite a bit so that possibly, maybe by election day slash prom, I might be able to tell them I'd decided on some place.

I think. Sort of.

I was in the middle of getting my Trig notes ready when I got an IM from J.P.

```
JPRA4:      Hey! How'd it go today? With
            finals, I mean.
>
FtLouie:    Good, I think. I just had World
            History and English Lit, so
            nothing too stressful. It's
            tomorrow I'm worried about.
            Trig! You?
```

It seemed so weird that we were IM-ing about finals, when in less than a week we're going to be . . . you know.

And we've never even been undressed in the same room together before.

```
JPRA4:      OK. I'm worried about tomorrow
            too . . . tomorrow night.
>
FtLouie:    Oh, right, your big performance
            in front of the senior project
            committee! Don't worry, I'm sure
            it's going to go great. I can't
            wait to see it!
```

How can he even care about his stupid senior project when we're going to have sex? What's wrong with boys?

```
JPRA4:      It'll go great as long as you'll
            be there.
```

WHAT IS HE EVEN TALKING ABOUT???? IS HE INSANE?????? SEX!!!! WE'RE GOING TO HAVE SEX!!!! WHY CAN'T WE TALK ABOUT IT?????
At least Michael would talk about it.

```
FtLouie:    You know I wouldn't miss it! And
            it'll be great.
>
JPRA4:      You?re the awesome one.
```

We went on like that for a while, each one saying who was the more awesome, but neither of us saying what we really NEEDED to say (or at least what I felt like we needed to say), until I got an IM from Tina, interrupting us.

Iluvromance: Mia, I know you said not to talk
about this any more, but this
isn't talking about it. It's IM-
ing about it. I really don't
think Michael left the party
last night because he doesn't
care about you. I think he left
because he DOES care about you
and he couldn't stand to see
you with another. I know you
don't want to hear that, but
that's what I think.

I do love Tina. So, so much.

But sometimes I want to strangle her.

Iluvromance: I mean, I was just wondering if
you've really considered *all*the
implications of what you're
about to do with J.P. on prom
night. Take it from someone
who's been there. I know Lana
and Trisha might make it sound
like it's nothing, but sex is a
deeply emotional experience your
first time, Mia - or it should be.
This is a really big step and you
shouldn't take it with just anyone.
>
FtLouie: Like with my boyfriend of almost
two years whom I love to distraction, you mean?

```
>
Iluvromance: OK, I see what you're saying,
             and you guys have been going out
             for a long time. But what if
             you're making a mistake. What if
             J.P. isn't The One?
>
FtLouie:     WHAT ARE YOU TALKING ABOUT? Of
             course J.P. is The One. BECAUSE
             HE HASN'T BROKEN UP WITH ME.
             LIKE MICHAEL DID. REMEMBER?
>
Iluvromance: Yes, but that was a long time
             ago. And now Michael's back. And
             I was just thinking . . . maybe
             you shouldn't make any hasty
             decisions. Because what if Lilly
             tells Michael what she heard in
             the bathroom today?
```

I knew Tina was lying today.

```
FtLouie:     YOU SAID SHE WOULDN'T.
>
Iluvromance: Well, she probably won't.
             But . . . what if she does?
>
FtLouie:     Because Michael doesn't *care*
             Tina. I mean, *he* broke up with
             *me*. *He* left the party last
             night. What would he care if I'm
             going around saying I'm still a
             virgin but I'm going to sleep
```

```
                        with my boyfriend after the prom
                        and that I only just got over
                        still liking him? If he cared,
                        he'd do something about it,
                        right? I mean, Michael has my
                        phone number, right?
>
Iluvromance:    . . . Right.
>
FtLouie:        And the phone's not ringing, is
                it?
>
Iluvromance:    I guess not.
>
FtLouie:        No. It isn't. So. No offence,
                Tina. I love romance too, but in
                this particular case, it's OVER.
                MICHAEL DOESN'T CARE ABOUT ME
                ANY MORE. As his behaviour at my
                party clearly illustrates.
>
Iluvromance:    Well, OK. If you say so.
>
FtLouie:        I do. I do say so. Case closed.
```

That's when I told both Tina and J.P. that I really had
to go. I had to log off, or I thought my head was going
to go spinning out into the courtyard of our building
and go whizzing off into space to be with all the space
satellites that keep hurtling down to rain upon us.

That's not what I told them, of course. I said if I don't
study, I won't pass Trig. Truthfully, if I don't pass Trig,
then maybe one of these colleges that let me in based

on my actual grades and essays and extra-curriculars and all really won't let me in.

J.P. IM-ed me a million goodbye kisses. I sent them back in return. Tina just IM-ed 'Bye'. But I could tell there were ten thousand more things she wanted to say. Like about how J.P. wasn't my One, undoubtedly.

Nice of her to mention that NOW. Not that there's anything I can do about it.

I suppose she thinks my One is Michael. Why does my best friend have to think my One is a guy who is categorically uninterested in me?

# Tuesday, May 2, 8 p.m., the Loft

Crud. There is stuff all over the gossip websites about my 'engagement' to J.P. Reynolds-Abernathy IV.

It's all tied in with how Dad is still losing in the Genovian election polls . . . and how maybe flying to the US for a day for his daughter's eighteenth birthday party wasn't the best idea, seeing as how he really can't afford to be spending time away from the campaign.

On the other hand, a lot of the articles say maybe if he did spend more time with his daughter, she wouldn't be getting herself engaged at such a young age.

I'm like the Jamie Lynn Spears of the Renaldo family! Minus the pregnancy!

I'm going to crawl under the covers and never come out.

It's a PROMISE RING! Who told them it was an engagement ring anyway?

Seriously, when is it all just going to go away?

Oh, that's right: never.

# Tuesday, May 2, 9 p.m., the Loft

Grandmere just called. She wanted to know if I had a dress for the prom yet.

'Um,' I said, suddenly remembering that in fact I didn't. 'No?'

'I figured as much,' Grandmere said with a sigh. 'I'll put Sebastiano on it, since he's here in town.'

Then she said if I'd just given J.P. the speech she'd made me memorize so long along, none of the gossip stuff would be happening. I guess they'd said something about it on *Entertainment Tonight*. Grandmere never misses an episode, since she's obsessed with Mary Hart's posture, which she says is perfect, and I should emulate it (I would, but I'd have to jam a broomstick up my butt).

'On the other hand,' she went on, 'if you had to get yourself engaged to anyone, Amelia, at least you picked someone with breeding and his own fortune. It could be worse. I suppose,' she added with a cackle, 'it could have been That Boy.'

By *That Boy*, Grandmere meant Michael. And I don't frankly see what's so funny about that.

'I'm not engaged,' I told her. 'It's a promise ring.'

'What in God's name,' Grandmere wanted to know, 'is a promise ring? And what is this your father tells me about you having written a romance novel?'

I really was not in the mood to discuss *Ransom My Heart* with Grandmere. I still had about twenty chapters of Trig to review. Oh, and my devirginization to map out. I had to figure out what I was going to buy at CVS to keep a whole *Juno* scenario from breaking out. The next novel I write does not need to be titled *Pregnant Princess*.

'You don't need to worry about that,' I snapped. 'Since no one wants to publish it anyway.'

'Well, thank the Lord for that,' Grandmere said. 'The last thing this family needs is some tawdry paperback-novel writer—'

'It's not tawdry,' I interrupted her, stung. 'It's a very humorous and moving romance about a young girl's sexual awakening in the year twelve ninety-one—'

'Oh my God.' Grandmere sounded as if she'd swallowed the wrong way. 'Please tell me if you do get published, you'll be using a pen-name.'

'Of course I am,' I said. How much can one person be expected to take anyway? 'But even if I wasn't, what's wrong with it? Why does everyone have to be such a prude? You know, I've put up with doing what everybody else wants me to do for nearly four years now. It's about time I got to do something *I* want to do—'

'Well, for the love of God,' Grandmere said. 'Why can't you take up skiing or something? Why does it have to be *novel* writing?'

'Because I like it,' I said. 'And I can do it and still have time to be Princess of Genovia, and not have paparazzi chase me around, and it isn't bad for me, and why can't you just be happy for me that I've found my calling?'

'Her calling!' I could tell Grandmere was rolling her eyes. 'Her *calling*, no less. It can't be your calling if no one will even *buy* the wretched thing from you, Amelia. Listen, if you want a calling, I'll pay for you to have cliff-diving lessons. I hear it's all the rage with the young people down in—'

'I don't *want* cliff-diving lessons,' I said. 'I'm going to write novels and there's nothing you can do to stop me. And I'm going to go to college to learn to do it better. I just don't know where yet. But I will by the election—'

'*Well,*' Grandmere said, sounding offended. 'Someone didn't get her beauty sleep!'

'Because I was at *your* party,' I said. Then I softened my tone, remembering what my dad had said about princesses being kind. 'I'm sorry. I didn't mean it that way. It was very nice of you to have that party for me, and it was lovely to see Dad, and you and Vigo did an awfully nice job. I just meant—'

'I suppose,' Grandmere said stiffly, 'I ought to be relieved I don't have to have an engagement party for you. No one gives *promise*-ring parties . . . do they? But I imagine you'll expect a *book* party some day.'

'If I get published,' I said, 'it would be nice.'

Grandmere sighed gustily and hung up. I could tell she was going to go have a Sidecar, even though her physicians have expressly ordered her to cut back on them (and I saw her with one in her hand throughout the night yesterday evening. Either her glass was magic and never emptied, or she had several).

So, yeah. Exactly what Dad DIDN'T want: looks like I'm a Princess with a Reputation.

On the other hand, at this point . . . I might as well live up to it, I guess.

# Wednesday, May 3, Trig final

OK. Barely passed that.
  Moving on.

# Wednesday, May 3, Lunch

OH MY GOD!

I was just about to sit down at our table in the caff with my tofurkey burger and salad when my phone rang and I saw that it was my dad.

Dad never calls me during school unless it's an emergency or massively important, so I practically dropped my tray and was all, 'WHAT?' into the phone.

Of course, J.P. and Tina and Boris and Lana and everyone stopped talking and turned to look at me.

The only thing I could think was:

a) Grandmere finally croaked from too many Gitanes, or

b) Somehow the paparazzi got wind of the fact that I'm going to have sex on my prom night and spilt the beans to my parents, and I was busted. Could Tina be right? Had they finally tapped my phone?

Then Dad went, in a completely calm voice, 'I thought you'd be interested to know that a brand-new CardioArm was just delivered to the Royal Genovian Hospital, with a card indicating it was a donation courtesy of Michael Moscovitz, President and CEO, Pavlov Surgical Industries.'

I almost dropped my phone into Lana's fro-yo. 'Hey, watch it,' she said.

'A programmer named Midori came with the CardioArm to teach our surgeons a two week course on how to use it,' Dad went on. 'She's at the hospital now, setting it up.'

Micromini Midori!

'I don't understand,' I said. I really was totally

confused. 'Why would he do that? We didn't ask for one. Did you ask for one? I didn't ask him for one.'

'I didn't ask him for one,' Dad said. 'And I already checked with your grandmother. She swears she didn't ask him for one.'

I had to sit down, my legs having suddenly given out from beneath me. I hadn't even thought of Grandmere. She had to have been behind this! She must have browbeaten Michael into giving Genovia one of his CardioArms! No wonder he'd left my party early! Poor thing.

And all this time I'd been thinking horrible thoughts about him . . .

'Mia,' J.P. said, looking concerned, 'are you all right? What's going on?'

'She must have said something to him,' I said into the phone, ignoring my boyfriend. 'She's got to be lying. Why else would he have done it?'

'Oh, I think I have a pretty good idea why,' Dad said in a strange voice.

'You do?' I was flummoxed. 'Well, why? Other than Grandmere having cornered him the other night at my party and demanding one? Dad, she had to have.' I lowered my voice so the lunch gang wouldn't overhear me. 'There's a huge long waiting list for those things. They cost over a million dollars! He's not just going to have one shipped over to Genovia for free, for no reason!'

'I think there's a reason,' Dad said drily. 'Why don't you call him to thank him? I imagine he'll probably tell you what it is over dinner.'

'Dinner?' I echoed. 'What are you talking about? Why would we go out to din—'

Comprehension dawned. I couldn't believe it had

taken me so long to figure out what my dad meant – that Michael had sent the CardioArm because he still liked me. *More* than liked me, maybe, even.

I could feel myself starting to blush. I was grateful everyone at the table couldn't hear both sides of the conversation. That is, if they hadn't figured it out already from my end.

'Da-ad!' I whispered. 'Come on! It's not *that*! I mean –' I lowered my voice even more, grateful for the din of the cafeteria – *'he broke up with me, remember?'*

'That was almost two years ago,' Dad said. 'You've both done a lot of growing up since then. One of you in particular.'

He meant me. I knew he meant me. He certainly didn't mean Michael, who'd never been anything but calm and understanding, whereas I'd been . . .

Well, not.

*Geek.*

'Mia, what's going on?' Tina wanted to know. She looked worried. 'Is your dad all right?'

'Everything's fine,' I said to them. 'I'll tell you in a minute—'

'Mia, I have to go,' Dad said. 'The press is here. I don't think I have to tell you that something like this . . . well, it's big news in a little place like Genovia.'

No, he didn't need to tell me that. People don't make donations of million-dollar, state-of-the-art medical equipment to Genovia's dinky hospital. Something like that was going to get major media coverage.

Way more, in fact, than René's efforts to open an Applebee's.

'OK, Dad,' I said in a daze. 'Bye.'

I hung up, feeling totally confused. What was going

on? Why had Michael done this? I mean, I knew why my *dad* thought Michael had done it.

But why had he *really* done it? I'd seen how he'd walked out of my birthday party like that. It didn't make any sense.

*Love Michael.*

'What's going on, Mia?' J.P. wanted to know.

'You look like you just ate a sock,' Tina said.

'It's nothing,' I said quickly. 'It was just my dad to say that the Royal Genovian Hospital got a donation of a CardioArm from Michael's company. That's all.'

Tina choked on the sip of Diet Coke she was taking. Everyone else took the news calmly.

Including J.P.

'Oh, hey, Mia,' he said. 'That's great! Wow. That's a generous gift.'

He didn't look a bit jealous.

And why should he? It's not as if there's anything to be jealous about. Michael doesn't like me like that, despite what Dad – and Tina – might think. I'm sure he just donated the CardioArm to be nice.

And Micromini Midori . . . the fact that he sent her to teach the surgeons how to use it? That doesn't mean she and Michael aren't going out. It just means they're in such a stable relationship that they can be away from each other for weeks at a time and it doesn't bother them a bit.

What am I blathering about? Who cares if Michael and Micromini Midori are dating? I'm wearing a promise ring from another guy! To whom I am going to lose my virginity after the prom this coming Saturday! What is wrong with me?

Really – What IS wrong with me? I shouldn't even be

thinking about any of this stuff! I have a French final in fifteen minutes!

WHAT AM I GOING TO DO ABOUT THE FACT THAT MICHAEL SENT A CARDIOARM TO THE ROYAL GENOVIAN HOSPITAL?????

And I can't stop thinking about him for even one second, and I'm due to lose my virginity to my boyfriend after the prom in four days (three if you don't count today)????

## Wednesday, May 3, French final

Mia - Are you done with the final? T

    Yes. That was horrible.

I know! What did you get for number 5?

    I don't know. Future perfect, I think. I don't remember any more. I'm trying to block it out.

Same here. So. I know you probably don't want to talk about it, but what are you going to do about Michael, and the fact that he did what he did? Because, no matter what you say, Mia, you can't deny - no guy is going to send a CardioArm to the country of a girl he doesn't like.

See, I knew this was going to happen. Tina takes everything and wraps it up in silver tissue paper and puts a big bow on it and calls it Love.
    And *I'm* supposed to be the romance writer

    He doesn't like me! Not *like* like me. He just did it to be nice. For old times' sake. I'm sure.

Well, I don't see how you can be sure when you haven't even spoken to him about it. Have you spoken to him about it?

    Well, no. Not yet. I'm not sure I'm going to either. Because, in case you don't remember, Tina, I'm promise-ringed to someone else.

That doesn't give you the right to be rude! When someone goes to all the trouble of donating a CardioArm to your country, the least you can do is personally thank him! Although that doesn't mean you have to sleep with him or anything. I'm sure Michael isn't expecting anything like that. You could kiss him though.

Oh my God.

Who's side are you on, anyway, Tina? J.P.'s, or Michael's?

J.P.'s, of course! Because that's who you've chosen, right? I mean . . . haven't you? It would be pretty weird if that's NOT who you've chosen, seeing as how you're wearing his ring and plan on spending the night with him on Saturday.

Of course I chose J.P.! Michael broke up with me, remember?

Mia, that was almost two years ago. Things are different now. You're different now.

WHY DOES EVERYONE KEEP SAYING THIS?

OH MY GOD YOU GUYS I JUST GOT OUT OF MY LAST GER-MAN FINAL EVER! No more German finals ever! At least for me! I think in college I'm going to take Spanish, because then I'll be able to order more things when I go to Cabo for break instead of just tacos.

— — — — — — — — — — — — — — —

Lana, don't you think Mia should call Michael to thank him for donating a CardioArm to the Royal Genovian Hospital?

Whatevs, she should just call him because he is HOT like a red hot chilli pepper like the kind I'll be learning about when I start taking SPANISH instead of GERMAN!!!!

— — — — — — — — — — — — — — —

See? Mia, just text Michael. Thank him for what he did. That's not hurting J.P. I mean, you already met with Michael and didn't tell J.P. And OK, maybe Michael did it because Lilly told him what she overheard us saying in the bathroom. But chances are he was going to send it anyway. So just call him.

You think he sent it because Lilly told him she overheard me say I still like him? I'm going to be sick!!!!!

No! I said MAYBE that's why he did it!

OH MY GOD that IS why he did it! I know it! Oh my God. OH MY GOD!!!!!!

Look, I'm sure that's NOT why. But . . . you should call him and find out.

Wait a minute . . . I'm going to Genovia for break from now on. I should take French next year. What's French for tacos?

_ _ _ _ _ _ _ _ _ _ _ _ _ _ _ _ _ _

Sent from my BlackBerry Wireless Handheld

When I go to college the first thing I'm going to do is pick out all new friends. Because the friends I currently have are a little bit psychotic.

## Wednesday, May 3, 4 p.m., Limo on the way to Grandmere's condo at the Plaza

Sebastiano has picked out a half-dozen gowns from his latest collection for me to try on to wear to the prom, and I'm meeting him at Grandmere's to check them out.

I have a feeling they're going to be horrible, but I guess I shouldn't be so judgemental. I really liked the last formal gown of his that I wore (to the Non-Denominational Winter Dance my freshman year. Can it really have been so long ago? It seems like yesterday). Just because Sebastiano's selling his stuff at Wal-Mart doesn't mean it's going to be awful.

Anyway, I've been writing and deleting texts to Michael the whole way up in the car. I've been trying them out on Lars (he thinks I'm nuts, clearly. But then, what else is new?). It's really hard to capture just the right casually breezy, yet still warmly sincere tone.

Lars thinks I should go with this:

Dear Michael. I can't tell you how surprised yet pleased I was to hear from my dad today about a certain delivery that arrived at the Royal Genovian Hospital. You can't even begin to imagine what you've done for him and for the people of Genovia. Your generosity will never be forgotten. I would so like to thank you on their behalf in person (when you have time). Sincerely, Mia

I do think this probably has just the right polite yet friendly tone. It's the sort of thing a girl who is

247

promise-ringed to someone else could send and not have misinterpreted. Or have intercepted by the paparazzi and get herself into trouble.

I added the stuff about meeting in person because . . . well, it just seems like you should thank someone in person for a gift that cost over a million dollars. Not because I want to smell him again. No matter what Lars thinks (I really wish he wouldn't eavesdrop on all my conversations. But I guess that's one of the hazards of having someone guard you).

I'm going to hit Send before I chicken out.

## Wednesday, May 3, 4.05 p.m., Limo on the way to Grandmere's condo at the Plaza

Oh my God! Michael got the text and texted me back already! I'm freaking out. (Lars is laughing even harder at me but I don't care):

Mia, Would love to see you 'in person'. How about tonight? Michael. PS No need to thank me on behalf of your father or Genovia. I only sent it because I thought it might help out your dad in the elections, and that, in turn, would make you happy. So you see my motives were completely selfish.

Now what do I do????

Lars has no answer for me. Well, he does, but it's completely unreasonable. He's like, 'Call him. Go out with him tonight.'

But I can't go out with him tonight! Because I've got A BOYFRIEND! Plus, I've got J.P.'s play tonight. I promised I'd be there to support him.

And I *want* to be there for J.P. Of course I do. It's just that—

What can Michael mean, his motives were entirely selfish? Does he mean what Lars says he thinks he means, that he only sent the CardioArm because he likes me?

And wants to get back together?

No. That's not possible. Lars has spent too much time in the desert sun, setting off explosives with Wahim. Why would Michael want to get back together with me, when I am so obviously a crazy person? I mean, when we were together last time, I went positively Britney on him. I can't imagine any boy would ever sign up for a second helping of that.

Even though of course, like Dad said, I have grown up a lot since then . . .

And we did have a nice time at Caffe Dante. But that was just an interview.

Oh! But he did smell nice! I don't suppose he thought *I* smelt nice too?

I've got to check with Tina . . . even though she's nuttier than I am, if you ask me.

But never mind about that. I'm forwarding his text to her . . . And, dang, we're at Grandmere's now. I've got to endure trying on clothes for hours. Who has the patience for fashion when all THIS is going on?

# Wednesday, May 3, 8 p.m., the Ethel Lowenbaum Theater

It's really very hard to write in here since the lights are down and J.P.'s play is going on. I'm doing this, in fact, by the glow of my cellphone.

I know I shouldn't be writing in my journal at all – I should be paying attention to the play, since the senior project committee is here (and so are J.P.'s parents and all our friends who didn't stay home to study for finals) and I should be trying to look like I support J.P. and all.

But I just have to write more about Michael's text.

Because of course I couldn't keep it to myself. I *had* to show everyone at Grandmere's.

Grandmere said it just proves that Michael harbours *une grande passion* for me. She says a million-dollar piece of medical equipment as a gift isn't quite as romantic as a three-carat diamond-and-platinum promise ring.

'But,' she went on, 'the fact that Michael donated it without your having asked for it is rather extraordinary. I'm starting to wonder if I wasn't wrong about That Boy after all.'

!!!!!!

Honestly, I nearly fainted on the spot. I have NEVER heard Grandmere say she was wrong about ANY-THING!!!!!

Well, hardly ever.

Anyway, this was such a startling thing to hear coming from Grandmere's lips that I nearly tumbled off the stool Sebastiano had me standing on while he stuck pins into the gown I was modelling. He said, 'Tsk, tsk,

251

tsk,' and asked me if I wanted to be stuck all over like a porcupine.

Only of course Sebastiano still hasn't grasped the basics of the English language, so he just called it a 'porc'.

'G-Grandmere,' I stammered, 'what are you saying? Sh-should I give Michael another chance? Should I give J.P. his ring back?'

I swear my heart was slamming so hard inside my chest, I felt like I could hardly breathe as I waited for her reply. Which is weird, because it's not like I particularly VALUE advice from Grandmere, as she is in fact a certified lunatic.

'Well,' Grandmere said, looking thoughtful, 'it is a terribly *large* ring. On the other hand, it's a terribly expensive piece of medical equipment. But you can't *wear* a robotic surgical arm.'

See what I mean?

'I know what you should do, Amelia,' Grandmere said, brightening. 'Sleep with both of them, and whichever young man performs better in the boudoir, that's the one you keep. That's what I did with Baryshnikov and Godunov. Such lovely boys. And so flexible.'

'Grandmere!' I was shocked. I mean, seriously: how evil is she? How could we even be of the same bloodline?

Honestly, I don't consider myself a prude. But I think you should at least be *in love* with someone before you do *that* with them (something I have tried unsuccessfully to impress upon Lana. Oh, and my grandmother).

Anyway, I told her not to be stupid, that I'm not sleeping with anybody. (<u>Mia Thermopolis's Big Fat Lie Number Nine.</u>)

But what *am* I going to do? I've gotten a confirmation IM back from Tina (she's here tonight with Boris. But of course we can't *talk* about it. Not with J.P. around. Oh, and Boris):

She thinks Michael's note meant what Grandmere thinks it did (but who even counts what Grandmere thinks, as she's clearly unhinged): Michael really did send the CardioArm for me. ME!

Tina says I've got to write him back and truly make some kind of arrangement to see him in person. Because, as she just texted from *her* seat:

You can't leave Michael hanging. He could just be flirting with you . . . but I doubt it. He went to a lot of trouble to send that CardioArm . . . not to mention Micromini Midori along with it.

And the only way to find out what's really going on with him is to see him in person. You'll know when you look him in the eye whether he's playing or for real.

This is serious, Mia: You could find yourself TORN BETWEEN TWO LOVERS!!!!

I know you're probably really upset about this, but is it wrong that I for one find it VERY VERY EXCITING?????? OK, I'm sorry, I'll stop bouncing up and down in my seat. Someone in the next row just shot me a very annoyed look, and Boris wants me to pay attention to the play now.

I'm glad someone's happy about it, but I personally am not. I honestly don't know how it happened. How could I, Mia Thermopolis, go from being the most boring person on the planet (except for the princess thing), who has basically never left her house for the past year and a half because she was always working on her senior project, a history of Genovian olive-oil pressing, circa 1254–1650 (and, OK, it was really a historical romance novel, but so what?), to a girl who is being sought after by two highly desirable men?

Really, how????

And, according to my best friend, what I'm supposed to do about it is arrange to meet the one to whom am I not engaged-to-be-engaged . . .

But how can I arrange to meet Michael now – knowing my weakness for him, especially the smell of his neck – when he might possibly *like* me . . . enough to send my country a CardioArm (and someone to teach our surgeons how to use it)?

I can't do that to J.P. J.P. has his faults (I still can't believe he hasn't read my book), but he's never met his exes behind my back (not that he has any exes, besides Lilly). He's never *lied* to me.

And admittedly I don't think that whole Judith Gershner thing is as big a deal now as I used to, considering it all happened before Michael and I ever went out. I never did flat out ask Michael if he'd ever been with anybody else before me, so technically it's not like he actually lied.

But there is no denying the fact that that was an important piece of information that he really ought to have shared with me. People in romantic relationships really are supposed to share their sexual history with one another. Their *complete* sexual history.

Although I guess he *did* share it with me. Eventually.

And I behaved with about as much maturity as a five-year-old. Just like he knew I would.

Oh God! I'm so confused. I don't know what to do! I need to talk this all out with someone sane – someone who is *not* related to me (see: previous statement re: someone sane) or who I go to school with.

Which just leaves Dr Knutz, I think, unfortunately.

But I'm not seeing him until Friday, for what will be our last appointment ever. So.

LUCKY ME!!!! I get to sit around and try to figure out what the right thing to do is on my own until then.

I guess this is how people who are eighteen and soon-to-be high-school graduates deal with things.

(You know, there's someone in this audience who looks so familiar and I've been sitting here trying to figure out who it is all night and it finally just hit me: it's Sean Penn.

No wonder J.P. was acting so nervous before.

*Sean Penn*, his favourite director, is here in the audience for the big performance of his play, *A Prince Among Men*. J.P. must have told him about the show when they were talking on the boat at my birthday party.

That's awfully nice of Mr Penn to come.)

Anyway. I know I've got to text Michael back. After all, I'm the one who said I wanted to meet him in person. I just left him hanging after that last text when he said that nice thing about how he did it for me and not my dad or Genovia.

But I don't know what to say exactly! *I can't tonight* seems obvious since it's after eight already.

On the other hand, people who've graduated from high school stay out really late, so maybe this wouldn't seem obvious to him.

But Tina's right. I do have to see him.

How about:

Hi, Michael! Tonight won't work (obviously), and tomorrow night is Boris's senior project (his concert at Carnegie Hall). Friday is Senior Skip Day. Are you free for lunch on Friday? Mia

Lunch is good, right? Lunch isn't sexy or anything. You can have lunch and still just be friends. Friends of the opposite sex have lunch all the time and there's nothing in the least romantic about it.

There. I sent it.

I think that was a good text. I didn't say *Love Mia* or anything like that. I didn't get into the stuff about how he gave the CardioArm to Genovia because of me and not my dad. I was just breezy and casual and –

Oh my God, he wrote back. Already!

Mia, Friday for lunch is great. Want to meet at the Central Park Boathouse, Lakeside, one o'clock? Love Michael

The Boathouse! Friends don't have lunch at the Boathouse. Well, I mean, they do, but . . . it's not casual or breezy. You have to have reservations to get a table, and the lakeside restaurant is sort of . . . romantic. Even at lunchtime.

And he signed it *LOVE MICHAEL*! Again! Why does he keep SAYING that?

Oh – everyone is clapping . . .

Ack! Is it intermission already?

# Wednesday, May 3, 10 p.m., the Ethel Lowenbaum Theater

OK.

OK, so J.P.'s play is about a character named J.R., who's pretty much exactly like J.P. I mean, he's a handsome, wealthy boy (played by Andrew Lowenstein), who goes to a fancy New York City prep school, which also just happens to be attended by the princess of a small European principality. At the beginning of the play, J.R. is very lonely, because his only hobbies include throwing bottles off the rooftop of his apartment building, writing in his journal, and picking corn out of the chilli the lunch ladies in his school cafeteria serve him. This makes his relationship with his self-centered parents very rocky, and he is teetering on the brink of wanting to move to Florida to live with his grandparents.

But then one day the princess, Rhia (played by Stacey Cheeseman, who wears a blue plaid school-uniform skirt in the play that by the way is much shorter than I've ever worn any of mine), goes up to J.R. in the caff and actually asks him to sit with her at lunch, and J.R.'s whole life changes. Suddenly he starts listening to his shrink about not throwing bottles off the top of his apartment building, and his relationship with his parents improves, and he stops wanting to move to Florida. Soon it's all about the beautiful princess, who falls in love with J.R., because of his wit and kindness.

I could tell that the play was about me and J.P. He had changed our names (barely), and a few of the details, but who else could it be about?

The thing was, I'm used to people making movies

based on my life, and with them taking little liberties with the facts about that life.

But the people who made those movies don't know me! They weren't there when the things they were showing actually happened.

But J.P. was. The things he had Andrew and Stacey saying in his play . . . I mean, they're things J.P. and I have actually said to each other . . . and J.P. has the actors in his play saying them completely out of context!

For instance, there is a scene where Princess Rhia drinks a beer and does a sexy dance and totally embarrasses herself in front of her ex-boyfriend.

Which, OK, totally happened.

But shouldn't that be something that stays private between a boyfriend and a girlfriend? Did J.P. *have* to go and share that with everyone we know (even if everyone we know pretty much already knew about it)?

And J.P. has J.R. nobly standing by the princess's side and supporting her (despite the sexy dancing, which I guess is supposed to make everyone hate her and think she's such a slut and all). Right now there's a scene going on where Stacey Cheeseman is tearfully explaining to Andrew Lowenstein that she could understand it if he didn't want to be with her, because he'll never be able to have a normal life with her, what with all the beer swilling and sexy dancing and the fact that there'll always be paparazzi chasing them around. And then if they were ever to get married (!!!!), of course he'll have to become a prince and lose all his anonymity, and as royal consort he'll always have to walk five feet behind her and never be allowed to drive racing cars.

But Andrew Lowenstein is saying, in a very patient

voice as he holds Stacey Cheeseman's hand and looks lovingly into her eyes, that he doesn't care, he just loves her so much he'd be willing to suffer any indignity for her, even her sexy dancing and his having to become a prince . . .

Oh, and now everyone is clapping like crazy as the curtain falls, and J.P. is joining the cast as they come out to take their bows . . .

I just . . . I just don't get it. I mean . . . his play is about *us*.

Only not really. Half the stuff in it didn't even technically happen the way he has it happening.

Can you *do* that?

I guess so. He just did.

# Wednesday, May 3, 11 p.m., the Loft

Dear Author

Thank you for submitting your manuscript, *Ransom My Heart*, to Tremaine Publications. Although your work shows promise, we don't feel we have a place for it at this time. We apologize for the fact that, due to the volume of submissions we receive, we cannot give you a more detailed critique of your work. Thank you for thinking of Tremaine!

Faithfully

Tremaine Publications


Thanks for nothing, Tremaine Publications.

Anyway, J.P.'s play was a huge success.

Of course, he passed the senior project committee with flying colours.

But that's not all:

Sean Penn wants to option it.

Which basically means Sean Penn – *Sean Penn* – wants to make *A Prince Among Men* into a movie.

Which I'm totally happy about. Don't get me wrong, I'm thrilled for J.P.

And there are already so many movies about my life. What's one more, right?

It's just . . . WHEN IS IT GOING TO BE MY TURN?

Seriously. When is someone going to recognize something *I've* done? Other than bring democracy to a small

European nation, which frankly no one seems to care about.

I don't mean to whine (which I know is hilarious, because it's basically all I ever do in my journal), but for God's sake. I don't think it's fair that a guy can write a play (which is basically a huge chunk of MY life, that he's more or less STOLEN), throw it up on to a stage, then get a movie deal with Sean Penn.

Whereas I slave – yes, slave – over a book for months, and I can't even get a publisher to look at it.

*Come on!*

And I'm going to tell you the truth: I didn't like that Sean Penn movie *Into the Wild* so much.

*Yes!* I know it was critically acclaimed! I know it won all those awards! It's very sad that boy is dead and all. But I thought the movie *Enchanted*, with the singing princess and the squirrel and the people dancing in Central Park, was cuter.

So there!

Anyway, J.P. came up and asked me how I liked *A Prince Among Men* ('I was exploring the theme of self-discovery –' he explained to me – 'a boy's journey towards manhood and the woman who helped him find his way from troubled childhood to the full realization of what it means to become a man . . . and eventually even to become a prince.' He didn't mention anything about exploring the theme of sexy dancing).

I told him I liked it a lot. What else could I say? I guess if it hadn't been about me, I really *would* have liked it. Except that the princess came off as this kind of kooky girl, who always needs her boyfriend to bail her out of the zany situations she gets herself into, and I don't actually think I'm like that. I don't think I need any rescuing at all actually.

But it seemed the wrong time to give him editorial notes. And I was glad I didn't, because he seemed so pleased to hear me say I liked it. He wanted me to come out with him and Sean Penn and his parents and Stacey Cheeseman and Andrew Lowenstein so we could all talk about his movie deal. Sean Penn was taking everyone, including the senior project committee, to Mr Chow's for a celebratory meal.

But I said I couldn't go. I said I had to go home and study for my Psych final.

Which I will admit was not very friendly of me. Especially since I don't have to study for my Psych final at all. I have Psych down cold. After all, I was best friends for most of my life with a girl whose parents were psychiatrists. Then I dated her brother. And now I'm *in* therapy.

But obviously this didn't occur to J.P., because he just went, 'Are you sure you don't want to come, Mia?' and kissed me when I said I was, then hurried to join Sean and Andrew and Stacey and his parents at the theatre door, where tons of paparazzi were waiting to take his photo.

Yeah. Because there were huge amounts of paps in front of the theatre. As I made my own way out, they asked me how I felt about my boyfriend having written a play about me that's going to be turned into a movie directed by Sean Penn.

I said I felt great about it, making that statement officially <u>Mia Thermopolis's Big Fat Lie Number Ten.</u>

Although I think I'm starting to lose track.

I don't know how I'm ever going to get to sleep tonight when all I can think about is this:

PS No need to thank me on behalf of your father or Genovia. I only sent it because I thought it might help out your dad in the elections, and that, in turn, would make you happy. So you see my motives were completely selfish.

EEEEEEEEEEEEEEEEEEEEEEEEEEEEEEEEEEEEE!!!!!!!!!!

An Excerpt from *Ransom My Heart* by
Daphne Delacroix

He felt her body tense, but when she tried to
back away from him, two things happened
simultaneously to thwart her escape. The first
was that she came up against Violet's solid
flank. The mare only looked back at them,
placidly chewing on some loose straw, and
would not move. The second was that Hugo's
arms went around her, half-lifting Finnula off
the ground even as his tongue slid into her
mouth.

Finnula let out a mew of protest that was
quickly stifled by his own mouth . . . but her
protest seemed short-lived. Either Finnula was
a woman who appreciated a good kiss, or she
liked him, at least a bit. Because a second
after his mouth met hers, her head fell back
against his arm, and her lips opened like a
blossom. He felt her relax against him,
her hands, which previously had been trying
to push him away, suddenly going around his
neck to press him closer.

It wasn't until he felt her tongue flick tentatively against his that he lost his careful
control. Suddenly, he was kissing her even
more urgently, his hands travelling down her
sides, past her hips, until they lifted her full
up against him.

Her firm breasts crushed against his chest,
her thighs clenched tightly around his hips,
Hugo moulded Finnula against him, kissing

264

her cheeks, her eyelids, her throat. The sensuous reaction he'd evoked from her amazed and excited him, and when she held his face between both her hands and rained kisses upon him, he groaned, both from the sweetness of the gesture and the fact that he could feel the heat from between her legs burning against his own urgent need.

Holding her to him with one arm, he swept open the collar of her shirt. Finnula let out another sound, this one a sigh of such longing that Hugo could not stifle a wordless cry, and he looked about for a pile of hay thick enough for them to lay in . . .

# Thursday, May 4, Psychology final

Describe major histocompatibility complex

This is so easy.

Major histocompatibility complex is the gene family found in most mammals that is responsible for reproductive success. These molecules, which are displayed on cell surfaces, control the immune system. They have the capacity to kill pathogens, or malfunctioning cells. In other words, MHC genes help the immune system to recognize and destroy invaders.

This is especially useful in the selection of potential mates. MHC has recently been shown to play a crucial role, via olfaction (or sense of smell) in this capacity. It has been proven that the more diverse, or different, the MHC of the parent, the stronger the immune system of the child. Interestingly, MHC-mate dissimilar selection tendencies have been categorically determined in humans. The more dissimilar a male's MHC to a female's (this was without deodorant or cologne), the 'better' he tended to smell to her in clinical studies. These studies have been duplicated time and again, with the same results. Mice and fish have shown similar –

Oh.
 My.
 God.

# Thursday, May 4, Psych final

*What am I going to do?*

Seriously. This can't be happening. I *cannot* be suffering from major histocompatibility complex for Michael. That is just . . . that is just *ridiculous.*

On the other hand . . . why else have I always been so drawn to – OK, completely obsessed with – the way his neck smells?

This explains everything. He is my perfect dissimilar MHC match! No wonder I've never been able to get over him! It's not me, or my heart, or my brain . . . it's my *genes*, crying out in longing for their complete and total genetic opposite!

And what about J.P.? This perfectly explains why I've never been that physically attracted to him . . . he's never smelt like anything but dry-cleaning fluid to me. We're too MHC compatible! We're *too* close of a genetic match. We even *look* alike . . . the blond hair, light eyes, same build. How did that person put it, so long ago, who saw us together at the theatre – *'They make a very attractive couple. They're both so tall and blond.'*

No wonder J.P. and I have never even gotten past first base. Our molecules are like, REJECTION! REJECTION! DO NOT MATE!

And here I am, demanding that we do it anyway.

Well, with a condom.

But still. Offspring *could* result, down the line, if J.P. and I get married.

OH MY GOD! I wonder what kind of genetic defects

our kids would have, considering I get no olfactory vibe from him at all! They'll probably be born all aesthetically perfect – just like LANA!!!!

Which, seriously, think about it, is a serious genetic defect. Being born perfect would turn any kid into a horrible *Cloverfield*-type monster, just like her (well, for the first seventeen years of her life, considering how awful she was until I tamed her a bit). I mean, if you're born perfect, like Lana, you never have to learn any coping mechanisms, the way I did growing up. Because beautiful people can often coast along on their looks, never having to develop a sense of humour, or compassion for others or anything like that. Why would they have to? They're perfect. If you're born aesthetically beautiful, the way J.P.'s and my kids would be, basically you're a monster . . . and my genes know it.

That's why whenever J.P. kisses me, I don't get that thrill I always did when Michael kissed me . . . MY GENES DON'T WANT ME TO GIVE BIRTH TO GENETIC MONSTERS!!!!!

What am I going to do?????? I am scheduled to have sex in less than two days with a guy with whom I am a complete MHC match!

AND THAT IS THE EXACT OPPOSITE OF WHAT MAJOR HISTOCOMPATIBILITY COMPLEX IS ALL ABOUT!

My MHC *mis*match is someone who broke up with me almost two years ago!

And who, despite what my grandmother and best friend seem to think, does NOT love me, but really does just want to be friends.

True, J.P. and I have so *much* in common personality-wise – we both like creative writing, and *Beauty and the Beast*, and drama.

While Michael and I basically have nothing in common except a deep and abiding love for *Buffy the Vampire Slayer* and *Star Wars* (the original three movies, not the prequels).

And yet I might as well admit I have an insufferable weakness for him. Yes! I do! I cannot resist the way he smells. I am drawn to him the way the American public is drawn to Tori Spelling.

I have got to fight this. I can't allow myself to feel this way about a boy who is so incredibly wrong for me (except, of course, genetically).

*But what if I'm not strong enough?*

# Thursday, May 4, Psych final

Mia, is it true? Is J.P.'s play really going to be a movie?

Ahhhhh! You scared me! I don't have time to talk about this now, Tina. I just figured out J.P. and I are total MHC mismatches . . . or, matches, really. Our children are going to be perfect genetic mutants, like Lana! And that Michael's my MHC match! That's why I've always been obsessed with how his neck smells! And why whenever I'm around him, I act like a total blithering idiot. Tina, I am a dead woman.

Mia . . . are you on drugs?

No – don't you see what this means? It explains EVERYTHING! Why I've never felt attracted to J.P Why I can't let Michael go . . . Oh, Tina, I'm being held hostage by my own MHC. I've got to FIGHT it. Will you help?

Do you need help? Because I could call Dr Knutz.

No! Tina – Look. Just . . . never mind. I'm fine. Pretend I never said anything.

*Why does everyone always think I'm crazy when I've never been saner in my life?* Can't Tina – can't everyone – see that I'm just a woman who's busy trying to take care of business? I'm eighteen now. I know what I have to do to get things done.

Or – as in this case – not done, I guess. Because there's nothing I can do about this.

Except stay far, far away from Michael Moscovitz.

I just can't believe I bought J.P. all that cologne. When it turned out cologne had nothing to do with it in the first place. It was his genes all along.

Who knew?

Well . . . me, I guess. I just didn't put it all together until the test today.

I guess I *have* had a lot on my mind, what with trying to get my dad elected and pick a college and all.

I blame the educational system in this country. Why did they wait until the last semester of my senior year to tell me all this – about MHC, I mean? This is information that might have been useful to me, oh, I don't know, round about ninth grade maybe!

The big question now is: how am I going to avoid smelling Michael during lunch tomorrow?

I don't know. I guess I'll just stay as far away from him as I can. I certainly won't hug him this time. If he asks for a hug, I'll just say I have a cold.

Yes! That's it. And I don't want him to catch it.

God. Genius.

I can't believe Kenneth is our class valedictorian. It should really be me. If they gave out class valedictorian for LIFE lessons, it would be.

# Thursday, May 4, Lunch

Dad just called with more Moscovitz news.

This time it was about Lilly.

Seriously, I should stop purchasing food here, since I'm only going to end up dropping it on the floor. Although since tomorrow is Senior Skip Day . . . I guess this is the last day I'm going to have this particular problem.

'Do you remember how she was filming everyone at your party?' Dad asked when I picked up the phone, convinced this time Grandmere really *had* keeled over.

'Yeah . . .' I was picking bits of salad out of my hair. Everybody else was giving me the evil eye, picking bits of salad out of their own hair. Though it wasn't my fault, really. I'd dropped my Fiesta Taco bowl.

'Well, she's crafted a campaign commercial from the footage. It began airing on Genovian television last night at midnight.'

I groaned. Everyone looked politely inquisitive – except J.P. He got a call on his own cellphone at that exact moment.

'It's Sean,' he said apologetically. 'I've got to take this. I'll be right back.' He got up to go take the call outside, away from the din of the caff.

'How bad's the damage?' I asked. Dad's numbers had gotten a little better since Michael's donation and the press Dad had received because of it.

But René was still leading in the polls.

'No,' Dad said. He sounded strange. 'You don't understand, Mia. Her commercial's in *support* of me. Not against me.'

'What?' I asked him breathlessly. '*What* did you say?'

'That's right,' Dad said. 'I just thought you should know. I've emailed you a link to it. It's really lovely actually. I can't imagine how she accomplished it. You said she has her own show in Korea, or something? I suppose she had her people there put it together, and then they had someone over here—'

'Dad,' I said, my chest feeling tight. 'I've got to go . . .'

I hung up, then went straight to my email. Scrolling through all the hysterical messages from Grandmere about what I was going to wear to the prom and then the next day to graduation (like it even matters, since I'll have my graduation gown on over whatever it is), I found Dad's email and clicked on it. The link to Lilly's commercial was there and I clicked on that. The ad began to play.

And he was right. It *was* lovely. It was a sixty-second clip featuring all the celebrities from my party – the Clintons, the Obamas, the Beckhams, Oprah, Brad and Angelina, Madonna, Bono and more – all saying sweet, very sincere-sounding things about my dad, about stuff he'd done for Genovia in the past, and how Genovian voters ought to support him. Interspersed between the brief celebrity endorsements were gorgeous shots of Genovia (which I realized Lilly had taken during her many trips with me there), of the blue sparkling waters of the bay, the green cliffs above it, the white beaches and the palace, all looking pristine and untouched by touristy schlock.

At the end of the ad, some curlicue script came that said, 'Preserve Genovia's historic wonder. Vote for Prince Philippe.'

By the time the music – which I recognized as a

ballad Michael had written, way back in his Skinner Box days – had ended, I was almost in tears.

'Oh my God, you guys,' I said, 'you have to see this.'

And then I passed around my cellphone and showed them all. Soon the whole table was almost in tears. Well, except J.P., who hadn't come back yet, and Boris, who is immune to emotion unless it involves Tina.

'Why would she do that?' Tina wanted to know.

'She used to be cool,' Shameeka said. 'Remember? Then something happened.'

'I have to find her,' I said, still blinking back tears.

'Find who?' J.P. asked. He'd finally returned from his Sean Penn call.

'Lilly,' I said. 'Look what she did.' I handed him my cellphone so he could watch the commercial she'd made. He did, a frown on his face.

'Well,' he said when it was over, 'that was . . . nice.'

'Nice? It's amazing,' I said. 'I have to thank her.'

'I really don't think you do,' J.P. said. 'She owes you. After that website she made up about you. Remember?'

'That was a long time ago,' I said.

'Yeah,' J.P. said. 'Even so. I'd watch out, if I were you. She's still a Moscovitz.'

'What's that supposed to mean?' I asked.

J.P. shrugged. 'Well, you of all people should know, Mia. You have to imagine Lilly wants something in return for her apparent generosity. Michael always did, didn't he?'

I stared at him in complete shock.

On the other hand, maybe I shouldn't have been surprised. He *was* talking about Michael, the boy who'd broken my heart into so many little pieces . . . pieces J.P. had so kindly helped put back together again.

Before I had a chance to say anything though, Boris said, from absolutely nowhere, 'Funny, I hadn't noticed that. Michael's letting me live with him next semester for absolutely nothing.'

This caused all of us to swivel our heads around to stare at him as if he was a parking meter that had suddenly, magically, begun speaking.

Tina was the first one of us to recover.

'WHAT?' she demanded of her boyfriend. 'You're living with *Michael Moscovitz* next semester?'

'Yeah,' Boris said, looking surprised she didn't know. 'I didn't hand in my housing registration to Juilliard on time, and they ran out of singles. And I'm not going to live with a ROOM-MATE. So Michael said I could crash in his spare bedroom until a single opens up for me on the waiting list. He's got a kick-ass loft, you know, on Spring Street. It's huge. He won't even know I'm there.'

I glanced at Tina. Her eyes were bigger than I'd ever seen them. I wasn't sure if it was with rage or bewilderment.

'So all this time,' Tina said, 'you've secretly gone on being friends with Michael behind Mia's back? And you never told me?'

'There's nothing secret about it,' Boris said, looking offended. 'Michael and I've always been friends, since I was in his band. It has nothing to do with Mia. You don't stop being friends with a guy just because he's broken up with his girlfriend. And there's lots of stuff I don't tell you about it. *Guy* stuff. And you shouldn't be stressing me out today. I have my concert tonight, I'm supposed to be taking it easy—'

'*Guy* stuff?' Tina said, picking up her bag. 'You don't have to tell me about guy stuff? Fine. You want to take it easy? You don't want to be stressed? No problem. Why don't I just relieve *all* your stress? By leaving.'

'Tee,' Boris said, rolling his eyes.

But when she stormed from the caff in a huff, he realized she was serious. And he had to hurry to chase after her.

'Those two,' J.P. said with a chuckle when they were gone.

'Yeah,' I said. I wasn't chuckling though. I was remembering something that had happened nearly two years ago, when Boris had come up to me and urged me to write back to Michael, when he kept writing to me, but I didn't trust myself to write back.

I'd wondered then how Boris even knew Michael had been writing to me. I thought it was because Tina had told him.

Now I wondered if I'd been wrong. Maybe *Michael* had told him. Because the two of them had been in communication.

About *me*.

What if Boris, scraping away on his violin in the supply closet while the two of us were in Gifted and Talented together, had been spying on me for Michael the whole time?

And now Michael's giving him free room and board in his fancy SoHo loft to pay him back!

Or am I reading too much into this – as usual?

And I don't think that's true, what J.P. said, about the Moscovitzes always wanting something in return. I mean, yes, Michael wanted to have sex back when we were dating (if that's what J.P. was implying . . . and I think it was).

But the truth is, so did I. Maybe I wasn't as ready for

it emotionally then as I am now. But we couldn't exactly help being attracted to each other.

And now I finally realize why!

This is all just so confusing. Honestly, *what* is going on? Why did Lilly make that commercial for Dad? Why did Michael donate the CardioArm?

*Why is everyone in the Moscovitz family being so nice to me all of a sudden?*

# Thursday, May 4, 2 p.m., the hallway

I'm cleaning out my locker.

Tomorrow is Senior Skip Day (although technically not an officially school sanctioned holiday), and I don't have any finals this afternoon, so this is basically the only time I'm going to be able to do this – also the last time I'll be inside this hellhole (aside possibly from graduation, which will be in Central Park, unless it rains).

It's really sad in a way.

I guess this place wasn't really a hellhole. Or at least, it wasn't always. I had some good times here. At least a few. I'm throwing away tons of old notes from Lilly and Tina (remember when we used to write notes, before we got cellphones and started texting?) and a lot of things that are stuck together that I can't identify (seriously, I wish I had cleaned this thing out once or twice before in the past. Also, I think a mouse has been in here).

Here's a flattened Whitman's Sampler (empty) someone once gave me. I seem to have eaten everything that was inside it. And here's a smushed flower of some kind that I'm sure had some kind of significance at some point but now it's kind of mouldy. Why can't I take better care of my things? I should have pressed it neatly between the pages of a book the way Grandmere taught me, and noted what kind of flower it was and who gave it to me so I could always treasure its memory.

What's wrong with me? Why did I jam it in my locker like that? Now it's rotten and I have no choice but to stuff it in this trash bag Mr Kreblutz, the head custodian, has given me.

I'm a terrible person. Not just because I don't take better care of my belongings, but because . . . well, all the other reasons, which should be obvious by now.

What am I going to do? WHAT AM I GOING TO DO?

I looked all over for Lilly, but I couldn't find her. I suppose she has finals this afternoon.

(I did find Tina and Boris though. They made up. At least if the fact that they were making out in the third-floor stairwell means anything. I snuck discreetly away before they noticed me.)

I guess I could call her (Lilly, I mean). But . . . I don't know what I'd say. Thank you? That seems so lame.

What I want to say is . . . *why*? Why are you being so nice to me?

Maybe I'll ask her brother at lunch tomorrow. I mean, if he knows. After I warn him about my cold. And to stay far away from me.

Anyway.

It feels so weird to be wandering around the halls of this place while everyone else is in class. Principal Gupta totally saw me too, but she didn't say anything like, 'Why aren't you in class, Mia? Do you have a pass?' She was just like, 'Oh, hello, Mia,' and kept walking by, all distracted. Clearly she was worrying about graduation (So am I – WHAT COLLEGE AM I GOING TO CHOOSE???) or whatever, and had more pressing matters on her mind than why a princess was roaming around loose in the halls of her school.

Either that or I didn't look like much of a threat. I guess that's what happens when you're a graduating senior.

With a bodyguard in tow.

Maybe some day I'll write a book about this. A senior girl experiencing conflicting emotions as she cleans out her locker, saying goodbye to the place of higher education she's known so long . . . her love/hate relationship with it . . . She wants to leave it, and yet . . . she's afraid to leave it, to spread her wings and start anew somewhere else. She hates the long, grey, smelly hallways, and yet . . . she loves them too. I mean, in a way.

*Einstein Lions, we're for you*
*Come on, be bold, come on, be bold,*
*come on, be bold*
*Einstein Lions, we're for you*
*Blue and gold, blue and gold,*
*blue and gold*
*Einstein Lions, we're for you*
*We've got a team no one else can ever tame*
*Einstein Lions, we're for you*
*Let's win this game!*

Goodbye, AEHS. You suck. I hate you.
And yet . . . somehow I'll miss you too.

# Thursday, May 4, 6 p.m., the Loft

*Dear Ms Delacroix*

*Enclosed please find your manuscript, which we are sorry to say we do not believe is the right fit for us at this time. We wish you the best of luck placing it elsewhere.*

*Sincerely,*

*Heartland Romance Publications*

I had to hide the above from J.P., who's here right now. He came over after school today. It's the first time in months he didn't have play rehearsal or I didn't have princess lessons or one of us didn't have therapy.

So. He came over.

He's out in the living room right now, talking to Mom and Mr G about his movie deal. I'm 'changing for Boris's concert'.

But obviously I'm not. I'm writing about what happened when he came over instead. Which is that I totally tried VERY VERY HARD to get my MHCs to respond to his. I did this by doing what Tina did when she saw Boris in his swimsuit.

Yes. I jumped his bones.

Or I tried to anyway. I just figured, if I could get J.P. to kiss me – *really* kiss me, the way Michael used to, when we were having a heavy-duty make-out session the way we used to in his dorm room – maybe everything would be all right. Maybe I wouldn't have to worry about pretending I have a cold tomorrow when I have lunch with Michael. Maybe I won't be so super attracted to him any more.

But it didn't work.

Not that J.P. pushed me away or anything. He kissed me back and stuff. He tried. He really did try.

But he kept stopping every thirty seconds or so to talk about his movie deal.

I'm not even joking.

Like about how 'Sean' had asked him to write the screenplay (I guess a screenplay isn't the same as writing a play. J.P. has to rewrite the whole thing from scratch now, in a different computer program).

And how J.P. is seriously considering moving out 'to the coast' so he can be there for the filming.

He's even debating putting school off for a year so he can work on the movie. Because you can go to school any time.

But you can only be one of the hottest young screenwriters in Hollywood once.

Anyway, he asked me to come with him. Out to Hollywood.

This completely killed the mood. The making out mood, I mean.

I guess some girls would love it if their boyfriend, who'd written a play about them that was soon to become a major motion picture directed by Sean Penn, asked them to defer college for a year and move out to Hollywood with them.

But I, being the ultimate loser that I am, just blurted out, 'Why would I do *that*?' before I could really stop myself. Mostly because I didn't really have my mind in the conversation. I was thinking about . . . well, not Hollywood film deals.

Also because I'm a horrible person, for the most part.

'Well, because you love me,' J.P. was forced to remind

me. We were lying on my bed, with Fat Louie glaring balefully at us from the windowsill. Fat Louie hates it when anyone but me lies on my bed. 'And you want to support me.'

I flushed, feeling guilty for my outburst.

'No,' I said, 'I mean, what would *I* do out in Hollywood?'

'Write,' J.P. said. 'Maybe not romance novels, because frankly I think you're capable of much more important work—'

'You haven't even read my book,' I reminded him, feeling hurt. We'd still never gotten to have our Stephen and Tabitha King editorial talk. And important work? Romance novels are important! To the people who like to read them, anyway.

'I know,' J.P. said, laughing. But not in a mean way. 'And I'm going to, I swear, I've just been so swamped with the play and now finals and everything. You know how it is. And I'm sure it's the best romance novel there is. I'm just saying, I think you could write something much weightier if you really put your mind to it. Something that could change the world.'

Weightier? What is he talking about? And haven't I done enough for the world? I mean, I made Genovia a democracy. Well, not me personally, but I helped. And if you write something that cheers someone up when they're feeling down, doesn't that change the world?

~~And let me tell you something. I have seen *A Prince Among Men* now, and it is not going to change the world OR cheer anybody up. I don't mean to sound like I've got sour grapes, but it's the truth. It doesn't even make you think — except to make you think that the guy who wrote it must think pretty highly of himself.~~

Sorry. I didn't mean that. That was uncalled for.

Anyway, I was like, 'J.P., I don't know. Moving to Hollywood with you isn't something my mom or my dad is going to approve of. They both expect me to go to college.'

'Right,' J.P. said. 'But taking a year off might not be such a bad idea. It's not like you got in anywhere that great anyway.'

Ouch. See, that would have been a great opportunity for me to say, 'Actually, J.P., I was kind of exaggerating when I said I didn't get in anywhere . . .'

Only of course I didn't. Instead I just suggested we go into the living room and watch *True Life: I'm Hooked on OxyContin*, because I didn't want to get into an argument.

Anyway, after watching *True Life*, I learned something. Not just that I am never going to do drugs (obviously). But that writing is my drug. It's the only thing I ever do that I really like.

I mean, besides kiss Michael, of course. But I can't do that any more, obviously.

## Thursday, May 4, 9 p.m., ladies' room, Carnegie Hall

OH MY GOD!

I thought this concert was going to be really boring, but I was wrong.

Oh, not the music. *That's* totally boring. I've heard it a million times coming out of the G and T supply closet (although I'll admit, it's kind of different to hear it coming from the centre of the Carnegie Hall stage, especially seeing all these fancy people turned out in their best clothes, clutching CDs with Boris – BORIS – on the cover, all saying his name in excited voices. I mean, it's just Boris Pelkowski. But these people seem to think he's some kind of celebrity. Which, hello, HIGHlarious).

But the fact that everyone I know from AEHS is here, including *both* Moscovitz siblings – *that's* exciting. I wasn't expecting that.

And I know it's wrong to be excited to see my ex-boyfriend when I'm out on a date with my current boyfriend.

However, that is not my fault. It's MHC.

Our seats are rows and rows apart so there's no chance of my being overpowered by eau de Michael. Unless somehow we bump into him later. Which I highly doubt is going to happen.

Anyway, Michael's alone. He didn't come with a date! Which may be because Micromini Midori is in Genovia.

Except that I can't help wondering if he came solo because I said in my text to him that I'd be coming.

But then I remembered what Boris said – about how

the two of them are going to be living together this year. So I guess that's why he's here actually. To support his friend.

Stupid me, getting my hopes up. AGAIN.

Anyway. I guess I should be getting back to my seat. I didn't want to be rude and write while I was supposed to be looking like I was paying attention, but –

WAIT.

Oh God.

I recognize those shoes.

## Thursday, May 4, 9.30 p.m., ladies' room, Carnegie Hall

Lilly just left here.

I was right: they *were* her shoes.

I totally confronted her when she came out of her stall.

Well, confronted isn't the right word. I *asked* her about the commercial she made for my dad. Why she did it, I mean.

At first she tried to get out of it by saying it had been a birthday gift for me.

And it's true, she had said, back in *The Atom* office when I turned in my story about Michael, that there was something she'd been going to give me for my birthday. And she'd said to give it to me she'd need to come to my party. She hadn't said she was going to give it to me at my party. I'd just assumed that part.

But . . . why now? Why a present *this* year? And such a *great* present?

At first she looked really annoyed that I wouldn't just let it go. Like she couldn't believe she'd walked into the bathroom and there I was.

I guess it probably *does* seem like every single time she goes for a pee, there I am.

Well, it's basically true. It's like I have some kind of Lilly Moscovitz Bladder Radar.

And this time Kenneth wasn't around to ask weird questions about whether or not I was still going out with J.P., and keep her from answering. For a second I thought she wouldn't anyway.

But then she seemed to make a decision within

herself. She sort of sighed and, looking a bit annoyed, went, 'Fine. If you must know, Mia . . . my brother said I had to be nice to you.'

I just stared at her. It took a few seconds for her words to register. 'Your *brother* said . . .?'

'. . . that I had to be nice to you,' Lilly finished for me, sounding exasperated, as if I should have been aware of this. 'He found out about the website see?'

I moved from staring to blinking. I was making progress. 'Ihatemiathermopolis.com?'

'Right,' Lilly said. She did look a little ashamed of herself actually. 'He was really mad. I'll admit . . . it *was* pretty childish.'

Michael found out about ihatemiathermopolis.com? You mean . . . he hadn't known? I thought everyone in the whole world had known about that stupid website.

And he'd told Lilly she had to be *nice* to me?

'But.' I was having trouble processing so much information at once. It was like I was a desert that was finally getting rain . . . only there was too much of it and I couldn't soak it all in. Soon I'd be experiencing mudslides. And flash floods. 'But . . . why were you so mad at me in the first place? I'll admit, I acted like a total jerk to your brother. But I regretted it, and I tried to get back together with him. He's the one who said no. So what were you so mad about it?' This was the part I could never figure out. 'Was it . . . was it just because of J.P.?'

Lilly's face darkened. 'You don't know?' she asked, sounding incredulous. 'You honestly don't know?'

I was definitely experiencing sensory overload. 'No,' I shook my head. She hadn't actually answered the question. 'What am I supposed to know?'

'I have never,' Lilly said flatly, 'met anyone so dense as you in my life, Mia.'

'What?' I still have no idea what she was talking about. I know I'm dense. I do! I'm a geek. She didn't have to rub it in. She could have helped me a little. 'Dense about *what*?'

But at that point an old lady came into the bathroom and I guess Lilly decided she'd said enough. She just shook her head and walked out.

Which just leaves me here to wonder, as I have a million times before: *What is it I'm supposed to know? What is it that Lilly thinks I'm so dense about?*

It's true I started dating J.P. right after the two of them broke up. But she was already not speaking to me by the time that happened. So that can't be it.

Why can't Lilly just tell me what it was I was so dense about? She's the genius, not me. I hate it when geniuses expect the rest of us to be as smart as they are. It's not fair. I'm of *average* intelligence, and I always have been. I'm creative and stuff, but I'm romance-novel-writing creative! I don't perform well on IQ tests and certainly not SATs (obviously).

And I've NEVER been able to figure out Lilly.

And I can't figure her brother out either. For instance, why does *Michael* care whether she starts being nice to me or not?

Oh great. I hear clapping! I'd better get back to my seat . . .

# Friday, May 5, Midnight, the Loft

I was wrong about being able to stay away from my MHC match.

Everyone went up on to the stage after Boris's fantastically successful concert (standing ovations all around) to congratulate him.

That's how I found myself standing next to J.P., talking to Tina and Boris, when Michael and Lilly came up to congratulate Boris as well.

Which wasn't a bit awkward.

Considering Lilly was Boris's ex (remember when he dropped the globe on his head over her?) and J.P. was Lilly's, and Michael was mine. Oh, and Kenny's my ex too!

Ah, good times.

Not.

Fortunately Michael didn't try to hug me. Or say anything like, 'Oh, hey, Mia, see you at lunch tomorrow.' It was kind of like he knew this wasn't something I'd discussed with my boyfriend.

Although he was perfectly cordial, and didn't storm off like he did the night of my birthday (why *did* he do that? It can't be because of what Tina said, because he couldn't stand to see me with J.P. Because he seemed just fine seeing me with J.P. tonight).

Lilly, on the other hand, stonily ignored J.P. – although she cracked a little bit of a smile at me.

Tina, meanwhile, was so nervous about the whole thing (which was weird, because she was the only person there who *didn't* have an ex present), that she began talking in a very high-pitched voice about the senior project committee – who were looking a little haggard, possibly from their night out with Sean Penn – and I had to take her by the arm and start steering her away, gently murmuring, 'It's going to be OK. Shhhh. It's all over now. Boris passed with flying colours . . .'

'But,' Tina said, flinging a glance over her shoulder, 'why are Michael and Lilly here? *Why?*'

'Michael's friends with Boris. Remember? They're living together next year until Boris gets his space through the waiting list.'

'I need a vacation,' Tina whimpered. 'I really need a vacation.'

'You're getting one,' I said. 'Tomorrow's Senior Skip Day.'

'Are you really going to sleep with J.P.?' Tina wanted to know. 'Are you really, Mia? Really?'

'Tina,' I whispered, 'could you say it a little louder? I don't think all Carnegie Hall heard you.'

'I just don't think you're doing it for the right reasons,' Tina said. 'Don't do it because you think you have to or because you don't want to be the last girl in our class who is still a virgin or because you don't want to be the only girl in your college who hasn't slept with someone. Do it because you *want* to, because you feel a burning passion to. When I look at the two of you together, I just don't think . . . Mia, I don't think you *want* to. I don't feel like there's any *passion*. You write about passion in your book, but I don't think you actually *feel* it. Not for J.P.'

'OK,' I said, patting her on the arm, 'I'm going to go now. Tell Boris he did a lovely job. Bye now.'

I got Lars and J.P., told everyone else we were leaving, stayed far enough away from Michael that I couldn't smell him, then left, dropping J.P. off at his place on our way home.

I tried really hard to feel passion as I kissed him good night.

I think I even did. I definitely felt something.

It might have been the staple from the dry-cleaner the Reynolds-Abernathy family uses on the back of J.P.'s shirt collar though. I think it was scratching my finger as I tried to cling to him passionately.

# Friday, May 5, 9 a.m., the Loft

I don't believe it.

Mom just poked her head in here and went, 'Mia. Wake up.'

And I was like, 'MOM. I'm not going to school. It's Senior Skip Day. I don't care if it's not an officially sanctioned school holiday. I'm a senior. I'm skipping. Which means I don't HAVE TO GET UP.'

And she went, 'It's not that. There's someone on the house line, asking for Daphne Delacroix.'

I thought she was joking. I really did.

But she swore she was serious.

So I crawled out of bed and took the phone she was holding and put it to my ear and was like, 'Hello?'

'Is this Daphne?' asked a way-too-cheerful woman's voice.

'Um,' I said, 'sort of.' I really hadn't woken up enough to be able to deal with the situation.

'Your real name isn't Daphne Delacroix, is it?' asked the voice, laughing a little.

'Not exactly,' I said, stealing a glance at the caller ID on the handset. It said Avon Books.

Avon Books was the name on the spine of half of the historical romances I'd read while doing research for my own. It's a huge publisher of romance novels.

'Well, this is Claire French,' the cheerful voice said. 'I've just finished reading your book, *Ransom My Heart*, and I'm calling to offer you a publishing contract.'

I swear I did not think I could have heard her right. It sounded like she said she was calling to offer me a publishing contract.

But that could not possibly be what she had said.

Because people don't call and offer me book deals. Especially first thing in the morning. Ever.

'What?' I said intelligently.

'I'm calling to offer you a publishing contract,' she said. 'We'd like to offer you a book deal. But we'll need to know your real name. What *is* your real name, if you don't mind telling me?'

'Um,' I said, 'Mia Thermopolis.'

'Oh,' she said. 'Well, hi, Mia.' She then went on to say some things about money and contracts and due dates, and some other things I didn't understand because I was in too much of a daze.

'Um,' I finally said, 'can I have your number? I think I'm going to have to call you back.'

'Sure!' she said and gave me her extension. 'I look forward to hearing from you.'

'OK,' I said. 'Thanks a lot.'

Then I hung up.

I lay back in my bed and looked at Fat Louie, who was staring at me, happily purring from my pillows.

Then I screamed as loud as I could, freaking out Mom, Rocky and, of course, Fat Louie, who darted off the bed (all the pigeons on my fire escape took off too).

*I cannot believe it:*

I got an offer on my book.

And OK . . . it's not for a ton of money. If I was an actual person who had to make a living doing this, I would not be able to survive – at least not in New York City – for more than a couple of months on what they offered. If you really want to be a writer, clearly, you have to write *and* do some other job too, in order to pay your rent, etc. At least when you're first starting out.

But since I'm going to be donating the money to Greenpeace anyway . . . who cares?

Someone wants to buy my book!!!!!

# Friday, May 5, 11 a.m., the Loft

I feel like I'm floating . . .

Seriously, I'm so happy! This has been the best day of my life. At least so far.

I really mean that. Nothing is going to ruin it. NOTHING. And NO ONE.

I won't let them.

The first thing I did, after I told Mom and Mr G about my book deal, was call Tina. I was all, 'Tina – guess what? I got an offer on my book.'

And she was like, 'WHAT???? OH MY GOD, MIA, THAT IS FANTASTIC!!!!'

So then we shrieked for like, seriously, ten minutes. After that I hung up and called J.P. Probably I should have called him first, since he's my boyfriend. But I've known Tina longer.

The thing is even though J.P. was happy for me and all, he wasn't . . . well. He had some words of warning. Just because he loves me so much though.

'You shouldn't accept a first offer, Mia,' he said.

'Why not?' I asked. 'You did, from Sean Penn.'

'But that's different,' he said. 'Sean's an award-winning director. You don't even know who this editor is.'

'Yes I do,' I said. 'I just looked her up on the Internet. She's published tons of books. She's totally legit, and so is her publishing house. It's huge. They publish all the romances. Well, a lot of them.'

'Even so,' J.P. said, 'you might get a better offer from someone else. I wouldn't rush into anything.'

'Rush into anything,' I echoed. 'J.P., I've had like sixty-five rejection letters. She's the only person who has expressed the remotest interest in my book. It's a totally fair offer.'

'If you'd just do what I said,' J.P. said, 'and try to sell it under your real name, you'd get a ton more interest and probably a much bigger advance.'

'That's just it,' I said. 'She wants to publish it without knowing who I am! That means she likes the book on its own merit. That means way more to me than money.'

'Look,' J.P. said. 'Just don't accept the offer yet. Let me talk to Sean. He knows people in publishing. I bet he can get you a better offer.'

'No!' I cried. I couldn't believe how J.P. was trying to ruin this beautiful moment for me. Although it wasn't his fault. I knew he was just looking out for my best interests. But he was being a total buzzkill, as they said on *True Life*. 'No way, J.P. I'm taking this offer.'

'Mia,' J.P. said, 'you don't know anything about publishing. How do you know what you're getting yourself into? You don't even have an agent.'

'I have the Royal Genovian lawyers,' I reminded him. 'I don't think I need to remind you that they are like a pack of rabid pit bulls. Remember what they did to that guy who tried to publish that unauthorized biography of me last year?' I didn't want to add, *And what I could have them do to you, for writing a loosely based bio-play on me?* Because I didn't want to be mean, and of course I'd never sic the Royal Genovian lawyers on J.P. 'I'll have them look over the contract before I sign it.'

'I think you're making a mistake,' J.P. said.

'Well, I don't think I am,' I said. I wanted to cry. I really did. I knew he was only being that way because he loves me, but come on.

I got over it though. Even though J.P. and I got into our first (albeit very minor) fight over it, I still think I'm doing the right thing. Because I called my dad and told him about it, and after he asked a lot of questions (in a sort of distracted way, because he's busy campaigning. I was sorry to bug him about something so unimportant when he has so much to do, but – well, this is important to me) he still said it was fine by him, and I could do what I wanted – so long as I didn't sign anything until I had his pit-bull lawyers see it first.

So I said, 'THANKS, DAD!'

Then I called Claire French and told her I accepted.

The only problem was, by the time I called back, she fully knew who I was.

She said, 'This is going to sound strange, but when you said your name was Mia Thermopolis, I thought it sounded familiar, so – please don't be offended – I Googled you. You wouldn't happen to be Princess Mia Thermopolis of Genovia by any chance, would you?'

My heart totally sank.

'Um,' I said.

The thing is, even though I'm a totally habitual liar, I knew there was no point in lying to her about this. She was going to find out eventually. Like when I sent in my author photo or met her for a fancy editor-author lunch or my pit-bull lawyers used the Genovian crest notary or whatever.

'Yes,' I said. 'Yes, I am. But I didn't send my book out under my real name because I didn't want it to be published just because of my celebrity, you know? I wanted to see if people liked it based on its own merits, not because of who wrote it. I hope you can understand that.'

'Oh,' Claire said, 'I completely understand! And you don't need to worry, I had no idea it was you when I read it, or when I made you the offer. The thing is, though . . . well, the name Daphne Delacroix . . . it actually sounds very fake, and the last name – Delacroix – is hard for Americans to pronounce correctly. Whereas your real name is much more recognizable and memorable. I assume you're not doing this for any sort of financial gain—'

'No,' I said, horrified. 'I'm donating my author proceeds to Greenpeace!'

'Well, the truth is,' Claire said, 'you'd have a lot more author proceeds to donate if you let us publish the book under your real name.'

I clutched the phone to my ear, feeling sort of stunned. 'You mean . . . Mia Thermopolis?'

'I was thinking Mia Thermopolis, Princess of Genovia.'

'Well . . .' My heart was beating kind of fast. I remembered what Grandmere had said, about being sure not to use my real name. She was going to hate this, I thought. She was going to hate it so much if I published a steamy romance novel under my real name!

On the other hand . . . everyone in school would see it. Everyone in school would see my book and go, 'Oh my God. I *know* her! I went to school with her.'

And it wasn't as if Claire had bought the book knowing it was by me . . . but readers would. Think of all the money that would go to Greenpeace!

'. . . I think that would be fine,' I said.

'Great!' Claire said. 'That's settled then. I look forward to working with you, Mia.'

It was the most fantastic phone call of all time. It

almost made me forget that J.P. and I had sort of had a little fight and that I was going to have a very scary lunch with Michael very soon.

I'm a published author. Well, soon to be.

And no one can take that away from me. NO ONE!

## Friday, May 5, 12.15 p.m., the Loft

M – Fashion 911, here to the rescue. You need to wear your Chip & Pepper jeans and your pink and black Alice + Olivia sequinned top with that purple motorcycle jacket we picked out at Jeffrey and those super cute Prada platforms with the fringy things. Got it? Don't overdo it on the make-up, because I think he likes the natural type (whatever) and not chandelier earrings this time, go for studs, oooooh what about those cute little cherries I got you for your birthday? So appropriate for you HA HA HA!

– – – – – – – – – – – – – – – – – –

Sent from my BlackBerry Wireless Handheld

> No! I think that's all too much! By the way I'm getting my book published!

It's not too much, just do what I say, don't forget to curl your eyelashes, YAY ON *PUT IT IN MY CANDYHOLE!* What colour are you wearing to prom?

– – – – – – – – – – – – – – – – – –

Sent from my BlackBerry Wireless Handheld

> I don't know yet, Sebastiano is sending over a couple things. The Prada platforms are too much. I think I'll go with boots. It's not called *Put It In My Candyhole*, I told you.

NO! IT IS MAY. NO BOOTS AT LUNCH. You may compromise with adorable velvet flats.

– – – – – – – – – – – – – – – – – –

Sent from my BlackBerry Wireless Handheld

OK, you're right about the flats. THANK YOU! I HAVE TO GO!!!! I'm late. I'm so nervous!!!!

**Don't worry. Trisha and I are going to be taking a boat out and may row by to check on you.**

\- \- \- \- \- \- \- \- \- \- \- \- \- \- \- \- \-

**Sent from my BlackBerry Wireless Handheld**

NO! LANA!!! NO!!!! DO NOT COME BY!!! If you do, I will never speak to you again.

**BYE!!! Have fun!**

\- \- \- \- \- \- \- \- \- \- \- \- \- \- \-

**Sent from my BlackBerry Wireless Handheld**

## Friday, May 5, 12.55 p.m., Limo on the way to Central Park

I will stay away from Michael.

I will not hug him.

I will not even shake his hand.

I will not do anything that could, in any way, result in my smelling him and losing control of myself and doing something I might regret.

Not that it matters, because he doesn't like me that way. Any more. He thinks of me as just a friend.

But I mean, I don't want to embarrass myself in front of him.

And anyway, I have a boyfriend. Who really, really loves me. Enough to want what's best for me.

So, in conclusion:

Stay away from Michael – Check.

Do not hug him – Check.

Don't even shake his hand – Check.

Do not do anything that could result in smelling him – Check.

Got it. I think I'm good. I can do this. I can totally do this. This is cinchy. We're just friends. And it's just lunch. Friends have lunch all the time.

Since when do friends give each other million dollar pieces of medical equipment though?

Oh God. *I can't do this.*

We're here. I think I'm going to be sick.

An Excerpt from *Ransom My Heart* by Daphne Delacroix

Finnula had been kissed before, it was true. But the few men who'd tried it had lived to regret it, since she was as swift with her fists as she was with a bow.

Yet there was something about these particular lips, pressing so intently against hers, that caused nary a feeling of rancour within her.

He was an excellent kisser, her prisoner, his mouth moving over hers in a slightly inquisitive manner – not tentatively, by any means, but as if he was asking a question for which only she, Finnula, had the answer. It wasn't until Finnula felt the intrusion of his tongue inside her mouth that she realized she'd answered that question, somehow, though she hardly knew how. Now there was nothing questioning at all in his manner; he'd launched the first volley and realized that Finnula's defences were down. He attacked, showing no mercy.

It was then that it struck Finnula, as forcibly as a blow, that this kiss was something out of the ordinary, and that perhaps she was not in as much control of the situation as she would have liked. Though she struggled against the sudden, dizzying assault on her senses, she could no sooner free herself from the hypnotic spell of his lips than he'd been able to break the bonds with which she'd tied him. She went completely limp in his arms, as if she were melting against him, except for her hands, which, as if of their own volition, slipped around his brawny neck, tangling in the surprisingly soft hair half-buried beneath the flung-back hood of his cloak. What was it, she wondered dimly, about the introduction of this man's tongue into her mouth that seemed to have a direct correlation to a very sudden and very noticeable tightening sensation between her thighs?

Tearing her mouth away from his and placing a restraining hand against his wide chest, Finnula brought accusing eyes up to his face, and was startled by what she saw there. Not the derisive smile or the mocking eyes she'd become accustomed to, but a mouth slack with desire and green eyes filled with . . . with what? Finnula could not put a name to what she saw within those orbs, but it frightened as much as it thrilled her.

She had to put a stop to this madness, before things went too far.

'Have you lost your reason?' she demanded through lips that felt numb from the bruising pressure of his kiss. 'Release me at once.'

Hugo lifted his head, his expression as dazed as a man who'd just been roused from sleep. Blinking down at the girl in his arms, he gave every indication of having heard her, and yet his hand, still anchored upon her breast, tightened, as if he had no intention of releasing her. When he spoke, it was with a hoarse voice, his intonations slurred.

'I rather think it isn't my reason I've lost, Maiden Crais, but my heart,' he rasped.

## Friday, May 5, 4 p.m., Limo on the way to therapy

I suck.

I am a horrible, terrible, awful person.

I don't deserve to be in J.P.'s presence, let alone wear his ring.

I don't know how it happened! How I *let* it happened.

Also, it was completely my fault. Michael had nothing to do with it.

Well, maybe he had *a little bit* to do with it.

But mostly it was me.

I'm the world's worst, most disgusting girl.

And I know now that Grandmere and I *DO* come from the same bloodline. Because I'm just as bad as she is!

Maybe all this really is from hanging out so much with Lana. Maybe she's rubbed off on me!

Oh God. I wonder if I have to give back my Domina Rei membership now? Surely a Domina Rei wouldn't have done what I did?

It all started out so innocently too. I got to the Boathouse and Michael was there, waiting for me. And he looked fantastic (no big surprise), in a sportscoat (but no tie), with his dark hair kind of messy like he'd just gotten out of the shower.

And the very first thing that happened – the *very* first thing! – was that he came over to greet me with a kiss on the cheek.

And even though I tried to back away, crying, 'Oh, no, I have a cold!', he just laughed and said, 'I like your germs.'

And that's when it happened. Well, the first time. I got a great big whiff of him, his fresh clean *Michael* smell, all those dissimilar molecules smacking me in the olfactory senses at the same time. I swear, it was so much I nearly fell over, and Lars had to reach out and lay a hand on my elbow and go, 'Are you all right, Princess?'

No. The answer was no, I was not all right. I nearly got knocked out. Knocked out by desire! Desire for forbidden dissimilar molecules!

But I managed to pull myself together, and laughed like nothing had happened (but something had! Something had happened! Something *very, very* bad!).

Then we were being led to our sun-dappled table (Lars took up a seat at the bar so he could keep one eye on some sporting event and one eye on me. Oh, why, Lars, why? Why did you sit so far off????), and Michael was chatting away, I had no idea about what – I was still all dazed by the pheromones or whatever that were tweet-tweeting around my head, and we had a table RIGHT BY THE LAKE, so I had to start keeping an eagle eye out for Lana and Trisha, in case they happened to row by.

But also I think I was dazzled by the sun twinkling on the water, it was all so beautiful and fresh and not like we were in New York at all, but in . . . well, Genovia or something.

I swear, I felt as if I was on drugs.

Finally Michael was like, 'Mia, are you all right?' and I shook my head like Fat Louie does when I've scratched his ears too much, and I went, laughing all nervously, 'Yes, yes, I'm fine, I'm sorry, I'm just a little distracted.'

But I couldn't tell him WHY I was so distracted of course.

Then at the last minute I remembered my excellent news, and I gushed, 'I got a phone call this morning from an editor – she wants to publish my book.'

'That's great!' Michael said, his face breaking out into this big smile. That wonderful smile that I remembered from back in my freshman year, when he used to slip into Algebra to help me with Mr G's assignments *during* class, and I thought I'd died and gone to heaven. 'We've got to celebrate!'

So then he ordered sparkling water, and he toasted my success, and I was totally embarrassed, so I toasted his success back (I mean, honestly, my romance novel isn't going to save any lives, but as he pointed out, while his CardioArm is saving a patient's life, the family members of that patient could very well be sitting in the waiting room keeping happy and calm by reading my book. Which is a very good point), and we sat there sipping Perrier by the water in the middle of a Friday afternoon in Central Park in New York City.

Until the bright rays of the afternoon sun caught on the diamond in the ring J.P. had given me, which I forgot to take off. Anyway, the resulting reflection sent an explosion of little rainbows all over Michael's face, making him blink.

I was mortified and said, 'I'm sorry,' and slipped the ring off and put it in my bag.

'That's some rock,' Michael said with a teasing smile. 'So are you guys like engaged now?'

'Oh no,' I said. 'It's just a friendship ring.' (<u>Mia Thermopolis's Big Fat Lie Number Eleven</u>.)

'I see,' Michael said. 'Friendships have gotten a lot more . . . expensive than when I was at AEHS.'

Ouch.

But then Michael changed the subject. 'And where's J.P. going to college next year?'

'Well,' I said carefully. 'Sean Penn's optioned this play J.P. wrote, so he's thinking about heading out to Hollywood next year, and doing college later.'

Michael looked very interested to hear that. 'Really? So you guys would be doing the long-distance thing.'

'Well,' I said. 'I don't know. We're talking about me going with him . . .'

'To Hollywood?' Michael sounded totally incredulous. Then he apologized. 'Sorry. You just . . . I mean, you've just never struck me as the Hollywood type. Not that you aren't glamorous enough now. Because you totally are.'

'Thanks,' I said, completely embarrassed. Fortunately the waiter had brought our salads by then, so I was able to distract myself by saying no, thank you, to ground pepper.

'But I know what you mean,' I went on when the waiter went away. 'I'm not really sure what I'd do all day in Hollywood. J.P. said I could write. But . . . I always thought if I put off college for a year, it would be to go out in one of those little boats that put themselves between the whaling ships and the humpbacks or something. Not hang around on Melrose. You know?'

'Somehow I don't see your parents giving the seal of approval to either of those plans,' Michael said.

'And then there's that,' I said with a sigh. 'I have some things I need to figure out. And not a whole lot of

310

time left to do it. The parental units want a decision on where I'm going by the election.'

'You'll do the right thing,' Michael said confidently. 'You always do.'

I just stared at him. 'How can you even say that? I so do not.'

'Yes you do,' he said. 'In the end.'

'Michael, I screw everything up,' I said, laying down my fork. 'You, more than anyone, should know that. I completely ruined our relationship.'

'No you didn't,' he said, looking shocked. 'I did.'

'No, *I* did,' I said. I couldn't believe we were finally saying these things . . . these things I'd been thinking for so long, and saying to other people – my friends, Dr Knutz – but never to the one person to whom they really mattered . . . Michael. The person to whom I ought to have said them, ages ago. 'I never should have made such a big deal over the Judith thing—'

'And I ought to have told you about it from the beginning,' Michael interrupted.

'Even so,' I said. 'I acted like a complete and utter psycho—'

'No, Mia, you didn't—'

'Oh my God,' I said, holding up my hand to stop him with a laugh. 'Can we please not try to rewrite history? I did. You were right to break up with me. Things were getting too intense. We both needed a breather.'

'Yeah,' Michael said, 'a *breather*. You weren't supposed to go and get engaged to someone else in the meantime.'

For a second after he said it, I couldn't inhale. I felt as if all the oxygen in the room had been sucked out of it or something. I just stared at him, not sure I'd heard

311

him correctly. Had he really said . . . was it possible he'd really . . .?

Then he laughed and, as the waiter came back to pick up his empty salad plate (I'd barely touched mine), said, 'Just kidding. Look, I knew it was a risk. I couldn't have expected you were going to wait around for me forever. You can get engaged – or, what is it? Right, friendship-ringed – to whoever you want. I'm just glad you're happy.'

Wait. What was happening?

I didn't know what to do or say. Grandmere had prepared me for tons of situations – from dealing with thieving maids to escaping from embassies during coups d'état.

But honestly, nothing could have prepared me for this.

Was my ex-boyfriend really intimating that he wanted to get back together?

Or was I reading too much into things (it wouldn't be the first time)?

Fortunately just then our main courses came, and Michael steered the conversation back to normal ground like nothing had happened. Maybe nothing *had* happened. Suddenly we were talking about whether or not Joss Whedon will ever make a *Buffy the Vampire Slayer* feature film and how much Karen Allen rocks and Boris's concert and Michael's company and Dad's campaign. For two people with relatively nothing in common (because, let's face it, he's a robotic-surgical-arm designer. I'm a romance writer . . . and a princess. I love musicals and he hates them. Oh, and we have totally dissimilar DNA) we have never, ever run out of things to say to one another.

Which is completely weird.

Then, without my knowing quite how, we got to Lilly.

'Has your dad seen the commercial she made for him?' Michael asked.

'Oh,' I said, smiling, 'yes! It was wonderful. I couldn't believe it. Was that . . . did you have something to do with that?'

'Well,' Michael said, smiling as well, 'she wanted to do it. But . . . I might have encouraged her a little. I can't believe you two still aren't friends again, after all this time.'

'We aren't *not* friends,' I said, remembering what Lilly had told me about how he'd said she had to be nice to me. 'We just . . . I don't know what happened really. She never would tell me.'

'She'd never tell me either,' Michael said. 'You really have no idea?'

I flashed back to an image of Lilly's face as we sat in G and T that day she told me J.P. had broken up with her. I'd always wondered if that had been it. Could this whole thing have been over a boy? Is that what I was being so *dense* about?

But that would be so stupid. Lilly wasn't the type of person to let something as dumb as a boy get in the way of a friendship. Not with her best friend.

'I really,' I said, 'have no idea.'

The dessert menus came, and Michael insisted on ordering one of each dessert so we could try them all (because this was a celebration), while he told me stories about the cultural differences in Japan – how one takeaway restaurant delivered meals in actual china bowls that he'd place outside his door when he was finished eating, and the restaurant would come back to pick them up, which takes recycling to another level – and some of the embarrassments he'd suffered because of them (karaoke ballad singing, which his Japanese co-workers had taken very seriously, high amongst them).

And as he talked, it became clear that he and Micromini Midori? Not a couple. He mentioned her boyfriend, who is apparently a karaoke champion in Tsukuba, several times.

Then I started giggling in a different way when, after all the desserts came, I noticed two girls in a boat in the centre of the lake, arguing fiercely with one another and rowing in circles, not getting anywhere. Lana's plan of spying on me completely and utterly failed.

It was later, after the cheque came – and Michael paid, even though I said I wanted to take *him* out, to thank him for the donation to the hospital – that things *really* started to fall apart.

Well, maybe they'd been falling apart all afternoon – steadily crumbling – and I just hadn't been paying attention. Things have a tendency to do that in my life, I've noticed. It was when we were standing outside the Boathouse, and Michael asked what I had to do for the rest of the day, and I admitted that – for once – I had nothing to do (until my therapy appointment, but I didn't mention that. I'll tell him about therapy some day. But not today), that everything disintegrated like one of the madeleines we'd been nibbling on.

'Nothing to do until four? Good,' Michael said, taking my arm. 'Then we can keep on celebrating.'

'Celebrating how?' I asked stupidly. I was trying to concentrate on not smelling him. I wasn't really paying attention to anything else. Like where we were going.

'Have you ever been in one of these?'

314

That's when I saw that he had led me over to one of those cheesy horse and carriages that are all over Central Park.

Well, OK, maybe they're not cheesy. Maybe they're romantic and Tina and I talk about secretly wanting to ride in them all the time. But that's not the point.

'Of course I've never been in one of these,' I cried, acting horrified. 'They're so touristy! And PETA is trying to get them banned. And they're for people who are on dates.'

'Perfect,' Michael said. He handed the carriage driver, who was wearing a ridiculous (by which I mean fantastic) old-timey outfit with a top hat, some money. 'We'll go around the park. Lars, get up front. And don't turn around.'

'No!' I practically screamed. But I was laughing. I couldn't help it. Because it was so ludicrous. And so something I've always wanted to do, but never told anyone (except Tina, of course), for fear of being ridiculed. 'I am *not* getting in there! These things are cruel to horses!'

The carriage driver looked offended.

'I take excellent care of my horse,' she said. 'Probably better than you take care of your pets, young lady.'

I felt bad then – plus, Michael gave me a look, like – *See, you hurt her feelings? Now you* have *to get in.*

I didn't want to. I really didn't!

Not because it was stupid and touristy and I was afraid someone would see me (of course I didn't care about that, because secretly it's something I've always longed to do). But because – it was a romantic horse-

and-buggy ride! With someone who wasn't my boyfriend!

Worse, with someone who was my ex-boyfriend! And who I'd sworn I wasn't going to get close to today.

But Michael looked so sweet standing there with his hand out all expectantly, and his eyes so kind, like, *Come on. It's just a cheesy carriage ride. What could happen?*

And at the time, all I could think was that he was right. I mean, what harm could one buggy ride around the park do?

Also, I looked all around, and I didn't see any paparazzi.

And the red velvet bench in the back of the carriage looked roomy enough. We could definitely both fit on it and not touch or anything. Like, I could easily sit there and not run the risk of smelling him.

And really, in the end, how romantic could a cheesy touristy buggy ride be to a jaded New Yorker like myself!? Despite J.P.'s portrayal of me in *A Prince Among Men* as a kook who is constantly in need of rescuing (which is completely inaccurate), I'm actually very tough. I'm going to be a published author!

So, rolling my eyes and pretending to be all *I'm So Over This*, I laughingly let Michael help me into the carriage, and sat down on the lumpy bench. Meanwhile, Lars climbed up beside the lady in the top hat, and she started the horse, and we got going with a lurch . . .

And it turned out I was wrong.

The bench was *not* that big.

And I'm *not* that jaded a New Yorker.

Even now, I can't really say how it happened. And it seemed to happen pretty much right away too. One minute Michael and I were sitting calmly beside one another on that bench, Not Kissing, and the next . . . we were in each other's arms. Kissing. Like two people who had never kissed before.

Or, rather, like two people who used to kiss a lot, and really liked it, and then had been deprived of kissing one another for a very long time. And then suddenly were reintroduced to kissing and remembered they liked it. Quite a bit.

And so they started doing it again. A lot. Like a couple of kiss-starved maniacs, who had been in a kissing desert for approximately twenty-one months.

We basically made out from like Seventy-second Street, all through the park, and up to Fifty-seventh. That's like twenty blocks, give or take a few blocks.

YES. WE KISSED FOR TWENTY BLOCKS. IN BROAD DAYLIGHT. IN AN OLD-TIMEY HORSE CARRIAGE!

Anyone could have seen us. AND TAKEN PIC-TURES!!!!

I have no idea what came over me. One minute I was enjoying the clip-clop of the horse's hoofs and the beautiful scenery of the lush green leaves of the park. And the next . . .

And yes, I will admit it did seem like Michael was sitting AWFULLY close to me on that benchy thing at first.

And, OK, I did sort of notice his arm went around me when the carriage first lurched forward. But that was only natural. I thought it was sweet. It was the kind of thing a friend – a guy friend – might do for a girl friend.

But then Michael didn't take his arm away.

And then I got another whiff of him.

And it was all over. I knew it was all over, but I turned

my head to tell him – in a polite way, of course, the way a princess would – not to bother, that I'm with J.P. now and that it's hopeless, I won't do anything to hurt or betray J.P. because he was there for me when I was at my most despairing, and Michael should just give it up, if that was what he intended. Which it probably wasn't. But just in case.

But somehow those words never came out of my mouth.

Because when I turned my head to tell Michael all that, I saw that he was looking at me, and I couldn't help looking back, and something in his eyes – I don't know. It was like there was a question there. I don't know what the question was.

OK. I guess I do.

In any case, I'm pretty sure I answered it when he brought his lips down over mine.

And, like I said, we kept on kissing, passionately, for twenty-something blocks instead. Or whatever. Math is not my best subject.

Actually, as long as I'm confessing everything, I should admit there was more than kissing. There was a little – *discreet* – below the neck action, as well. I really hope Lars did what Michael asked, and didn't turn around.

Anyway, when the carriage stopped, I finally came to my senses. I guess it was the fact there was no more clip-clopping sound. Or maybe it was just the final lurch that practically threw us both off the bench.

That's when I was like, 'Oh my God!' and stared up at Michael, all horrified, realizing what I'd just done.

Which was make out with a boy who wasn't my boyfriend. For a really long time.

I guess the most horrifying part was how much I'd liked it. Which was a lot. A whole lot. That major histocompatibility complex thing? It does NOT mess around.

And I could tell Michael had felt the same way.

'Mia,' he said, looking down at me with his dark eyes filled with something I was almost afraid to put a name to, and his chest going all up and down like he'd just been running. His hands were in my hair. He was cradling my head. 'You *have* to know. You have to know I lo—'

But I smashed my hand over his mouth just like I'd done to Tina. My hand that used to have the three-carat diamond ring on it. From another boy.

I said, '*DO NOT SAY IT.*'

Because I knew what he was going to say.

That's when I said instead, 'Lars, we're leaving. *Now.*'

And Lars hopped down from the top of the carriage and helped me from the bench. And the two of us went to my waiting limo.

And I climbed inside. And I totally did not look back. Not even once.

And there's a message on my phone from Michael, but I'm not looking at what it says. I'm NOT.

Because I can't do this to J.P. I *can't*.

Oh my God though. I love Michael so much.

Oh, thank God. We're here.

Dr Knutz and I have a *lot* to talk about today.

## Friday, May 5, 6 p.m., Limo home from Dr Knutz's office

When I walked into Dr Knutz's office, Grandmere was there. AGAIN.

I demanded to know why. WHY she keeps insisting on violating my doctor–patient confidentiality. And OK, today was supposed to be my last therapy session ever, but still. Just because I'd invited her to join me a few times before didn't mean she could keep showing up to my appointments ALL the time.

She tried to used the excuse that this is the only place she knows she can find me (too bad she didn't look out of her window at the Plaza a little while ago. She could have seen her granddaughter going around Central Park in a horse and carriage in a liplock with a boy who is not her boyfriend).

Which I supposed (then) was a reasonable excuse. But that still didn't make it RIGHT, and I told her that.

Of course she fully ignored me. She said she needed to know if it was true I'm getting a romance novel published and if so how I could do this to the family and why didn't I just shoot her if I wanted to kill her, and get it over with? Why did I have to do it this way, by slowly humiliating her in front of all her friends? Why couldn't I be more like Bella Trevanni Alberto, who is such a perfect granddaughter (I swear if I have to hear this *one more time* . . .)?

Then she started on about Sarah Lawrence (again) and how she knows I have to pick a college by election day (also prom), and if I'd *just pick Sarah Lawrence* (the college she would have gone to if she'd bothered going to college), then everything would be all right.

I let out a shriek of frustration and stormed right past Grandmere and straight into Dr Knutz's office without waiting to hear any more. Because really, how ridiculous can that woman be? Besides, I was in crisis mode, what with this thing with Michael. I don't have time for Grandmere's histrionics.

Anyway, Dr Knutz listened calmly to what had just happened – with me and Grandmere, I mean – and said he was sorry, and that obviously, since this was my last session, it wouldn't happen again, but that he'd speak to Grandmere if I wanted. For what good that will do.

Then he listened to me describe what had just happened with Michael.

And his response was to ask me if I'd given any thought to the story he'd told me last week about his horse, Sugar.

'Because as I was explaining, Mia,' Dr Knutz went on, 'sometimes a relationship that seems perfect on paper doesn't always work out in reality, just like Sugar looked like a perfect horse on paper, but in real life we just didn't click.'

SUGAR! I pour my heart out about my romantic travails (and pain-in-the-butt grandmother), and Dr Knutz still can't talk about anything but his stupid horses.

'Dr K,' I said, 'can we talk about something else besides horses for a minute?'

'Of course, Mia,' he said.

'Well,' I said. 'My parents have told me I have to pick out a college to go to by Dad's election – and my prom.

321

And I can't decide. I mean, it seems as if every school that let me in only did so because I'm a princess—'

'But you don't *know* that to be true,' Dr Knutz said.

'No, but with my SAT scores, it's pretty obvious—'

'We've discussed this before, Mia,' Dr Knutz said. 'You know you're supposed to be concentrating on not obsessing over things you have no control over. What, in fact, are you supposed to do instead?'

I raised my gaze to the painting behind his head, of a herd of stampeding mustangs. How many hours have I gazed at that painting over the past twenty-one months, wishing it would fall on his head? Not enough to hurt him. Just enough to startle him.

'Accept the things I cannot change,' I said. 'And pray for the courage to change the things I can, as well as the wisdom to know the difference.'

The thing is . . . I know this is good advice. It's called the Serenity Prayer, and it really does put things in perspective (it's supposed to be for recovering alcoholics, but it helps recovering freakoutoholics, like me, as well).

But honestly, it's something I could have told *myself*.

What's becoming more clear to me every day now is that I've graduated. Not just from high school and princess lessons, but from therapy too. Not that I'm self-actualized or anything, because Lord knows I'm not . . . I don't believe anyone can ever achieve self-actualization any more. Not and still be a thinking, learning human being.

I've just realized the truth, which is: no one can help me. My problems are just too weird. Where am I going to find a therapist with the experience to help an American girl who finds out she is, in fact, the princess of a small European country, who also has a mother who married her Algebra teacher, a father who can't commit to romantic relationships at all, a best friend who won't speak to her, an ex-boyfriend she can't stop kissing in Central Park carriages, a boyfriend who wrote a play revealing intimate details about her, and a grandmother who is certifiably insane?

Nowhere. That's where.

I have to solve my own problems from now on. And you know what? I'm pretty sure I'm ready.

But I didn't want Dr Knutz to feel bad, because he had helped me a lot, in the past. So I said, 'Dr Knutz. Would you mind looking at a text message with me?'

'Not at all,' he said.

So we opened Michael's message together.

It said:

Mia, I'm not sorry. And I'll wait. Love Michael

Wow.

Also . . . *wow.*

Even Dr Knutz agreed. Although I doubt Michael's note made *his* heart pound faster – *Mi-chael, Mi-chael, Mi-chael* – the way it did mine.

'Oh my,' Dr Knutz said about Michael's text. 'That's very direct. So. What will you do?'

'Do?' I said sadly. 'I'm not going to *do* anything. I'm going out with J.P.'

'But you aren't attracted to J.P.,' Dr Knutz said.

'I am too!' I said. How did *he* know that? I'd never admitted that. To him anyway. 'Or at least . . . Well, I'm working on it.'

Science. The problem is, it's science. Which I've never been very good at.

But there are ways to beat science. That's what scientists, like Kenneth Showalter, do. All day long. Find ways to beat science. I have to beat this thing with Michael. Because I can't hurt J.P. I *can't*. He's been too kind to me.

'Mia,' Dr Knutz asked with a sigh, 'are we not actually done here?'

Uh . . . yeah. We totally are.

'I can't break up with a perfectly nice guy,' I said, wondering if I was going to have to explain my dad's theory about me being a tease, 'just because my old boyfriend wants to get back together with me.'

'You not only can, but must, if you're still in love with that old boyfriend,' Dr Knutz said. 'It isn't fair to the perfectly nice guy otherwise.'

'Oh!' I dropped my face into my hands. 'Look, I know, OK? I don't know what to do!'

'You do,' Dr Knutz said. 'And you'll do it, when the time is right. Speaking of time . . . ours is up.'

AAAAARGH!!!!

And what is he talking about, I'll know what to do when the time is right? I have no idea what to do!

Actually, I do: I want to move to Japan and have food on real plates delivered to my door, and live under an assumed name (Daphne Delacroix).

# Friday, May 5, 8.30 p.m., the Loft

Tina just called. She wanted to know how my lunch date with Michael went. She's called a few times before actually, but I didn't pick up (J.P.'s called a few times too). I just couldn't face speaking to either of them. The shame, you know? How could I possibly tell her?

And how can I possibly ever speak to J.P. again? I know I'll have to eventually. But . . . not now.

Anyway, I didn't tell her now when I spoke to her either. I just went, 'Oh, lunch was fine,' all breezy and casual. I didn't say a word about old-timey carriages or making out for blocks on end or anything about below-the-neck fondling.

GOD! I'm such a slut!

'Really?' Tina said. 'That's so great! So . . . what about MHS?'

'MHC, you mean? Oh, fine, fine. All under control.'

A slut and a LIAR!

'Well . . .' Tina sounded like she couldn't believe it. 'That's great, Mia! So, you and Michael really can just be friends then.'

'Sure,' I said. (<u>Mia Thermopolis's Big Fat Lie Number Twelve.</u>) 'No problem.'

'That's great,' Tina said. 'It's just that . . .'

'What,' I said. Oh no. What had she heard? Had Lana and Trisha finally gotten their rowing under control and followed us? I'd gotten a text from Lana that just said, )(&$#! Which I took to mean Lana had had too much sake at Nobu, a usual event on a Friday.

'Well, I was talking to Boris,' Tina said, 'and did you know, he was telling me that the whole time Michael was in Japan – you're going to laugh when you hear this,

I suppose – he had Boris kind of . . . well, keeping an eye on you. You know, while you guys were in Gifted and Talented together? I can't believe Boris didn't tell me before. But he said Michael said not to say anything to me. They're better friends than I thought, I guess. Anyway, Boris says he thinks Michael's seriously in love with you and always has been. That he never stopped loving you, even after you guys broke up. I guess he just thought it wasn't fair to ask you to wait for him while he was away, trying to prove himself to your dad or whatever, you know? God, it's just . . . it's so romantic.'

I had to move the phone away from my face, because I'd started to cry. And I was afraid Tina would hear my sniffling.

'Yeah,' I said. 'That *is* romantic.'

'Not like Boris was spying on you or anything,' Tina said. 'I mean, I've never told him any of the stuff you and I have talked about. Anyway, Boris told me the reason Michael left your birthday party the other night when J.P. pulled out that ring was exactly why I said . . . because he couldn't stand seeing you get engaged-to-be-engaged to another guy. Boris didn't say Michael said this, but I don't think Michael likes J.P. very much. On account of him being jealous, because J.P.'s with you now. Isn't that just the sweetest thing you ever heard?'

Tears were totally streaming down my face. But I pretended like they weren't.

'Uh-huh,' I said. 'Sweet!'

'But he didn't say anything about that at lunch?' Tina asked. 'You guys didn't talk about it at all?'

'Nope,' I said. 'I mean, Tina . . . I'm with J.P. now. I would never do that to him.'

Liar!

'Gee,' Tina said. 'Well, of course not. You're not that kind of girl!'

'Nope,' I said. 'I gotta go. I'm gonna hit the hay early to get my beauty sleep for the prom.'

'Oh, sure,' Tina said. 'Me too! Well, see you tomorrow!'

'See you,' I said, and hung up.

Then I bawled like a baby for like ten whole minutes, until Mom came into my room looking all bewildered, and was like, 'What's the matter now?'

And I just went, 'Hold me, Mommy.'

And even though I'm eighteen and a legal adult, I crawled into my mom's lap and stayed there for like ten minutes, until Rocky came over and went, 'YOU'RE not the baby! I am!'

And Mom said, 'She gets to be the baby sometimes.'

So then Rocky thought about it, and finally said, 'OK,' and patted me on the cheek and said, 'Good baby.'

Somehow, this made me feel better.

At least a little bit.

# Saturday, May 6, Midnight, the Loft

I just got the following email from J.P.:

Mia

I've tried to call you a few times, but you aren't picking up. I know you're probably really mad at me, but just, please, listen to what I have to say . . . I know you asked me not to, but I spoke to Sean anyway about your book. Please dont be mad. I only did it because I love you, and I want what's best for you.

And when you hear what Sean just called and told me, I think you're going to be pleased that I spoke to him. He's good friends with the president of Sunburst Publishing (you know, they do all those novels that get reviewed in *The New York Times* that you never read, the ones that got turned into movies starring all Sean's friends). And they would LOVE to publish your book (providing they can do so under HRH Princess Amelia Renaldo of Genovia). Sean says they'd be willing to offer a quarter of a million dollars for it.

Isn't that fantastic, Mia? Don't you think you should reconsider that other offer you got? I mean, it's a tiny percentage of that.

Anyway, I just thought I'd try to help. Sweet dreams, and . . . I can't wait until tomorrow night.

I love you
J.P.

So.

The thing is, I probably *should* take Sunburst Publishing's offer. That quarter of a million dollars . . . that's a ton more money that I could donate to Greenpeace. But . . . Sunburst Publishing has never even *read* my book. They have no idea if it's any good. They're just offering to publish it because of who I am.

And that's just not how I want to get a publishing contract. That's like . . . writing a play about your girlfriend, the princess. In a way.

I know baby seals and the rainforests are going to suffer because of my selfishness but . . .

I just can't do it. I CAN'T.

I suck. I suck more than any human being on the planet.

## Saturday, May 6, 10 a.m., the Loft

All I could think about all night long was J.P. and the baby seals I'm not saving by not taking Sunburst Publishing's money.

And Michael of course.

I don't think I slept for more than few hours. It was terrible.

I woke with a splitting headache and still no idea what I'm going to do about the two of them, to find exit polls in Genovia showing my dad totally tied with René in today's election for prime minister.

Almost all the news outlets I've seen credit Lilly's commercial (although they don't name her of course) and the donation of new state-of-the-art medical equipment to the Royal Genovian Hospital as reasons for Dad's sudden boost in the polls.

I seriously can't believe it if it's true. The *Moscovitzes* saved the prime ministry for my dad?

And yet . . .

Has there ever been anything either of them hasn't been able to accomplish if they've set their mind to it?

No. Not really. It's scary actually.

The polls close at noon our time (which is six Genovia time). So we've got two more hours to go. Mr G is making waffles (regular ones this time, not heart-shaped) while we wait for the call.

I'm keeping everything I have crossed for luck.

There's no way René can win. I mean . . . no *way*. Not even Genovians can be that stupid.

Oh, wait. Did I just write that?

Tonight is the prom. I know I have to go . . . I can't get out of it.

330

And yet there's never been anything I've least wanted to do in my entire life.

And that includes becoming a princess.

## Saturday, May 6, Noon, the Loft

The polls are closed.

Dad just called.

It's officially too close to tell.

I wish I hadn't eaten so many waffles. I feel totally sick.

# Saturday, May 6, 1 p.m., the Loft

Grandmere is here. She brought Sebastiano and all the dresses I'm supposed to choose from for the prom as her excuse for why she showed up.

But you can tell she's here because she just didn't want to wait alone in her condo at the Plaza for the results.

I know how she feels.

Rocky is thrilled of course. He's all, 'Gwanmare, Gwanmare,' and blowing her air kisses the way she taught him. She's pretending to catch them, and clutch them to her heart.

I swear, when she's around babies, Grandmere is a totally different person.

We're all just sitting here waiting for the phone call.

This is excruciating.

## Saturday, May 6, 6 p.m., the Loft

Still no word from Dad.

I finally told them all I had to go. Get ready, I mean. Paolo was coming by with all his equipment to give me the perfect blow-dry. Plus I had to shave my legs and do all the other stuff you have to do to get beautified before an evening out . . . purifying mud mask, Crest White strips, Bioré strip etc. (I didn't even want to think about what might be coming after my evening out tonight).

Every twenty minutes or so I poked my head out of my room and asked if they'd heard anything though.

But Dad didn't call. I can't tell if this is a good sign or a bad sign. The vote shouldn't be this close. Should it?

Finally I was ready to choose a dress. I had my hair done – Paolo put the front up in the diamond and sapphire clips Grandmere had given me for my birthday, but left the back hanging loose in a sort of flip – and everything was clean and moisturized and polished and shaved and smelt nice.

Not that it matters really, because I've already decided no one is going to get close enough to inspect any of those parts of me. I mean, I have enough problems as it is – I don't need sex compounding them.

Actually, I was trying very hard not to think about what was going to happen *after* the prom – or what I was getting myself into. I mean, the whole after-prom thing just had this big DO NOT ENTER sign over it in my brain. I had decided the only way to get through this night was to take it – literally – one minute at a time. I had even emailed J.P. back and said 'Thanks!', for his Sunburst Publishing offer.

I didn't say that I'd already taken the other offer or decided against taking his or anything like that. It just didn't seem worth arguing about. We were going to have a nice, worry-free evening at our senior prom, I'd decided.

Because I owed him that much, at least.

Everything was going to be OK. No one had to know I'd spent a big chunk of yesterday making out with my ex-boyfriend in an old-timey horse carriage. Except my ex-boyfriend and bodyguard and the carriage driver.

Who I really, really hoped wouldn't turn out to have recognized me and gone running to TMZ about it.

I tried on a bunch of Sebastiano's dresses and did a little mini fashion show for Grandmere, Mom, Mr G, Rocky, Lars, Sebastiano and Ronnie from next door, who'd come over (and kept going, 'Girl, you look *pop*pin' fresh!' and, 'I can't believe how much you've grown since you were just a knock-kneed little thing in overalls and Ralph Nader buttons!').

In the end, everyone agreed on this short, tight black lace kind of retro eighties cocktail number, which isn't very princessy or very promlike, but sort of suited the fact that I'm a girl who yesterday totally cheated on her boyfriend (even though of course, nobody knows but me and Lars, and possibly the carriage driver).

If kissing counts as cheating. Which technically I really don't think it does. Especially if it's with your ex.

We won't even get into the below-the-neck fondling part.

So now I'm just waiting for J.P. to show and pick me up. And then we'll be off to the Waldorf to fulfil all my prom-night dreams of rubbery chicken and dancing to lame music. Just like I always said I didn't want to be doing tonight. Yay! I can so not wait.

Hang on, someone's knocking on the door to my room. That can't be . . . Oh. It's Mom.

# Saturday, May 6, 6.30 p.m., the Loft

I should have known Mom wouldn't let me go off to as momentous occasion as my senior prom without a meaningful speech. She's given me one at every other turning point in my life. Why would the prom be any exception?

This one was about how, just because I've been going out with J.P. for almost two years, I shouldn't feel *obligated* to do anything I *don't feel like doing*. That boys sometimes put pressure on girls, claiming that they have *needs*, and that if girls really loved them they'd help them fulfil those needs, but that boys won't really explode or go insane if those needs aren't met.

Not that J.P. is that kind of boy, Mom hastened to explain. But you never know. He might turn into one. The prom does funny things to boys.

I had to try really hard to keep a straight face the whole time she was talking, because I took Health in tenth grade, so I already know boys won't explode if they don't have sex. There was also the small fact that what she was talking about was SO NEVER GOING TO HAPPEN IN A MILLION YEARS.

Except of course the day before yesterday it actually kind of sort of was, since having sex with J.P. after the prom had been my idea in the first place.

So she did have a point. Not of course that I was going to have sex with him *any more*. At least, if there was the slightest chance that I could get out of it, which of course there was. By just saying no. Which I had every intention of doing.

Although I really didn't want to hurt his feelings.

I really wished I could ask her how I could do that,

but then of course she'd know I'd been thinking about Doing It, and there was no way on God's green earth I was bringing THAT up, even though of course she was.

Then Mom went on to say that the prom does funny things to girls too, and that although she knew that I'm a very different kind of girl than *she* was when *she'd* been a teen (back in the eighties, when no one had ever heard of abstinence, and Mom had lost her virginity at the age of fifteen to a boy who'd later gone on to marry a Corn Princess), she hoped that if I got carried away tonight – though she'd prefer it if I didn't – I'd at least practise safe sex.

'Mo-o-om,' I said, cringing with embarrassment. Because this is the only appropriate response to such a statement.

'Well,' Mom said, 'give us parents some credit, Mia. When you come straggling home after breakfast the day after the prom, we all know where most of you have been, and it isn't an all-night bowling alley.'

Busted!

'Mom,' I said in a different voice, 'I – er – uh – OK. Thanks.'

Thank GOD the buzzer just went off. Here he is.

And here I go.

Saved by the bell.

Literally.

Or not.

I really don't know actually.

I can do this. I can totally do this.

## Saturday, May 6, 9 p.m., ladies' room, the Waldorf-Astoria

I can't do this.

Don't get me wrong, J.P. is being totally sweet. He even got me a corsage – just like he said he would – to wear on my wrist.

Fortunately Grandmere remembered to get J.P. a boutonnière (I never thought I'd be so grateful to her), since I completely forgot. Mom got a lot of pictures of me pinning it on to his lapel.

Which wasn't too embarrassing or anything.

I guess she *can* be like a normal moms when she wants to.

Anyway, we got here – I managed to act pretty normal on the ride over, not giving away that I'd been making out with my ex-boyfriend yesterday – and the room is beautiful. The Waldorf-Astoria ballroom is gorgeous, with it's huge high ceilings and lusciously set, foofy tables and sumptuous decor and thick carpets. The prom committee have outdone themselves with the welcome signs and the AEHS memorabilia and the DJ and whatnot.

And J.P. is *totally* into it. I mean, I thought *I* used to be into it, back when I was a freshman and I lived and breathed prom, *prom*, PROM!

But J.P. *loves* it. He wants to dance every single dance. He ate every bit of his chicken (rubbery, just as I suspected) and he ate mine too (I'm a flexatarian, but not *that* flex). He brought his digital camera and he's taken 8,000 pictures – we're all at a big table together: Lana and her date (a West Pointer, in full uniform), Trisha and Shameeka with theirs, Tina and Boris, and Perin and Ling Su and some guys they dug up somewhere for the benefit of their parents. Every five minutes, J.P. is like, 'Smile!'

Which isn't so bad. But as we were coming in, he made me stop and pose for the *paparazzi* with him outside the hotel (which . . . I'm trying to understand. How is it that the paparazzi only shows up when I'm with J.P.? I mean, first Blue Ribbon . . . then my party . . . then his play . . . now the prom. Is it just me or is it like TMZ has LoJack on my boyfriend?).

But that's not the worst part. Not by a long shot. Oh no. The worst part is, the boys at the table were all bragging about what hotel rooms they'd gotten for after prom (which, no offence, but except for J.P. and maybe Boris, I happen to know the GIRLS all made the hotel room reservations), and showing off their keys, and J.P. whipped his Waldorf key out like it was nothing – *right in front of everybody.*

I wanted to die. I mean, I don't even know Lana's, Trisha's and Shameeka's dates! Can we not show a *little* discretion? Especially since—

Wait a minute.

How *did* J.P. get a room at the Waldorf, when Tina said the hotel was sold out so many weeks ago? And J.P. only called this past week?

## Saturday, May 6, 10 p.m., table number 10, Waldorf-Astoria

I just marched back up to our table and asked J.P. about the hotel reservation.

And he told me, 'Oh, I called and they had a room. It was no problem. Why?'

But when I asked Tina what she thought about it later, after J.P. had gone to get me some punch, she said, 'Well, I guess . . . maybe . . . they had a cancellation?'

But wouldn't they have had a waiting list?

And how could J.P. have been at the top of the waiting list, calling *that day*?

Something just didn't seem right about his answer. It's not that I don't trust J.P. But that . . . that seemed weird to me.

So I went to my source for all evil and duplicitous scheming (now that Lilly is basically out of my life): Lana.

She stopped sucking face with her date long enough to go, 'Duh. He must have made the reservation *months* ago. He was obviously planning on getting with you tonight all along. Now go away, can't you see I'm busy?'

But that can't possibly be true. Because J.P. and I never even discussed the possibility of having sex tonight – until I texted him about it the other day. We've never even gotten to second base before! Why would he assume I'd want to have sex on our prom night? He didn't even *ask me* to go to the prom until last week. I mean, isn't making a reservation for a hotel room on our prom night without even having asked me to go to the prom a little bit . . . *presumptuous*?

341

So. Yeah. I started freaking out. Just a little. About that. I mean, could J.P. really have been planning, all this time, for us to have sex tonight? When we've never even *talked* about it?

The thing is . . . I can tell by his play and all that he's planning on marrying me and becoming a prince some day. He even called his play *A Prince Among Men*. So . . . it's not like he doesn't plan for the future. He's even gotten me a gigantic ring.

And maybe it isn't an engagement ring.

But it's the next closest thing.

And that's not all. When we were dancing just now, I said, just casually commenting, really, because it's something I've been thinking about since my close call with the carriage ride yesterday, 'J.P., do you think it's weird how everywhere you and I go together, the paparazzi show up? Like tonight, for instance?'

And J.P. said, 'Well, it's good press for Genovia, don't you think? Your grandmother's always saying every time you appear in the papers, it's like a free tourism ad for your country.'

And I said, 'I guess. But it's just strange, because they show up so randomly. Like when I went to Applebee's the other night with Mamaw and Papaw, I was terrified the paps were going to show up and get a shot of me. And that would have ruined Dad's chances in the election. Can you imagine if TMZ or whoever had gotten a shot of me eating in an Applebee's? But they didn't.'

And they didn't show up yesterday, when I was in the old-timey horse carriage with Michael. But I didn't add that part out loud. Obviously.

'I just don't get how sometimes they know where I'm

going to be and sometimes they don't,' I went on. 'I know Grandmere's not tipping them off. She's evil, but she's not *that* evil—'

J.P. didn't say anything. He just kept holding me close and dancing.

'In fact,' I said, 'they mostly only seem to show up when I'm with . . . *you*.'

'I know,' J.P. said. 'It's so annoying, isn't it?'

Yeah. It is. Because it only started happening, really, when I started going out with J.P. My very first date with J.P., when we went to see *Beauty and the Beast* together. That was the first time the press got a shot of us, coming out of the theatre, looking like a couple, even though we weren't.

I'd always wondered who'd called and told them we were there together. And every other subsequent date we'd gone on, many of which there'd been no way they could have known about in advance – like when we'd gone to Blue Ribbon Sushi the other night. How had they known about that, a casual sushi date around the corner from my house? I go out to eat around the corner from my house all the time, and the paps never show up.

Unless J.P. is there.

'J.P.,' I said, looking up at him in the blue and pink party lights, 'are *you* the one who's been calling the paps and telling them where they can find us?'

'Who, me?' J.P. laughed. 'No way.'

I don't know what it was. Maybe it was that laugh . . . which sounded just slightly nervous. Maybe it was the fact that after all this time, he still hadn't read my book. Maybe it was the fact that he'd put that sexy dancing scene in his play, for everyone to laugh at. Or maybe it was the fact that his character, J.R., seemed to want to be a prince so very, very badly.

But somehow, I just knew:

That 'No way' was <u>J.P. Reynolds-Abernathy IV's Big Fat Lie Number One</u>. Actually, make that <u>Number Two</u>. I think he was lying about the hotel room reservation too.

I couldn't stop staring at him, gazing down at me with that nervous smile on his lips.

This, I thought, wasn't the J.P. I knew. The J.P. who didn't like it when they put corn in his chilli and who kept a creative-writing journal that was a Mead composition notebook exactly like all mine and who'd been in therapy for way longer than I had. This was some different J.P.

Except it wasn't. This was the exact same J.P.

Only I knew him better now.

'I mean,' J.P. said with a laugh. 'Why would I do that? Call the paparazzi on myself?'

'Maybe,' I said, 'because you like seeing yourself in the paper?'

'Mia,' he said, looking down at me with the same nervous smile on his face, 'come on. Let's just dance. You know what? I heard a rumour we might get voted Prom King and Queen.'

'My foot hurts,' I said. This was a lie. But for once I didn't feel guilty about it. 'These are new shoes. I think I have to sit down a minute.'

'Oh no,' J.P. said. 'I'll go see if I can find you a Band-Aid. Stay here.'

So J.P. is looking for a Band-Aid.

And I'm trying to figure this out.

How could J.P. – J.P., who is so big and blond and

good-looking, the guy with whom I have so much common, the guy everyone liked so much better for me than Michael – be someone it turns out I may have nothing in common with at all?

It can't be possible. It *can't* be.

Except . . . what was Dr Knutz talking about the other day?

His story about his horse, Sugar. The thoroughbred who looked so good on paper, but in whose saddle he could never find a comfortable place? Dr Knutz had to give Sugar up, because he never wanted to ride her, and it wasn't fair to Sugar.

I get it now. I so get it.

Some people can *seem* perfect . . . everything about them can, on paper, be just right.

Until you get to know them. *Really* know them.

Then you find out, in the end, while they might be perfect to everyone else, they just aren't right for *you*.

On the other hand . . .

What's so wrong about a guy who loves his girlfriend getting a hotel room for the two of them on prom night, months in advance? Oh, big crime.

So he screwed up with the play? If I ask him to, I'm sure he'd change it. I—

Oh my God. There's Lilly.

She's in black from head to toe (well, so am I actually. Only somehow I don't think I look like a trained assassin the way she does).

She's heading for the ladies' room.

OK, I think this might constitute stalking. But I'm going in after her. She dated J.P. for six months.

If anyone will know if my boyfriend's a great big

phoney, she will. Whether or not she'll even speak to me is another story.

But Dr Knutz *did* say, when I figured out what the right thing to do was, I'd do it.

I really hope this is it . . .

## Saturday, May 6, 11 p.m., ladies' room, the Waldorf-Astoria

OK. I'm shaking. I have to stay in here until my knees stop trembling long enough for me to stand up again. For now I'm just going to sit here on this little velvet settee and try to write this down so it makes some kind of sense—

In any case . . .

. . . I guess I finally know now why Lilly was so mad at me for so long.

I walked into the bathroom and there she was putting bright red lipstick on in the mirror.

It looked exactly like blood.

She glanced at my reflection and sort of raised her eyebrows.

But I wasn't going to back off, even though my heart was pounding. *Pray for the courage to change the things I can.*

I checked to make sure we were the only people in the room. We were. And then I went, to her reflection, before I could lose my nerve, 'Is J.P. a total fake or what?'

She very calmly put the lid back her lipstick and slipped it into her evening clutch. Then she said with an expression of total disgust, turning around to look me in the eye, 'Took you long enough.'

I won't say it was like she plunged a knife into my chest, or anything dramatic like that. Because the part of me that used to think I loved J.P. had stopped thinking that as soon as I spilt the hot chocolate on Michael last week, and I realized that whole loving J.P. thing had just been wishful thinking. I mean, I guess I *could* have trained myself to fall in love with J.P. eventually, if Michael Moscovitz had never come back from Japan and then been so nice to me and made me realize I'd never fallen out of love with him.

And if J.P. had been someone else completely.

But that will never happen now.

'Why didn't you tell me?' I asked Lilly. I wasn't mad really. Too much time had passed – and water gone under the bridge – for me to be mad. I was just curious, more than anything.

'Oh, what,' Lilly said, letting out a sarcastic laugh. '*You*'re the one who started going out with him the day he dumped me, practically – dumped me for *you*, by the way.'

'He did not dump you for me,' I said, shaking my head. 'That's not how it happened. Way to rewrite history.'

'I beg your pardon,' Lilly said. 'I was there, you were not. I think I would know. J.P. most assuredly dumped me because, as he said, and I quote, he was hopelessly in love with you. I didn't mention that part, did I, the day I told you about our break-up?'

I stared at her, feeling colour creep up my face. 'No—'

'Well, that's what he told me. That he was dumping me like a hot potato the minute it looked like things were over with you and Michael because now he, quote, had a chance with you, unquote. But I told him there was no way in hell my best friend would ever give him the time of day, because you would never do something like go out with the guy who'd broken my heart.' Her look of disgust deepened. 'Oh, but . . . I guess I was wrong about that, wasn't I?'

I was so shocked I didn't know what to say. I couldn't believe it. *J.P.?* J.P. had told Lilly he loved me . . . before he and I had even started going out? J.P. had dumped Lilly because I'd become available?

That was worse – way worse – than calling the paps on me and telling them where I'd be having dinner.

Or getting a publisher to agree to print my book without even having read it.

'Don't try to deny it, Mia,' Lilly went on, her upper lip curling. 'Not five minutes after I told you about our break-up – our next class period, practically – I saw you two kissing.'

'That was a mistake!' I cried. 'He turned his head at the last minute!' On purpose, I knew now, beyond a shadow of a doubt.

But then, I shouldn't have been flinging my arms around boys in the hallway anyway.

'Oh, and it was a *mistake* that you two went out on a date the same night my brother left for Japan?' she asked with a sneer.

'It wasn't a date,' I said. 'We went as friends.'

'That's not how the press saw it,' Lilly said, shaking her head.

'The press?' I inhaled, a single, horrified breath as the truth finally sank in . . . after twenty-one long months. 'Oh God. He called them that night. The night we went to see *Beauty and the Beast*. That's why the paparazzi showed up. J.P. called them himself.'

'Oh, NOW you finally realize it.' Lilly shook her head. Now that the blindfold had been lifted from my eyes at last, she'd stopped looking so disgusted. 'He played us both. He only went out with me because it was a way to be closer to you . . . although I'm not entirely sure what *sleeping* with me had to do with you—'

'Oh my God!' That's when all the bones in my body turned into jelly and I had to sit down before I fell down. I collapsed on to one of the velvet couches the Waldorf-Astoria hotel staff had helpfully supplied for this purpose, and sunk my head into my hands.

Also, I would just like to add, *I knew it*! I knew they Did It! Way back at the beginning of eleventh grade, I knew it.

'Lilly!' I cried. 'You told me you never slept with him! I specifically asked you, and you said he could have taken advantage and he never did!'

'Yeah,' Lilly said, sinking down beside me and slumping against the wall. Her face was devoid of expression. 'Well, I lied. I still had *some* pride, I guess. And anyway, it's not like I didn't get something out of it too. I was totally warm for the guy's form. I just would have appreciated it if, in the end, he hadn't have turned out to be lusting for my best friend the whole time.'

'Oh my God,' I said again. I was having a whole lot of trouble picturing J.P. and my best friend – Lilly – doing . . . well. *That*.

Also, what about all those times J.P. said he was a virgin, just like me? About how he was so glad he'd waited for the right girl, and how that girl was me? <u>J.P. Reynolds-Abernathy IV's Big Fat Lie Number Three.</u> Or was it <u>Four</u> now? Wow, he was going to start beating *my* lying record soon.

'Lilly,' I said. My heart felt like it was twisting in my chest, I felt so bad. Not for myself. For Lilly. I understood now. Everything . . . even about ihatemiathermopolis.com. This didn't make it right.

But it made it more understandable.

'I'm so, so sorry,' I said, reaching out to take her hand, with it's black-painted nails. 'I had no idea. And . . . well, about him dumping you for me. I had no idea about that either. Honestly, though . . . why didn't you just *tell* me?'

'Mia, come on.' Lilly shook her head. 'Why should I have had to? As my best friend, shouldn't my ex have been off-limits? You should have known better. And what were you doing, breaking up with my brother over that dumb Judith Gershner thing in the first place? That was just so . . . psychotic. Most of the beginning of last year, *you* were psychotic.'

I bit my lower lip. 'Yeah,' I said 'I know. But the things you did didn't help, you know.'

'I know,' Lilly said. When I glanced at her, I saw there were tears in her eyes. 'I guess I was pretty psychotic too. I . . . well, I loved him, you know. And he dumped me for *you*. And I . . . I was just so *angry* with you. And you were being so stupidly blind about who he really was. But . . . you seemed happy. And by then I had Kenny, and *I* was happy . . . and how do you apologize for something like that . . . what I did?'

She looked at me and shrugged helplessly. I looked back at her, my own eyes filled with tears as well.

'But, Lilly,' I said, sniffling a little, 'I missed you. I missed you so much.'

'I missed you too,' Lilly said back. 'Even though I kind of hated your guts for a while.'

This made me sniffle harder.

'I hated your guts too,' I said.

'Well,' Lilly said, the tears sparkling like jewels in the corners of her eyes. 'We *both* acted like idiots.'

'Because we let a boy come between our friendship?'

'Two boys,' Lilly said. 'J.P. *and* my brother.'

'Yeah,' I said. 'Maybe we should agree never to do that again.'

'Agreed,' Lilly said, and snagged my pinky with hers. We pinky swore. Then, sobbing a little, we hugged.

And it's weird. She doesn't smell like her brother.

But she smells really good just the same. She smells like something that reminds me of . . . well, of home.

'Now,' Lilly said, wiping tears from her eyes with the backs of her hands when she let go of me, 'I have to get back to the party, before Kenny blows something up.'

'OK,' I said with a shaky laugh. 'I'll be right out. I just need . . . I just need a minute.'

'See you later, POG,' Lilly said.

I can't even tell you how good it felt to hear her call me that. Even though I used to hate it. I couldn't help laughing as I wiped away my own tears.

And she got up and left, just as two girls who looked only kind of familiar to me came in and went, 'Oh my God, aren't you like Mia Thermopolis?'

And I was like, 'Yeah.' What now? Seriously. I don't know how much more I can take.

And they went, 'You better get back out there. People are looking for you. Everyone is saying they're going to name you Prom Queen. They're just like waiting for you to come back out so they can start the ceremony.'

So. Yeah. Looks like I'm Prom Queen.

Sadly, if J.P. is Prom King, he's in for a big surprise.

## Sunday, May 7, Midnight, Limo on the way Downtown

I walked out of the ladies' room and, sure enough, they were calling out the names of the Albert Einstein High School Prom King and Queen: J.P. Reynolds-Abernathy IV and Mia Thermopolis.

I'm not even kidding.

How did I go from the geekiest girl in the whole school my freshman year to Prom Queen my senior year? I don't get it.

I guess turning out to be a princess might have helped.

But I don't think that had all that much to do with it really.

J.P. came through the crowd and found me and smilingly took my hand and steered me up to the stage, where the lights were shining so brightly down on us. Everyone was screaming. Principal Gupta handed him a plastic sceptre and put a rhinestone tiara on my head. Then she made a speech about positive moral values and how we exemplified them, and how everyone should look up to us.

Which was a pretty big joke, if you consider what we'd both planned on doing after the prom. Oh, and what I'd been doing in an old-timey horse carriage yesterday with my ex.

Then J.P. grabbed me and dipped my body back and kissed me, and everyone cheered.

And I let him because I didn't want to embarrass him by having Lars taser him right there in front of the entire senior class.

Although that's really what I felt like doing.

Except if you think about it, it's not like I'm all that morally superior to him. I mean, I'm wearing his ring, and yet I'm not a bit in love with him. At least, not any more. And I lie all the time too.

Except that my lies were to make people feel better. His lies? Not so much.

But at least I intend to do something about it.

Anyway, right after our kiss, a lot of balloons came down from the ceiling and the DJ put on a super fast punk version of The Cars' 'Let the Good Times Roll', and everyone started dancing like mad.

Except for me and J.P.

That's because I pulled him off the stage and said, 'We need to talk.'

Only I had to shout it to be heard above the music.

I don't know what J.P. thought I said, but he went, 'Great, yeah, OK, let's go.'

I guess he was in a really good mood on account of being made Prom King. Our whole way out of the ballroom, we kept getting congratulated by all the girls, and J.P. kept getting high-fived by all the guys – when he wasn't getting chest-bumped, like by Lana's West Pointer date – for his mad Prom King skills. That made our progress out the doors to the lobby, where it was quieter, very slow.

But we finally made it.

'Look, J.P.,' I said, dragging the plastic tiara off my head. It was really uncomfortable and I'm pretty sure had ruined my pretty hairdo. But I didn't care. I checked to make sure Lars was nearby. He was, sticking his fingers in his ears to check his hearing, which he apparently feared had been damaged by the din inside the ballroom. 'I'm really sorry about this.'

The thing is, Dad had only said I had to go to the prom with J.P. And as far as I was concerned, the prom was over now. I mean, they'd crowned the King and Queen. So, I felt like that meant the evening was complete.

Which meant, as far as J.P. was concerned, I was done.

'Sorry about what?' J.P. had walked me over towards a bank of elevators. I had no idea why at the time, because the hotel exit was on the ground floor, and so was the ballroom. But later I figured it out. 'This is actually the perfect time to leave. That music was driving me crazy. I don't know what's wrong with a little Josh Groban. And there's no better time to go than with everybody wanting more, right? How's your foot? Does it still hurt? Look—' He dropped his voice – 'Shouldn't you tell Lars he can go now? I can take it from here.' He smiled knowingly, then stabbed the elevator button UP.

I had no idea what he was doing. Or what he was talking about. At least, not then. I was completely focused on what I had to do.

'It's just . . .' I said. I didn't want to hurt him. Grandmere had given me a speech to use for letting down suitors gently.

But honestly. What he'd done to Lilly? That was unforgivable. And I didn't see any reason to let him down gently.

'I think it's time we were honest with one another,' I said. '*Really* honest. I know it's you that's been calling the paparazzi every time we go out. I can't prove it, but it's pretty obvious. I don't know why you do it. Maybe you think it's good publicity for your future career as a writer or something. I don't know. But I don't like it. And I'm not going to put up with it any more.'

J.P. looked down at me with a shocked expression on his face. He said, 'Mia, what are you talking about?'

'And the thing with the play?' I shook my head. 'J.P., you wrote an entire play about me. How could you do that – drag my personal life, like the thing with the sexy dancing, out into the public like that – and let Sean Penn make a movie out of it? If you really loved me, you'd never do something like that. I once wrote a short story about you, but that was before I got to know you, and once I did get to know you, I had all the copies of it destroyed, because it's not fair to take advantage of people that way.'

J.P.'s jaw dropped a little lower. He started shaking his head. 'Mia, I wrote that play for us. To let the world know how happy we are – how much I love you—'

'And that's another thing,' I said. 'If you love me so much, how come you haven't read my book? I'm not saying it's the greatest book in the world, but you've had it a week, and you still haven't read it. You couldn't have skimmed it and told me what you thought? I appreciate your trying to get me this fantastic book deal, which I don't need because I already got one on my own, but you couldn't have just glanced at it?'

'Mia.' Now J.P. was starting to look defensive. 'This again? You know I've been busy. We had finals. And I was in rehearsal—'

'Yeah.' I folded my arms across my chest. 'I know. You've told me. You have a lot of excuses. But I'm curious to know what your excuse is for why you lied about the hotel room.'

He took his hands out of his pockets and spread his palms, face out, towards me, in the age-old gesture of innocence.

'Mia, I don't know what you're talking about!'

'The rooms in this hotel were sold out weeks ago. Seriously, J.P.' I shook my head. 'There's no way you called this week and got a room. Be honest. You made the reservation months ago, didn't you? You just assumed you and I would be hooking up tonight.'

J.P. dropped his hands. He also dropped the pretence.

'What's so wrong with that?' he wanted to know. 'Mia, I know good and well how you and your friends talk about prom night – and *everything* that entails. I wanted to make it special for you. So that makes me a bad guy all of a sudden?'

'Yeah,' I said. 'Because you weren't honest with me about it. And OK, J.P., I wasn't honest with you about a lot of stuff either, like about the colleges I got into and my feelings and . . . well, a lot of stuff. But this was big. I mean, you lied to me about why you broke up with Lilly. You told her you loved me! That's the whole reason she was so mad at me for so long, and you knew it, and you never told me!'

J.P. just shook his head. Shook it *a lot*.

'I don't know what you're talking about,' he said. 'If you've been talking to Lilly—'

'J.P.,' I said. I couldn't believe it. I couldn't believe what he was saying. I couldn't believe he was lying. *To my face!* I'm a liar. I'm the *princess* of liars. And he was trying to lie to *me*? About something that mattered this much? How dare he! 'Stop lying. Lilly and I are friends again. She told me *everything*. She told me you slept with her! J.P., you aren't a virgin at all. You were never

357

saving yourself for me. You *slept* with her! And you never thought that was something you ought to mention to me? How many girls *have* you slept with, J.P.? I mean really?'

J.P.'s face was turning so red it was almost purple. Still, he kept trying to salvage the situation. As if there was anything left to salvage.

'Why would you believe *her*?' J.P. cried, shaking his head some more. 'After what she did to you? That website she made up? And you believe her? Mia – are you crazy?'

'No,' I said. 'One thing I absolutely am not, J.P., is crazy. Lilly made up that website because she was angry. Angry at me, for not being a better friend to her. And yes . . . I believe her. *You're* the one I can't believe, J.P. Just how many lies have you told me since we started going out?'

He stopped shaking his head. Then he said, 'Mia—'

And he looked . . . well, terrified is the only word I can think of to describe it.

Just then, the elevator doors opened in front of us. And Lars came over to check to make sure the car was empty. Then he asked drily, 'You two aren't going anywhere, correct?'

J.P. said, 'Actually, we—'

But I said, realizing just then where those elevators went – upstairs, to the hotel rooms – 'No.'

And Lars backed away again.

And the elevator doors closed.

Here's the thing: I'm not going to say that I don't think J.P. ever cared about me. Because I think he did. I really do.

And the truth is, I cared about J.P. too. I did. He was

a good friend at a time when I needed friends. Maybe we'll even be friends again some day.

But not right now.

Because right now, I think a big part of the reason he liked me so much is because he wants to be a famous playwright, and he thought hanging out with me could help make him that way.

It sucks to have to admit this. That a guy really only liked me because I'm royal. How many times am I going to fall for this anyway?

But you know what else sucks sometimes?

Actually *being* a princess. And having people who are so fascinated by this that they can't see the person you are behind the crown. The kind of person who wants to be judged on her own merits. The kind of person who doesn't care if someone offers her a quarter of a million dollars for her book. She'd rather have less money if it's from someone who really values her work.

Oh, sure. People will *claim* they like you for who you are. They might even do a really good imitation of it. So good, you'll even believe it. For a while.

The thing is, if you're smart, there'll be clues. It may take you a while to pick up on them.

But you will. Eventually.

And in the end, it all boils down to this:

The people who were your friends before you got the crown are the people who are going to be your best friends no matter what. Because they're the ones who love you for you – you, in all your geekiness – and not because of what they can get out of you. Weirdly, in some instances, even the people who were your enemies before you got famous (like Lana Weinberger) can end up being better friends to you than the people you become friends with after you become famous. And even when those friends get mad at you – like Lilly was at me – you still need them, even more than ever. Because they might just be the only people who are willing to tell you the truth.

That's just the way it is. It's lonely on the throne.

Luckily for me, I had fabulous friends before I ever found out I was the Princess of Genovia.

And if there's one thing I've learned in the past four years, it's that I better do my best to try to hold on to them.

No matter what.

Which is why I found myself giving J.P. the speech Grandmere had taught me – the one for letting suitors down gently.

'J.P.,' I said, pulling the ring he'd given me off my finger, 'I care about you. I really do. And I wish you the best. But the truth is, I think we're better off as friends. Good friends. So I want to give this back to you.'

And I lifted his hand, put the ring back in the centre of his palm and closed his fingers around it.

He looked down at his hand with an expression of abject misery on his face.

'Mia,' he said, 'I can explain why I didn't tell you about Lilly. The thing is, I didn't think you—'

'No,' I said. 'You don't need to say another word. Don't feel bad.' I reached up and patted him on the shoulder.

I guess I could have felt sorry for myself because my prom had gotten totally and completely ruined. I'd gone to it with a guy who'd turned out to be a total phoney.

But I remembered what my dad said about how it's the duty of royalty always to be the stronger person and to make everyone else feel better. So I took a deep breath and said, 'You know what I think you should do? Call Stacey Cheeseman. I think she has a total crush on you.'

J.P. looked down at me as if I was nuts. 'You do?'

'I totally do,' I lied. But it was a white lie. And I was pretty sure she had a crush on him. All actresses adore their directors.

'This is completely embarrassing,' J.P. said. Now he was looking down at the ring.

'No it's not,' I said, patting him on the shoulder some more. 'Now, are you going to call her?'

'Mia,' J.P. said, his expression stricken, 'I'm sorry. But I thought if you knew the truth, you'd never—'

I held up my hand to indicate he should say no more. Really, would you think a man of the world such as he would know better than to keep trying to get me back when I had made it so clear I was done.

I wondered how much of his reluctance to call Stacey was rooted in the fact that she isn't really that famous. Yet.

But I decided this thought was ungenerous of me. I'm really trying to be more princesslike in my thoughts and actions.

I also wasn't trying to let my gleefulness over the situation show. You know, that even though my prom was a total bust, I'd gotten my best friend back, and I hadn't been even a bit in love with my prom date, with whom I was breaking up, in the first place.

I tried to keep a solemn expression on my face as I stood on my tiptoes and kissed him.

'Goodbye, J.P.,' I whispered.

Then I hurried away before there was any chance he

could start begging, which is so unattractive in a suitor (well, so Grandmere says. It hasn't happened to me . . . yet. But I had a feeling it was about to).

And as I was hurrying, I flipped open my cellphone and made a quick call to the Royal Genovian lawyers. Their offices weren't open yet, because it was only around seven in the morning, Genovia time.

But I left a message asking them to put a cease and desist on J.P.'s play, or whatever they had to do in order to stop it from ever getting made into a movie, or even a Broadway show.

I mean, I know I was princessy and gracious during our break-up. And I do completely forgive what J.P. did to me.

But for what he did to Lilly? He's going down.

He really ought to have remembered that several of my ancestresses are known for strangling and/or chopping off the heads of their enemies.

It was as I was putting my phone away that I crashed right into Michael.

Yes, *Michael*.

I was totally flabbergasted of course. What was *Michael* doing at the AEHS prom?

'Oh my God,' I cried. 'What are *you* doing here?'

'What do you *think* I'm doing here?' he demanded, rubbing his shoulder where I'd walked into him, plastic tiara prongs first.

'How long have you been standing there?' I was seized with a sudden panic he might have overheard what J.P. and I had been discussing, vis-à-vis Lilly. On the other hand, if he had, surely there'd have been a murder already. J.P.'s, to be exact. 'Wait . . . what did you hear?'

'Enough to make me feel nauseous,' Michael said. 'Nice move with the call to the lawyers, by the way. And is that really how you guys talk to each other?' His voice rose into a falsetto. '*You know what I think you should do? Call Stacey Cheeseman. I think she has a total crush on you.*' He lowered his voice again. 'Cute. What does that remind me of exactly? Hold on. Wait, I know . . . the TV series *Seventh Heaven*—'

I grabbed his arm and dragged him around the corner, well out of earshot of J.P. (who hadn't yet noticed a thing, because he'd already gotten on the phone with Stacey).

'Seriously,' I said, dropping Michael's arm when we were far enough away. 'What are you doing here?'

Michael grinned. He looked so cute in his black Skinner Box T-shirt with his messed up hair, and his jeans fitting him just right. I couldn't help remembering all that making out we'd done yesterday. It came back as such a visceral memory, it was almost like a punch.

Of course, that might have been because I'd also gotten a big whiff of him when I'd crashed into him. That major histocompatibility complex is strong stuff. Strong enough to knock a girl out, practically.

'I don't know,' he said. 'Lilly told me a couple of days ago I was supposed to show up here and meet you by the elevators at around midnight. She said she had a feeling you were going to need, er, my assistance. But you seemed to be handling the situation just fine, if that whole ceremonial giving-back-of-the-ring thing was any indication.'

I could feel myself turning bright red, realizing what Lilly must have meant. Having overheard my conversation with Tina in the girls' bathroom at school about my getting a hotel room with J.P. tonight, Lilly had sent her brother down here to stop me from doing something she knew I'd regret . . .

. . . only she hadn't told him exactly *what* he was supposed to be stopping me from doing. Thank God.

Lilly really *was* a friend, after all. Not that I'd ever doubted it. Well, very much.

'So are you going to tell me why Lilly felt my presence was so urgently needed here tonight anyway?' Michael wanted to know as he wrapped an arm around my waist.

'You know,' I said quickly, 'I think it's because she knew I always wanted to spend my senior prom with you.'

Michael just laughed. Sort of sarcastically.

'Lars,' he called over the top of my head, to my bodyguard. 'Tell me the truth. Do I need to go back over there and turn J.P. Reynolds-Abernathy the Fourth into Cream of Wheat?'

Lars, to my total mortification, nodded and said, 'In my opinion, most definitely.'

'Lars!' I cried, starting to panic. 'No. No! Michael, it's over. J.P. and I just broke up. You don't have to hit anybody.'

'Well, I think maybe I do,' Michael said. He wasn't teasing either. There was no smile on his face as he said, 'I think maybe the earth would be a better place if somebody had turned J.P. Reynolds-Abernathy the Fourth into Cream of Wheat a long time ago. Lars? Do you agree with me?'

Lars looked at his watch and said, 'It's midnight. I

don't hit anyone after midnight. Bodyguard union regulations.'

'Fine,' Michael said. 'You hold him down and I'll hit him.'

This was terrible!

'I have a better idea,' I said, taking Michael by the arm again. 'Lars, why don't you take the rest of the night off? And, Michael, why don't we go back to your place?'

Just as I'd hoped, this completely distracted Michael from his Kill J.P. Death Mission. He stared down at me in shock for nearly five seconds.

Then he said, 'That sounds like a completely excellent idea.'

Lars shrugged. What else could he do? I'm eighteen and a legal adult now.

'I am fine with this idea too,' he said.

And that's how I ended up in this limo, speeding downtown to SoHo and to Michael's loft.

And now Michael has suggested that I stop writing in my journal and pay attention to him for a little while.

You know what? This sounds like a completely excellent idea to me too.

An Excerpt from *Ransom My Heart* by
Daphne Delacroix

'Finnula,' he said again, and this time she recognized the need in his voice. It matched the
need she felt in her own heart, in the thrum
of her own pulsing veins. 'I know I gave you
my word I wouldn't touch you, but—'

Finnula wasn't at all certain how what happened next transpired. It seemed as if one
minute she was standing looking up at him,
wondering if he'd ever stop talking and just do
it, for heaven's sake . . .

. . . and the next she was in his arms. She
didn't know if he'd moved or she had.

But suddenly, her arms were around his
neck, drawing his head down towards hers,
her fingers tangled in his soft hair, her lips
already parted to receive his.

Those strong golden arms, the ones she'd
longed to have round her, imprisoned her,
clasping her so close to his broad chest that
she could hardly breathe. Not that she could
catch her breath anyway, since he was kissing
her so deeply, so urgently, as if she might at
any moment be torn away from him. He
seemed to fear that they'd be interrupted
again. Only Finnula realized, with a satisfaction that surely would have shocked her
brother, had he known of it, that they had all
night long. Accordingly, she lengthened the
kiss, conducting a leisurely exploration of
those arms she'd so admired. Why, they really

were every bit as perfect as she'd imagined.

Abruptly, Hugo lifted his head and looked down at her with eyes that had gone an even deeper green than the emerald around Finnula's neck. She was panting from lack of breath, her chest rising and falling quickly, colour bright over her high cheekbones. She saw the question in his glance and understood it all too well. He didn't know that she had already made her decision, that it had been irrevocably made for her the second she'd seen him without that beard, and her heart – or something very like her heart anyway – had been lost for good.

Well, maybe her decision had been made the second that bolt had slid into place. What did it matter? They were strangers in a strange – well, strange enough – place. No one would ever know of it. Now was no time for his oddly misplaced sense of chivalry.

'Not now,' she growled, knowing full well why he'd stopped kissing her, and what his questioning look implied. 'God's teeth, man, it's too late –' Whatever Hugo had been planning to say, her impatient cry silenced him upon the subject forever. Tilting her body back in his arms, Hugo rained kisses upon her cheeks and the soft skin beneath her ears, his mouth tracing a fiery path down the column of her throat to the neckline of her gown. Finnula, still anxious for the taste of his lips on hers, drew his head towards hers again, then gasped as his fingers closed over first one firm breast, and then the other.

The sensation of his mouth devouring hers, his hands on her straining breasts, was threatening to overwhelm Finnula. It was everything she'd suspected it would be . . . only so much more. The room seemed to sway around her, as if she'd drunk too much, and Hugo remained the only stationary, solid mass within her line of vision. She clung to him, wanting something . . . she was only just beginning to understand what that something was.

Then, when his knee slipped between her weakening legs, and she felt his hard thigh against the place where her legs joined together, the resulting spasm that shot through her was like nothing she'd ever experienced before.

Suddenly, she understood. Everything.

# Sunday, May 7, 10 a.m., Michael's Loft

I HAVE MY SNOWFLAKE NECKLACE BACK.

It turns out when I dropped it in that hotel room that horrible night so long ago, Michael found it where it fell.

And he's kept it ever since.

Because (he says) he's never stopped loving me and thinking of me and hoping . . .

. . . just like I was hoping, that tiny ember I was keeping alive inside.

It turns out Michael was keeping one alive inside too. He knew things had gone horribly wrong between us, but he thought time apart – for both of us to come into our own – might help.

He never thought another man would come along and split us permanently asunder (OK, he didn't put it quite like that, but it sounds more dramatic than saying he never thought I'd starting going out with J.P. Reynolds-Abernathy IV).

And that's when he *did* ask Boris to keep an eye on me (*not* spy on me. Just keep him informed).

Michael thought (because of what Boris reported back to him) that J.P. and I were madly in love. And I guess for a time, we might have looked that way. To an outsider (especially to Boris, who doesn't understand actual live human beings, including – and perhaps especially – his girlfriend).

But still Michael wouldn't give up hope. That's why he kept the necklace– just in case.

It wasn't until Michael saw me at the Columbia event that day and I acted so shy that he says he began to dare to dream that maybe Boris was wrong.

But then when J.P. gave me the ring for my birthday, he knew drastic measures were called for. *That's* why he'd left my party – to get busy making arrangements to send my dad the CardioArm (and also, as he put it, 'Because I knew I had to leave before I wiped the floor with that guy's face.').

It's all just so romantic! I can't wait to tell Tina.

Some day. Not now though. For now I'm keeping it a secret just for Michael and I to share – at least for a little while.

He told me if I want he'll get me a diamond snowflake necklace as a replacement for the old silver one I have on now. But I said no way.

I love this one just the way it is.

EEEEEEEEEEEEEEEEEEEEEEEEEEEEEEEE!!!!!!!!

Anyway, I don't want to want to go into too much detail about what happened between us here in his loft last night, because it's private – too private even for this journal, because what if it to fall into the wrong hands?

But I do want to say something important, and that is this:

If Dad thinks I'm spending this summer in Genovia, he's totally nuts.

Oh my God, *DAD*! I forgot to check and see how the election is going!

# Sunday, May 7, 1.30 p.m., Limo on the way to Central Park

OK, so Dad WON THE ELECTION!

Yeah, I'm still not sure how that happened. I accused Michael, on top of all the many other wonderful things he's done for me lately, of rigging the Genovian voting machines.

But he swears that, although he is a computer genius, he is not capable of rigging voting machines in a small European country many thousands of miles from where he lives.

Besides, in Genovia they use Scantron.

It actually turned out Dad won by a significant majority. The problem was that they're unaccustomed to voting there, so it took them a long time to count them all. Voter turnout was quite a bit higher than expected.

And then René couldn't believe he didn't win, and demanded a recount.

Poor René. It's OK, though. Dad's promised a place for him on the cabinet. Probably something to do with tourism. Which I think is very decent of him.

I found all this out from Dad on the phone. It wasn't a transatlantic call, though. He was phoning from Grandmere's. Dad's back here for my graduation ceremony. Which is in half an hour.

It's too bad he doesn't fly commercially, because he could really rack up the frequent-flyer miles with all the time he's put in, jetting between New York City and Genovia in this past week. I've already spoken to him about his carbon footprint.

371

Anyway, everyone acted totally cool when I showed up at the loft wearing my prom clothes, with Michael in tow. Like nobody said anything to embarrass me, like, 'Oh, hey, Mia, how was it at the all-night bowling alley?' or 'Mia, didn't you leave the house last night with a *different* guy?'

Mom seemed pretty pleased to see Michael actually. She knows how much I've always loved him, and she can tell how happy Michael makes me, which, in turn, makes *her* happy.

And she never made it much of a secret that she couldn't stand J.P. At least she doesn't have to worry about *Michael* being a chameleon. *He* has an opinion about everything.

And he's not shy about expressing it either, *especially* when it's the opposite of my own, since that gets us arguing, which gets us . . . well, in the mood for kissing. That's major histocompatibility complex for you.

Sadly, I'm not sure Rocky actually remembers Michael at all. Which makes sense, since the last time he saw him was almost two years ago, and Rocky's not quite three.

But Rocky seems to really like him. He right away showed Michael his drums, and how adept he is at pulling out tufts of Fat Louie's fur if Fat Louie doesn't run away fast enough.

Anyway, we're all headed uptown to the graduation ceremony now, where we're going to meet Dad and Grandmere. I've got on the dress everyone chose for me to wear today (another one of Sebastiano's creations, exactly like the one I wore last night, only pure white) under my graduation gown. I'm trying to ignore the 80,000 text and phone messages I've gotten from Tina and Lana, most of which, I'm pretty sure, have to do with where I disappeared to last night. Well, OK, Lana's are probably all about her West Pointer.

But come on. A girl's got to have *some* privacy.

One of my text messages, I see, is from J.P. But I'm not opening it with Michael in the car.

Another one is from Lilly. But whatever. I'm going to see all these people in like five minutes! So whatever it is, they can just tell me in person.

And now I have to go, because Rocky's discovered the buttons that control the moon roof. My little brother has a lot in common with his cousin Hank.

## Sunday, May 7, 2.30 p.m., Sheep's Meadow, Central Park

Oh my God, Kenny – I mean, Kenneth – is giving the most boring valedictorian speech I have ever heard. All valedictorian speeches are boring (at least, the ones I've heard).

But this one takes the cake. Seriously, it's about dust particles or something. Or maybe not dust particles. But some kind of particles. Who even cares? It's so hot up on these bleachers.

And no one is paying the slightest bit of attention to him. Lana is actually sleeping. Even Lilly, the valedictorian's own girlfriend, is texting someone.

I just want to get out of here so I can go have cake. Hello? Is that so wrong?

Yeah. I guess it is.

Ack – someone is texting me . . .

Mia, what is going on? I've been texting you all morning. Is everything all right? I saw J.P. last night with STACEY CHEESEMAN! They went up the elevators together. Where were U?????

Oh, hey, T! It's all good! J.P. and I broke up. But it was a hundred per cent mutual. I actually went over to Michael's last night.

EEEEEEEEEEEEEEEEEEEEEEEEEEEEEEEEEEEEEEEEEEEEE!!!!
!!!!!!!!!!!!!!!!!!!!!!!!

That's what I said!!!!!!!!!!!!

OMG that is so romantic!!!! I'm so happy for you!!!!!!!!!!!!!!!

I know! Me too. I love him so much!!!! And he loves me!!!!!!!!!!! And everything is perfect. Except I wish this stupid speech would be over so we could all go eat cake.

Yeah, me too. The only thing is, this morning on my way here I could have sworn I saw Stacey Cheeseman making out with Andrew Lowenstein at a Starbucks downtown. But no way right, cos she's with J.P. now. Right?

Um. Right!

Oh, another text—

Hey, POG. I saw you leave the hotel last night with my brother.

It's Lilly!!!!

Is that a problem? He said you sent him!!!!

It's cool. But you better not break his heart again. Or this time I really WILL break your face.

Nobody's heart is going to get broken this time around, Lilly. We're all grown up now.

Ha. Not likely. But . . . I'm glad you're back, POG.

Awwww . . .

Glad to be back, Lilly.

Uh-oh . . . here's the message from J.P.:

JPRA4:     Mia. Just wanted to say again
           how sorry I am about . . . well,
           everything. Even though the word
           'sorry' seems so inadequate. I
           hope you meant it when you said
           we could be friends. Because
           nothing would mean more to me.
           And thanks too for suggesting
           I call Stacey. You were right
           - she really is a wonderful
           person. And you don't have to
           worry about the play. Sean's
           company called this morning and
           it looks like there's a problem
           with the option. Something to do
           with some lawyers. So I guess he
           won't be producing it after all.
           But don't worry, I'll be all
           right. I have another idea for a
           play, a really great one about a
           playwright who is in love with
           an actress, only she - well,
           it's complicated. I'd love to
           talk to you about it if you get
           a chance. You know how valuable
           I find your editorial input. Call
           me. J.P.

Really. You just have to laugh. Because what else can you do?

OMG, why won't this guy shut up? I'm totally getting a sunburned sitting out here. If I get freckles, I'm suing this stupid school. Wait a minute . . . Geek, did you have SEX last night? You look like you had SEX last night! Don't try to deny it! OMG, the geek had SEX! HA HA HA! Isn't it FUN, geek?????

_ _ _ _ _ _ _ _ _ _ _ _ _ _ _

Sent from my BlackBerry Wireless Handheld

# Sunday, May 7, 4 p.m., table 12, Tavern on the Green

Everyone is making speeches and taking pictures and carrying on about how this is a day we'll never forget.

It's certainly a day Lana's never going to forget . . . that's because Mrs Weinberger (at my urging, though I'll never tell Lana of course) presented Lana with the thing her heart most desired as a graduation present:

That's right, the Weinbergers tracked down Bubbles, Lana's pony that they gave away so many years ago, and gave it back to her. Bubbles was waiting for Lana in the Tavern on the Green parking lot when we all walked up here for our post-graduation reception.

I don't think I've ever heard anyone scream so joyously.

Or so loudly.

It's a day Kenneth's not going to forget either. That's because his parents just handed him an envelope containing a letter from Columbia. He's been taken off the waiting list.

So it looks like he and Lilly won't be separated by a state any more. They'll only be separated by a dorm – if that. There was a lot of joyous hugging and screaming over by that table too.

At first I was kind of afraid to go over to where the Moscovitzes were sitting, even though Michael was totally hanging out with my parents. But I was shy about how the Drs. Moscovitz were going to feel about me. It was true I'd already seen them at the reception at Columbia, but that seemed so long ago and, I don't know, things seemed different now, on account of what had gone on last night (and this morning too)!

But of course, they didn't know about that. And Michael had been brave in coming over to my house (not to mention hanging out with Dad and Grandmere now). So the least I could do was return the favour.

So I did.

And of course, it turned out fine. The Drs Moscovitz – not to mention Nana – were totally delighted to see me. Because I'd made their son happy. And so that made them happy.

What was scary was when J.P. came over to our table with his parents to say hello. Now THAT was awkward.

'Well, Prince Philippe,' Mr Reynolds-Abernathy said all sadly, shaking my dad's hand, 'looks like our kids won't be going to Hollywood together after all.'

But of course my dad had NO idea what he was talking about, because he'd never been let in on that plan (thank God) in the first place.

'Excuse me?' he said, looking totally confused.

'Hollywood?' Grandmere cried, looking appalled.

'Right,' I said quickly. 'But that was before I decided on Sarah Lawrence.'

Grandmere sucked in so much air it was a wonder there was any left for the rest of us to breathe.

'Sarah Lawrence?' she cried in joyous wonder.

'Sarah Lawrence?' Dad echoed. It was one of the schools he'd mentioned, way back when, as one of his top choices for me. But in a million years, I'm pretty sure he never thought I'd actually take him up on it.

But as it happens, like Michael said, Sarah Lawrence is one of the colleges that doesn't count SAT scores towards its entrance requirements. And it's got a strong writing programme. And it's really close to New York City. Just in case I have to pop back into Manhattan to visit Fat Louie or Rocky.

Or smell my boyfriend's neck.

'That's a great choice, Mia,' Mom said, looking super happy. Of course, she's been looking super happy ever since she noticed the diamond ring on my left hand was gone, and I'd come home from the prom with Michael and not J.P.

But I think she really is happy about Sarah Lawrence too.

'Thanks,' I said.

But no one was happier than Grandmere.

'Sarah Lawrence,' Grandmere kept murmuring. '*I* was to go to Sarah Lawrence. If I hadn't married Amelia's grandfather. We've got to start planning how we'll decorate her room. I think buttercup-yellow walls. *I* was to have buttercup-yellow walls . . .'

'OK then,' Michael said to me, eyeing Grandmere as she waxed on about buttercup-yellow walls. 'Wanna dance?'

'Do I ever,' I said, relieved to have an excuse to leave the table.

Which is how we ended up on the dance floor with my mom and Mr G, dancing with Rocky and having a blast together, as usual; Lilly and Kenneth, doing some kind of new wave dance they seem to have invented themselves, even though the music was sort of slow; Tina and Boris, just holding each other and gazing up into one another's eyes, the height of romance, as one would expect, since it was Tina and . . . well, Boris; and . . . my dad and Ms Martinez.

'No,' I said, coming to a standstill when I saw this. 'Just . . . no.'

'What?' Michael looked around. 'What's the matter?'

I should have expected it. I mean, they'd been dancing together at my birthday party, but I thought that had been a one-time thing.

It was at that point that my dad said something to Ms Martinez and she slapped him across the face, then stalked off the dance floor.

I don't think anyone could have been more stunned than my dad . . . except maybe my mom, who started laughing.

'Dad!' I exclaimed, horrified. 'What did you *say* to her?'

My dad came over, rubbing the side of his face, but looking more intrigued than actually hurt.

'Nothing,' he said. 'I didn't say anything to her. Well, nothing more than I usually say when I dance with a beautiful woman. It was a compliment actually.'

'*Dad*,' I said. When would he ever learn? 'She isn't a lingerie model. She's my *former English teacher*.'

'She's intoxicating,' Dad said thoughtfully, gazing after her.

'Oh my God.' I groaned, and buried my face in Michael's neck. I could see clearly what was going on. It was all too obvious. Not again! 'Tell me this is not happening.'

'Oh, it's happening,' Michael said. 'He's following her, calling after her . . . Did you know her first name was Karen?'

'I think I'm about to become very well acquainted with that fact,' I said, still keeping my face in his neck and inhaling deeply.

'Yeah, now he's heading across the parking lot after her . . . She's trying to hail a taxi to get away, but . . . oh, he's stopped her. They're talking. Oh, wait. She's taking his hand . . . .So, are you going to call her Ms Martinez after they get married like you do Mr Gianini, or do you think you'll ever be able to call her Karen?'

'Seriously. What is wrong with my family?' I asked with a groan.

'The same thing that's wrong with everybody's family,' Michael said. 'It's made up of human beings. Hey, quit sniffing me a minute and lift your head up.'

I lifted my head and looked at him. 'Why?' I asked.

'So I can do this,' he said. And kissed me.

And as we were kissing, and the late afternoon sun was pouring in all around us, and the other couples were swirling around us on the dance floor, laughing, I realized something. Something I think might be really important:

This princess thing, which nearly four years ago I was convinced was going to be the ruination of my life, had turned out to be just the opposite. It's actually taught me things, some of them very important. Like how to stand to up for myself and be my own person. How to get what I want out of life, on my own terms. And to never sit by my grandmother while crab is being served, since it's her favourite dish, and she simply can't eat it and talk at the same time, and half of it will end up all over whoever she's sitting next to.

It's taught me something else too.

And that's that as you get older you lose things, things you don't necessarily want to lose. Some things as simple as . . . well, your baby teeth when you're a little kid, as they make way for your adult teeth.

But as you age you lose other, even more important, things, like friends – hopefully only bad friends, who maybe weren't as good for you as you once thought. With luck, you'll be able to hang on to to your true friends, the ones who were always there for you . . . even when you thought they weren't.

Because friends like that are more precious than all the tiaras in the world.

I've also learned that there are the things you *want* to lose . . . like that hat you throw into the air on graduation day. I mean, why would you want to hold on to it? High school sucks. People who say those were the best four years of your life – those people are liars . . . Who wants the best years of their lives to be in *high school*? High school is something *everybody* should be ready to lose.

And then there are the things you thought you wanted to lose, but didn't . . . and now you're glad you didn't.

A good example of this would be Grandmere. She drove me crazy for nearly four years (and not just because of the crab thing). Nearly four years of princess lessons, and nagging, and insanity. I swear, there were moments during some of those years when I gladly would have beat in her face with a shovel.

But in the end I'm glad I didn't. She taught me a lot, and I don't just mean how to use the appropriate cutlery. In a way, she's the one – well, with Mom and Dad's help of course . . . not to mention Lilly and all my friends really – who taught me how to appreciate this royalty thing . . . another thing I wanted desperately to lose, but didn't . . .

And, yes, in the end . . . I'm glad.

I mean, yeah, it sucks sometimes, being a princess.

But I know now there are ways I can work it so I can help people, and maybe, in the end, even make the world a better place. Not in huge ways necessarily. Sure, I'm not going to invent a robotic surgical arm that's going to save people's lives.

But I've written a book that might, like Michael said, make someone whose loved one is being operated on by that arm forget about how scared she is while she's in the waiting room.

Oh, and I brought democracy to a country that's never known it.

And OK, these are small things. But one baby step at a time.

Still, the most important reason I'm glad I turned out to be a princess and that I'm going to stay one forever?

If I hadn't, I highly doubt I'd have gotten this majorly happy ending.

# Mediator

# LOVE YOU TO DEATH & HIGH STAKES

Meet Susannah Simon — the sassiest ghost-hunter ever!

In *Love You to Death*: Suze has just arrived in California and needs to unpack, make friends, look around . . . and exorcise a vicious ghost, hell-bent on making her life a complete nightmare. Oh, and the sexiest spook in existence just happens to haunt her new bedroom . . .

In *High Stakes*: When a screaming spirit wakes Suze in the middle of the night with an important message, she finds herself on the trail of a very creepy businessman. One who doesn't like sunshine and only drinks a weird red liquid . . . Suze may have met her match, but his cute son Tad makes it hard for her to stay away.

# air head

## meg cabot

She's a brainiac trapped inside the body of an airhead...

Teenagers Emerson Watts and Nikki Howard have nothing in common. Em's a tomboy-brainiac who couldn't care less about her looks. Nikki's a stunning supermodel, the world's most famous airhead. But a freak accident causes the girls' lives to collide in the most extraordinary way – and suddenly Em knows more about Nikki's life than the paparazzi ever have!

The first book in a spectacular romantic trilogy with a spine-tingling twist!